Alison Roberts has been lucky enough to live in the South of France for several years recently but is now back in her home country of New Zealand. She is also lucky enough to write for the Mills & Boon Medical line. A primary school teacher in a former life, she later became a qualified paramedic. She loves to travel and dance, drink champagne, and spend time with her daughter and her friends. Alison is the author of over one hundred books!

Susan Carlisle's love affair with books began when she made a bad grade in mathematics. Not allowed to watch TV until the grade had improved, she filled her time with books. Turning her love of reading into a love for writing romance, she now pens hot Medicals. She loves castles, travelling, afternoon tea, reading voraci
readers. Join h

Also by Alison Roberts

City Vet, Country Temptation
Paramedic's Reunion in Paradise
Midwife's Three-Date Rule

A Tale of Two Midwives miniseries

Falling for Her Forbidden Flatmate
Miracle Twins to Heal Them

Also by Susan Carlisle

A Kiss Under the Northern Lights

Atlanta Children's Hospital miniseries

Mending the ER Doc's Heart
Reunited with the Children's Doc
Wedding Date with Her Best Friend
Second Chance for the Heart Doctor

Kentucky Derby Medics miniseries

Falling for the Trauma Doc
An Irish Vet in Kentucky

Discover more at millsandboon.co.uk.

THEIR FAKE DATE RESCUE

ALISON ROBERTS

SECOND CHANCE WITH HIS CITY NURSE

SUSAN CARLISLE

MILLS & BOON

All rights reserved including the right of reproduction in whole or in part in any form. This edition is published by arrangement with Harlequin Enterprises ULC.

This is a work of fiction. Names, characters, places, locations and incidents are purely fictional and bear no relationship to any real life individuals, living or dead, or to any actual places, business establishments, locations, events or incidents. Any resemblance is entirely coincidental.

Without limiting the author's and publisher's exclusive rights, any unauthorized use of this publication to train generative artificial intelligence (AI) technologies is expressly prohibited. HarperCollins also exercise their rights under Article 4(3) of the Digital Single Market Directive 2019/790 and expressly reserve this publication from the text and data mining exception.

® and TM are trademarks owned and used by the trademark owner and/or its licensee. Trademarks marked with ® are registered with the United Kingdom Patent Office and/or the Office for Harmonisation in the Internal Market and in other countries.

First published in Great Britain 2025
by Mills & Boon, an imprint of HarperCollins*Publishers* Ltd,
1 London Bridge Street, London, SE1 9GF

www.harpercollins.co.uk

HarperCollins*Publishers* Macken House, 39/40 Mayor Street Upper, Dublin 1, D01 C9W8, Ireland

Their Fake Date Rescue © 2025 Alison Roberts

Second Chance with His City Nurse © 2025 Susan Carlisle

ISBN: 978-0-263-32512-6

07/25

This book contains FSC™ certified paper
and other controlled sources to ensure responsible forest management.

For more information visit www.harpercollins.co.uk/green.

Printed and Bound in the UK using 100% Renewable Electricity
at CPI Group (UK) Ltd, Croydon, CR0 4YY

THEIR FAKE DATE RESCUE

ALISON ROBERTS

MILLS & BOON

CHAPTER ONE

CLAIRE CAMPBELL LET out her breath in a long, contented sigh.

Walking away from her old life and coming to this isolated country on the opposite side of the globe had most definitely been the best decision she'd ever made in her life.

August might be the last month of winter in the southern hemisphere but it felt far more like spring with this small town's hospital garden a glowing swathe of bright yellows and oranges with hundreds of daffodils already in full bloom.

If she wasn't still holding the mug of coffee she'd brought outside with her, having decided to get a breath of fresh air on her break, Claire would have been tempted to throw her arms out sideways and do a three-hundred-and-sixty-degree twirl to embrace this new patch of the planet she'd discovered. Being well up one of Kaikōura's hills meant that she had the best of both worlds as far as the extraordinary views this coastal town could provide. The sea was a glorious stretch of an almost turquoise blue and, behind her, the southern Alps still had an impressive coating of snow on their peaks.

A puff of wind made goosebumps come up on her

arms, though. Okay…maybe there was still a hint of winter in the air. She was reminded of her first day in town, only a week or so ago, when ominously dark clouds had unleashed a very unpleasant amount of rain as she tried to find the address of the rental property she'd organised online from the UK.

Claire turned to go back inside but, just as the path curved to go around the corner to where the general practice clinic was attached to one end of the small hospital, she came to a sudden halt. She could hear voices coming from one of the rooms of the clinic. A consulting room? No…if it was this close to the hospital wing, it had to be the office of Tom Atkinson—Claire's new boss, who was the consultant physician and director for the hospital and senior GP for the medical centre.

They were angry voices.

The window had to be open for her to be able to hear the voices this clearly. The people could well be standing right beside it, in fact, and if she walked past she would be somewhere she really didn't want to be—in the middle of an altercation her new boss was having with someone. She could be quite sure that Tom would not want the newest member of his staff to overhear a private conversation.

A very private one, by the sound of it.

'I cannot *believe* you've done this, Hanna. I'm… I'm lost for words. I'm…appalled…'

'Someone had to do it.' The woman's voice was defensive. 'You were never going to do it for yourself, were you?'

'Did it not occur to you that there's a very good reason for that?'

'It's been seven years, Dad. Seven *years*... If you don't do it now, you're never going to and...and you'll be sorry when you're old and lonely.'

'I'm not lonely. And even if I was, what on earth makes you think I'd want to do *online dating*?'

'It's how you find people these days, especially when you live in a town that's not big enough to even have traffic lights. Stop being such a *dinosaur*. Look...it's only been live since this morning and you've been sent fourteen kisses already. All you have to do is click on them and you can send a message back and start getting to know someone.'

'Oh, my God...' The words were slightly muffled, as if Tom might have put his head in his hands. Then they sharpened. 'You haven't put my name on that site, have you?'

Claire knew she shouldn't be listening to this. She had turned, knowing that she could take the long way round to get to the main doors of the medical centre, and she was poised to move. It was just that her feet were not co-operating quite yet.

She had to admit she was fascinated. She'd noticed that Tom was wearing a wedding ring when she'd finally met him in person last week. Why on earth had his daughter signed him up for online dating? And what had happened seven years ago? Had his wife—Hanna's mother—deserted them? Or died? That was more likely, wasn't it. She might have only just met him but she could be quite sure that Tom was not the kind of man any woman in her right mind would walk away from.

'I haven't even put your photograph on it yet. I used an avatar.'

'Show me.' The words were an icy command. 'What's the name of the site?'

'Ahh...' This Hanna sounded a bit embarrassed now. *'Find The One.'*

The short silence suggested that Tom was tapping and then scrolling on a computer screen. The sound he made to break the silence was a groan.

'You've *got* to be kidding... *That's* my username? *TrustMeI'maDoctor*?'

'I thought it was good.' Hanna sounded like she might be about to burst into tears. 'I'm sorry, Dad...' Yes, she was sobbing now. 'Please don't be angry with me...'

Her choked words faded as Claire finally began walking briskly back the way she'd come.

'I was only trying to help... I'll take it down...'

It was just as well Tom, along with his colleagues, had to get on with a busy afternoon surgery. There was no time to dwell on the mischief his daughter had been up to. Hopefully, by the time he got home, she would have already deleted his embarrassing profile on that dating site and no harm would have been done. The argument, and the undercurrents, could be pushed back under the carpet where they belonged. With a bit of luck, it would be another seven years before they emerged again.

And, in the meantime, he could tap into the space that made it so much easier to deal with anything that was emotionally disturbing on a personal level. He could simply let it be pushed into the background by thinking about other people rather than himself. He'd learned that the pain of even the worst things could fade eventually and thinking about them too much only added to their power. He'd developed a new mantra all those years ago.

It's not all about me...

How good was it that the waiting room was full of people that made it so much easier to instantly divert his attention from himself. There were several elderly patients, a pregnant woman, a crying baby, two toddlers fighting over a truck from the toybox and others who were probably trying to ignore what was going on around them by perusing magazines or their phones.

His young receptionist, Kaia, was looking a little flustered as she sorted patient notes between taking phone calls and welcoming patients but his new practice nurse, Claire, seemed admirably calm. She was helping Edward Bramley to negotiate the toddlers with his walking frame, no doubt heading for the nurse's room where she would take Edward's vital signs and a blood test before he came in for his routine appointment to monitor a myriad of health issues he'd collected in his ninety-three years of being alive. Tom could feel her gaze on him as he headed to the desk to collect the pile of case notes Kaia had ready but when he turned to smile at her, she looked away so quickly it made her smooth, shoulder-length bob of silver-grey hair swing. It almost felt as if she was avoiding eye contact with him.

Which was ridiculous. Claire was old enough to be Kaia's grandmother and she hadn't seemed at all shy or retiring in the short time he'd known her so far. Quite the opposite. She was confident, friendly and adventurous. Good grief...she was in her early sixties, a time when most people might be starting to think about slowing down and enjoying a life they'd spent decades building, but Claire Campbell had set off on an adventure to start a whole new life in a foreign country. She also seemed to be very good at her job as a general practice and community nurse, a quick learner for finding her way around a new environment and getting up to speed with different protocols, with decades of experience and common sense to draw on. Exactly the person he'd been searching for to join the staff here at the Seaview Hospital and Medical Centre.

Tom picked up the first set of notes in the basket with his name on it. Through the window of the waiting room, he could see his daughter Hanna walking away from the building. Striding, in fact, as if *she* was the one who had the right to be upset.

And maybe she did. Maybe this really *wasn't* about him?

Hanna had driven a very long way so that she could have a few days with him while she was on study leave and, after overhearing part of a phone call she'd made yesterday, he knew that she was missing a close friend's birthday party in Dunedin. She was a young adult now and she had her own life to live but she'd been thinking about him when she'd decided to set up that profile on a dating site. Had she been fretting, perhaps, that he was lonely now that she'd left home to go to university?

With an inward sigh, Tom firmly pushed his personal life aside. He found a genuine smile as he looked for a familiar face amongst the waiting patients.

'Olivia? Come on through…'

The young woman with long blonde hair stood up. So did the small girl beside her, slipping a hand into her mother's as they followed Tom to the waiting room.

Lucy, who was three years old, went straight to the toybox in the consulting room. Olivia sat down in the chair in front of the desk.

'It's lovely to see you, Liv. How can I help today?' He glanced towards Lucy, who didn't look at all unwell. She was stroking the mane and tail of a small plastic unicorn she'd found in the box.

'It's probably nothing,' Olivia said with an apologetic smile. 'But Sam said I had to come and see you. I've… well…it's weird but I've fallen over a few times recently.'

'You've tripped?'

'No. It just seems to happen.'

'Have you injured yourself?'

'I had a sore wrist for a few days but that's okay now. Except…my arms get really tired when I brush my hair. And maybe it's just that Lucy's getting heavier but it's getting harder to pick her up.'

Tom's eyes narrowed a little as he focused on his patient. He'd known Olivia virtually all her life. He'd come back to work here for the two years of his advanced GP training and she'd been one of his first patients.

'You won't remember this,' he said, 'but you were one of my first patients here. You were a bit older than Lucy and you'd come in for your vaccinations.'

'I do remember. You gave me a lollipop.'

Tom laughed. 'Imagine the outrage if we were seen to be contributing to poor dental health these days?' His smile faded. 'The last time I saw you was for your repeat prescription for your reflux medications. Are those symptoms causing you any more issues?'

Olivia shrugged. 'They're a bit worse, I guess. I'm taking more antacids as well as the pills. It would be good to get the hernia fixed but there's no point if it's going to just come back when I get pregnant again.' Her smile was shy. 'We're trying for a second baby. Sam said that was another reason for me to come and see you—to make sure I'm a hundred percent.'

'He's quite right. Come and jump on the bed for a minute and let me give you a quick check.'

Tom was quick but thorough. He asked questions about any changes to diet or lifestyle as he did his physical examination. He found Olivia's heart rate, blood pressure and temperature were normal. So was his percussion of her chest and her breath sounds. Palpation of her abdomen revealed some epigastric discomfort.

'On a scale of one to ten with one being no pain and ten being the worst you can imagine, what score would you give this abdominal pain?'

'Maybe a four or five? But only when you push on it. Or if I've eaten too much.'

'Okay...lift your leg for me.' He put gentle pressure on her ankle. 'Try and keep it up.'

Tom did find a noticeable weakness in both her arms and legs, however, which was a concern.

'Watch my finger,' he instructed, as he concluded the brief neurological check. 'Keep watching it.' He moved his finger to the right and left, up and down. The ocular muscles were also weak and Tom's level of concern was rising. Despite how well Olivia was looking, instinct was telling him that these could be the first signs of something serious. He really hoped he was wrong.

'I'm going to get you to see our new practice nurse and get some blood tests taken before you leave,' he said, as

Olivia got off the bed and straightened her clothes. 'Have you got time?'

'Sure. We're just heading home again after this.' Olivia sat down again. 'Mum said the new nurse went to see Gran to change the dressings on her ulcers the other day and Gran really liked her. She said she was very kind and it didn't hurt as much as usual.'

'Good to hear,' Tom said. 'Her name's Claire and she's come over from England to live in New Zealand for a while. I think she's going to be a real asset to the team.' He was tapping his computer keyboard as he spoke and request forms for the blood tests were starting to emerge from the printer. 'I'd also like to refer you back to the specialist you saw in Christchurch for the hernia. She might want to do a gastroscopy rather than just the barium swallow test you had initially.'

Olivia was helping Lucy put the toys back into the box. 'Okay. That'll be fun, won't it, Lucy? We could go to the big playground while we're there. We might take Daddy with us if he can get a day off work and have a family fun day.'

'Can we get burgers, Mummy? And fries?'

Oliver shared a smile with Tom. 'It makes life easier to live in a place that's too small to have any fast-food outlets.' She led Lucy to the door but then looked over her shoulder with a smile. 'It's a shame about the lollipops though.'

Tom thought so, too. 'I might look into sourcing some sugar-free ones,' he said.

'Now you're talking...' Olivia was still smiling as she left.

The rest of the afternoon clinic passed swiftly, with

examinations and prescriptions given for a chest infection that was exacerbating respiratory issues, Edward's slowly increasing level of heart failure, a sprained ankle, different medication for someone whose high blood pressure wasn't responding to current treatment, a new diagnosis of atrial fibrillation and two toddlers, one with an ear infection and the other with an impressively snotty nose and a cough. His final patient was a girl that Hanna had gone to school with who wanted to start using contraception because she and her boyfriend had decided to take their relationship to the next level. Tom gave her a pamphlet.

'There are lots of options, Sasha. Condoms, both internal and external, different types of pills, injections, intra-uterine devices and implants. It can be a lot to take in all at once and there are more things to consider than simply not getting pregnant.'

'Yeah… I know. Like STIs.'

'And whether or not the options have side-effects or risks or use hormones which can affect your periods. Have a read, maybe talk to your boyfriend about it and come back to have a chat with me and we'll get you sorted. You can go and see our practice nurse as well, if there are things you'd rather talk about with her.' His smile was sympathetic. 'It's one of the downsides of living in a small town, isn't it, when your doctor's known you all your life and you're likely to meet him in the supermarket?'

Sasha laughed. 'Everybody knows you're a vault, Dr Atkinson. But yeah…it's a bit weird talking to you about anything to do with sex.'

Tom spent a few minutes typing a summary of the visit into Sasha's digital notes but he found he was thinking just as much about his own daughter. As far as he knew, Hanna did not have a steady boyfriend, but it would be unusual if, as a nineteen-year-old, she did not have a sex life. Was that another reason, on top of assuming he was lonely, why she was suddenly more interested in her father's longstanding lack of female companionship?

Not that it would excuse her misguided decision to put him onto that dating site without his knowledge. Tom's initial shock might have worn off and he knew that Hanna had probably had the best of intentions when she'd put her plan into action, but he still was a long way from being happy. He suspected Hanna felt the same way so it might be a good idea to give things more time to cool down before he went home. She would, hopefully, have distracted herself by focusing on studying for her final exams and he wouldn't want to interrupt that. He had plenty to do here, with a ward round of the inpatients in the hospital and making sure he was up-to-date with any new test results or referral notes that had arrived this afternoon.

It would be nice to be able to look forward to going home, however. Perhaps he could offer some kind of truce so that they could patch up their disagreement more easily?

He flicked her a text.

Be home by seven. I'll pick up some fish and chips for dinner.

He added a lip-licking emoji. There might not be any of the big chain, fast-food restaurants in town but this takeaway meal had been a Friday night treat for Tom and Hanna for many years. Eaten sitting outside in summer on the lawn or maybe down on the beach or on the rug in front of the fire in winter—always straight off the paper, with a puddle of tomato sauce near the chips. A time for just the two of them.

He knew that Hanna would be able to read the hidden message in this offer.

I still love you...

The practice nurse's room, which was also the medical centre's treatment room, at the end of the corridor leading away from the reception area was becoming a familiar space for Claire.

She knew where all the different vaccines were stored in the fridge, the cupboard that held the urine test dipsticks and the jars for specimen collection and could find any kind of dressings, disinfectant or bandages instantly. She could remove stitches or assist one of the doctors to insert them, take blood samples or chase up results. She had everything she needed to test blood glucose levels, take a blood pressure or do a twelve-lead ECG. It was her job to alert the doctors to abnormal results to see if another appointment needed to be made or to send a text message to the patient to reassure them that nothing abnormal had been found on a blood test, biopsy or scan. She also needed to be available at any time if she was needed as part of a response to an emergency like a cardiac arrest or a local accident.

Claire loved the variety her job offered. The community visits that took her out in the mornings to housebound patients in town or on farms were even more of a bonus in what had to be one of the most spectacular places she could have dreamed of ending up in.

Not that she had ever dreamed about it, mind you. It had taken a catastrophic implosion of the comfortable, if a little unfulfilling, life she'd been living just outside of London to shake her world up to this extent but she was finally at the point where anxiety about whether she was doing the right thing was being buried by the volume of sheer gratitude that she'd been forced into making such a dramatic change.

The cute little cottage she'd rented for the next six months was also a delight but she wasn't in too much of a hurry to get home. Maybe she should just double check that she hadn't missed any results that might have come in while she'd been so busy in the last couple of hours.

Booting up the computer in her room, Claire remembered the altercation she'd overheard earlier this afternoon between Tom Atkinson and his daughter. What was the name of that online dating site again?

Ah…yes… *Find The One*. Not particularly original. Claire's lips twitched. Neither was *TrustMeI'maDoctor*.

Claire was mystified. Having noticed the ring, she'd assumed that her new boss was married when she'd met him and why wouldn't he be? He was a good-looking middle-aged man who gave the impression of being very happy in his work and his life. An exceptionally good-looking man, in fact. Had he really been single for seven years?

She could hear the echo of a snippet of that conversation.

Someone had to do it… You were never going to do it for yourself, were you?

Okay…that did it.

She could no longer resist doing an internet search for

both the dating site and the profile for Tom Atkinson—if it hadn't been taken down already.

It hadn't.

Claire found herself smiling as she discovered that Hanna had chosen a superhero avatar for her father. Cute...

The profile gave a bare minimum of information.

Gender: male
Looking for: female
Age: 54
Marital status: widowed
Location: South Island

Claire blinked. So his wife *had* died. Presumably seven years ago. But he was still wearing his wedding ring? Why...? Had he been so in love with his wife that he couldn't bear to take it off? Or go dating again? No wonder he'd been so horrified by what Hanna had done on his behalf.

But it was kind of cute that she'd done it. She'd kept his description short but attention-grabbing as well.

Small town guy with a big heart who saves lives for a day job and goes scuba diving for fun. Be nice to have someone's hand to hold for a walk on the beach.

Send a kiss, the site invited its members, with a red heart button to click. *Get one back and you can start talking to the person who might just be 'The One'.*

Tom might have had fourteen kisses a few hours ago but there were twenty-six of them now. Each one came with a thumbnail profile picture to click on. Claire hovered the cursor over one of the pictures—a woman with a wild mane of peroxide blonde hair who seemed to be wearing only underwear—but something stopped her clicking.

Perhaps it was the feeling that she was being watched...

Her head turned so fast she felt something crack in her neck.

How on earth had she not heard someone coming into the room?

Someone who was now staring at the screen of the computer, where it was so very obvious that she wasn't doing anything remotely work-related. She was, in fact, snooping on the private life of one of her new colleagues.

Claire froze. It was possible that she'd never felt quite this mortified in her entire life.

Because this person was none other than the colleague in question, the only person, in fact, who could know who she was snooping on.

It was Tom Atkinson himself.

CHAPTER TWO

TALK ABOUT AWKWARD!

How on earth did the newest member of the staff of this medical centre know that he was enrolled on an online dating site?

Or was this simply a coincidence?

Maybe she'd joined up herself, which might make sense, being in a new town and a new country and wanting to meet people.

Except... Tom suddenly remembered the way Claire had apparently avoided eye contact with him in the waiting room earlier this afternoon. And she was looking... well, as guilty as if she'd been caught with her hand in the proverbial cookie jar. The cursor zipped across the screen to find the X that she clicked on to shut down the website.

'I'm so sorry,' she said. 'I should know better. I *do* know better but...' A corner of her mouth twitched. 'I couldn't help myself.'

'How did you find out about it?' Tom had the horrible thought that maybe he was the last person to know. Was he going to go to the fish and chip shop this evening and find everybody in the queue giving him knowing glances? The 'wink, wink' kind?

'I'd gone outside for a breath of fresh air and the window to your office was open,' Claire said. 'I didn't want you to know I'd overheard any part of what was obviously a private conversation, but by the time I'd realised I could turn around and go the long way back, it was too late. I knew what your username was and…' Her gaze slid sideways to the computer screen. 'I got curious.' She looked up at him. 'I'm really sorry…'

She was. Tom could see the apology in her eyes. Brown eyes, he noticed, but not a really dark brown. More like a dark hazel. His gaze only held hers for a split second but he still managed to catch a glimpse of something other than the colour or a genuine apology in her eyes. There was a spark of…what was it…interest? Mischief, even?

Perhaps there was more to this older, reliable and apparently very competent new staff member than he'd realised. It seemed to be his turn to feel curious.

She seemed to be finding this amusing rather than embarrassing, judging by the way she was biting her lip now, trying not to smile. 'It's certainly attracting a lot of attention.'

'She said she was taking it down.'

'It can take a while,' Claire said. 'Or so I've heard,' she added hastily. 'I've never put a profile up on a dating site, personally.'

'*I* didn't put this one up,' Tom said. 'In case you missed overhearing that part of the conversation. It was my daughter, Hanna, who did that.'

Claire nodded. 'It seems that it's becoming a normal way for young people to meet others these days.'

'I don't want to meet people,' Tom growled. 'And I certainly don't want to *date* anybody.'

Claire actually appeared to shudder at the thought.

'You and me both,' she said. 'Couldn't think of anything I'd like less, to be honest.'

Tom blinked. Why was she so vehement about it? He'd had enough experience with people to know that there had to be a story behind a reaction like that and he suddenly realised how little he knew about his new staff member, other than her age, professional qualifications and how impressed her referees had been.

He cleared his throat. He was relieved that this escapade of Hanna's might not be common knowledge. Perhaps the best way to bury the subject was to simply ignore it and move on.

'How are you settling in here?' he asked. 'I'm hearing good things about you.'

'Really? I've only been here for a week.'

'I had a visit from Olivia Jamieson. You did a house visit to her grandmother to dress her ulcers. She really liked you.'

'I liked her, too. What a character! I can't believe she's nearly a hundred years old and still living in her own home. Nasty diabetic ulcers, though.'

'Don't spread it around, but…' Tom lowered his voice as though he was about to impart something very confidential. 'She said the dressing change didn't hurt as much as it usually did.'

Claire's smile grew until it could only be described as a beam. It lit up her face and even the air surrounding her. 'I love this job. I love the people I'm meeting and I love my wee house and…oh, my goodness—the scenery is extraordinary. I can't wait to get out on a boat and go whale watching.'

'Sometimes,' Tom told her, 'you don't even need to go

out on a boat because the whales come in so close. There's a massive submarine canyon that's less than a kilometre from the shore in places. I saw some Southern right whales once, down by the tavern on the esplanade. We ended up with a huge crowd on the beach and the people sitting in the windows of the bar having a glass of wine that day certainly got a bonus.'

'Oh, wow!' Claire seemed thoroughly distracted. 'How amazing would that have been? I've been wanting to go into that bar and see what's it like,' she added, ducking her head. 'It's just not something I do...you know? I'm not brave enough to go somewhere for a drink by myself.'

'But you're brave enough to go to the other side of the world for a new job?' Tom laughed but then shook his head. 'We should have welcomed you properly by arranging something there.' He looked at his watch. 'I don't have to be home for a while yet. Why don't I see how many of the troops I can round up and we'll go right now.'

The way Claire wrinkled her nose was something he might have expected Hanna to do, not a mature woman, but it was kind of cute.

'It's a bit short notice. And late in the day. Anyone who's still here is likely to be on call, aren't they?'

'True. You should be heading home yourself.' He turned to leave but then turned back. 'Don't you live down that way? Off the esplanade?'

'I do.'

'Why don't I walk down with you and we could have a glass of wine and keep an eye out for a whale or two. To be honest, I could do with winding down a bit more before I get home. I was a bit...annoyed with Hanna about...' he took a furtive glance over his shoulder—there was no one else in the treatment room but he lowered his voice again anyway '…the dating site thing.'

Claire caught her bottom lip between her teeth for a moment. 'I don't blame you,' she said as she released it. 'I would have felt the same way.'

'Have you got a daughter?'

Her expression faltered. 'I did have,' she said. 'She… um…died ten years ago.'

'Oh, God… I'm *so* sorry…' Tom flinched and then groaned. Why hadn't somebody warned him so he wouldn't say something completely insensitive?

'It's okay…you weren't to know. It's not something I put on my CV.' Claire was smiling again, though it looked as if it was more of an effort. 'How 'bout we just rewind anything awkward either of us has said so far and we can start over?'

'Deal.' Tom blew out a sigh of relief. 'But I still owe you a glass of wine, by way of apology for putting my foot in my mouth like that.'

Claire was shaking her head but smiling at the same time. 'Maybe it's me who owes you one—*my* apology for the very unprofessional snooping.'

'In that case, let's just resolve the issue right now, along with dissolving any of the awkwardness we've managed to create. We can go and buy a drink for each other.'

Claire laughed. 'Is that the opposite of going Dutch?'

'Could be.' Tom was holding the door open as Claire picked up her coat. 'But it's friendlier because you're not paying for your own drink.'

Tom ended up paying for both their glasses of white wine, but Claire simply thanked him rather than protesting.

They both knew that he had, albeit inadvertently, trodden on ground that was even more personal than someone's sex life and it was important that they reached a space in which there were no obstructions to working well together.

The nautically themed bar and restaurant—Beachcombers—had comfortable chairs near the bar that afforded a view out to sea over the road, past the trunks of trees that lined the stretch of grass leading to the stony beach.

'Do you know what those trees are?' Claire asked as they sat down. 'They look like really overgrown Christmas trees.'

'They're Norfolk Island pines,' Tom told her. 'Planted well over a hundred years ago now. I believe they're closely related to the monkey puzzle trees that are native to South America.'

Claire eyed him over the rim of her glass as she took a sip of an excellent white wine and Tom grinned.

'Sorry... I didn't mean to sound like some kind of tree nerd. I grew up here and you kind of absorb a lot of local knowledge. It would have made Hanna roll her eyes, too.'

'It would take more than that to make me roll my eyes.' Claire returned his smile. 'How old is Hanna?'

'Nineteen. She's finishing her pre-med course in Health Sciences at university in Dunedin. Up here on study leave for a few days before the rest of her final exams. She's hoping to get into medical school next year.'

'Hoping? Is it very competitive?'

Tom nodded. 'But she's working hard and her marks are great, so fingers crossed.'

He was clearly very proud of his daughter but Claire

could see it was making him uncomfortable talking about her. They were both too aware of the elephant in the room. She swallowed hard.

'Ten years ago, my daughter Sophia was in her first year of university,' she told him quietly. 'She was living in a residential hall and she caught meningitis but she was told she just had the flu and got sent home from the campus medical centre. Her roommate called an ambulance in the middle of the night, but by the time we got to the hospital she was deeply unconscious. She never woke up.' Claire cleared her throat before she could sink too far into the past and do something embarrassing like burst into tears. 'She wasn't planning on becoming a doctor, though. She had her sights set on being a marine biologist.' She fixed her gaze on the sea view. 'She would have loved Kaikōura.'

Tom was silent for a long moment. 'Lives can change in a heartbeat,' he said quietly. 'My wife, Jill, died when Hanna was only twelve—a time when a girl really needs her mum the most, I think. It's just been the two of us since then.'

Claire couldn't help shifting her gaze to his left hand.

'I know…' Tom grimaced. 'I kept wearing it to start with because I couldn't bear to take it off. And then I kept wearing it because I didn't want anyone to think I was making myself available. I have no desire to put myself back out there. That's why I might have overreacted a bit to what Hanna did.'

'I totally understand,' Claire told him. 'I might have kept wearing my wedding ring except…' She took a deep breath. 'I threw it away. As far as I could. I pulled it off my finger and hurled it into the Thames.'

'Really?' Tom's eyes widened. 'That's rather dramatic.'

'So was finding my husband in bed with his secretary. A woman half his age. In *our* bed. During my sixtieth birthday party, no less.'

Tom opened his mouth to say something but then closed it again, clearly lost for words.

'It's not as bad as it sounds.' Claire shrugged as she broke the silence. 'It wasn't even the first time he'd had an affair. Our marriage had been over long ago, really. Looking back, losing Sophia was probably the real end. We just kept going out of habit. Or maybe it was too hard to find the energy to do something about it. I should thank Richard to some degree, I guess. He made it impossible for me *not* to do something.'

The silence was longer this time.

'Sorry,' Claire said with a grimace. 'That was way too much information, wasn't it? You're the first person I've ever said that to.' She eyed her glass and tried to find a smile. 'How strong is that wine?'

'Don't worry about it,' Tom said. 'I've never told anyone why I've kept wearing my wedding ring either.' He wasn't smiling but his glance was kind. Understanding. 'Sometimes it's easier to say things to people who don't know you very well. Or maybe we just feel comfortable with each other? That wouldn't be a bad thing, would it?'

'Not at all.'

And magically, her embarrassment about oversharing evaporated. Comfortable was exactly how she was feeling.

'So…here you are,' Tom said. He sounded comfortable, too. 'On the opposite side of the world, with a totally new life.'

Claire's smile felt real this time. 'My first adventure,' she agreed. 'But definitely not the last. I'm going to make the most of whatever time I've got left and…it's all about me from now on. I'm not going to complicate my life by including anybody else. Does that sound incredibly selfish?'

'It sounds both brilliant and brave.' Tom raised his glass to clink it against Claire's. 'Go you.'

His smile held a note of admiration and it was warm enough to make the corners of his eyes crinkle. Very blue eyes, she noticed for the first time. Dark blue—like the sea here became further out when it was, presumably, too deep to have that turquoise hue. She took a larger swallow of her wine this time.

'So…' Claire raised her eyebrows. 'Scuba diving, huh…?'

'I got into it at high school. My best mate Pete was passionate about it. He runs a dive school now. It's only a hobby for me. I like going out to play with the seals and get a few crayfish.'

'They're like our Cornish lobsters, yes? Or crawfish?'

'Do you like them?'

'I have to confess, I've never actually tasted them.'

'I'll get you one next time I go out. How 'bout you? What are your hobbies, Claire?'

'I have a new hobby,' Claire said decisively. 'Making the most of every adventure that comes my way. And if it doesn't come my way, I'll go out and find it.'

They clinked almost empty glasses this time and then drank the last of their wine.

A young woman had been collecting empty glasses

from a nearby table. She paused as she carried the tray past Tom and Claire. 'Can I get you guys another drink?'

'Not for me,' Tom said. 'I'd better get going. I told Hanna I was going to pick up some fish and chips for dinner. Claire—would you like anything else?'

She shook her head. 'No, thank you.'

'This is Kerry,' Tom told her. 'She was Hanna's best friend right through school.'

'BFFs,' Kerry confirmed. 'And you're the new nurse at the medical centre, aren't you? From England?' She grinned at Claire's expression. 'Word gets around,' she said unapologetically.

She picked up their empty glasses. 'Tell Hanna I'll call her tomorrow,' she said to Tom. 'We need to catch up properly before she heads back to uni.'

And then, to Claire's astonishment, Kerry winked at Tom and lowered her voice to a stage whisper. 'She's going to be thrilled that you're out on a date. Last I heard, she was going to surprise you by putting your profile up on *Find The One*. Now she won't have to.'

She grinned at Claire as she turned to head back to the bar. 'Welcome to Kaikōura,' she said. 'I'm sure you're going to be very happy here.'

Tom was more than lost for words as Kerry headed back to the bar. Claire was almost certain that the poor man was blushing. He wasn't making any move to go and order dinner either.

He made a sound like a stifled groan.

'Looks like I need to apologise again,' he said. 'You must be starting to wonder what you've been dragged into.'

'It's not a problem,' Claire assured him. 'I'm kind of

liking the village feel I'm getting here. And I think it's sweet that Hanna doesn't want you to be lonely.'

'I guess. But I don't want her worrying about me. It's hard enough coping with university and living away from home for the first time. I'm the one who's supposed to worry about her, not the other way round.'

He made a kind of growling sound this time. 'I'm going to make sure she's deleted that membership as soon as I get home. And that it never happens again.' He glanced over his shoulder. 'Want me to go and let Kerry know that this is definitely *not* a date? It might be half-way around town by now.'

'I'm not bothered,' Claire said. '*We* know it's not a date and that's all that really matters. And—'

Tom's eyebrows rose. 'And *what*?'

'It just occurred to me that if Hanna does think you were out on a date, she'll be more than happy to delete your profile. She might even stop worrying about you.'

'You wouldn't mind people thinking that we're going out with each other?' He cleared his throat. '*Dating...*?'

'Don't get the wrong idea,' Claire said hurriedly. 'I don't *want* to date anybody. And if I did, it wouldn't be my new boss. But if it's the solution to your...um...personal issue that I accidentally managed to get involved in today, I'm quite happy to go along with people *thinking* that we might be dating.'

Tom was staring at her. 'It might work both ways,' he said slowly.

'How?'

'A new, unattached and attractive woman in town is not going to go unnoticed in a small place like this. If it gets around that *we're* getting to know each other, nobody's going to hit on you.'

A silence fell between them that stretched on.

And on.

Or maybe it was just Claire's attention had caught so completely on something Tom had said that she wasn't hearing anything else.

He thought she was *attractive*?

Yep. He was still talking.

'...so we could both adopt a "neither confirm nor deny" policy and we'd be the only ones who knew the truth. But it's not as though we'd be doing something dishonest and... I don't know about you, but I'd be more than happy to spend some more time in your company.'

There was no hint of anything more than friendliness in either Tom's tone or expression. If he considered her to be attractive it was purely an impersonal observation. She had, after all, considered him to be an exceptionally good-looking man, hadn't she?

And she was on a side of the world where she didn't know a soul. It would be stupid to find reasons to not make a friend.

So she smiled at Tom.

'Same,' she said.

'Ooh... Fish and chips? It's not even Friday.'

'I felt too lazy to cook.' These days, they tended to eat at the kitchen table rather than lounging on the floor or the lawn. Tom unfolded the white newsprint paper as Hanna got the bottle of tomato sauce from the fridge.

'How's the study going?'

'Good. I need to do a practice multi-choice test for

microbiology on genes, inheritance and selection next. Want to help? You could ask me the questions and explain anything I get wrong.'

'I might have forgotten a lot of that stuff.'

'Doubt it.' Hanna leaned past Tom to squirt the sauce into a puddle on a corner of the paper. 'What sort of fish is it?'

'Tarakihi. We got lucky—it was fresh in today.'

They both knew this flaky white fish was Hanna's favourite. She caught her father's glance.

'I'm sorry, Dad…about…the dating site thing. I've deleted your profile but it might take a day or two to disappear.'

'Okay. Thanks…'

Hanna sat down, picked up a piece of battered fish and broke it in half to release fragrant steam. 'Sounds like you don't need it anyway.'

'Oh?' Tom had turned back to the kitchen bench to rip off some paper towels to use as serviettes. He knew exactly what Hanna was referring to but it was easy to play dumb.

'Yeah… Kerry sent me a pic of you having a drink at the Beachcombers. Who was your date?'

Tom opened his mouth to deny that it had been a date but stopped himself just in time. Neither confirm nor deny, he reminded himself. This was it. The moment where he would find out whether Hanna would stop worrying about him. If she could focus on enjoying her own life and not feel any need to interfere with his.

'I was with Claire Campbell.' He kept his tone casual. 'Our new practice nurse.'

'The English lady?'

'Yes.'

'So she's single then? She's quite attractive, isn't she?'

Tom remembered telling Claire she would be seen as an unattached and attractive new woman in town and… yes…that shiny, silvery hair and her soft brown eyes *were* a very nice combination. The way her face could light up with that eye-catching smile was more appealing, however. So was her attitude to life.

Claire had been through a personal loss in life as crushing as his own but her response—now, at least— was very different to his own. Tom had made his life smaller. He had focused on his daughter and his work and, apart from his hobby of scuba diving, he'd deliberately shut other pleasures out of his life. Like companionship. And sex. Anything that had the risk of emotional complications or, worse, loss associated with it, in fact. His mantra had been that it wasn't all about himself because putting someone else first made it easier to protect himself from risk.

Claire's new mantra was that it was *all* about herself and she intended to make the most of the rest of her life. She was out to have fun. Adventures.

Adventurous people were always interesting.

If they had to spend some time in each other's company now and then to keep up the smokescreen that would prevent Hanna worrying about his personal life, it wasn't going to be a hardship. Maybe it wouldn't hurt if a bit of her attitude to life rubbed off on him. He was probably overdue for a bit of fun himself.

He'd almost forgotten what Hanna's question had been.

'Yes,' he said aloud. 'She's definitely single and she *is* a very attractive woman but she's only just arrived in the country a week or so ago.' Tom reached for one of the crispy battered fish fillets. 'Don't you or Kerry go starting any rumours. Give the poor woman a chance to get settled in.'

'Don't worry... I get it.' Hanna tilted her head. 'It's early days... We'll make sure we don't scare her off.'

She probably thought her smile was hidden as she ate another chip but Tom could almost feel her breathing a sigh of relief and see a thought bubble forming over her head.

My work is done...

CHAPTER THREE

'Claire, can I get you to give me a hand, please?'

'Of course.' Claire was only too happy to help. It had, in fact, made her happy just to see Tom appear in the doorway of the treatment room. 'I was just about to start sending test result text messages but they can wait.' She got to her feet as Tom stood back from the open door.

'Come on in, Carl. Claire's not going to bite.'

A man with curly grey hair and grizzled stubble on his face entered the room. He was wearing an oilskin vest over a heavy knitted jumper with one sleeve pulled up. What looked like an oily rag was wrapped around his hand. His attempt at a smile was enough of a failure to let Claire know he was in severe pain.

'Let me help you,' she said, going towards him. She caught Tom's gaze. 'Bed or chair?'

'Bed,' Tom said. 'Carl might look as tough as old boots but he's just the kind to faint at the sight of a needle.'

'Yeah…right…' Carl gave a dismissive huff. He evaded any help from Claire as he climbed onto the bed and lay back against the pillows, the rag-wrapped hand being held protectively by the wrist at head height.

'Carl is one of the favourite boat skippers in town,' Tom told her. 'He does dive trips and whale watching tours. He's managed to get a finger caught in a pulley this morning, though, and he's done a good job of squashing it. Might well lose the tip. Could be lucky to keep the rest of it.'

Claire lifted her eyebrows. Tom gave a single shake of his head.

'Not the kind of minor surgery we can do. I've called for an ambulance to transfer him to Christchurch but I want to get a ring block in to deal with the pain and clean things up a bit. That rag from the boat is not going to cut it as a sterile dressing. When did you last have a tetanus booster, Carl?'

'No idea.'

'I'll check your notes but I'm pretty sure you're going to need a top-up.'

Claire was opening cupboards to grab supplies as Tom went to the basin to scrub his hands. She'd had another week or so to get to know where everything was in this room so she could work more swiftly now. She put alcohol wipes, syringes, needles and local anaesthetic into a kidney dish that she put on a trolley. She also collected disinfectant, dressings and bandages. Finally, she pulled a couple of plastic-backed sterile sheets from a box like an oversized packet of tissues. By the time Tom was drying his hands and then reaching to pull gloves from the box on the wall, she had the trolley positioned beside the bed and was pulling on gloves herself.

She'd also had another week or so to get used to working with Tom in the wake of their agreement to let Hanna think he didn't need any assistance in his love life. The extra time had confirmed how good he was at his job, how respected and valued he was in this close-knit community, but it had also become apparent that Hanna wasn't the only one who believed the pretence that there might be something simmering between herself and Tom. So far it had been easy to stick to the 'neither confirm nor deny' tactic and nobody pushed her when she simply smiled and said how much she was enjoying working with everybody at the medical centre and how lovely it was to be making new friends.

That hadn't stopped a few envious glances coming her way from other women, mind you, which was understandable. She slid a sideways glance at Tom, who had picked up an ampoule of lidocaine and was starting to draw the drug up into a syringe. He *was* a very attractive man. Even better, he was a very *nice* man.

'If you can get rid of the rag, it would be helpful,' he said to Claire. Then he smiled at Carl. 'We'll have you sorted in no time, mate.'

'Sorry...' Claire apologised in advance. 'I know it hurts to move your hand. I'm going to put one of these waterproof sheets on the bed beside you here, and if you can hold your hand over it, I'll take the cloth off before you put your hand down.'

Carl's hands had oil ingrained into the skin and under his nails. Claire carefully unwrapped the cloth to reveal the badly squashed ring finger on his left hand.

'Put the hand palm down,' Tom instructed Claire. 'I'll get you to hold the wrist and help keep his hand steady, please.'

Tom ripped open a small foil package to remove an alcohol wipe and swab the area around the base of the finger.

'We have to do something about that wedding ring,' he

noted. 'It's almost disappeared under the swelling already. We'll cut it off once we've numbed your finger, Carl.'

'The missus won't be too happy about that.' Carl was staring up at the ceiling, clearly not wanting to see how bad the finger injury was.

'Can't be helped,' Tom said. 'And it needs to come off as soon as possible before that finger gets any more swollen or I won't be able to use my ring cutter.'

'You'll be able to get the ring fixed,' Claire assured him.

'Might keep it as a souvenir,' Carl muttered. 'In case I don't get to keep my finger.'

Tom was about to inject into the web on each side of the finger where it joined the palm. A quick glance was a silent query as to whether Claire was ready to counteract any movement from Carl during what was going to be the most painful part of this procedure. She settled her hands across his forearm and wrist and tried to think of something to distract him.

'I'm really looking forward to doing a whale watch boat trip, myself,' she said. 'What's the name of your boat so I'll know who to book with?'

'*Time and Tide.*'

'As in you don't wait for anybody?'

'More like make the most of today.' Carl winced as the needle went into his hand,

'I like that philosophy,' Claire told him as she tightened her grip on his arm a little. 'I'm guessing a really calm day is best?'

Carl's voice was strained. He could feel the anaesthetic being injected. 'You wouldn't believe how many people get sick out there. Especially on a smaller boat like mine.

It's a catamaran. Sits nice and low in the water so you're closer to the action and I only take out about ten people at a time. Twelve, max.' He was still gritting his teeth as Tom inserted the needle for a second time on the other side of his finger.

'What sort of whales might I get to see?' Claire asked. 'Tom told me he saw some really close to the shore—what were they? Southern something?'

'Southern right,' Tom said. 'But giant sperm whales are the stars of the show, aren't they, Carl?'

'My favourites are the humpbacks,' Carl said. 'They can really put on a show, if you're lucky.' He let his breath out in a sigh which suggested that he was already noticing a difference in his pain level. He opened his eyes to look at Claire. 'How 'bout I keep an eye on the weather and give you a heads-up whenever it's looking good. Should coincide with a day off for you, eventually.'

'That would be great. Thank you!'

'Not sure when I'll be back on deck, mind you. Ooh… that's feeling a lot better, Doc. Pain's almost gone.'

'It can take up to ten minutes for the full effect and it should last long enough to get you to specialist care in the big smoke. Don't move. Can you find the ring cutter for me, please, Claire? It should be on the bottom shelf of the cupboard in the far corner—it's a black plastic box about the size of a laryngoscope kit. Should be labelled.'

Claire hadn't seen the specialist tool that Tom got out of the case. He inserted a thin, flat metal plate under the ring on Carl's finger.

'Protection,' he said. 'So I don't go too far and cut more than the ring.'

Carl shook his head. 'Hope you know what you're doing, Doc.'

Tom grinned. 'I don't get to play with this toy very often but I have done it before. Claire, can you get a syringe and fill it with saline? The metal gets hot so it'll be useful to cool it off occasionally.'

It took time to use the battery-powered disc cutter and then a tiny pair of spreaders that opened the ring far enough to remove. It left a deep mark between a normal-looking hand and a finger that had ballooned into a large sausage shape.

'Flush the wound as best you can, Claire, and then we'll dress the finger and splint the hand. I'm going to check Carl's notes and get a tetanus booster sorted.'

Claire cleaned and dressed the finger and then bandaged the whole hand into a splint. She was tying the knot of a sling behind Carl's neck as Tom came back in. 'Our ambulance will be here in a minute,' he said. 'Just time to give you that booster. They'll take you halfway and a crew from Christchurch will take over.'

Minutes later and Carl was walking out to the ambulance.

'I'll get a report from the specialists,' Tom said. 'But come and see me when you get back if you're worried about anything.'

'Will do.'

'I'll look forward to hearing from you, too,' Claire told Carl. 'I'm going to wait for my whale watching until you are back on deck.'

Tom followed Claire back into the clinic.

'Is there something else you need?' she asked. 'Aren't you due to do a ward round?'

Tom wasn't really surprised that Claire was obviously becoming as familiar with his routine as she was with all aspects of her own job. She was, hands down, the best practice nurse he'd ever worked with.

'I am, yes...but I'm hoping I'm going to find an urgent appointment's been made by the gastroenterology department in Christchurch for Olivia Jamieson. If there isn't, I might need to chase my referral up. I would really prefer her to be seen as soon as possible.'

'I've got the link open on my computer in the treatment room. Not sure I've seen anything about Olivia, though.'

'I'll come in for a minute and check.'

Tom sat down at the desk tucked in behind the door. He could hear Claire busy dealing with contaminated rubbish like swabs that had to go into the hazards rubbish bag and the sharps like needles that went into the plastic wall container as he scrolled through the clinic email marked for his attention.

'How did Hanna go with her exam yesterday?' Claire asked.

'She's happy. She's got a couple more next week and then she'll start the summer job that she's really excited to have scored.'

'What is it?'

'An entry-level position as a medical laboratory technician. They'll give her on-the-job training.'

'Sounds great. She'll be learning a lot and getting paid for it as well. I hope she'll get some time off, though. You must be missing her.'

'I hear from her most days.' Tom turned away from the screen. He'd have to check again later or try ringing the specialist, although he knew how busy they would be. 'She's been asking about you.'

'Oh…?' Claire had her back to him as she put the kidney dishes into the benchtop steriliser. She sounded… wary?

As well she might. Hanna wanted details of the embryonic relationship she believed he had with Claire.

'She wants an update,' Tom said.

'What kind of update?' Claire looked over her shoulder. 'A full report on an *actual* date?'

'That would work.' Tom got to his feet. He felt slightly uncomfortable at the thought of having anything *like* an actual date with Claire because it made him instantly more aware of her as a woman than as his colleague. She was more than simply attractive he'd decided at some point since Hanna's visit when the plan to let her think he was dating Claire had been hatched. That shiny silvery hair was like moonlight and it made her brown eyes look even darker. Warmer. She looked at least a decade younger than he knew she was. Younger than him, even. Not that he was thinking about her age. Or her attractiveness. He needed to think of a pretend date that he could tell Hanna about.

'It might not be a good look if we're only meeting to have a drink,' he said. 'Maybe we could do something that looks like a healthier kind of date.'

'Such as?'

'A movie? A walk? A visit to the lookout?'

'Ooh… The lookout on the hill where you can see both sides of the peninsula? I haven't been up there yet. I drove up to Blenheim on my last day off.'

'Let's go after work. A quick selfie with the wind in our hair and the view behind us will be more than enough to keep Hanna happy.'

He was feeling rather happy about the prospect himself, in fact. Tom headed for the door. It was definitely time he went and got on with that ward round.

It was only a thirty-minute walk up to the lookout, which should have warmed them up very well but there was an icy wind blowing on the top of the hill that felt like it was coming straight off those snow-capped mountains. They could see over South Bay on one side of the peninsula but the view they needed as a background was in the opposite direction where the ocean swept out to one side and the dramatic peaks of the mountains towered over the township and made the distinctive pointy tips of the Norfolk pines look the size of toothpicks.

'The mountains are called the Seaward Kaikōura Range,' Tom told her. 'But they're really the northernmost section of the Southern Alps that go all the way down to Queenstown in Central Otago. That's another part of the country you need to explore on this adventure you're having.'

'Is Mount Cook part of the Southern Alps? That's the tallest mountain in New Zealand, isn't it?' Claire was trying not to let her teeth chatter. She couldn't feel her cheeks or her nose now but the view was definitely worth it.

'Sure is, even though ten metres fell off it in an earthquake back in the nineties.' Tom didn't seem to be feeling the cold as much as Claire was. He was fishing his phone out of his pocket.

'You any good at taking selfies?'

'I've never taken one in my life,' Claire confessed.

'And I suspect my fingers would be too cold to push the button, anyway.'

'Can't say I've taken many either, but let's see what we can do.'

They turned so that the mountains and ocean would be behind them and Tom held his phone up as far away as he could reach. Only half of their faces were on each edge on the screen.

'We need to be closer.' Tom's arm was pressed against Claire's but then he lifted it and put it around her shoulders.

She instantly felt warmer.

And it felt...nice. How long had it been since she'd had a man's arm around her like this?

'Okay...try and look happy,' Tom instructed. 'This is supposed to be a date, remember?'

Claire could see both their faces in the phone's screen. Tom was grinning, as if he was having the best time. Claire tipped her head a little as she practised a big smile and it ended up against Tom's shoulder as he took the photograph.

'This is great,' he declared. 'But let's do another one just to make sure.'

Claire was getting used to the feeling of Tom's arm and her smile felt way more genuine now. She found herself looking up at Tom rather than at the phone. He seemed taller up this close.

Astonishingly good-looking with the way the wind was whipping his hair into a rough tumble of waves. And that smile...

Oh, my goodness...it was one of the loveliest smiles Claire had ever seen. She'd totally forgotten how cold she'd been feeling only a minute or two ago. Maybe because of the warm glow that her body was suddenly producing?

It was a glow she hadn't experienced in too many years to count, but Claire knew instantly what it was and she found herself moving away from the touch of Tom's body. Being attracted to him was definitely not part of the plan. Being attracted to anyone was not in any plan Claire had in her life going forward. Been there, done that and she didn't even want to wear the tee shirt any longer.

If she just ignored it, would it quietly go away?

Tom didn't seem to have noticed. He was checking out the photos.

'I don't want to blow my own trumpet,' he said, 'but this one's great. Look at that view.'

It *was* a great photo. Good enough for a travel blog with that backdrop of mountains and ocean. What Claire noticed more, however, was that the way she was gazing up at Tom, with her head against his arm, could be seen as blatantly advertising how attracted she was to the man.

How inappropriate was that?

At least Tom would think she'd only been acting for the sake of the staged photo he'd requested so that they could give Hanna the impression that they were on a real date. This was for Hanna's benefit, after all, so that she could stop worrying about her dad and focus on her own life, but it was a win-win situation for everybody involved, wasn't it? Tom could avoid having any interference with the way he wanted to live *his* life. And Claire had her own reasons to be grateful for this unexpected playacting—the protection of declaring herself unavailable for dating with the bonus of having a new friendship in her life. A platonic one that had strong enough boundaries to render it completely safe.

They were doing this because the last thing Tom wanted was to be genuinely dating anyone and Claire was just as keen to avoid becoming romantically involved with anyone again. If she ever changed her mind about that, it certainly wouldn't be happening with a man who was her boss, with the additional risk of making her professional life uncomfortable if it turned to custard. Not only that—Tom was seven years younger than she was, for heaven's sake. Young enough to be her…okay, not her son, of course, but…little brother?

'That photo's the one,' Claire declared. 'It should be more than enough to keep Hanna happy for a while.'

Tom didn't seem so sure. 'Next time,' he said, 'we'll go to the movies. It'll be a whole lot warmer, I promise.'

It was actually far more pleasant than Tom had expected to have a companion to…well, *do* stuff with. Things that his mate, Pete, might have thought it was strange to spend his time off doing. The kind of things that Tom hadn't done since Hanna became old enough to want to hang out with her friends rather than spend too much time in her dad's company.

Things like grabbing last-minute tickets to go to the latest blockbuster being screened in the only movie theatre in town. The selfie he took outside the iconic old pink art deco building got a response from Hanna by way of a text message that consisted of a whole line of heart emojis. It was like getting an A+ on a report card for the project of making Hanna think he was happy enough in his personal life that there was no need for her to interfere.

He could possibly have relaxed his efforts a bit after that but…this was fun. Claire was great company, and they both knew that this was never going to be anything more than a friendship, so it was…

Completely safe. That's what it was. So why not enjoy it?

There was absolutely no danger of it being considered as anything significant. On either side. Claire had only recently escaped a marriage that had clearly been less than ideal and she was embracing the freedom to do whatever she wanted without…how had she put it? Oh, yeah…that she wasn't going to complicate her life by including anybody else.

Tom could understand that. Why would she want to risk getting trapped in another less-than-ideal relationship? Was his aversion to the risk of getting too close to someone even stronger because his marriage *had* been so good? Because he couldn't face the idea of having to pick his life up after having had it completely shattered?

Not that it mattered. They both had very valid reasons for not wanting anything more than a friendship and that was what made this safe enough to embrace.

He took Claire to the most famous of the crayfish caravans that were dotted along the coastline and sold freshly caught crayfish, cooked or still alive if you wanted to do the cooking yourself. That would have been Tom's choice, given that he hadn't had a chance to go diving for a while, until he saw how fast Claire took a backwards step when he held one up to show her. The waving long antennae, too many legs and the claws were obviously way too close for comfort and, while her expression made him have to stifle laughter as he apologised, he made a mental note to be more considerate when he'd caught his own to cook on the barbecue or under the grill for her at his house.

The thought made him blink and he was still thinking about it when they sat at one of the picnic tables beside the caravan to share a freshly cooked crayfish tail served with garlic butter and lemon. Was he really thinking of inviting Claire home for dinner? *Just* Claire?

Maybe he should make it a work thing and invite everybody for a casual get-together?

Nah… Tom lifted another delicious mouthful of the white meat from the bright orange shell of the crayfish tail. It would be harder to keep up the pretence of this being anything more than a friendship if it was out of work hours and they had an audience. He might have to start giving some thought to how this was going to work when Hanna came home for a visit, however. She would be an even sharper-eyed audience than anyone they worked with.

Not that he needed to worry about that yet. He could keep enjoying being alone together with Claire in the meantime.

On another shared day off, they drove even further north to have lunch at a popular café in Kekerengu that had a gift shop full of tempting locally made products. Claire stopped on the way out to admire a blanket that had a pattern of small woolly sheep woven into it.

'That's such a Kiwi blanket,' she said.

The urge to give her something that she might treasure was unexpectedly strong, 'Let me buy it for you,' Tom offered. 'As a thank you gift.'

'What for? You've just taken me out for a lovely lunch.

And consider this fair warning that I'm definitely paying next time.'

'I just wanted to say thank you for going along with this... I don't know what to call it...this fake dating? Hanna's so happy about it. I'm totally off the hook for any future online capers.'

Claire went quite still. 'Do you know, I'd almost forgotten about that,' she said. 'It's started to feel like...spending time with a friend. Our friendship isn't fake, is it?'

Tom's smile was fading rapidly. 'Of course not. I'm enjoying this as much as you are. I'd still like to get the blanket for you, though.'

But Claire shook her head. 'I'm travelling light,' she said. 'Who knows when I'll get itchy feet to set off on my next adventure? I don't want to be accumulating luggage on the way.'

'Fair enough.'

They stopped on the way back to Kaikōura that day to visit the seal colony. A fenced walkway provided the perfect viewing point to get close enough to watch without disturbing the seals. He got his phone out to take pictures of the adults sunbathing like giant brown slugs on top of rocks big enough to keep them safe from being annoyed by the tribe of playful babies that were rock scrambling, sliding over piles of kelp or learning to swim in the rock pools but he ended up taking photos of Claire laughing at their antics.

And they were both laughing in that selfie.

Tom looked at it later, intending to send it to Hanna, but something made him pause. Was it because he was struck by how gorgeous Claire was, with the sunlight caught in her hair making it look like a halo? And that *smile*... He was smiling now, just looking at the image of it. Not as widely as he was smiling in the photograph, however. He hadn't seen himself looking *this* happy in years and, for some peculiar reason, it suddenly made him feel sad enough to bring a lump to his throat.

Why? Because it was reminding him of the companionship and support of a happy marriage and a beloved wife? Underlining what was missing from his life now? Even the pretence of having found someone new was making him happier.

So maybe he needed to think about that. About whether he was finally ready to invite someone else into his life again.

Not Claire, of course. She'd made it very clear that she was only here on a temporary basis. Kaikōura was simply the first stop on the series of adventures she was going to pack into her life. The worst thing he could do would be to fall for someone when it was inevitable that he would lose her in the near future. That would put him back to square one and if that happened Tom knew how unlikely it was that he would ever want to try again.

But could that also be why he was feeling sad looking at this photo? Because it was recording a relationship that could never be anything more than fake?

No. Tom remembered what Claire had asked earlier today.

'Our friendship isn't fake, is it?'

He cleared that lump from his throat. It certainly wasn't. Their friendship was becoming very special. Important. Potentially life-changing, even?

Tom tapped the share button and sent the image to Hanna.

We had a great day today. Hope you did, too.

CHAPTER FOUR

MAYBE THE STARS weren't aligned quite right today.

Claire had felt like something was out of kilter ever since she'd woken up this morning, even though she couldn't think of any good reason to feel this way. It was probably just life, she told herself as she arrived at work to start her community house calls. Some days were simply better than others.

Mabel Jamieson certainly wasn't having a good start to her day, as Claire had to spend more time cleaning the infected ulcers on her feet and the antiseptic solution on what was nothing more than raw flesh had to be excruciatingly painful.

'I'm so sorry, Mabel. We'll get some fresh dressings on very soon and they should stop hurting so much.'

'You just do what you need to do, love. I'm not complaining.'

'You never do.' Claire looked up with a smile for a patient she had become very fond of in a matter of only weeks. 'You're a legend.'

Mabel shook her head. 'You expect things to go wrong at my age. What's you don't expect is that a darling young one like our Livvy is going to get sick. She had to have all sorts of tests done last week in Christchurch. She said she got put right inside some enormous machine. For a scan.'

'It would have been a CT scan. Or maybe an MRI. Did she say if there were strange noises happening?'

'No. But she had to go back the next morning and they put her to sleep to put a camera down her throat to take a biopsy of something. She did say she was nervous about getting the results. She thinks she might have an ulcer herself, in her gullet, and that's why she gets such bad indigestion. At least I can keep my weight off my feet to give things a chance to heal. She's a busy young mum—she can't stop *eating*, can she?'

'Ulcers *are* treatable,' Claire said, trying to sound reassuring. 'And Olivia might need to avoid certain foods, but she wouldn't need to stop eating completely if that *is* what's causing her problems.' She found a smile for Mabel. 'This infection is starting to respond to the antibiotics, I think. Tom will be happy to hear that.'

Tom had been worried that if things got any worse, Mabel might well need to be admitted to hospital and when you were nearly a hundred years old there was no guarantee that you would get to go home again.

'Sorry,' she said again, as Mabel winced beneath her hands at the sting of the liquid. 'That's the last one.'

Her elderly patient was much happier a few minutes later as Claire began applying the specialised absorbent dressings that were also impregnated with beneficial medications.

'So what's this I hear about you and young Tom Atkinson?' Mabel queried, her tone much brighter. 'Is he courting you?'

'Good heavens, no.' Claire's laugh was genuine. 'What

a wonderful old-fashioned expression that is. No,' she repeated, more decisively. 'We're just good friends.'

'I've heard that one before.' Mabel chuckled but didn't pry any further. 'Enjoy yourself,' was all she said. 'Make the most of still being young enough to have that kind of fun.'

Claire pretended to be too busy with securing the dressings to respond but she was smiling. Mabel had reminded her of why the not so good things in life had their purpose—they made you appreciate the really good things even more.

Like the day she'd spent with Tom last weekend and they'd gone halfway to Blenheim to have lunch and then watched the baby seals playing on the way home.

She'd been regretting not buying that sheep blanket, though. Was her decision not to acquire something that she would love to have on her bed, or cuddle up under on the couch, really about not collecting too many possessions for when she moved on?

Or was it because Tom had offered to buy it for her and that felt like a gift that would be too significant?

A gift that might make her start believing things that had no basis in reality? Like how Tom felt about her, for instance. And whether there might be something happening that was more than purely a friendship.

Claire shook the thought off as she put her kit back into the back hatch of the hospital car she used for her community visits and slammed the door shut.

Mabel was old and wise.

She should just enjoy this friendship she'd found with Tom. He'd made it very clear there was nothing more on offer. Heavens above…this had only started because he was so determined to avoid going anywhere near that type of relationship with someone.

And thank goodness for that.

It was the last thing she wanted as well. What if she repeated the mistake she'd made before and settled for a marriage based on nothing more than friendship? One that seemed good enough because she'd never found something that was as magical as she thought falling in love was supposed to be? It hadn't been good enough, though, had it? Richard's affair with his secretary hadn't been his first but Claire had chosen to ignore her suspicions until it became blatant enough to make that impossible. Had it been that she hadn't tried hard enough not to let grief push them so far apart there was no way back? That she didn't want confirmation that the mediocrity of this marriage was her fault? That *she* wasn't good enough?

She'd certainly been left with that impression after finding him with a woman who was so much younger than herself. So much more attractive. No wonder her husband had fallen so madly in love.

He'd found what she'd never been able to find when she was young enough to believe it could happen.

But to expect a fairytale romance at this stage in her life?

How ridiculous would *that* be?

Tom read the report that had just arrived in his inbox during his lunch break.

He put down the sandwich he'd been about to take a bite of, his appetite gone. He closed his eyes for a long, long moment. And then he opened them and read it again. He looked at the scan images and his heart sank even further.

He picked up the phone.

'Dr Atkinson...hey! Oops...hang on a sec... Lucy, that's only one shoe. You need *two* shoes to go to kindy, darling. Go and find the other one. Sorry...' Olivia sounded a bit breathless now. 'It's always a bit of a rush to get her off to afternoon kindy. Is this about my results?'

'It is. Can you come in this afternoon and I'll go over the test results and scan images and things with you. Maybe while Lucy's at kindy?'

'Um...okay...what sort of time?'

Oh, help...how obvious was it that the news wasn't good when reassurance couldn't be given over the phone? How great would it have been to be able to open this conversation by saying something like 'Look, it's nothing to worry about, but could you come in...'

Lucy calling in the background covered Tom's slight hesitation.

'You find it, Mummy...*now*... I want my *shoe*...'

'How does two o'clock sound?' Tom took a breath, trying to keep his tone upbeat. 'You might like to bring someone with you. Like Sam? Or your mum?'

The silence felt fragile now. As if something, or some*one*, could break at any moment.

'Yeah...okay. I guess Mum's just down the road. She could get away from the shop for a bit.'

'Great. Just tell Kaia when you get to Reception and she'll come and find me.'

It was another busy afternoon clinic in the medical centre.

Claire took blood samples and a urine dipstick test

for someone who probably had a urinary tract infection. She took blood pressures for people who needed regular monitoring and administered a vaccination for shingles for someone in their sixties and one for whooping cough for a woman in her fifties who was about to become a grandmother for the first time.

'I'd never forgive myself if I passed something horrible on to the baby,' she told Claire. 'Are there any other vaccinations I should get?'

'The MMR is recommended,' Claire said. 'That's measles, mumps and rubella.'

'I definitely had a measles vaccination when I was a kid.'

'Yes, but immunity fades over time. The pneumonia vaccination is another one that's on the list you might like to consider. I've got a pamphlet I can give you to read.'

She took a twelve-lead ECG that had been scheduled for ninety-three-year-old Edward Bramley.

'I'll give this to Dr Atkinson and he can tell you about it in your appointment,' she told him as she helped him manoeuvre his walking frame through the door of the treatment room. She saw Kaia, further down the corridor, showing Olivia Jamieson and an older woman into Tom's consulting room and she caught her breath. Had the results from the numerous investigations that Mabel had said Olivia had been subjected to finally come in? The older woman was about Claire's age so she assumed that it might be her mother that had come to the appointment with her. Her heart went out to her if it was. What was worse, she wondered—to be without family completely, as she was, or to be sandwiched between trying to support a sick parent and child at the same time?

Oddly, it made her feel very lonely.

Claire was hoping she could catch up with Tom and find out what was happening for Olivia but he was nowhere to be seen whenever she went out to Reception to collect the next person who had an appointment booked with her. She spent one time slot with someone who was taking part in a smoking cessation programme and then she had stitches to remove and a dressing change for Carl the boat skipper, who had ended up only having the tip of his ring finger amputated after the accident with the pulley.

'That's healing really well,' she told him. 'You'll still need to keep it dry a bit longer, though.'

'I'm wearing a rubber glove on the boat. A bright pink one.' He grinned at Claire. 'Get some funny looks from the tourists. When are you going to come out and do some whale watching?'

'As soon as I get some time off that coincides with some good weather. I haven't forgotten, I promise.'

She did forget almost as soon as Carl had gone, however, as her next patient arrived. Even after clinic hours were well over she was still busy, writing up notes for all the appointments she'd done that afternoon and tidying up and restocking the treatment room so that it was ready for any emergency that might come in.

What she hadn't forgotten was that Mabel's granddaughter had been to see Tom, but he wasn't in his consulting room when she went to look for him. She'd send him a text message later, she decided, but when she was walking out of the medical centre's front door to head home for the day she saw him coming out of the hospital wing.

She hadn't been wrong about the stars not being aligned very well today, had she? And someone else had been affected far more than she had. Tom was far enough away to not be able to read his expression clearly but she didn't need to. She could sense that he was carrying a weight on his shoulders that had been caused by a very bad day. What took her completely off-guard was the way that made *her* feel. It was a squeeze on her heart that was hard enough to be physically painful.

Hard enough to be a warning?

The kind of complications that came with caring too much about other people was something Claire had resolved to leave behind in her old life. Tom Atkinson might have enlisted her assistance to pretend that there might be something more than friendship between them but that was all it was. A pretence.

This was taking the sheep blanket disquiet to a whole new level. Friendship was acceptable. Anything more was not. Surely caring about someone else enough to make it feel as if their wellbeing was far more important than her own was stepping into unacceptable territory?

She could already guess that the news about Olivia wasn't good. She hadn't seen any results come through so maybe they'd been emailed directly to Tom, which would suggest that it was something really serious. Would Tom want her poking her nose into his personal feelings about it? They barely knew each other. This was Tom's hometown and Olivia Jamieson was probably one of many patients he'd known for a significant part of their lives. He must have had to deal with countless difficult emotional situations, professional and personal, and many would have been a mix of both, given this small community.

He had managed without Claire in the past and he would manage without her in the future when she'd moved on to her next adventure.

She needed her freedom to be able to do that without feeling guilty. Or regretful.

And Tom needed his privacy.

The general practitioners in this small town still made house calls on a regular basis but they weren't usually at this time of the evening when it didn't involve an emergency.

Tom had just made two such visits, the second one because Olivia's mother, Yvonne, had asked if he could be the one to break the news to Mabel that her granddaughter was going to need surgery for something a lot more serious than the hiatus hernia they already knew she had.

The sun was already setting by the time he was heading home but he still parked along the esplanade and got out of his car to go towards the beach. He needed to breathe some of that cool, salty air and listen to the waves tumbling pebbles as they rolled onto the shore for a while. He barely noticed the person getting up from a wooden bench seat as he walked past until he heard the woman's voice, even though it was little more than a surprised whisper.

'Tom...?'

'Claire... Good heavens—' He stopped himself from saying that she was the last person he would have expected to see here but it wasn't entirely true, was it? He knew she lived close to this end of the esplanade. And saying that might make her think she was the last person he *wanted* to see here and Tom realised in that split second that that was a long way from being true as well. She was probably the only person he would have chosen to see just now. Because she would know exactly how hard this was but she wasn't so involved that it would be hard to think clearly. She could be, in fact, the kind of rock Tom very much needed in this moment.

She didn't ask him what *he* was doing here. The graze of eye contact made him think that perhaps she already knew.

'I came out for a bit of a walk on the beach,' Claire said. 'But I didn't realise how dark it was getting and I decided it probably wasn't a sensible thing to be doing on my own when there's no moonlight. I might end up in trouble if I tripped over a bit of driftwood and broke my ankle.' He could hear the smile in her voice. 'Would you like some company? You don't have to talk or anything, if you don't feel like it.'

Talking was the last thing Tom wanted to do. It took a good ten minutes of walking in a companionable silence, with only the wash of the waves and the crunch of pebbles under their feet to break it before he changed his mind.

'Olivia Jamieson was one of the first patients I ever saw at Seaview,' he told Claire quietly. 'I'd come back here to do my advanced GP training and her mum, Yvonne, brought her in for some of the usual childhood vaccinations.' He cleared his throat. 'She's got oesophageal cancer,' he said.

'Oh, no…' Claire's words were a groan. 'The worst she was expecting, according to Mabel, was that she had an ulcer from her reflux.'

'I had my suspicions that it was more than that,' Tom said quietly. 'It's rare, but neurological symptoms like the weakness and falls she presented with can be associated with an altered immune system response to a tumour. The more normal symptoms that would have raised a red flag, like a feeling that something was stuck in her throat, were masked by the issues caused by the reflux. She's booked in to start an aggressive surgical and chemotherapy regime next week in the hope of getting control.' He let his breath out in a heavy sigh. 'I'm sure I don't need to tell you what the five-year survival statistics are like.' His voice was tight. 'Yvonne asked me to go and tell Mabel and it was one of the hardest things I've ever done.'

'I'm so sorry, Tom,' Claire said.

'It broke my heart,' Tom said, his voice cracking. 'She said, "It should be me, not Livvy. I've lived my life but she's barely started. It's really not very fair, is it?".'

'No…it really isn't.' He could hear tears in Claire's voice.

They both stopped walking. He wasn't sure who initiated the hug, it just seemed to happen. They stood there in the dark, the foam of waves just catching the muted light from the streetlamps on the esplanade, simply holding each other tightly, offering and accepting comfort. An acknowledgment that they were both very personally aware of just how hard life could be sometimes.

The last of the soft strip of light on the horizon had faded by the time Claire stepped back from what was, without doubt, *the* most sincere hug she could remember getting since…well, since those unbearably dark days in the aftermath of losing Sophia.

The shared connection of that kind of pain had possibly been the beginning of the end for her marriage but with Tom it felt like the complete opposite—as if it gave them a link that was as strong as a padlock that had just been snapped shut. They both knew, too well, what it was like to have a family broken by loss and the strength that was needed to hang on long enough to rediscover the joy that was still there in being alive yourself.

One of the skills Claire had learned along the way was to deliberately look for that joy and it had become an automatic response to the touch of grief. She didn't have to look far to find it either. She just needed to tilt her head up.

'Oh, wow...' The words were an awed whisper.

Tom tilted his head back as well. 'Gorgeous, isn't it?'

'I used to think I could see the stars quite well sometimes in London, but I had *no* idea...'

'Did you know that Kaikōura has recently been officially designated as an international Dark Sky sanctuary?'

'I read something about that online. Didn't it start with some rare birds?'

Tom nodded. 'It's a type of shearwater found around Australia and New Zealand. They're the only sea bird in the world to come ashore to breed up in the mountains and this is the only place they do it. They get attracted to artificial light at night and there were too many crashing and killing themselves so a few passionate people decided to do something about controlling it. A big bonus for us is that the stars are even easier to see.'

'I wish I knew more about them,' Claire confessed. 'I can recognise the Southern Cross but everything else still looks upside down for me. That smudgy bit is the Milky Way, yes?'

Tom was just as distracted as she was, now. 'You can see it even better if you get away from the streetlights.' He caught her gaze. 'Are you up for a bit of a walk? I could show you something rather special.'

'Oh, yes, please…' The glow of something warm and happy inside Claire had finally melted that knot that had been hanging around ever since she'd noticed that Tom had been struggling with his day.

'We'll have to go up on the road, it gets a bit stony on the beach further along.' He was smiling at her. 'I wouldn't want you to fall over and break your ankle.'

There was no traffic to make it dangerous to walk along the side of the road in the dark and it became even darker as they left the last of the houses behind.

'We're heading for the oldest surviving building in Kaikōura,' Tom told her. 'It's built on a foundation of whale bones and just across the road, right on the foreshore—in the waves sometimes—is an ancient chimney which is the only part left of an old customhouse.'

He didn't take Claire onto the rocky shoreline in the dark. They leaned against the fence on the other side of the road, with Tom taking particular care to choose the exact spot to stand.

'Can you see the Milky Way now?'

'Yes…' Claire ignored the chill of the night settling around them as they stopped moving. She gazed up at the brilliance of what looked like an infinite number of stars and it was easy to find the distinctive area where the light of so many stars seemed to merge to make bright patches that emphasised the dark, smudgy band across the centre.

'Follow it down.' Tom's voice was a murmur, close to her ear. 'Until you get to the chimney.'

Claire's inward breath was a gasp of astonishment a moment later. 'It looks exactly like smoke,' she whispered. 'Coming out of the chimney.'

'Cool, isn't it?' She could hear the smile in Tom's voice. 'I remember the first time I brought Hanna out to see this. She sounded just as amazed as you do.'

They both got their phones out to take photographs of the extraordinary illusion. Then they stood for another minute, just soaking it in. Claire finally managed to drag her eyes away to look up at Tom.

'Thank you,' she said softly. 'I might never have seen this if you hadn't shown me and it's something I'll remember for ever.'

Tom just smiled. 'Thank *you*,' he said. 'Bringing you here to see this has been the best thing to happen on a really bad day.' His sigh was visible in the cold night air. 'It's the downside of spending your life as a small-town GP. You get too emotionally involved with your patients.'

'I knew it was going to be bad news when I saw you earlier today,' Claire said. 'I think that was why I ended up on the beach this evening. I was thinking about Mabel…' She paused for a heartbeat. 'I've only been here for a few weeks,' she added, 'and I already feel involved with this family myself. I can't imagine how hard it is for you.'

'I'm not very good at hiding it, am I?'

'No.' Claire smiled at him. 'You're a doctor who really cares. You're a lovely man, Tom. And a totally genuine person.'

'It's kind of my own fault that it hits me this hard.'

'What makes you think that?'

'It was my way of coping. After Jill died, I buried my own feelings by focusing on other people. Mainly Hanna, of course. But patients as well. I dealt with their problems and ignored my own. Not exactly a good way to deal with grief, is it?'

'You do whatever works,' Claire said quietly. 'Other people think they understand, but they can't, can they? Unless it's happened to them.'

'No...'

It was a negative word but somehow, it felt like an affirmation of the connection *they* had and it brought them even closer.

'It's really not a bad thing that you can't hide everything you feel for other people,' Claire said. 'It's why people love you.'

'It will be a bad thing when Hanna comes home next week for a break. If she sees us together, she's going to know straight away that I've been lying to her about you. She might be really upset about that.'

'You haven't been lying, exactly,' Claire said carefully. 'It's not as though we weren't out together when we took those photos you've been sending her. Or that we're not friends...' She hoped that was true, anyway.

'But she thinks we're more than friends. And I don't think I can pretend that it's any more than that.' Tom pushed his fingers through his hair. 'I wouldn't even know how to *begin* pretending. I haven't even *kissed* a woman since Jill died.'

His words fell into a somewhat stunned silence from Claire which she broke without thinking.

'Maybe that's a good place to start, then.' The words

were out of her mouth before she could filter them. 'You never know what might happen if you push through a barrier like that. You might even meet someone you end up wanting to share your life with.'

The shocked look on Tom's face made her shake her head. 'Not me,' she said hastily. 'In the future. Hanna doesn't want you to be lonely for the rest of your life and…maybe she's right. You deserve to find whatever happiness you can in life, Tom—and…if you're hanging back because you think you've forgotten how to kiss someone then…' her heart skipped a beat '…here's your chance. There's no one to see and…it's perfectly safe.' She smiled up at him. 'I know it's purely for…um…experimental reasons. Or maybe therapeutic?'

Tom's expression had been changing as she spoke. His gaze dropped from her eyes to her lips and Claire knew he was thinking about kissing her.

Suddenly, it was exactly what she *wanted* him to do. And it had nothing to do with helping him break any self-inflicted barriers. The knot of empathy might have melted from around her heart but there was a new knot deep inside her now. Much lower down. Hotter.

Dear Lord…she fancied Tom Atkinson, didn't she?

She hadn't felt a physical attraction like this since… since for ever. It felt like it had been bottled up for her entire life and she had unwittingly just pulled the cork from the bottle.

Claire stood on tiptoes. She put her fingertips on Tom's cheek and she touched his lips with her own. Just briefly. Lightly.

'There you go,' she said very softly. 'See how easy it is?'

Tom was still staring at her lips. Then he raised his gaze to look into her eyes and she knew that it had happened for him as well. He was also feeling a potentially long-forgotten awareness of something very physical. He lifted *his* hand, but he didn't touch her cheek. He slid his hand under her hair until it was circling the back of her neck. Supporting her head as he leaned closer to put his lips on hers again.

And this time it wasn't brief. It might have started out just as light—a soft exploration of the pressure and warmth—but then it became something very different as Claire felt her lips part under Tom's and the touch of his tongue against hers.

Oh...*my*...

The barrier had well and truly been broken, hadn't it?

This was a kiss that was going to be just as memorable as seeing the Milky Way rising from a ruined chimney.

CHAPTER FIVE

FOR THE FIRST time ever, Tom Atkinson was feeling decidedly reluctant to get out of his car and start his working day at the Seaview Hospital and Medical Centre.

How on earth was he going to face Claire after last night?

After that...*kiss*.

Oh, they'd brushed it off at the time. They'd laughed about how unexpectedly successful the experiment had been and then, by tacit consent, they'd very carefully not mentioned it again for the whole of the walk back to where Tom had left his car on the esplanade, which seemed to take an inordinately long time.

And then he'd lain awake for most of the night, dealing with the emotional aftermath of embarrassment that he'd let it happen at all and guilt that he'd...well...that he'd enjoyed it so much. He was also doing his best to ignore the physical reaction that his body was trying to force him to acknowledge.

It had seemed like such a harmless idea. A practice kiss. Dipping a toe into the sea of water that actual dating might represent—because, at some level, Tom knew there was an element of truth in the idea that he was missing out on something in his life. If only he'd left it at that light, sweet brushing of lips that Claire had initiated.

But he hadn't, had he? Oh, no... Something had washed over him and rinsed away the usual impeccable self-control that Tom had put considerable effort into perfecting when it came to any interactions with women in his personal life. He'd let himself go and he'd initiated the *real* kiss. The one that had swept them both into very dangerous waters.

Good grief... How far would those currents have taken them if they hadn't both abruptly broken it off at exactly the same moment?

How on earth had it even happened? Maybe it was because he'd been totally alone with Claire, under a magically starry night sky. Or perhaps it was because they'd been pretending to go on all those dates so it almost felt...natural?

Or had it simply been because he liked Claire and he felt completely safe in her company?

No... Tom knew the reason. It had been the feeling of that touch of Claire's lips. The feeling of them moving beneath his. Alive. Responsive. The *taste* of her mouth. After so many years of being stifled—totally ignored, even—his libido had suddenly woken up and come roaring out of hibernation. Liking, laced with an undeniable appreciation of this woman's attractiveness, had suddenly morphed into something far less acceptable— like a cringemaking level of lust. The kind of hormonal overload that a teenage boy might experience.

He could only hope that Claire could excuse his lack of control. That they could, hopefully, keep it in a vaguely surprised and amused category of their friendship and sweep it firmly under the carpet. If it had been designed to counteract his inability to act like he and Claire were actually dating if they were in the same space when Hanna was visiting it had been an unmitigated failure.

If Hanna saw him being this awkward at even the thought of being in Claire's company she would, understandably, laugh out loud at the idea they'd been on any kind of date. Tom was going to have to give up the idea of using this fake dating as a protective mechanism and just confess to the deception.

He was also going to have to give up the safe cocoon of being alone inside his car. There would be patients who were already in the waiting room, ready for their appointments with him. Taking a deep breath, during which he sent up a silent plea to the universe that Claire was already busy in the treatment room or had gone on any morning house calls, he marched inside, grabbed the first set of notes Kaia held out to him and read the name on the front.

'Daphne Morris?'

'I'm here.' A middle-aged woman stood up from her chair in the waiting room.

'Come on through, Daphne,' Tom invited. The corridor looked clear, thank goodness. He could delay the moment he would have to make that first eye contact with Claire Campbell for just a little longer.

He felt even safer when he had closed the door of the consulting room behind him. 'Have a seat,' he told Daphne. 'What's brought you in today?'

'I'm feeling a bit off, Doctor. Not all the time, but quite often.'

'In what way?' Tom had opened Daphne's notes. She

was a relatively new patient and he noted that she was sixty-three years old and on medication for her blood pressure and for high cholesterol.

'I get a bit dizzy and sweaty and I can feel my heart going really fast.'

Tom put his fingers on Daphne's wrist. 'It's a normal rate at the moment,' he told her. 'But let's check your blood pressure as well.' He took the cuff off the hook on the wall to wrap it around Daphne's arm and pushed the button for the automatic measurement to start. 'How often are these episodes happening?'

'At least once every day. Sometimes more.'

'Do they happen at a particular time, like when you wake up or you're exercising or after a meal?'

'I don't think so.'

'Is there anything that makes it better?'

'I usually sit down and have a glass of water or something and it just goes away slowly.'

'Your blood pressure's fine.' Tom had been watching the figures settle. 'I'd like to listen to your chest and check your heart and lung sounds if that's okay?'

'Of course.'

Tom fitted his stethoscope to his ears. 'I might get our nurse to take an ECG as well.' He could do it himself, of course, but given the exposure needed to attach electrodes to his patient's chest, it would be preferable for it to be done, or at least chaperoned, by a female staff member. And Tom couldn't deny that there was relief to be found in the idea of a professional interaction to break the ice that seemed to have suddenly formed in his relationship with Claire. If nothing else, he'd be able to gauge how justified his worry was about the aftermath of that kiss.

Maybe he was overthinking things and there was actually nothing to worry about at all?

'Take a deep breath for me, Daphne. And another one…'

There was something else he wanted to try before doing the ECG, he decided, after finding nothing of concern in what he was hearing. Or seeing. Daphne's respiration rate and skin colour were quite normal and there was no evidence of any other abnormalities like a new tremor in her hands or swelling in her ankles.

'Could you stand up for me, please, Daphne?'

His patient blinked. She looked down at the cuff still wrapped around her arm. 'Do I need to take this off?'

'No. I want to take your blood pressure and your heart rate when you've been standing up for a few minutes.'

Her blood pressure hadn't changed much after she'd been standing and answering more of his questions for several minutes but her heart rate certainly had. It had gone up from eighty to nearly a hundred and twenty beats per minute and Daphne was starting to look pale.

'I can feel it now,' she said. 'My heart's really pounding.'

'Come with me.' Tom led the way to the treatment room.

Claire had a drawer open and was taking out blood collection tubes with differently coloured tops to put into a kidney dish. There was a laboratory request form on the bench beside the dish. She looked up as Tom tapped on the door.

'You busy?'

'Just getting ready for some routine blood tests. Do you need me?'

The eye contact was brief enough to suggest that Claire was feeling just as awkward as he was. Dammit...he hadn't been overthinking things, had he?

'This is Daphne Morris,' he said, his tone a little crisper than he'd intended it to be. 'I'd like an ECG on her, please.'

'Of course.' Claire's smile was warm but it was directed at Daphne, not him. Her glance at Tom was a question. She had clearly noticed that Daphne wasn't looking so well.

'Tachycardia on standing,' he told her. 'With some vasovagal symptoms and palpitations.'

'Do come in, Daphne. This won't take long and you might feel better lying down for a few minutes.'

Claire took Daphne back to Tom's office but gave her the ECG printout to take inside by herself.

Which was fine. She did, after all, have at least one patient waiting to have their blood tests taken.

No. It wasn't really fine, was it? It would have been more professional to hand the printout of quite an impressive sinus tachycardia to Tom herself and make sure there wasn't any other assistance he required from her for this patient even if her rapid heart rate and other symptoms had subsided with rest.

But it felt so...awkward.

Claire had come to work this morning knowing that a small bomb had gone off in their personal relationship but determined not to let it affect the way they could work together. If it did, it would make what had happened last night even more of a disaster.

What on earth had made her imagine that it was an acceptable suggestion that he kissed her?

What *had* she been thinking?

Witnessing a peck on the cheek would have probably been quite enough to persuade Hanna that her father was involved in a meaningful friendship. She hadn't needed to kiss him on the lips at all, even though it had only been intended to be light enough to be insignificant.

What had happened after that, exactly?

It was a bit of a blur, to be honest. She remembered the tingling sensation that had come from that light touch and she remembered the way she couldn't look away from his eyes but she couldn't remember who had actually initiated that astonishingly passionate kiss.

Oh, dear...even the thought of it made her skin tingle. Not just on her lips but all the way down to her toes. How horrified would Tom be if he knew the effect that his kiss had had on her? Everyone knew she'd only just arrived in town. How appalled would some of them be to think that she was throwing herself at her boss? If they found out how much older than Tom she was, it would only make the gossip more juicy, wouldn't it? How had something that had been intended to make the pretence of fake dating easier gone so very wrong?

And how on earth were they going to be able to get things back to the way they *had* been? Claire didn't want to lose what she'd found with Tom. The company of someone she could have fun with. The connection with someone who really understood what she'd been through in life because he'd been there himself. Someone she enjoyed being with so much that it would leave a huge hole in her life if it vanished.

Tom's approach to sorting it became apparent later that morning, when they found themselves getting a cup of coffee in the staffroom at the same time.

'I'm going to get Daphne to come in on a regular basis for a while,' he said to Claire. 'I'd like you to do a sitting and standing blood pressure and repeat ECG. I suspect she has POTS but we'll need to monitor it for a while before I can make a definitive diagnosis.'

Claire nodded, spooning instant coffee into the mug. 'Postural Orthostatic Tachycardia Syndrome,' she said. 'Interesting...'

The condition, where the body couldn't coordinate the balancing act of blood vessel constriction and heart rate response to postural changes, was interesting. Enough to make Claire realise that Tom probably had the right idea. Focusing on their professional connection was the way to go to get things back to normal. 'Do you know what might have triggered it?'

'She hasn't had any trauma or surgery recently but she did have trouble shaking off a viral illness a while back.'

'There's no real treatment for it, is there, apart from lifestyle changes like using compression clothing and avoiding sitting or standing for too long?'

'Increasing salt intake is useful. Apparently, people who have POTS need up to three times as much sodium as the recommended limit to keep a sufficient circulating volume. Daphne was a bit horrified by that—she was more than happy to try increasing how much water she's drinking but she's been on a health kick and trying to reduce the salt and sugar in her diet.'

Keeping things professional seemed to be working, Claire decided, but then she risked a glance at Tom over the rim of her mug as she took a sip of her coffee. Just one heartbeat's worth of eye contact was enough to let her know that it wasn't actually working on anything other than a very superficial level. She didn't even need to drop her eyes to his lips to be thinking about that kiss.

Worse, to know that Tom was also thinking about it.

'I'd better get back to work.' Claire's tone was overly bright. 'I need to make some calls before the rest of my appointments for today.' She moved so quickly she was in danger of slopping her hot drink. 'I'm hoping to drop in on Mabel Jamieson on my way home and check on how she's coping after the news about Olivia.'

'Good idea.' But Tom's voice sounded as though some of his coffee might have gone down the wrong way.

Oh, help...why had she said something that was going to remind them both of the intense conversation about Mabel's granddaughter last night, which was how they'd ended up snogging like a pair of teenagers under the Milky Way?

It felt like she was scuttling out of the staff room.

If anything, the awkwardness had just got more pronounced.

Something needed to be done to break the tension that seemed to be growing rather than fading as Tom and Claire navigated their way through the afternoon surgery hours at the same time and he found himself doing his best to avoid being in the same space at the same time, or at least avoiding eye contact if it was unavoidable. He could never have engineered the circumstances that ended up making the awkwardness suddenly becoming totally irrelevant, however.

The police car, with its lights flashing, skidding to a halt out the front door of Seaview's medical centre was dramatic enough to have the few people still in the waiting room on their feet, staring out of the windows. Tom was standing by the reception desk and Claire was coming into the room from the corridor as one of the local senior sergeants, Ngaire, rushed inside.

'We need you, Tom,' she said. Then she lowered her voice. 'Someone's been shot.'

Tom's nod was swift. So was his glance in Claire's direction. 'Can you grab the emergency kit from the treatment room, please, Claire? You'd better come too.' He turned back to Ngaire. 'Where are they?'

'Well...that's the thing. They're well up in the high country. It's an accident in a group of guys that went out deer hunting.'

Claire's steps faltered. She looked confused. So was Tom.

'What's happened to the usual emergency response via helicopter?'

'There are no rescue helicopter aircraft or crews available any time soon,' Ngaire informed them. 'We don't even have a local ambulance crew available—they're on a transfer with your man with chest pain.'

Tom nodded. He'd arranged that transfer himself.

'A Search and Rescue team, including a police officer, have already been dispatched by road,' Ngaire said, 'but it's going to take them at least an hour to reach the scene using quad bikes via the track and we've got one of the local scenic tour helicopter pilots on standby to take you there as first response. Apparently, there's a hut and an area big enough to land about a ten-minute walk away from where the victim is. There's only room for two medics and your gear but hopefully one of the rescue choppers should be available before too long for evacuation of someone on a stretcher.'

'Do you know how badly the person's injured?'

'Doesn't sound good. It's an older man who's been shot and it's a chest wound. He's having some trouble breathing but he's still conscious.'

The decision was a no-brainer. 'How soon can the pilot get to the hospital helipad?'

'Less than five minutes.'

'Right...' Tom was thinking fast. This was by no means the first time he'd been involved in a rural emergency rescue situation. He knew his colleagues would cope with any patients he couldn't see for the afternoon and he didn't want to take another doctor away from the medical centre or hospital but another qualified pair of hands might be essential. 'Change of plans, Claire,' he said. 'We'll need some extra medical supplies and some overalls and boots. For you as well. I need you to come with me. Let's see how quickly we can get sorted and out to the helipad, yes?'

If Claire Campbell was fazed by the dramatic twist in her professional duties that afternoon, she wasn't showing it. If anything, Tom had the impression that she was not only embracing the challenge but revelling in it. She moved decisively and efficiently to gather everything they had available to stabilise and monitor a critically injured patient, like a life-pack and IV gear and even a cool bag with its isothermal lining designed to keep blood products like packed red cells and fresh, frozen plasma stable for hours. She pulled on the slightly scratchy overalls on top of her scrubs with no complaints and if the sturdy boots weren't a great fit she didn't mention that either.

She did look slightly perturbed when their pilot, Jonno, did some very tight turns to show them the accident scene before going back to land on a small patch of flat ground beside a rustic mountain hut. With her eyes closed, Tom suspected that Claire probably hadn't seen the very relieved-looking hunters waving up at them.

Jonno helped them unload their gear. 'You've got the GSP coordinates loaded into your phone, yes?'

'Yep. And we've got satellite radios. If we lose the track we'll stay put and get in touch with the Search and Rescue team. They won't be too far away by now.'

'I'll keep myself available,' Jonno told them. 'But I'm guessing you'll be picked up to travel with your patient.'

Tom put the straps of a backpack over his shoulders and picked up the heavy life-pack. Claire had the container of blood products. They both reached for the oxygen cylinder at the same time.

'You've got enough to carry,' Tom said. 'I can take that.'

'I'm fine,' Claire insisted. 'I've done a lot of hiking in my time, Tom. It's not far.' She picked up the cylinder. 'And the sooner we get there, the better, yes? You lead the way. I'll be right behind you.'

They saw the group of five men huddled amongst the first line of trees on the edge of a tussock covered slope. The man on the ground was well covered with extra jackets as blankets and more clothing folded up to provide a pillow. One of them—a younger man—was sitting a little further back, his head in his hands.

'Tom!' One of the men recognised him as they got closer. 'Thank goodness *you're* here.'

'Hey, Harvey.' Tom knew him as one of their local plumbers.

'It's Bruce who's hurt,' Harvey told him. 'He's a mate of mine who came down from Wellington for a few days hunting, with his son, Mason.'

'Fill me in,' Tom said as he approached the patient. 'What happened exactly?'

'He's been shot. From a range of maybe twenty to thirty metres.' The man cleared his throat. 'One shot. Left side of his chest. No exit wound that we could see.'

The young man sitting to one side looked up, his face tear-streaked. 'It was an accident,' he said, his voice raw. 'I could see a deer in my scope. I could see its antlers…'

''Course it was, son.' The man paused to grip the younger man's shoulder. 'We all know that. We just don't know why your dad decided to leave his own patch.'

'He's going to be okay, isn't he?'

'He's got the best doctor around these parts. If anyone can help, he can… Get a bit closer, lad. Your dad'll want to see that you're here.'

From the corner of his eye, Tom could see Mason edging closer to his father as he knelt down beside the man on the ground, his fingers on the man's wrist.

'How's it going, Bruce? I'm Tom, one of the local doctors, and I've got my colleague Claire with me. We're going to get you sorted and into hospital.'

He could see, and hear, how short of breath Bruce was.

'Hurts…' he said succinctly. 'Hard…to…breathe…'

'We'll give you something for that pain asap,' Tom promised. He could see Claire attaching an oxygen mask to the cylinder and he nodded at her choice of a non-rebreather mask. Bruce had a patent airway because he was talking but they needed to try and improve his breathing before they moved on with their primary survey of how badly injured he was.

'Let's get some leads on, too,' he said calmly. 'And a set of vital signs, please, Claire.' He already knew that Bruce's blood pressure was very low because he hadn't been able to feel a radial pulse in his wrist.

'I'm going to put a mask on your face,' Claire told Bruce. 'The oxygen should help your breathing, okay?'

Bruce nodded and Claire slipped the elastic band around his head and turned on the oxygen cylinder. She clipped a saturation monitor clip on his finger. Tom had opened the long zip on the backpack and folded it out flat to reveal all the clear plastic pouches containing supplies inside. He took out a stethoscope. Claire was folding back the layers of coats keeping Bruce warm to attach ECG electrodes below his collarbones and on the left side of his abdomen—a basic three-lead view to monitor heart rhythm and rate. Tom could see the entry wound of the bullet on the left side of Bruce's chest. Had it penetrated deeply enough to have injured his heart as well as having caused potential internal bleeding and lung damage that was affecting his ability to breathe? He would need to look for an exit wound very soon.

The screen of the life-pack was already settling as Tom placed the disc of his stethoscope on Bruce's chest and he could see that the heart's rhythm was normal but the rate was far too high at a hundred and forty beats per minute. The rate of respiration was also too high and...

'Decreased breath sounds, left side,' Tom told Claire quietly.

'SpO2 is ninety-two,' she responded. 'Up from eighty-six since the oxygen first went on.'

The level of oxygen in Bruce's blood was still too low. Already, in the space of only seconds, things were adding up and they both knew that Bruce was in trouble. The puncture wounds from the shotgun pellets were causing air, or blood—probably both—to accumulate in his chest and affect the function of his heart and lungs, which meant that not enough oxygen was reaching his vital organs. The clock was ticking and they were not in the best place to try and deal with a major resuscitation.

Bruce needed pain relief, fluids to try and increase his blood volume, drugs to try and slow any internal bleeding, to help his veins constrict to make the most of what blood was circulating and to help his heart pump more effectively.

Tom draped the stethoscope around his neck as he turned to open more pouches in the backpack.

'Have we got a blood pressure?'

'Seventy-six over forty,' Claire said. 'Also dropping.'

Tom eyed the IV cannula he'd just picked up. The only way to deliver everything was intravenously but a low blood pressure meant that access was going to be a challenge and he couldn't afford the time to try and chase a peripheral vein that might have already collapsed. He dropped the cannula and reached for a sterile package containing the device he needed to get access to the centre of a bone that could provide fast and reliable access for the infusion of both fluids and medications.

Claire was watching him. 'Insertion site?' she queried.
'Proximal tibia.'

Claire picked up a pair of shears. 'I'm going to have to cut your clothes,' she told Bruce. 'Tom's going to put a needle into your leg, just below your knee. We'll be able to give you something for that pain then. Hang in there, Bruce. You're doing well...'

Tom could feel the encouragement and warmth in her voice. If he was in as much pain as Bruce and probably terrified, he would love to hear a voice like that. It would make him feel cared for. Hopeful. Safe, even...?

Bruce made a grunting noise that sounded as if he was thinking the same thing Tom was. He had his eyes closed but he was nodding his head. 'All good,' he whispered.

'Mason's right here, too,' Claire added. 'He's the one who's holding your hand right now.'

'All...good...' Bruce repeated. 'Not...your fault... son... Mine... I forgot...where I was...'

Mason had tears streaming down his face.

'I'll need a giving set and a litre of saline,' Tom told Claire. 'And draw up a flush, too, please.'

'Onto it.'

With swift movements Tom inserted and then twisted the intraosseous needle into the tibia just below Bruce's knee and secured it. He flushed the line, attached the tubing of the giving set and asked one of the men standing around them to hold up the bag of fluid.

'Not allergic to any medications, are you, Bruce?' he asked. 'Like morphine?'

'Don't...think...so...' It sounded like it was getting harder for their patient to speak.

Tom drew up and administered pain relief. An alarm on the life-pack sounded as he was drawing up other drugs.

'Oxygen saturation is below ninety again,' Claire said. 'Heart rate's one forty and we're getting more than a few ectopics.' She gripped Bruce's shoulder. 'Can you hear me, Bruce? Can you open your eyes?'

There was no response this time.

Tom could hear other sounds from behind them. The Search and Rescue team had clearly arrived on scene now. There would be extra hands, trained in first aid to assist if needed and support Mason, who might need to be moved further away from his father very soon. The group would have carried a stretcher to the scene that could be used to carry Bruce out and get him to an emergency department and operating theatre. Hopefully fast, if a rescue helicopter became available.

They would have to stabilise him first, however, and Tom's heart sank as he discovered that breath sounds had vanished from one side of the hunter's chest and were reduced on the other side. Bruce was now unconscious and gasping for air with shallow, overly rapid respiratory efforts. His heart was throwing off unusual beats that suggested his rhythm could change, at any moment, into one that was potentially fatal, like a ventricular fibrillation.

Tom glanced up, the stethoscope still on Bruce's chest, to find Claire's steady gaze on him. She was poised to do whatever he was about to ask because she knew as well as he did that they were going to have to try something a lot more dramatic.

Bruce was in imminent danger of going into a respiratory or cardiac arrest.

And the fight for his life had just become a whole lot harder.

CHAPTER SIX

CLAIRE HAD SPENT the early years of her nursing career working in a big London hospital's emergency department.

She had seen medical experts fighting to save lives against the odds and she knew she was watching someone who knew exactly what he was doing, in an environment far more challenging than a well-equipped and staffed hospital department, as Tom worked on their patient.

Not that she was simply watching. She was as involved with this case as Tom was. His assistant. His partner.

She removed the makeshift pillows from beneath Bruce's head and positioned his arm as if to put the palm of his hand behind his head. She prepped the skin on his chest, first one side and then the other, to allow Tom to perform finger thoracostomies, where he made an incision with a scalpel and then used his finger and a pair of forceps to do a blunt dissection between ribs to reach the pleural space around the lung. A rush of air and blood escaped the channel he had created as he removed his finger. A lot of blood.

'Claire, can you find a unit of packed red blood cells and get it running, please? I'm going to decompress the other side of the chest.'

The bag of Group O blood product was smaller than the bag of saline but would be far more effective in carrying oxygen. Claire attached it to the connection on the intraosseous IV access and gave the bag to one of the men in orange overalls, who stepped forward to assist without being asked. Behind the member of the Search and Rescue team, she could see a police officer talking to the other hunters in the group. Bruce's son, Mason, was sitting to one side again, his face white as he watched what was happening around his father. Claire's heart went out to the young man, who was probably only in his late teens. He was not only afraid of losing his dad, he knew he was responsible for the accident.

It was only moments later that things started happening so fast they became almost a blur, but all Claire needed to do was to listen for Tom's voice and to do exactly what he wanted her to do.

To use an Ambu-bag to deliver breaths for Bruce, who was no longer breathing for himself, and check for a pulse that was no longer there. Even though they could see the electrical impulses on the screen of the life-pack, the heart was no longer able to pump blood.

To do chest compressions until someone else took over because she was getting tired, even if she didn't feel like she was and didn't want to stop.

To draw up and check the drugs that Tom was administering.

To do another round of chest compressions.

To hang more blood and tell the person holding it to squeeze as hard as they could to get it in faster.

To sit…much later, as daylight was beginning to fade, with her arms around Mason as he sobbed against her shoulder, while the Search and Rescue team secured Bruce's body to the stretcher so that they could carry him down the track to where they'd left their quad bikes. She only heard snatches of the orders being given and radio calls being made. It was Tom who came and crouched beside Claire and Mason.

'Hey, Mason.' His tone was so gentle that Claire felt tears spring to the back of her own eyes. 'I'm so very sorry about this. We did everything we could for your dad.'

Mason nodded without saying anything.

'We've got a helicopter coming back to collect me and Claire and our medical gear but there's enough room for you, if you'd rather come back with us.'

'But...' Mason's voice was strangled. 'What about Dad?'

'These guys, including your dad's friend Harvey, are going to carry him down the track and they've got some four-wheel drive vehicles to get back out to the main road. The police will take charge then and your dad will be taken to Christchurch and looked after while they do the kind of stuff that has to happen in cases like this.'

'I want to stay with Dad,' Mason whispered. His voice broke. 'I can help carry him.'

'That's a brave thing to do.' Claire could see the squeeze of Tom's hand as it rested on Mason's shoulder. 'Your dad would be proud of you. Harvey will look after you and your mum's going to fly down to Christchurch to be with you, too. She might even get there before you do.'

Mason nodded again. He rubbed at his nose and then scrambled to his feet. The strength he found, to not only meet Claire's gaze but to then look at Tom and even hold out a hand to shake his, was heartbreaking.

'Thanks,' he said. 'For everything you guys did. I... I know how hard you tried to save him.'

Tom took Mason's hand in his but didn't shake it. He used it to pull the younger man closer and wrap him in a brief, hard, hug.

Claire could feel the genuine empathy in that hug herself. She couldn't hold back her tears any longer but she swiped at them with her fingers and then blinked them away as she watched the team pick up the basket stretcher and start their sad journey. Mason was one of the six men who had taken hold of a cut-out hand grip.

There was a moment's heavy silence as the group vanished down the track. It was broken by Tom's voice.

'Are you okay?' he asked softly.

Claire could feel the squeeze on her heart that came from the fact that Tom had room to be concerned about *her*.

She nodded. 'I'm okay. How're you doing?'

'Oh...you know...'

She did. 'It's Mason I really feel for,' she said. 'How could it be anything other than a tragic accident? From what I picked up, they'd arranged to be hunting in totally separate blocks. Bruce had come into Mason's and he was wearing camouflage clothing. Amongst those trees it would be too easy to make a mistake. Some of those branches look exactly like antlers. And...'

With a sigh, Claire turned back to start the clean-up and packing of their gear. 'I know what it's like to feel responsible even when something isn't your fault. I spent years trying to get past the feeling of guilt that I wasn't there to help Sophia.' She put on some gloves to start picking up the bloodstained packaging and swabs but then glanced up at Tom. 'I'm guessing you know that feeling, too.'

'Yeah...' Tom echoed her sigh. 'Let's get this cleaned up and get back to the hut or Jonno will get there before us. I'll take you out for a drink when we get home—I suspect we both need a bit of a wind down. Losing a patient never gets easier, does it, even when you know you've done everything you could?'

'No...it never does...'

Claire found she could meet Tom's gaze. And hold it. As she would any colleague that she was more than happy to work with. As she would with someone who was a trusted friend as well as a colleague. She couldn't find a smile yet—the loss of their shared battle to save Bruce's life was still too raw, but being with someone who was feeling exactly the same way was possibly the only comfort to be found right now.

'A drink sounds good,' she added.

And it did. Because that awkwardness that had been there between them this morning felt like ancient history.

Along with that kiss.

Having a defined task that had to be done made it easier to cope with the aftermath of a failed resuscitation. Tom made sure that every scrap of rubbish was picked up from this patch of forest. Nobody who came this way in the future would have any idea of the tragedy that had happened here.

It was nearly dark by the time they reached the small clearing beside the hut. They piled their gear onto the small veranda of the simple wood and corrugated iron structure because there were gathering clouds and they didn't want expensive equipment like the life-pack getting wet if it started raining. They sat on the veranda step then, waiting to hear the chop of helicopter rotors in the distance and see the lights of the aircraft approaching.

Instead, they heard the crackle of the radio that Tom had.

'Tom…are you receiving? It's Jonno.'

'Receiving loud and clear,' Tom responded. 'How far away are you, Jonno?'

'I'm still in town, sorry,' he replied. 'We've got a bit of an issue with a warning light. Probably nothing but I won't be taking off until I know for sure. There's also a bit of weather blowing in and we're losing light fast so if I can't get it sorted very soon, it could be first thing in the morning before I can get back to collect you.'

'So we'll walk out?'

'Not on your own. Or in the dark. We could send the Search and Rescue guys back up the hill but it might be a bit of a wait.'

Of course it would. The team of mostly volunteers would still be coping with their own duties and there would be protocol to follow with police interviews, probably a debriefing meeting and definitely some reports to file. The last thing those men needed was to be heading back into the mountain wilderness when it wasn't an emergency.

'We'll sit tight,' Tom told Jonno. 'We've got shelter and we can wait till morning if necessary. I don't want anyone taking any risks on our behalf.' He glanced sideways to see Claire nodding her head in agreement. 'It won't be a problem if we have to wait till first light.'

'Thanks, mate. I'll keep you posted.'

When the radio call ended there was a silence so deep it felt like he and Claire were the only people left on the planet. He caught Claire's gaze and could see that this was daunting for her but he could also see a spark of determination to cope with this challenge. To embrace it, even?

Yeah…she had an adventurous spirit, this woman.

Tom liked that.

'We may as well make ourselves at home,' he said. 'Can I make you a cup of tea?'

'You're kidding, right?'

Tom shrugged. 'You never quite know what you're going to find in a DOC hut but I wouldn't be surprised if there's a kettle and some tea. There might even be food if we're lucky.'

Claire followed his example and got to her feet. 'DOC?' she queried.

'Department of Conservation. It's a government department that oversees the care and preservation of everything to do with the land and our history. That includes the national parks and walking tracks and hundreds of huts like this one.' He turned the handle on the door and pushed it open.

'It's not locked,' Claire exclaimed.

'They're never locked. They might be needed in an emergency, if someone's injured or caught in bad weather.' He looked over his shoulder. 'Speaking of which, let's get our gear inside. That rain's going to be here any minute.'

It was more than rain by the time they got everything

inside and shut the door. Hailstones were falling thickly enough to sound like machine gun fire on the corrugated iron roof and it was suddenly dark enough to feel like night had fallen.

'I get the feeling we're not going anywhere in a hurry,' Tom said.

'No.' But Claire was actually smiling as she looked around in the dim light of the hut that might have bare, rough-hewn wooden walls but it was tidy and clean. Bunk beds with sponge mattresses were on each side. In the middle was a very old potbelly stove standing on a base of red bricks and it had a pile of twigs on one side and small split logs in a box on the other. Beside that was a bench, with shelves above it that were cluttered with an eclectic mix of mugs, plastic and tin bowls and plates, a jug full of cutlery and even a wine bottle with a half-burnt candle stuck in its neck. There were bottles of water and boxes of matches, pots and frying pans and a kettle on top of the bench and cupboards underneath that revealed treasure when Tom opened them.

'There's baked beans on this restaurant's menu,' he announced. 'Or…wait for it…spaghetti. With *sausages*. That's gourmet, isn't it?'

He turned as the hiccup of Claire's laughter changed into something he recognised all too easily—the release from bottled-up emotion after an intense medical battle that hadn't been won. He'd seen Claire fighting back tears when he'd released Mason from the hug he'd used to try and convey his heartfelt sympathy but they were appearing again now and…maybe they both needed that kind of release.

'I know…' he said, holding out his arms. 'It's okay…'

He didn't need to say anything else. Tomorrow, they could talk it through properly as they wrote the reports that would be needed into the investigation of the tragic accident and he knew they would both be left knowing they'd done their absolute best in a hopeless situation of major chest trauma and hypovolaemic shock so far away from an emergency department or operating theatre.

Offering a hug right now was the best thing he *could* do—for both of them—and he liked that Claire came straight into his arms. He knew he shed a tear or two himself as he held her for as long as it took for her to cry it out, but then it was time to be more practical.

'I'll see if I can get hold of Jonno,' he said, unclipping his radio. 'I'm guessing we're stuck here for tonight but I'm not going to light the fire until we know for sure.'

The hot tinned spaghetti in tomato sauce with the tiny, over-processed but surprisingly tasty sausages was quite possibly one of the most delicious meals Claire had ever had.

Tom had got a fire going in the little iron stove as soon as she'd finished crying all over him and the hut was now so warm she unzipped the overalls she was wearing. It was almost a surprise to realise she was still wearing her work scrubs underneath the overalls. It was only a few hours ago that she'd been in the Seaview Medical Centre doing something as mundane as taking someone's blood pressure and now, here she was in a completely different world, so far up in the mountains the rest of the world might as well have vanished.

Tom had taken a couple of the mattresses off the bunks and put them on the floor in front of the stove.

'It'll get cold in the middle of the night,' he'd warned Claire. 'I'll get a couple of foil blankets out of our kit, too, but it might be a good idea to stay here. I'll keep the fire stoked during the night. Hopefully, I'll have enough time to restock the hut before we get picked up in the morning.'

It was only then that it really hit Claire.

She was about to spend the night with Tom Atkinson. Alone.

So far away from anyone else that they were in a world that was entirely their own.

Maybe it hit Tom at the same moment because his gaze slid sideways and his face was scrunched into lines of… was it embarrassment?

Oh, help…had that awkwardness about the kiss reared its head again?

'Sorry,' Tom muttered.

'What for?'

'You know…it's been a bit…weird today, hasn't it?'

Claire shifted her gaze to the kettle that was on the flat top of the stove, a wisp of steam curling from its spout. She wondered if she should offer to make another cup of tea which might distract them both so they could avoid this conversation. Instead, she found herself saying something else.

'It's me who should apologise. That kiss was my idea, after all.'

'Your intentions were good,' Tom said. 'Maybe I'm overreacting by being so embarrassed about it.'

'No "maybe" about it,' Claire said firmly. 'There's nothing to be embarrassed about. We're both adults, Tom. And it was just a *kiss*, for heaven's sake.'

There was a moment's silence and then Claire let her

breath out in a huff. 'No...that's not entirely true, is it?' She could feel Tom's shock, but she waited a beat to deliver her punchline and turned to catch his gaze again. 'It wasn't just a kiss,' she added. 'It was a *great* kiss.'

That made Tom smile. 'It was, wasn't it? Not that I can imagine trying it with anyone else.'

'Why not?'

'The kiss made things awkward enough. How excruciating would it be if someone wanted more than a kiss and it turned out to be a disaster?'

'Why would it be?'

'I don't even know if I *could* do it.' Tom's voice was as quiet as if he was talking to himself. 'It's been more than seven *years*.'

Claire was silent. Tom could obviously sense her astonishment.

'The world got tipped upside down,' he said. 'There was so much grief. So much effort needed to try and keep things together for Hanna. I could only focus on two things—trying to be a good enough parent to raise our beautiful girl by myself and doing the best I could for every patient that I cared for. There was no room for anything else for years and by then it was my life.' He shrugged. 'It was working. I wasn't going to risk trying to fix something that didn't actually feel broken.'

Claire nodded. 'I get it. My life fell apart too. I haven't kept count but it might have been more than seven years since *I've* had sex.'

It was Tom's turn to be astonished. 'But you only left your marriage after your sixtieth birthday party! That was only last year, wasn't it?'

Claire simply nodded. Tom could join those dots without her going into the details of a relationship that had become so distant that the thought of physical intimacy had lost any appeal.

He didn't say anything for some time. He stoked the stove and then made them a mug of tea and they sat there in a silence that was perfectly companionable.

More than companionable, really. They'd shared a rather intimate confession that gave them rather an unusual connection, hadn't they?

It was Tom that finally broke the silence. 'Do you think you could ever get that close to someone again?' he asked.

Claire thought about that for a long moment. 'A year or so ago I would have definitely said no, but...you know what?'

'What?'

This was a new thought for Claire. A seed that had only just sprouted—possibly thanks to this conversation, even.

And it was a thought that was...rather thrilling, to be honest.

'I'm starting to think that I can do anything I want with the rest of my life,' she said, a little shyly. 'Look at me—I'm living on the other side of the world and right now, I'm nearly on top of a mountain in the middle of nowhere. If I meet the right person, at the right time, I might just forget that I'm too old to be doing anything as silly as sex and I might just jump in and have some fun.'

'You're not too old.' Tom was smiling, as if he was picking up on the embryonic excitement that Claire was feeling. 'And you *can* do whatever the hell you want. Hey...isn't sixty the new forty?'

Claire snorted. 'Not according to my bathroom mirror when I get out of the shower every morning.'

'You're beautiful, Claire,' Tom said quietly. 'Inside and out. We should both be past an age where what we look like matters. Who cares about a few wrinkles or scars or flabby bits?'

'I *don't* care,' Claire said. 'Not really. I'm happy and healthy and that's what really matters.' But she hunched her shoulders in an extreme wince. 'It's just the thought of some stranger judging me when I take my clothes off that's really off-putting.'

'That doesn't bother me as much as what happens after that,' Tom confessed. 'The…ah…performance factor? Especially the first time. What if it's too much to handle and…*nothing* happens? It would be the first *and* last time for me.'

'You can't let that happen.' Claire was shaking her head. 'The first time *is* going to be huge and if it's too much, so what? If you're with someone that you trust—someone that understands how huge it is, you can just try again. Take it slowly. Take as long as you need.' She offered Tom a slightly apologetic smile. Who was she, after all, to be offering advice on a subject like this? 'I'm older and wiser than you,' she added. 'And…and I think you deserve to have more in your life. Maybe Hanna's right to give you a push. This is *my* push.'

Tom was staring at her. 'You kissed me,' he said finally, so softly she could barely hear the words over the crackle of the fire as he opened the door of the stove to add more wood. 'I didn't expect that it would make me feel like it did.' He closed the door and turned to face Claire. 'Like… I wanted more.'

Claire swallowed hard. She'd wanted more, too, hadn't she? She could remember every detail of that kiss. She could feel the curl of sensation deep in her belly that was the spark of desire that was about to catch fire like those logs in the little potbelly stove.

She had no idea how long they simply stared at each other. She could see something in Tom's eyes that told her he was feeling something similar but he wasn't going to say anything more, she realised. This was her choice. If she didn't say anything herself, the whole subject of sex would never be spoken about again.

She dropped her gaze so that she could think about this without being distracted by how unbelievably attractive this man was and she discovered that there was something more than just the fizz of simmering desire that she was aware of. It was that thought she'd told Tom about—that she could do anything she wanted with her life from now on. If she wasn't brave enough to do something that scared her, how on earth would she know whether she was really making the most of her life?

Judging by the way her heart had picked up enough to feel like it was hammering against her ribs, this was absolutely scary. But what was the worst that could happen here?

Something embarrassing, that's what. But they were friends. They trusted each other. They could laugh that off, surely?

Her voice sounded oddly rough when she spoke.

'If you wanted,' she said slowly, thinking out loud. 'We're in the perfect place to have a trial run. Nobody else would ever have to know.' She let her gaze touch his. 'What happens in the hut would stay in the hut, wouldn't it?'

Tom was staring at her again. She could see the muscles in his throat moving as he swallowed. Carefully.

'Of course it would,' he agreed.

The candle in the wine bottle was giving its final flickers but neither of them got up to find a new one from the supply on the shelf beside the matchboxes. The light coming through the grilles of the metal door in the stove was bright enough to give things in close range a rosy glow, but it was soft enough for Claire to be confident that most physical imperfections would be almost invisible. The shadows further back made the bunk beds and everything else in the hut irrelevant and the sound of heavy rain on the iron roof was a barrier to the outside world that made this little patch of warmth and light the only patch of the planet that mattered in this moment.

And they were the only people that mattered.

This was crazy.

But all Tom could think of in this moment was *that* kiss—and how it had made him feel as if he wanted more.

As if he wanted *everything*...

And here it was, being offered to him with no strings attached whatsoever. With the most complete privacy you could ever imagine and a promise that nobody else would need to know about it if it didn't work.

There was a flicker of something in Claire's eyes that he'd never seen before. Not fear exactly, but he had the impression that it had taken rather a lot of courage for her to make this offer.

And maybe...she needed a trial run as much as he did?

Claire Campbell had left an unhappy marriage and her old life behind and she was planning to have adventures and make the most of whatever life she had left to live. He'd heard that shy note of hope in her voice when she'd confessed that maybe she *would* be happy to find someone to get close to again. To have some fun with.

To have *sex* with.

Maybe she was as nervous as he was at the prospect, even if it was for different reasons. Claire had no reason to feel like her body would be less than desirable in any way but he could understand why she might need reassurance. Like him, she hadn't been physically intimate with anyone in a very long time.

They could help each other.

It could, in fact, be a gift that would keep giving for the rest of their lives.

He held her gaze. 'Are you sure about this?'

Her eyes looked enormous and so dark they were unreadable but her expression was very serious. 'Yes.' Then a hint of a smile lifted the corners of her mouth. 'Fortune favours the brave,' she said.

'Nothing ventured, nothing gained,' Tom responded. He could feel a smile of his own trying to emerge.

Claire was really smiling now. 'Who dares wins,' she offered.

'No guts, no glory,' Tom countered.

'Do one thing every day that scares you.'

'Good grief…we're starting to sound like social media memes.'

They were both laughing now, but the sound faded and their faces stilled at the same time as well, until they were both simply looking at each other in the semi-darkness with no more than the glow of the firelight.

Tom reached out to brush strands of Claire's silver hair back from her face. She tipped her head to nestle her cheek into the palm of his hand and the movement was so trusting, so *welcoming*, that Tom could feel his whole body responding. He kept his hand there, cupping her face, and leaned closer to touch her lips with his own.

It was like that kiss on the beach under the millions of stars. A whisper of sensation that was all that was needed to conjure up the swirling currents of waters that didn't seem nearly as dangerous now. They knew what they were doing. They didn't have to control themselves and back off because they both wanted this. They undressed each other in the warmth still radiating from the stove. They smiled about not needing to worry about protection.

'Don't they say that you're a born-again virgin when it's been so long since you've had sex?'

'No need to worry about an accidental pregnancy either. There's a plus side to getting older, isn't there?'

There was certainly a plus side to the laughter. The fear of embarrassment was evaporating with every kiss. Every touch. Tom's body was letting him know that it remembered exactly how this worked and Claire seemed to be as lost in this almost forgotten world as he was rapidly becoming. His last coherent wish was that this would give Claire all the confidence she needed to know that she could do anything she wanted in the future.

His wish for himself was very simple.

He wanted *this*…

This moment. This feeling of being truly alive again for the first time in too many years.

And he wanted *this* woman.

Claire…

He didn't realise he'd spoken her name aloud until she responded.

'I'm here,' she whispered. 'Oh, Tom… I want you… *Now…*'

CHAPTER SEVEN

JONNO ARRIVED IN his helicopter to collect them not long after dawn the next day.

'Sorry about that,' he said. 'Turned out it was the warning light that was faulty but by the time we discovered that, the storm was on top of us.' He shook his head as he looked from Tom to Claire and back again. 'Doesn't look like you guys got much sleep.'

Claire made sure she didn't catch Tom's gaze by stooping to pick up the oxygen cylinder in one hand and the life-pack in the other. They hadn't got much sleep, but if Jonno knew the real reason why he would be horrified. Their pilot was still young enough to probably think that people her age wouldn't even be interested in sex any longer, let alone stay awake long enough to repeat—and embellish—what had been the best sex ever as far as Claire was concerned, anyway.

They landed at Seaview Hospital's helipad and found people waiting for them as they walked through the doors of the medical centre. One of them was Ruby, who was in charge of the hospital's kitchen.

'You must be starving,' she said. 'I've got bacon and eggs waiting for you in the kitchen. Unless you want a shower first?'

'A quick shower would be great,' Claire said. Did she look as dishevelled as she felt? Like a woman who'd thoroughly enjoyed an unexpectedly passionate sexual adventure?

Which was all it had been. A trial run for both of them. There was no need for it to ever happen again, so there was no need for anyone else to know anything about it…

What had happened in the hut was definitely going to stay in the hut.

But it had not only been a revelation for Claire, it had opened up a whole new level in her plan to make the most of the rest of her life. She'd never had any idea that sex could be *that* good…

'Sorry, what…?' She realised she'd completely missed what Ian, one of the other doctors in the team, had just said.

'You've got about an hour to get cleaned up and have something to eat. Lots of coffee might be a good idea, too. There's a specialist police team from Christchurch who are already on their way here to interview you both about your part in the incident.' He shook his head. 'Sounds like a real tragedy. Any hunting accident is awful, but for a son to have killed his father…how could anyone get past that?'

Claire suddenly felt guilty that she and Tom had managed to distract themselves from the tragedy so effectively for those night-time hours. Not that it mattered, but had that been partly why it had happened at all? Because they both needed an escape from the worst aspects of their work and something overwhelmingly physical was guaranteed to stop them lying awake and thinking about the awful moments of losing their fight to save a life?

Tom's response was a grunt that let Ian know he wasn't ready to discuss it yet.

'Thanks for stepping in for me,' he said. 'Any emergencies or issues with our inpatients?'

'Only Mrs B sleepwalking again. She thought someone had left the gate open and the sheep were all out on the road. She almost got as far as the road before Cathy noticed her bed was empty. It's probably time to think about transferring her to a secure dementia care facility.'

Tom nodded. 'In the meantime, we need an alarm of some kind. One of those mats that can go beside the bed and gets activated with any weight going onto it should do the trick. But the doors were all locked, weren't they?'

'She figured out how to open the fire door.'

'Let's make sure it's on the agenda for our next staff meeting. I'll have a chat to the family later today. Was that the only excitement?'

'Thankfully, yes…but there is another patient I want to talk to you about…'

Claire left them to it. She went into the staff locker room that included a shower and stood under the rain of hot water for quite some time. She was tired, of course, and emotionally drained after the adrenaline rush of yesterday's mission. Her body felt different, too—her arm and leg muscles were a bit sore after the unfamiliar activity of carrying heavy gear over a rough track. She could feel other parts of her body, too, that had been well-used for the first time in too many years.

But…she felt better than she had in even longer than that. As if she'd ridden an emotional—and physical—rollercoaster and the buzz hadn't yet worn off. She felt exhilarated and more alert than she could believe possible after so little sleep.

After the shower, she got dressed in the clothes she'd come to work in yesterday and used a comb and a lipstick that were in her bag to try and make herself look presentable for the interview that was going to happen before she could go home to start what was rostered to be a day off for her. She checked her reflection in the mirror as she turned to leave the locker room and she saw something that made her blink. And then smile.

She looked…alive, she decided. Really alive.

And happy.

Really happy.

Tom and Claire were interviewed separately. Claire had been first and had been told she could go home afterwards, which was good because she had to be as exhausted as he was.

Not that Tom was going to allow himself to think about why they were both so tired. He needed every ounce of his concentration to detail everything that had happened from the moment they'd arrived at the scene of the dreadful hunting accident. The interview was being recorded. Questions were being asked.

'The man who organised the hunting trip—Harvey Blakely, is a local plumber. You know him, yes?'

'I do.'

'We interviewed him last night. He was a close friend of the deceased and came to Christchurch to support the son, who is allegedly the person who fired the fatal shot.'

Tom gave a single nod although he hadn't been asked a question.

'Harvey told us that he could see the machine you were using to record vital signs and that he could see a heartbeat on the screen. He said he had complete faith in how you were treating the victim—that your reputation as a doctor is second to none—but he couldn't understand why you started doing CPR.'

'There was no pulse,' Tom explained. 'Which meant that there was no blood circulating so there was no oxygen to keep cells alive. He wasn't breathing. And yes, there was a rhythm to be seen on the screen for some time, but it's a rhythm called PEA. Pulseless Electrical Activity. The electrical signal for the heart to pump was still being generated but it wasn't making the heart pump.'

'Why not?'

'In this case, I suspect it was hypovolaemic shock from internal bleeding. Despite our efforts to replace fluid volume with saline and the blood products, he was still bleeding into his chest cavity. Has the autopsy been done yet?'

'It's happening today.'

'I'd appreciate a copy of that, if that's okay.'

'Of course. We'll supply the coroner with all the details you've given us of your treatment and the drugs administered etcetera. We also have your assistant, Claire Campbell's statement.' The police officer looked up at Tom from the papers in front of him on the table. 'She thinks very highly of your judgement and capabilities.'

It was the first gleam of something warm in what had been a difficult interview, going over every tiny detail of a resuscitation that had failed. Knowing that Claire respected his abilities this much gave him a glow of pride.

'I would say the same about hers,' Tom said. 'She

hasn't been working here very long, but she is the best practice nurse I've ever had the privilege of working with.'

'That's the impression everyone seemed to have at the scene.' The other police officer was nodding. 'They all said you seemed to be a great team. That you knew what you were doing. And that it was obvious you did everything you could to save the victim.' Her face creased into lines of sympathy. 'I'm sorry it was unsuccessful. I'm also sorry you had to be left out there for the night. I hope it wasn't too much of an ordeal.'

Tom merely shook his head, with a smile that dismissed the experience as something prolonged and memorably unpleasant.

He had to admit, as he walked to his office a few minutes later, that it had certainly been memorable. And it had been prolonged enough to leave him feeling distinctly sleep-deprived. But it had been the polar opposite of unpleasant. The very thought of it was enough to make his entire body tingle.

There was a twinge of regret to be found in the thought that it was never going to happen again. That what had happened had been left behind where it had happened. In the hut.

He almost bumped into Claire in the corridor as she was coming out of the treatment room.

'How did it go?' She grimaced. 'Silly question, sorry. I think I'm too tired to be thinking straight.'

'It's your day off, isn't it?'

'Yes, I'm just heading home. I'll sleep for a while and then have a long walk on the beach, I think.'

'Sounds good.'

Claire opened her mouth as if she was about to say something else, but then she bit her lip as if she felt she shouldn't. Tom knew she'd been about to invite him to join her. And that tingle in his body had suddenly ramped up into something else—a stab of sensation that was strong enough to be almost a physical pain.

It felt like he'd hit a wall that was stopping him from being able to do something that he really, really wanted to do and he also knew what that was. He wanted to touch Claire again.

To make love to her. Again.

Was it possible that what he was feeling was so strong that it was radiating into the air between them?

Because when he held Claire's gaze for a heartbeat too long, it felt like she was feeling it as well.

Tom tried, and failed, to keep his tone light. Friendly, even.

'I'd love to join you,' he said. 'But I need to have some more coffee and a shower and get on with my day.'

A cold shower might be a good idea, he thought as the corners of Claire's mouth turned up into the softest smile he'd ever seen on her face.

'Maybe next time,' she murmured, turning to walk away.

Tom watched her disappear into the waiting room. He wasn't quite sure whether that had been an actual invitation but he was sure of something. There *was* going to *be* a next time.

And that made him feel good.

Really good.

It was there every time they were breathing the same air.

Claire could feel the chemistry actually happening.

The mix of components was far more powerful than it had been when she'd first been aware of how attractive Tom was, because there were memories stirred into it now. Memories of that first kiss under the stars and of making love in the glow of a small potbelly stove in a mountain hut. Memories that never failed to spark a physical reaction. Claire could feel her heart rate pick up every time she saw Tom in the days following that night in the hut. She could feel something melty happening in her gut if she was close enough to pick up the scent of his skin or if he was holding a door open for her to walk through, perhaps. It was felt more fiercely if their hands happened to brush, like they had when they'd reached for a set of patient notes on the reception desk at the same time, for example. It was astonishing that nobody else seemed to be aware of what had happened and the new level of connection there was between herself and Tom.

Apart from Tom, of course.

Claire knew he was not only aware of it, he was feeling it himself. She could see a flash of it in even the briefest eye contact. She could feel it in some indefinable difference in the way he smiled at her. They were both doing their best to ignore it, however. Were they both hoping it would simply fizzle out? Or were they waiting so as not to be the one to suggest...

What...another fake date?

Except...there would be nothing fake about what would happen if they ended up alone together again, would there? And maybe that was what was stopping them. Now that they'd included sex in the pretence, it felt different. More complicated.

Dangerous?

No... Nobody was going to end up getting hurt. A serious relationship was the last thing Tom wanted. That had, after all, been the whole point of starting the fake dating in the first place. And Claire? Well, she didn't want anyone getting in the way of all the adventures she intended having, thank you very much.

So...while there wasn't any real reason to repeat what had happened in the hut, there wasn't really any reason *not* to either. *Que será, será*, she decided. And in the meantime she intended to quietly enjoy the frissons of physical attraction that hummed in the air between herself and Tom. She was blissfully confident that nobody around them had any idea of what she might be thinking—until the following week when she finished a brief conversation with Tom at the desk as he was searching for a patient's email address and turned to find his daughter Hanna in the waiting room.

Watching them.

Her smile felt oddly wary. 'Hey...it's Hanna, isn't it? Hi! I don't think we've ever been properly introduced.' They'd never been introduced at all, had they? She'd just eavesdropped on this young woman having an altercation with her father. 'I'm Claire...'

'Oh, I know...' Hanna's smile was amused. 'I'd recognise you anywhere after all the photos Dad's been sending me.'

'I'll be out in two minutes,' Tom told his daughter as he finished scribbling down the address he'd been searching for on a scrap of paper. 'I just need to flick off a quick email.'

'I'm taking the afternoon off,' he told Claire as she followed him out of the reception area. 'Hanna wants to fish from the boat and I'm going to go diving for some crayfish.' He paused by his office door. 'She also wants you to come for dinner,' he said quietly. 'At our place.' He raised an eyebrow. 'If you're not busy?'

He held Claire's gaze long enough to let her know that Hanna had decided it was time for her to meet the woman her father was supposedly dating. This could be the end point in this pretence if Hanna guessed the truth. No wonder Tom was looking as wary as Claire had felt when she saw that Hanna was back in town.

But things were different now. The awkwardness of that kiss was long gone. In its place was this simmering attraction that made it more than pleasant to be close to this man. It shouldn't be at all difficult to convince Hanna that their dating wasn't fake.

'I'd love to come,' she said. She held *his* gaze for a moment longer, hoping to convey a reassuring message. 'Crayfish? Yum… I hope it's a very successful fishing trip.'

The crayfish were lined up on the kitchen bench as Tom prepared to cook them. He had a pot of water coming to the boil to blanch them and the grill was on in the oven to finish them off. He would heat the frying pan as well soon and melt the butter to cook the fish fillets waiting on a plate beside it.

Hanna and Claire were at the kitchen table, sipping white wine and finishing off the preparation of a salad to go with their dinner. They'd been talking about Hanna's plans for her future studies.

'I'll know before Christmas if my application to med

school has been successful. If it isn't, I'll have to do something else.'

'What would you do?' Claire asked.

'Keep going with a science degree and reapply as a graduate. Or maybe I'll become a nurse, like you. You like your job, don't you?'

'Love it,' Claire said. 'Nursing is a fabulous career. Especially these days, when you can become a nurse practitioner and get to do a lot of what used to only be done by doctors. I suspect you really want to be a doctor, though, like your dad?'

'I do.' Hanna sighed. 'I hope I get in.'

'I'm quite sure you will,' Tom said. 'But it wouldn't be the end of the world if you had to wait a bit longer, would it? I know you're the same age I was when I went into medicine, but seeing you sitting in the boat this afternoon, waiting to feel your fishing line announce a catch, you looked exactly like you did when you were about fourteen years old and we'd take the boat out at least twice a week.'

'They were good days.' Tom saw Hanna glance up, from where she was about to start slicing a sourdough loaf, to smile at Claire, who was now crumbling some feta cheese on the top of the salad. 'It became our thing, after Mum died. When we'd had a bad day, we'd go out on the boat for hours. Sometimes we didn't catch anything but it didn't matter. We always felt better when we got back and usually we had crayfish for dinner. Like tonight.'

He liked the soft way Claire smiled back at Hanna.

It stirred something very deep and his breath caught as he realised what it was. The last time he'd been in this kitchen with Hanna and a woman had been when

Jill had still been alive—and well enough to be eating at the kitchen table.

It brought back such powerful memories of…family that Tom braced himself for the familiar shaft of grief that could still catch him unawares. But it didn't come. Was that because he knew he wasn't betraying the memory of Hanna's real mother by having any intention of replacing her? Claire was here as a friend, nothing more, so perhaps that was why he wasn't feeling sad. Or guilty. If anything, he was feeling grateful for being reminded of something special.

That bond between people that only family could create.

He turned to flick on the gas burner beneath the frying pan. He couldn't see Claire's smile now but he could hear its gentleness in her voice.

'Sounds like the perfect way to deal with grief. I can see why you and your dad have such a close bond. Did you get into scuba diving, too?'

'I tried it when I got older but I prefer sitting on top of the waves and breathing real air.'

'I'd be the same,' Claire said fervently. 'I went snorkelling once and I hated breathing underwater for just a single breath at a time—it felt *so* wrong. Terrifying, even.'

She got up and came close to Tom to rinse her hands under the kitchen tap. So close, his arm brushed hers as he reached for the garlic and butter he would need to add to the crayfish when they were under the grill. The touch of her skin gave him what felt like a mild electric shock and, judging by the way Claire's glance caught his so quickly, she'd felt it as well.

Maybe it was just as well Hanna was visiting. It might

be inevitable that he and Claire were going to enjoy the kind of pleasure they'd reminded themselves about in that mountain hut but it wasn't going to be tonight.

It was Claire that broke that rather intense eye contact. She eyed the shellfish as she reached for a paper towel to dry her hands.

'They're enormous,' she said. 'Were they hard to catch? Do they try and nip you with their claws?'

'It can be a challenge,' Tom said. 'They hide under rocks and all you can see are the antennae. You have to sneak up on them and get as close as you can before you try and grab them—behind the horns at the bottom of the antennae. You have to have a good hold, too, or they can scoot backwards and escape.'

Claire laughed. 'You sound like you love the chase.'

'You're not wrong there.'

He loved the sound of Claire laughing, too. It was impossible not to smile himself.

'Maybe you should have a go at proper diving,' he said. 'Pete's a great teacher. You might change your mind about breathing underwater and learn to love it, too.'

She shook her head. 'Don't think so. I'd like to go out on a boat soon, though. I'll have to chase up Carl and remind him to let me know when it's going to be a good day to go whale watching.'

Tom used tongs to take the crayfish from the boiling water and then cut them in half to put under the grill.

'Dinner's going to be ready in about five minutes,' he said. 'Could you set the table, please, Hanna?'

'That was *so* good, Dad. You've become a really good cook, you know that?'

'Oh...thanks, Hanna. Glad you liked it. I think Claire did, too.'

He'd rebuffed Claire's offer to help clean up, persuading her to go home before it got too late. The dinner had been a resounding success and he'd been delighted that Claire and Hanna had got on so well with each other, but the more time they spent together, the higher the risk that Hanna might pick up on something and realise that things weren't quite what they might seem.

Hanna was nodding happily. And then she smiled broadly. 'She likes more than just your cooking, that's for sure.'

Tom threw her a swift glance. 'What do you mean?'

Hanna laughed. 'I saw the way you two were looking at each other when she was washing her hands. I almost offered to disappear and give you some alone time but I was enjoying getting to know her. She's really nice, Dad. I like her.'

'Yeah...' Tom put another plate onto the rack for Hanna to dry. 'I do, too. She's great company.'

'Looked like more than just great company to me. I reckon I could see some pretty decent sparks flying around between you two.'

Oh, *man*...they'd been too successful in trying to convince Hanna that something was going on, hadn't they? And, as far as he'd thought, they hadn't even been trying to pretend they were dating this evening. If anything, they'd been trying to hide how close they'd accidentally become last week.

'And didn't I hear that you were both stuck overnight in that mountain hut?'

Tom almost dropped the plate he was lifting from the sink. Was Hanna reading his mind?

'Where did you hear *that*?'

'Everybody's been talking about it. Harvey the plumber was in Beachcombers the other night and when I had coffee with Kerry this morning she gave me a run-down about what he'd been saying to some of his mates when he got upset after a few beers. The helicopter pilot who was supposed to pick you up was there, too, but they weren't just talking about you and Claire getting stuck. Did you really poke huge holes in the chest of that guy who got shot?'

Tom sighed. 'He had major injuries. I did finger thoracostomies to try and decompress his chest.'

'Wow... I'm going to go and look for some videos on-line. That sounds like some hardcore first aid.'

'You could say that.' Tom's tone was dry and at least Hanna had been diverted from trying to find out just how close he had become to Claire.

Or had she?

'So...you and Claire...'

Tom didn't want to discuss it. Giving the impression that he had indeed been dating Claire had been surprisingly effective this evening but Hanna was his daughter. She'd see through any pretence if she asked too many questions. And then he'd have to confess the deception and she'd be really hurt, even if he explained that he'd done it because he didn't want her to be worried about him.

But she'd also be hurt on *his* behalf if she thought he was in a real relationship and it ended in the not-too-distant future, wouldn't she?

'It's early days,' he said, carefully slotting the last of the cutlery into the rack and pulling the plug from the sink. 'We're good friends, that's all. I don't even know how long Claire's going to be here. She's planning on having adventures for the rest of her life. She might not want to stay in one place.'

'She might change her mind,' Hanna said. 'Especially if you stop giving her mixed messages.'

'What's that supposed to mean?'

'You're still wearing your wedding ring, Dad.' She caught his gaze, her voice soft. 'That's like a "No Trespassing" sign for most women. A barrier to being anything more than good friends, that's for sure.' She put the dry cutlery into the drawer in front of her. 'I'm assuming Claire's been married. She's not wearing a ring.'

'No. She threw it away. Into the Thames. Her husband was cheating on her.'

Hanna looked impressed 'Go Claire.' She grinned. 'I like her even more now.' Then her tone softened. 'Don't you think it might be time to take yours off?' she suggested. 'Mum would have wanted you to be happy, you know. And I think Claire makes you happy.'

Tom pulled in a slow breath. It was true. He did feel happy when he was with Claire. This certainly wasn't the moment to confess that they'd only been pretending to be dating. And...hadn't he thought that maybe he was ready to think about the possibility of another relationship? Removing his wedding ring would be the logical first step in that direction but...

'I *can't* take it off,' he told Hanna. 'See?' He tugged the gold band, which didn't get anywhere near his knuckle.

'It's too tight and I don't want to damage it by cutting it off.'

'But would you take it off if you didn't have to cut it?'

'I...' Tom thought of how happy he'd looked in that photo on the day they'd gone to see the baby seals. How he'd felt the yearning to have that kind of companionship in his life again. 'Yes...' he said slowly. 'I think I would.'

'It's been a shield,' Hanna said. 'Be honest. You've used it to put women off. You're still using it.'

He couldn't deny it. And he knew that Hanna could see the truth in his face by the look she gave him. 'Don't move,' she commanded. 'I'll be right back.'

She came back, holding a dental floss dispenser. She broke off a long thread and pushed one end of it under Tom's ring by putting pressure on the ring from beneath to create a gap. She wound the length tightly around his finger from the ring to his fingernail.

'You do realise you've cut off my circulation? Look—my nail's gone completely blue. I'd quite like to keep this finger.'

'Hold your horses. This is the magic bit.' Hanna picked up the loose end on the other side of the ring and began to unwind it. The thread pushed the ring further along the compressed finger with every new loop, over the knuckle and then...and then it was off. His finger was bright red and there was a deep groove where the ring had been for more than twenty years, but it was off. Hanna handed it to him and then gave him a fierce hug.

'Put it somewhere with your other treasures that remind you of Mum,' she said. 'But it's okay to move on, Dad. It's okay to fall in love again and not be lonely for the rest of your life.' She let him go and swiped at a tear that was trickling down the side of her nose. 'I really hope it lasts with you and Claire,' she said. 'For what it's worth, I think she'd make an awesome stepmum. And, more importantly, I think you're perfect for each other.'

Tom watched her walk out of the kitchen.

What on earth had just happened?

And why did it feel like Hanna might be right?

Not about him and Claire being perfect for each other, but about it being time to be honest.

Pretending to still be married by continuing to wear that ring had not been honest.

Pretending to be in a genuine relationship with Claire was not being honest either.

But Hanna was so happy about it. And she was proud of him for making an effort to move on with his life. He'd hate to see that replaced by disappointment at his being less than honest.

Maybe Claire would have a good idea of how to fix this?

CHAPTER EIGHT

'I DON'T THINK it really needs fixing.'

Claire and Tom were using the bonus of a longer than normal lunch break to have a brisk walk up to the lookout and back. They'd invited everyone else in the staffroom to join them for some fresh air and exercise before the afternoon surgery began but nobody was keen. Kaia said she would be getting all the exercise she needed when she went to her line dancing class in the evening and Ian said he was going surfing after work.

Thanks to it just being the two of them, and possibly because they were retracing their footsteps to the site of the first fake date photo that they'd taken for Hanna's benefit, Tom had told Claire about the conversation he'd had when he and Hanna had been washing the dishes after the dinner she'd been invited to a few days ago.

'And I'm starting to think she's right—it's dishonest to let her think we're really dating. It's been playing on my mind a lot. I've never been anything less than honest with her—even when it was the hardest thing in the world—like when I had to tell her that her mother wasn't going to get better.'

'I wouldn't say it's dishonest.' Claire was having to push herself to keep up with Tom's long strides and her breathing rate was increasing. 'All you've done is send her photos of places we've actually been to together.'

'It was easier when it was only text messages. Before she'd met you. She really likes you, by the way.'

'I really like *her*.'

The look she received was a question she knew Tom was unlikely to ask aloud. So she told him, anyway.

'It used to be so hard to talk to girls who are around the same age that Sophia was when she died. She'll be eighteen for ever in my heart. But now, with enough time that's gone past, there's a special kind of joy in being reminded. It's new and different but it's familiar enough to fill a hole with something that I've missed *so* much.'

The question in Tom's eyes had vanished. Instead, the softness suggested that he understood completely. That he was happy his daughter could do that for her.

'She's a credit to you, Tom,' Claire added. 'And I'll bet she'll end up being just as brilliant a doctor as her dad is.'

'She knows about the night in the mountain hut.'

'*What?* You told her about that? That we'd…?' She couldn't bring herself to finish her sentence. What would she call it? Having sex? Having a trial run to see whether they'd forgotten how to do it? Making love…?

'*No!*' Tom sounded horrified. 'Of course I didn't. She'd heard about it from her friend Kerry—the one who works at Beachcombers. Apparently, Harvey got a bit tearful when he was having a few beers with his mates and he was telling them how traumatic it all was. And Jonno was there, too, but it was already common knowledge that he hadn't been able to get back to pick us up.'

'What did *you* say?'

'That we're just good friends. That you'd probably be

moving on at some point to have a new adventure somewhere else.'

'There you go, then… You were perfectly honest.'

'She told me I wasn't being honest by still wearing my wedding ring. So I took it off. Or rather, she did. I think she wanted to see if the dental floss trick would work.'

They'd reached the top of the hill now and Claire really needed to catch her breath so they stood there in silence for a minute or two. There was less snow on the mountains than there had been the last time they'd come up here and the cool breeze was welcome after the speed of their walking. In the sunshine, the sea was an even more glorious shade of turquoise near the shore.

Claire had noticed the day after that dinner that Tom wasn't wearing his wedding ring any longer but she hadn't said anything. It had, in fact, given her an odd sensation—as though she'd taken too deep a breath, too quickly. As if the road she was on had suddenly turned an unexpected corner. She'd wondered if the decision had had anything to do with her. She'd even wondered if she *wanted* it to have anything to do with her.

What if the age gap between herself and Tom wasn't as important as she thought it was?

What if she didn't really want to be floating from one place to another for the rest of her life, having adventures but never putting down roots or sharing her life in a meaningful way with anyone else?

What if fake dating could turn into *real* dating?

No…she didn't want that. Did she? But even if she did, Tom didn't feel the same way. He was feeling guilty that he hadn't been honest enough with his daughter—that she should know this was not a real relationship. And it never would be? That thought took her right back to her first comment about his concerns.

'I still don't think it's something that needs fixing,' she said. 'It's going to fix itself without you having to confess anything because I *will* be moving on eventually. There's too much to see out there. Have you seen that video that's gone viral? The one that was filmed from the cockpit of a plane as it dodged mountains and then followed the lake to land at Queenstown Airport? You were absolutely on point when you said it's a place I shouldn't miss.'

Tom threw her a smile. 'We were standing right here when I said that, weren't we? Feels like a long time ago.'

It had felt fake then. Claire remembered how she'd pasted that big smile on her face and tilted her head so that it was touching Tom's shoulder while he took the selfie. She remembered how nice it had felt to have his arm around her for the first time.

She'd had *no* idea how it was going to feel to be even closer to him.

And, dammit...she wanted to be that close again.

She tried to shake off the longing. She shaded her eyes with her hand and stared out to sea. 'Can't see any whales.'

'Maybe next time. We'd better start heading back, anyway.'

'We'd get fit if we did this a bit more often.' Claire pulled in a deep breath of the clear air. 'We could start climbing those mountains if we kept it up.'

'That's not a bad idea. I've been thinking I should get up there and restock the firewood we used. And take a box of canned food to go in the cupboards in case someone else needs it one day.'

'Sounds like we'll be carrying some heavy packs. We'll have to get really fit.'

It would take lots of long walks up hills to do that. Afternoons or whole days off spent on the tracks near the rivers and forests of the wilder country that was on their doorstep. The prospect was more than appealing but Tom's expression was almost a grimace.

'Yeah… That might be stretching things a bit. I could get hold of someone at DOC and get them to take the supplies next time they go to do maintenance on the hut.'

The disappointment that the prospect of another night in the wilderness with Tom had just vanished was powerful enough to slow Claire's steps. Then she took a deep breath and increased her pace to catch up with Tom again. She'd just remembered something else.

Something she'd told Tom when they were sharing that first glass of wine and getting to know each other. She'd told him what her new hobby was, hadn't she?

'Making the most of every adventure that comes my way. And if it doesn't come my way, I'll go out and find it…'

Adventures didn't have to be going to a particular place or doing something amazing. Her time with Tom was an adventure and if she didn't make the most of it, she might regret it for the rest of her life.

'Do you know anything about the Marlborough Garden Festival?' she asked as she lengthened her stride to walk by Tom's side. 'Mabel Jamieson told me that I shouldn't miss it while I'm here. And that I really should have a whole weekend in Blenheim and go on as many of the tours as I can.'

'People have been telling me that for years,' Tom said.

'They've given up now, probably because they think I'm not interested in gardens, but it's more that it's not the kind of thing I'd want to do by myself.'

'Like me going into a pub.' Claire looked up to smile at Tom but also to catch her breath before she took what felt like it could be a big step. 'Maybe it's something else we could do together?'

She held his gaze. Tom knew perfectly well that the suggestion was about a lot more than touring beautiful gardens. She'd reassured him that he didn't need to make any confessions to Hanna because this—whatever seemed to be pulling them together again—had a limited shelf life.

Would he think, like her, that it might be something they should make the most of?

The way his gaze was locked on hers felt like that could be exactly what he was thinking.

'Why not?' he said softly as he broke that gaze. 'I love gardens.'

Right from the start it was a weekend that Claire knew she was never going to forget. They booked two full-day tours and the first one let them experience far more than gorgeous manicured gardens. They were lucky enough to get tickets to join a tour that took them out onto the Marlborough Sounds in a boat which had been part of a service that had been running for more than a hundred years, to deliver mail and groceries to remote locations. There were beautiful farm gardens included in the tour but they also got to walk in native forest and along the most stunning beaches Claire had ever seen in her life. The weather was kind, the waters blue and calm and the bonus of a playful pod of dolphins around the boat on the way back to Havelock was almost too perfect.

Claire actually had tears in her eyes as she stood beside Tom on the deck watching the dolphins.

'I don't think I've *ever* been this happy,' she told him.

'I can't believe I've never done this before.' Tom held her gaze for a moment and then bent his head to place a soft kiss on her lips. 'Thank you,' he added.

'What for?'

'This was your idea. I might never have done this, if it wasn't for your adventurous spirit.' He was smiling now. 'You've changed my life, Claire Campbell.'

She hugged those words close as they left the boat, picked up a few supplies in a supermarket in Blenheim and then went to find their accommodation for the night. It was what she'd set out to do when she'd suggested that he kissed her, wasn't it? And when she'd offered to help him rediscover the joy of sex. She'd simply wanted to give Tom more options in his future by restoring his confidence in having a female companion.

She'd had no idea that she might be receiving as much, if not more, than she was giving.

Tom had booked a boutique bed and breakfast location that offered small rustic cottages dotted amongst a leafy vineyard with a backdrop of the dramatic peaks and valleys of the mountains in the distance. The self-catering cottages looked as though they had belonged to early settlers but offered an impressive level of luxury, including a welcoming grazing platter of cheeses, olives and other nibbles, accompanied by a choice of local wines, that was waiting for them on a private veranda so that they could enjoy the sunset and lingering dusk. A few sheep nearby had lambs that were making the most of the last daylight to frolic, which was a delight to watch, and as it started to get darker Claire heard an unexpectedly haunting bird call.

'That sounds like an owl. I didn't know New Zealand had owls.'

'We do. It's the morepork—our only native owl. Its Māori name is ruru, which I believe translates as "big eyes".'

Claire was smiling as she listened to the calls that were being made and answered around them.

'Morepork sounds exactly like the call. As if they're introducing themselves.'

'They could be saying goodnight. We've got another full day's tour tomorrow. Maybe we should get some sleep?'

'Good idea.'

They finally went inside, but as Tom shut the door behind them they caught and held each other's gaze for a long, significant moment as a totally silent conversation played out.

There were two beds in this cottage but they were silently agreeing that they were only going to need one of them and that they might not get as much sleep as they probably should.

And that turned out to be the most perfect part of this garden tour adventure. Claire hadn't been at all bothered by the lumpy old mattress on the floor of that hut the first time she and Tom had been together—that had been perfect in its own way. Perhaps the imperfections of the setting were a reflection of the inevitable hesitations and fumbles of two people who were not only strangers to each other's bodies but hadn't had sex at all for a very long time.

But this was very different. A gorgeously comfortable bed. Two people who had reason to be far more confident and this wasn't their first time with each other. Tom seemed to know exactly where and how to touch Claire that would make her gasp with the pleasure of it and, because she wanted it to be just as good for him, she was remembering everything she could that he had responded to with murmurs of appreciation and she got brave and added to where and how she touched *him* and was rewarded with a groan of ecstasy.

And then they were both lost. It wasn't until Claire was lying in Tom's arms and they were both trying to catch their breath that she realised she'd been wrong earlier. Watching the dolphins hadn't been the moment she'd been the happiest in her entire life.

This was…

It hadn't just been so very different this time because they were getting to know each other's bodies or that the bed was so comfortable. It was because it had been—for her, at least—far more than simply a physical act.

It had been making love…

She was falling in love with Tom Atkinson. Or perhaps it had already happened and it was the bump at the end of the fall that she was feeling now. Maybe she hadn't recognised it for what it was because she'd never experienced it before and it was the last thing she'd expected to find at this time of her life.

She turned her head just a little. Just far enough for her nose and her lips to be against the soft skin under his collarbone. She wanted to soak in the scent and taste and feel of him while she absorbed the realisation of how she was feeling. She wasn't brave enough to say anything. Or maybe she just wanted to keep it secret so there was no chance of Tom reminding her that falling in love again or finding a new partner in life was the last thing he wanted.

It was supposed to be the last thing *she* wanted and maybe, in the cold light of day, she would remember why with more definitive clarity. She would embrace the freedom she'd gifted herself and be grateful that she had the chance to choose exactly where she would go and what she would do to make the most of her life. She would remember what it was like to fall *out* of love and find herself trapped and...diminished. She would never want to risk feeling like that again.

What she did want was the rest of this night, however. She wanted to fall asleep in Tom's arms and dream of a future that could be as perfect as this moment.

CHAPTER NINE

Tom and Claire had the whole of the next morning to explore acres of a breathtaking classically designed garden in Kekerengu.

They walked along a path of velvety grass, with pointed cypress trees creating a guard of honour on either side. They looked through the round hole under the central arch of a brick wall to the long, thin pond that was still enough to reflect the nearby trees. They wandered through the magic of a pathway with brick pillars and wooden beams overhead, dripping with the long racemes of white wisteria, and they found a wooden bench to sit on and look out to sea when they needed time to let it all sink in.

'I can't believe I've never been here before,' Tom said. 'I've heard about it. I knew it was amazing but I wouldn't be here if it wasn't for you.'

'I would have come on this tour anyway,' Claire admitted. 'But it's so much better being able to share it with someone.'

'That's so true.' Tom nodded slowly. 'You know... I'm beginning to think that Hanna was right in giving me a push. Maybe I do want to find someone to share my life with. To grow old with.' He gave a huff of laughter. 'Old*er*, that is.'

'You're still young,' Claire told him. There was a note in her voice that Tom hadn't heard before. 'But maybe Hanna could see something you were ignoring. That you are lonely sometimes?'

'I had forgotten how good it is to share something like this. To just *be* with someone.' Tom touched Claire's hand where it lay on the bench between them. He felt her go very still and then she turned her hand over and linked her fingers with his. 'It's because of you I know it would actually be possible to have a relationship again. You've...' He paused to let his breath out slowly. 'You've quite possibly changed my whole future, Claire.' His lips curled into a smile. 'By giving me that trial run.'

Claire caught his gaze and held it. She took in a deep breath and opened her mouth but then she didn't say anything and Tom couldn't read her expression. She looked nervous...scared, even?

For a moment he didn't understand and then it hit him. She was thinking that he was going to ask her to stop the pretence. To see them being together as a real couple. To stay here. With him.

For ever...

Of course she was worried. She was probably trying to think up a way to tell him kindly that it was the last thing she'd want. She wasn't going to give up her dreams and her hard-won freedom to chase them. To do exactly what she wanted to do so that she could make the most of the rest of her life and not be held back by the anchor of someone who didn't have the same dreams.

'I'm not as adventurous as you,' he added quickly. 'I

admire you so much for having the courage to go and live life exactly the way you want to and I can't wait to hear about all the new and exciting adventures you're going to have.' He shook his head. 'I'd never be brave enough to just walk away to start a new life. To go hunting for new places to live and people to meet.'

'You're more adventurous than you think,' Claire said quietly. 'I'd never be brave enough to go scuba diving. And why would you want to start a new life, anyway? You have a job you love and family and a home. You have a whole community that you're an important part of. You belong here.'

Claire let go of his hand, standing up as if she wanted a better view of the cliff below them and the sea stretching to the horizon.

'It's an incredible place to belong,' she added. 'And you don't have to leave your life behind if you want to meet new people. Maybe Hanna wasn't completely wrong about the online dating. Who knows—you might find someone that would love to go scuba diving with you. Someone your own age, perhaps, so you can grow older at the same rate. Or stay young together for longer.'

Tom blinked. What on earth was Claire talking about? Oh…was she trying to remind him that she was a few years older than him? Why would that make a difference?

Her voice sounded different but he couldn't figure out why. She didn't sound relieved that he'd let her know he wasn't going to ask for anything more than she'd already given him. It was more strained than that. Maybe embarrassed was closer to the truth. She was probably wishing he hadn't started this conversation. He was beginning to wish that himself.

He got to his feet as well. 'Anyway,' he said. 'It's almost time for us to go and have that lunch down the hill at the café. It's included in the tour, isn't it?'

'It is.' Claire did sound relieved as she started moving. 'And I don't know about you, but after all this walking and a bit of sea air, I'm *starving*.'

It wasn't true.

Claire had actually lost her appetite completely.

She almost felt a bit sick, in fact.

She'd come so close to telling Tom that she felt the same way about how good it was to be sharing parts of her life with him. That she was changing her mind about travelling the world in search of new adventures.

Thank goodness she hadn't said anything before he made it so clear that she wasn't the person he wanted to share *his* life with. He didn't want anything more than friendship. To stay in touch and hear about what she was doing in whatever part of the world she moved on to.

That had been her plan so maybe she just needed to get back on track. There were so many other parts of New Zealand she'd love to see, like Central Otago and the North Island. Australia was practically next door, with its vibrant cities and astonishingly vast spaces like the Outback. And what about all those Pacific Islands? She could go and spend as much time as she wanted in a tropical paradise.

It should be such an exciting prospect.

And it would be. She just needed to pretend she was still perfectly happy with her original plan until she could embrace it properly again.

When they arrived at the café she joined the queue

where the tour group was invited to help themselves from an impressive buffet of seafood and meat and a huge variety of salads and fresh bread. Tom was just ahead of her, talking to an older woman and her husband about the garden they'd just visited.

'I'm so inspired,' she heard the woman saying. 'I'm going to go home and do something gorgeous with my own garden. Bob will help, won't you, darling?'

Her husband feigned resignation with a sigh. 'I'd better start warming up now,' he said. 'If I know Janice, I'm going to be on the end of a spade as soon as we get home. Or building brick walls or something.'

Claire picked up a serving spoon on top of a huge bowl of Greek salad. If anything was going to tempt her to eat, it would be this mix of tomatoes, cucumber, olives and feta cheese. She didn't get as far as putting any on her plate, however. The sound of a plate shattering as it hit the tiled floor made her turn sharply—just in time to see the woman in front of Tom crumpling as she collapsed against her husband and then slid to the floor.

'Janice!' Bob's cry was panicked. 'Oh, my God... what's happening?'

'Janice?' Tom was shaking the woman's shoulder. 'Can you hear me?'

There was no response.

Tom turned her onto her back. He tilted her head to open the airway and then bent over her, the fingers of one hand on her neck, feeling for a carotid pulse, and his other hand resting on her diaphragm as he watched and felt for any signs of breathing. Claire was beside him as he looked up.

'No pulse, no breathing,' he said. 'Cardiac arrest. Call

an ambulance, please, Claire. I think they may have an AED here so grab that, too.'

She nodded, pulling out her phone as she moved to meet the staff members coming towards the commotion. She could see Tom positioning his hands on the woman's chest, starting compressions. He was talking to her terrified-looking husband at the same time.

'Janice's heart has stopped,' he told him. 'Doing CPR will keep her blood moving until we can do more to help her. Does she have any history of heart problems?'

'Yes...' Bob's voice was choked. 'She's had angina for a couple of years now. Not badly. The pain goes away if she has a rest and some of her spray.'

Claire's phone call to the emergency services was swift. An ambulance was being dispatched from Kaikōura and a rescue helicopter would also be dispatched as soon as one was available. Café staff were lifting the buffet tables out of the way and encouraging everybody to move away from the emergency to create space. The manager got the AED from the cabinet on the wall and immediately handed it to Claire.

'I've never used it,' he said. He was looking very pale. 'I'm so glad you guys are here. I've done a first aid course but it's completely different when it's for real, isn't it?'

'You'll be surprised how easy it is,' she told him. 'Just watch and you'll be ready if there's ever a next time. Good for you on having one available—it could well be what saves her life.'

She knelt opposite Tom, who paused his compressions to help her cut the woman's clothing free so that the sticky pads could be attached to bare skin on her upper right chest and lower left side and the heart rhythm could be analysed to determine whether it was appropriate to provide a shock.

They didn't need the instructions the automatic device was giving them but they were loud enough to almost echo in the shocked silence inside the café.

'Call for help now.'

'Apply the pad exactly as shown in the picture.'

'Evaluating heart rhythm. Stop compressions.'

'Shock required. Stand back. Do not touch the patient.'

Claire wriggled her knees further back and Tom held out his arms. 'Stay clear,' he warned.

'Shock delivered. Provide chest compressions.'

Two minutes later they stopped compressions for another rhythm check. Another shock was delivered. But this time, just as Claire was about to take over the next two minutes of compressions, Tom held up his hand.

'Stop! Look...she's moving.'

Claire was holding *her* breath as she watched Janice's mouth open and her chest rise and then fall. Bob had one hand pressed to his mouth and the other was gripping his wife's hand.

'It's all right, Jan,' he said. 'It's going to be all right. You're alive...' He had tears streaming down his face but he was still as white as a sheet. He looked up at Tom. 'She *is* going to be all right, isn't she?'

Tom had his fingers on Janice's wrist. 'She's got a palpable pulse, which means that her heart's working again. We're going to put her into a comfortable position and watch her very carefully until the ambulance gets here. Then we'll be able to do more tests and we'll have everything we need to take the best care of her.'

Janice groaned as Claire helped Tom move her into the

recovery position. One of the café staff grabbed a cushion and then a blanket from the shop area. It was one of the blankets with the cute little sheep woven into them that Claire had admired the last time she'd been here.

Janice was semi-conscious by the time the ambulance arrived.

'Where am I?' she asked. 'What happened?'

They put her in the back of the ambulance and worked with the crew to get an IV line established, take a twelve-lead ECG and a full set of vital signs.

'Look at this.' Tom showed Claire the record of the ECG that the life-pack had produced.

'STEMI,' Claire murmured. The elevation of ST segment on the trace was high enough to make the next wave look like small mountains. It was more than enough evidence that Janice was suffering a heart attack that had caused the cardiac arrest. She needed to get to a hospital that could perform angioplasty as quickly as possible.

'I'll travel with her,' Tom told Claire after making another call to the emergency services. 'I've transmitted the ECG to the cardiology department and they'll have a catheter lab on standby for when we arrive. The helicopter's going to meet us at Kaikōura and take her through to Christchurch. Claire, can you drive my car back?'

'No problem.'

'Can I go with Jan too?' Bob begged. *'Please?'*

'Of course you can,' Tom said. 'She needs you right by her side and that's exactly where *you* need to be.'

The expression on his face told Claire that he understood exactly how this man felt, having watched his wife die and then be brought back to life. She caught his gaze as the back doors of the ambulance were being closed and her heart suddenly felt so full it hurt.

So full of love.

She loved everything about Tom. His skill, his compassion, his ability to love. He deserved to find every happiness possible for the rest of his life. It shouldn't feel heartbreaking that it wouldn't be with her because she'd been so sure that it wasn't what *she* wanted for the rest of her life but…

…but maybe she'd been wrong. And it wasn't simply that she loved Tom. She was *in* love with him.

Should she tell Tom that?

Would it change anything?

Claire went back inside, where the staff were doing their best to restore normality and look after their guests. They were all due to move on to the afternoon tour of another garden as soon as they'd had their lunch but Claire decided not to join them. Nothing could beat the last garden she'd seen—with Tom—and she wanted that to be the one she remembered in years to come.

She would go and sit on the beach for a while and be grateful that she was alive and that she'd rediscovered how amazing it was to fall in love with someone. And then she'd drive back to Kaikōura.

Back home.

But first, she'd go and buy one of the sheep blankets. Because it would remind her of…well, everything.

Of the first time they'd come here for lunch.

Of the lambs near the cottage they'd stayed in last night. Where they'd made love and it had been everything she'd ever dreamed it could be.

Of helping Tom save a woman's life and the genuine connection he'd felt with her husband.

Most of all, it would remind her of Tom.

She picked up one of the folded blankets that was tied with a braid of unspun wool. She held it to her cheek for a moment before taking it to the counter. It was soft and warm and she would be able to wrap it around herself and remember it all.

It might even give her the courage to tell Tom that she'd changed her mind. That she didn't want to stay single and travel the world seeking exciting things to do. That maybe she'd found what she was really looking for, without even knowing that she was looking for it.

When Claire took Tom's car back to the Seaview Hospital she was told that he'd ended up going to Christchurch on the helicopter with Janice and Bob. She left his car keys with the senior nurse on duty and walked home, carrying her overnight bag and the sheep blanket.

She draped the blanket over the back of the couch later that day and was standing there admiring it when her phone rang.

'Hey… Tom. Where are you?'

'I just got home after getting a bus back from Christchurch. Thanks so much for bringing my car home.'

'It was no problem at all. Thanks for coming to the garden festival with me.'

'That was absolutely my pleasure. Did you get to the last garden we had booked?'

'No. I didn't think I would have been able to relax enough to enjoy it. How's Janice?'

'Discharged. Good as new. Better than she'd been for some time, anyway.'

'What?' Claire sank onto the sofa. 'She's been discharged already? I thought her ECG showed that she was having a massive anterior infarct. Isn't that the one that's so likely to be fatal it's called the "widow-maker"?'

'I know. Amazing, isn't it? I was invited to observe in the catheter laboratory. I've sent so many patients to get stents but I've never actually seen it done. I think both Bob and Janice were happy that she was going to have someone that wasn't a total stranger in there with her and I was more than happy to stay.'

Tom sounded like he was still buzzing from the experience. Claire curled her legs beneath her. 'Tell me about it.'

'It was so slick. We landed on the roof of the hospital and went straight to the emergency department and the cath lab was all ready by the time Janice was seen by the cardiology registrar and another ECG and blood tests were taken. It was amazing, Claire. They put the catheter into the radial artery in her wrist and—'

'Her wrist?' Claire interrupted. 'I thought they put it in the femoral artery in the groin. Why the wrist?'

'Much easier to find,' Tom told her. 'And easier to manage after the procedure. You have to keep pressure on a femoral puncture manually for about thirty minutes and then patients have to lie still for up to six hours. They've got a band that can go around the wrist like a mini blood pressure cuff and it gets pumped up and stays there for a couple of hours and then the patient can go home. Bob and Janice were planning to stay in Christchurch overnight because they felt safer staying close to the hospital, just in case. They'll hire a car to get home again tomorrow.'

'Wow… I guess the procedure was successful, then?'

'Textbook,' Tom confirmed. 'They put the catheter in and injected dye and you could see on the X-ray screen exactly where the artery was pretty much a hundred percent blocked—like a dead-end road. The stent got placed and then the balloon was inflated to open it and there it was. You could see the blood flow looking perfectly normal again. Did you know about the drug-eluting stents they can use? They slowly release drugs that can prevent the narrowing that happens after implantation sometimes.'

Claire could hear Tom's breath being released in a sigh. 'It's been quite a day.'

'It was good you were there,' she said. 'Poor Bob looked terrified when he knew that Janice was having a heart attack.'

'Yeah…' There was a note in Tom's voice that told Claire she'd been right in thinking that he had more than empathised with Bob's fear at that point. That he had been remembering the devastation of losing his own wife. 'And…there's something else I should tell you.'

'Oh…?' Claire's heart skipped a beat. Had being with someone who was afraid of losing their life partner made Tom realise what was missing from his life? Had he been thinking about *her* in a different way? Was he going to tell her that he wanted her in his life even before she could tell him how she was feeling about *him*?

'I had a long text conversation with Hanna on the bus trip home,' Tom said. 'I told her the truth. About the fake dating. I didn't want her to be getting her hopes up too much.'

It felt like Claire's heart stopped for a moment then.

'She's coming for another visit before too long,' Tom added, 'and...what happened today was a sobering reminder that life can be too short. I don't want to be dishonest, even if it's not outright lying. About anything. With any*one*—but especially not with the people I love.'

'I understand,' Claire said quietly. 'Was she upset?'

'She was a bit shocked that people our age would behave like that, but in the end she thought it was funny. She said it would be our secret and she wouldn't tell Kerry so it didn't get around, which might be embarrassing for both of us. She reckoned that it might be better if people just assumed that we didn't want to take it any further. She also said that maybe, one day, I'll listen to her advice about the online dating, but I have my doubts about that. And I'm not going to even think about any kind of dating while you're in town, Claire. I enjoy your company too much.'

There was a tiny pause, as if Tom was taking the time to choose his words carefully.

'I hope we'll always be good friends,' he said. 'No matter where you end up in the world.'

Her voice was even quieter this time. 'I hope so, too.'

Claire stayed on the couch after the call ended. She pulled the sheep blanket down and wrapped it around herself because she needed the touch of something warm and cuddly to comfort her.

She felt as if a door had been slammed in her face. Or maybe it was in her heart.

A dream that had only just formed had just evaporated.

The idea of her finding a fairytale romance at her age was, indeed, ridiculous.

But this didn't have to be a big deal, did it? She had, after all, known that all along, hadn't she?

CHAPTER TEN

THERE WAS NO reason for Tom and Claire to be seen out together now.

No reason to take photographs to be sent to Hanna in order to keep up the pretence that they were dating. They could still go for walks on the beach together or share a meal or a drink together. They could probably still spend the night together, like people did with those friendships that came with 'benefits'. But in the wake of Tom telling Hanna the truth, something had changed.

It felt like they had both taken a step, not backwards—because they knew each other so well now—but sideways. The connection was still there, but there was a bigger gap between them. It felt like an elastic gap, as if it could change in either direction, and sometimes Claire got the impression that Tom would like to make it smaller. It felt like he was missing that intimate time they'd had together.

Claire was certainly missing it, but the kind of courage needed to chase an adventure she'd particularly wanted that had led to her inviting Tom to go to the garden festival with her was nowhere to be found now. She wasn't about to make things any harder for herself by getting that close to Tom again. She only had to remember him telling her that he hoped they would remain friends no matter where she was in the world to stop herself saying, or doing, anything that might reveal how she felt about him.

Because...if Tom had felt anything like that himself, he wouldn't have bothered telling Hanna the truth about the fake dating, would he? How it had all begun could have been *their* secret if it had morphed into a real relationship and telling Hanna later really would have made it funny. The kind of funny story that got told at weddings?

Oh, *help*...where had that thought come from? Claire had been confident that she was getting past the discomfort of having let herself get in too deep. She was focusing on work and getting more involved with her new community by joining a book club and a yoga class. She was keeping an eye out for any interesting nursing positions that were being advertised. Not that she wanted to leave Kaikōura any time soon, but if she couldn't get perfectly comfortable with the idea of nothing more than a friendship with Tom, it might become wise to move on. What if he did take Hanna's advice to start dating? Or he might decide he wanted to but was trapped by having said he wouldn't while Claire was still in town.

She still had more than half the lease of her little cottage left, however. There was no rush, was there?

Claire loved it here.

She really didn't want to be anywhere else.

The patients she saw on a regular basis, especially the ones she visited in their homes, were becoming an important part of her life. Mabel Jamieson was a delight and now that her granddaughter, Olivia, was home from hospital after the surgery on her oesophageal cancer, Mabel was determined to be as involved as everyone else in the family to provide the core of the wraparound support that the whole community was wanting to contribute to.

She was there when Claire made her first home visit, sitting in a big armchair in the corner of Olivia's bedroom, reading a story to Lucy, who was sitting on her lap. Yvonne was perched on the end of her daughter's bed.

'How are you feeling, Liv?' Claire asked.

'It's good to be home. But I'm *so* tired. I can't get out of bed for more than a few minutes at a time.'

'You've been through major surgery,' Claire reminded her. 'It's going to take time, but it will get easier.' She checked Olivia's temperature and heart rate and how the skin around her surgical wounds was looking, happy to record that there was no sign of infection. 'Try and get up as often as you feel up to it,' she said. 'And go outside, even if it's just for a minute. A bit of sunshine and fresh air can be a real boost.'

'Lucy's desperate to show her the sunflower plants we put in while Liv was in hospital,' Yvonne said. 'She thinks they're nearly as big as she is.'

Olivia's smile looked like an effort. 'I'll try later, Mum.'

'How's the eating going?' Claire asked. 'Dr Atkinson said you were finding it a bit difficult when he saw you yesterday.'

'It hurts to swallow. He's given me some new painkillers and something for the reflux that he thinks might help.'

'You know to try and eat small amounts often and stay sitting up for an hour or so after eating?'

'Yeah…and I can only eat baby food mush for the next six weeks.'

'It can be tasty, though.' Claire put a waterproof cloth on the side of the bed and started to collect what she needed for today's visit, which was to remove Olivia's stitches. 'What's your favourite meal?'

Yvonne responded when Olivia simply shrugged. 'She's always requested roast chicken for any special meals like birthdays. With lots of potatoes and gravy.'

'There you go.' Claire smiled. 'You can make that and put it in the blender until it's the consistency of mashed potatoes. It might feel like baby food but the flavours should still be there.' She touched Olivia's hand. 'It *will* get better,' she said gently. 'But, like the shampoo ads, it won't happen overnight.'

Olivia's small smile felt like a win.

'Now…let's get these stitches out, shall we?'

The surgery had involved incisions in her abdomen, the side of her chest and in her neck. Claire took the dressings off each site and cleaned the wounds with an antiseptic swab. She held the knot of each stitch in tweezers, pulling it up far enough to snip the suture beneath the knot with her sterile scissors. Then she pulled the stitch out gently and laid it on a gauze square to check that it was intact.

Yvonne stayed on the end of the bed, rubbing Olivia's leg occasionally in support. They could all hear the soothing sound of Mabel in the background, reading a story that Lucy clearly loved because she was able to join in every sentence with her great-grandmother. It made Olivia smile every time she heard her daughter's voice as she lay back against her pillows, with her eyes closed. Claire didn't want to interrupt something that was providing comfort so she stayed quiet as she got on with what was an easy, automatic task.

She knew Tom had been in to visit the family yesterday, when Olivia had arrived home, and plans had been made for her to start her chemotherapy sessions in a few weeks' time. They could be done in Seaview Hospital and would only happen once a week in three-week cycles. A central venous line had been inserted to provide painless IV access and it would be one of Claire's duties to watch for any signs of infection around that site on her upcoming visits. She would also be providing whatever other support she could in her role as a community nurse. For Olivia. And Mabel, who needed a dressing change on her ulcers today as well.

The gauze square was almost covered with the tiny black threads of the sutures. Claire would be able to clean the wounds again when all the stitches were out and then apply some sticky strips to protect the skin from tension as it continued to heal.

She wanted to be here to see more than just these wounds heal, Claire realised. She wanted to be here as part of the support team for the whole Jamieson family—as Tom would be. Olivia had been one of his first patients when he'd started his career as a doctor. He had probably delivered her daughter, Lucy. He would be here to share the sadness when the family had to say goodbye to Mabel and, even if he was retired, he would still be here to share the joy of Lucy growing up and maybe starting her own family.

How wonderful would it be to belong somewhere like that?

It would be far more fulfilling than moving from place

to place, searching for…what? A fleeting experience that could qualify as an adventure? A place or activity that would bring pleasure?

That wasn't what Claire wanted at all.

She wanted to belong, too.

Not necessarily to a single person. Maybe a place would be enough. Somewhere beautiful—like here. Or a community, where she could build connections to people—like Mabel and Olivia and Carl and…yes…to Tom and Hanna.

She wanted to feel needed. *Wanted*, even.

To know that she *was* good enough.

'Are you okay, Dad?'

'I'm fine, Hanna. More than fine. I'm delighted that you've managed to squeeze in a couple of days to come home.'

'Hmm…' Hanna didn't sound convinced. 'You just don't seem as happy as you were the last time I was here.'

'I am at work. I'll be my usual happy self when I get home later. Want me to bring some fish and chips home for dinner?'

'No, I'll make something. I'm going to catch up with Kerry and then I'll do a supermarket run. Is there anything you want me to pick up for you?'

'I forgot to get any oat milk in for you, I'm sorry.'

'No problem. Anything you'd like for a treat? Your favourite ice cream, maybe?'

Tom shook his head. 'I'm good.'

But Hanna was giving him a thoughtful look. 'I heard about Livvy Jamieson,' she said quietly. 'And I know how involved you always get with your patients.'

Tom shuffled some papers on his desk. 'It's not easy,' he agreed. 'But it's a privilege to be part of looking after her—and the family.'

'You've got to look after yourself, too, Dad.' Hanna frowned. 'And get some time away from work. Have you been out with Pete for a dive?'

'Not for a while. We've both been busy.'

'Have you and Claire gone out lately? For dinner, or a movie or something?'

Tom shook his head. 'I told you we were never really dating, remember?'

'You also told me that you'll always be great friends. Friends get to spend time together. They get to make each other feel better if they're having a tough time.' Hanna got to her feet. 'I'll get out of your way and let you get on with work. We'll have plenty of time to talk later.'

She walked around the desk to plant a kiss on her father's cheek. 'And I've changed my mind. Fish and chips for dinner is exactly what I feel like.'

Tom finished clearing his desk in preparation for the afternoon clinic hours. He wasn't surprised that Hanna had noticed he didn't seem as happy as the last time she'd been here.

He *wasn't* as happy. And it wasn't simply because he was worried about some of his patients, like Livvy. He was missing spending time with Claire but could that be fixed by simply going out for a coffee or a movie with her, as a friend? Tom was hesitant to even suggest it, in fact, now that Hanna knew they weren't actually dating. Neither could he forget that look on Claire's face when she'd thought he was about to say that she was the person he'd like to share his life with.

And if she was missing spending time with him, as a friend, she'd suggest something, wouldn't she? She'd been the one to suggest that he went on the garden tour with her, after all.

With a sigh, Tom got to his feet and headed towards Reception so he could pick up a set of notes and call for the person who had the first appointment this afternoon. If his path crossed with Claire's he knew they would both smile and, to all outward appearances, nothing had changed. He knew better, however. He just wished he knew how to fix the odd tension that was between them. Maybe having Hanna here for a visit would make a difference. The weather was looking settled for the next few days so perhaps they could put on a barbecue at home. She could invite all her friends and he could invite his.

Including Claire.

Especially Claire.

The barbecue was a great idea. There was a real hint of approaching summer and the weather was warm enough for the group of Seaview medical staff, family and friends to be enjoying the Atkinsons' garden and the aroma of the meat and seafood cooking on the grill. Tom had been out with his mate, Pete, and there were crayfish and snapper on the menu, along with the ubiquitous sausages and steak.

Best of all, there didn't seem to be any awkwardness when Claire met Hanna again as she went inside to add her contribution of a dessert to the shared meal. She got a warm hug from Tom's daughter and then a wink.

'Your secret's safe with me,' she said. 'I did tell Kerry

that you're not an item any longer but I didn't say why. And I said that you're still good friends.'

'We are,' Claire said. 'He's a lovely man, your dad. I must go and meet Pete properly. I've heard a lot about him.'

She enjoyed a glass of wine as she was introduced to Pete and chatted with her colleagues and met their partners. She stood by Tom for a while as he basted the crayfish tails with garlic and butter. She could still feel the hum between them. The warmth in Tom's eyes as he smiled at her suggested that he could feel it too and Claire decided it would only take a nudge for one of them to step over that invisible line and say something that would make that gap between them shrink enough to vanish.

Just a small nudge would do the trick. Like arranging to meet for a coffee and a walk on their next shared day off.

'Could you find Hanna and let her know we'll be ready in a few minutes?' Tom asked. 'She and Kerry went inside to sort the salads, I think.'

'Sure.'

Hanna *was* in the kitchen with her friend Kerry but they weren't doing anything with the salads. They were both peering at Hanna's phone.

'Ah... Claire... Just the person we need.'

'Oh...?'

'Yes.' Hanna bit her lip. 'Don't tell Dad about this, will you?'

'About what?'

'Well... I didn't exactly delete that profile I made for him on that dating site. I just snoozed it.'

Her smile was a mix of being apologetic and conspiratorial. 'I think he's feeling lonely now that you two aren't spending so much time together so Kerry and I were just looking at the profiles of all the women that sent him kisses in the first place to see if we can choose someone. You're probably a better judge than we are about who he might fancy.'

Claire blinked. Really? They wanted her to help choose a potential partner for Tom to share his life with? Someone that he would be *attracted* to? It was the last thing she wanted to do but it was too late. The girls were on either side of her now and Hanna's phone was in front of her.

'Look... This Penelope is rather gorgeous, isn't she?'

'Mmm...' Claire tried to keep her tone neutral. 'But how old is she?'

'Forty-five. That's only nine years younger than Dad and he doesn't really look his age, does he?'

'No.' Claire had to agree. 'I would have guessed he was in his late forties when I met him.'

'I like that one...' Kerry said. 'Jasmine. She's got a cute dog.'

Jasmine also looked to be in her early forties.

Young enough to be Claire's daughter, in fact. Definitely young enough to remind her of the person her husband was now happily sharing his life with.

Tom would have no problem attracting someone like Penelope or Jasmine or any of the dozens of hopeful women on this dating site. Thanks to Claire, he wouldn't have any misgivings about knowing where to start in getting to know them.

He should have all the confidence he needed to kiss them.

And that would, no doubt, inevitably lead to—

Thank goodness her thoughts were abruptly unable to go any further in that direction because Tom had just walked into the kitchen. Hanna hastily shoved her phone into the back pocket of her jeans and Claire held her breath, hoping that it wasn't obvious they'd been talking about him.

Hoping even more that her own thoughts were completely invisible.

Tom didn't seem at all perturbed.

'Where have those salads got to?' he asked. 'There's a hungry crowd out there.'

It was in the evening when she was alone at home, nearly a week later, that Claire received a text message from a number she didn't recognise.

Hey, Claire. Hanna here. Dad gave me your number. Hope you don't mind?

Claire sent a message back.

Not at all. How are you?

She got a smiley face emoji in return. And a short plea.

I need your help.

Is this about your dad?

Yes. I think I've found someone for him. She even lives in Kaikōura and loves scuba diving!! He's never going to agree to a blind date but I have a plan. I've given it a code name. Happy Ever After.

The emoji was a winking face this time. Closely followed by a pair of crossed fingers.

Claire could feel a chill run down her spine as she tapped the letters on her phone.

And it involves me?

You are the only way it could work. Are you up for it?

Was she? Did Claire want Tom to live happily ever after?
Of course she did.
With another woman?
Well...it would have to be, wouldn't it? Because it wasn't going to be with her.
She texted back.

I need more info. Give me five minutes to make a cup of tea and call me?

The response pinged in instantly—a 'thumbs up' emoji.

CHAPTER ELEVEN

THE PLAN WAS SIMPLE.

On their next shared day off, Claire would text Tom and suggest meeting for a coffee at one of the trendy cafés in town.

Tom would arrive at the café and sit down to wait for her but Claire was going to be late. She was, in fact, not going to turn up at all.

'You'll think of a reason,' Hanna assured her. 'Maybe you get a phone call from the UK, or an old lady falls over in the street and needs your medical expertise? You can text him to say sorry, but you can't make it.'

The woman who wanted to meet him—Lorraine, her name was—would be in the café as well. When Claire failed to show up, she would use the opportunity to strike up a conversation with Tom.

'It might well come to nothing,' Hanna admitted. 'But at least it's a way of getting him to say hello to someone, isn't it? And who knows? They might really like each other.'

Claire hadn't felt great about the plan but Hanna had been very persuasive and she'd promised to think about it. A sleepless night led her to the conclusion that, while Tom had thought her new motto in life of everything being all about herself from now on was brilliant and brave, she'd been the one who'd raised the real truth of the matter.

How incredibly selfish would it be to stand in the way of Tom's happiness to spare her own feelings?

She regretted her decision to play her part in the scheme a few days later, however, the moment she received Tom's text saying he'd love to meet for coffee and suggesting that they went for a walk on the beach afterwards. When the time came that she had arranged to meet Tom in the café and she was supposed to simply leave him waiting alone and then send a message to say she wasn't going to come after all, it was suddenly overwhelmingly unacceptable to have been so deceptive. This wasn't about her. It was about Tom's integrity and need for honesty in his life.

The cottage door banged shut behind her as she left a short time later. Maybe she could catch up with Tom before he got there and let him know that his daughter was up to a bit of mischief again. What she couldn't do was stand him up and then make up a story as an excuse. He deserved better than that from both her and Hanna. He deserved to know the truth, not just about being set up on a blind date but how she felt about him. It might make absolutely no difference at all but Claire wouldn't have to spend the rest of her life regretting that she hadn't found the courage to do that.

She had to pause as she reached the beach, to find her sunglasses in her bag. Life in London had not prepared her for how bright the light could be here. It felt like summer today and the sun seemed to be reflecting off a sea that was the calmest she'd ever seen it. Claire increased her pace after that but she didn't get to the café in time to intercept Tom.

He was already there. She paused again, waiting to cross to the other side of the street, and she could see him sitting at one of the outside tables. She saw the woman who casually sat down at the next table but turned almost immediately to talk to Tom. It had to be Lorraine and it only took a heartbeat for Claire to get a first impression. The star of this setup was wearing tight jeans that were rolled up to her calves and a tee shirt that showed off the rest of her gorgeous figure. She had sun-streaked blonde hair and a wide smile and…and she looked even younger than the profile pictures that had caught Hanna's attention on the night of the barbecue.

What was worse, however, was that Claire could see that it was Tom's attention that was firmly caught right now as he smiled and said something back to the stranger.

Her feet felt stuck to the footpath. There was no way she could walk over the road and interrupt them. For all she knew, this might be Tom's first conversation with the woman he was going to spend the rest of his life with.

Claire swallowed hard and then pulled out her phone before she could change her mind.

I can't make it after all. So sorry.

She stayed where she was for a moment, watching Tom read the text message. Even from this distance she could see him frown but then he turned as Lorraine said something else to him. And then, as smoothly as if she'd rehearsed her part in this charade, she saw the beautiful, *young* woman get up and move to sit at Tom's table.

That was when Claire felt the prickle of tears and the shaft of something painful that felt like a piece breaking off her heart. That was when she turned and started walking back the way she'd come. She was grateful for the sunglasses for more than the protection from bright light now. Nobody was likely to recognise her and, even if they did, they wouldn't be able to see how upset she was.

But, disconcertingly, she could hear someone calling her name.

'*Claire*… Wait up…'

She had to turn her head to glance over her shoulder. And then she had to stop.

'Carl!' It was impossible not to respond to the cheerful grin the boat skipper was giving her. 'How are you?'

He waved his hand at her. 'I've ditched the glove. Look… Almost as good as new.'

'That's great, Carl.' She noted the watertight latex dressing over the tip of the finger. 'Good to see you're still looking after your scar.'

'Keeping it covered reminds me to be careful. It hurts if I put too much pressure on it and I don't want to cause any more damage but…' Carl shook his head, talking fast '…that's not what I wanted to talk to you about. There's been a sighting of a giant sperm whale earlier today. The conditions are perfect and I'm taking my boat out right now. There's one space left on it and I knew as soon as I spotted you that it's got your name on it. Are you up for it?'

Oh… Those were the exact words Hanna had used when she'd wanted Claire to help her set her dad up on a date. Claire couldn't help looking past Carl to where she could still see Tom. Still sitting with Lorraine. A staff member was standing beside the table now, with a notepad in her hand, clearly taking their orders for coffee and maybe one of the cookies the café was known for.

That did it.

Claire had been promising herself the treat of going out whale watching ever since she'd arrived in this town. Maybe it was time to return to Plan A and make life all about herself again. But first, she had to get over this ridiculous pain of losing something—a future with Tom Atkinson—that had only ever existed in her imagination and Carl, bless him, had just offered her the perfect first step.

'I'm so up for it,' she told him.

The catamaran had two powerful outboard motors, a cabin that contained indoor seating, a table and the skipper's cockpit and an outside area with padded bench seats on either side and a solid canopy for shelter. Lifejackets had been provided for the passengers and there was a sound system so everybody could hear the snippets of information Carl was telling them as they sped away from the wharf. He congratulated people on choosing such an awesome day to go whale watching, talked about the different varieties of whales they might be lucky enough to encounter and threw in some housekeeping rules for safety, when afternoon tea would be served and that there was a toilet available down a step near the front of the boat. Claire was particularly pleased to hear that but, despite the calm sea, she didn't want to try moving around the boat while they were travelling at speed.

By the time they slowed down, she'd forgotten about wanting to go to the toilet. While everyone else, including Carl, who was using a pair of binoculars, looked out to sea to try and spot a whale's tail or a spout of water, she was looking behind the boat, where the township of Kaikōura nestled under the mountains across a stretch of impossibly blue sea.

How lucky was she to have discovered this tiny, astonishing patch of the world. She loved it. She felt happier here than she ever had in London.

Tom was somewhere in the middle of that idyllic scene, she thought.

Was that why it felt so much like home?

A call from someone made her turn her head. People were shading their eyes as they peered over the open sides of the boat. Inside, Carl was holding his binoculars in place with one hand. With the other, he reached for his microphone.

'That, my friends,' he said, 'looks to me like the blow of a blue whale. They're baleen whales, like humpbacks, which means they have two blowholes, but the blue's the only one that can send a cloud of water high enough to hang in the air like that, even after the whale's made its dive. We'll head in that direction and see if we're going to be lucky enough to get another glimpse.'

There was an air of excited anticipation amongst the passengers now that only grew as Carl kept the speed of the boat much lower. He even lowered his voice as he spoke—as if this was a momentous occasion.

'We do get blue whales in these parts all year round,' he told them, 'but spotting them is pretty special. They were hunted almost to extinction in the nineteen-thirties and they tend to be solitary creatures unless it's mating season.'

Claire was fascinated now. She leaned over the rail at the back of the boat, trying to spot another cloud of whale breath.

'They're the biggest—and loudest—animals on the planet,' Carl said. 'Their heart weighs about one hundred and eighty kilos. That's two of me, folks. And their tongue weighs as much as an elephant. They can be up to thirty metres long—that's three times as long as this boat.'

There was a collective gasp from the passengers, loud enough to be heard over the engine noise, when the enormous whale broke the surface of the sea not far ahead of the boat. Carl cut the engine and they floated in silence as they watched the head coming further out of the water until the blowholes were clear to expel a huge cloud of moisture into the air. Then its body kept rising before beginning to gently curve as the head went below water. Everybody had their phones out, taking videos or photographs as they waited for the magical moment of the tail coming up until the flukes were the only visible part of the magnificent creature.

And then it vanished below the surface and the white foam of the disturbed sea gradually faded.

'It might breach again,' Carl said. 'I can't start the engine again until I know where it is. Be prepared. It could come up a lot closer to the boat this time.'

They waited, *Time and Tide* rocking gently on the ocean. Another whale watching boat was approaching the area carefully and a helicopter could be seen coming from the shore. Word of the special visitor was obviously spreading. Minutes ticked past and there was still no sign of the whale.

That was when Claire's bladder gave her a much stronger reminder of how full it was so she ducked into the cabin of the boat. Carl was standing between his chair and the steering wheel, screens and dials of his instrument panel, scanning the ocean in front of them. Claire could see the step down on the other side of the boat.

'The loo's down there, yes?'

'Yep. Use the handrail. It's a big step.'

It was a small space, built partly below floor level to make it tall enough to stand up in comfortably, and it had a metal door that shut firmly. Claire was about to unlock the door to let herself out again when it happened.

She felt the impact through the wall of this space as something hit the boat so hard she was thrown against the small basin on the opposite wall. The sound of the impact was followed by the even more horrific sound of people screaming. And then, too fast for Claire to feel frightened, she could feel her feet leaving the floor. She clung to the taps of the basin as her whole body twisted. She lost her grip on the taps and tried to reach the door but she was totally disoriented. She couldn't even *find* the door.

And that was when fear took hold—just as cold and inescapable as the water enveloping her.

Tom read the text message from Claire saying she couldn't make it to the café for coffee again and he could feel his frown deepening. This was so unlike her that he was sure something untoward must have happened, but why hadn't she told him what it was and whether she was okay?

'You on your own?' It wasn't the first time the woman

had spoken to him. They'd exchanged a friendly comment about what a lovely day it was when she'd arrived at almost the same time he had and they'd chosen neighbouring tables.

'Apparently so. I was supposed to be meeting a friend for coffee but she can't make it.'

'Oh, no...you've been stood up?' The attractive blonde woman was smiling at him. 'I feel like I'm getting the death glare from people in that queue waiting for a table and I'm on my own as well. Can I join you? That way I might look like a local and not a tourist that's taking up too much space.' She was getting out of her seat and moving to sit on the other side of his small table before Tom had a chance to say anything. 'I'm Lorraine, by the way. And I'm not a tourist. I've just moved here.'

Tom's manners prevented him from ignoring his new companion to focus on his phone enough to send a message. It would have been even more rude to tell the staff member who came to their table with her notepad that he'd changed his mind about having coffee when he was already sitting here. Lorraine had ordered a cappuccino but Tom asked for a simple flat white.

'To have here?' she checked.

Inspiration struck and Tom shook his head. 'To take away, please.'

If it wasn't possible to spend some time with Claire, the next best thing would be to catch up with Pete. He could drive over to the marina where Pete kept the boat he used for any chartered fishing or diving expeditions. If his friend wasn't out with some clients, he would undoubtedly be messing about on his boat.

'Make that two coffees,' he added. 'And throw in a

couple of your delicious chocolate chip cookies.' He got to his feet. People didn't usually sit at the tables when they were ordering a takeaway coffee. 'I'll come in with you and wait for them.' He smiled at Lorraine. 'Enjoy your coffee. And welcome to Kaikōura.'

Her smile didn't reach her eyes and Tom suddenly realised that this woman might have been hoping for more than a companion to drink her coffee with. He should be flattered that such an attractive woman had approached him, he thought. But he didn't feel flattered. He felt... uncomfortable. He'd been looking forward to spending some time with Claire. He didn't want to spend that time with another woman. It felt almost as if it would be cheating, but that was ridiculous, wasn't it? They weren't in any kind of relationship.

So why did he find himself thinking about Claire now? Feeling concerned about what had prevented her getting to the café. He should drop in on his way home, he decided. Just to make sure she was okay. He'd pay for Lorraine's coffee as well before he left the café and maybe that small kindness would make her day a little better.

Finding that Pete was on his boat made Tom's day instantly better.

'Want to head out for a spot of fishing?' Pete asked as he finished his coffee. 'I don't have anyone on the books for this afternoon.'

'Why not?' Tom nodded.

They made a plan to head north to Ohau Point and try for some snapper or gurnard, but changed their minds before they rounded the tip of the peninsula, when they heard the chatter on the common VHF radio channel which allowed boats to communicate with each other.

'Sounds like they've spotted a blue whale,' Pete said. 'Want to hang around here instead?'

'Too right,' Tom said. 'That's an opportunity not to be missed. I've never seen a blue.'

Word was clearly spreading. They could see a helicopter taking off from the airport to head towards them and one of the bigger whale watching boats was doing a U-turn from the popular tourist attraction of the local seal colony. An excited voice came over the radio.

'Thar she blows!'

The spout of water was easily big enough to be seen from shore as the massive whale began to surface. But then someone was shouting.

'That's Carl's boat!'

Another voice was on the channel now. A calm voice that was following standard procedure for an emergency.

'*Mayday, mayday, mayday!* Boat *Time and Tide* capsized. Looked like it got swiped by a whale.'

'I can see people in the water,' came another panicked-sounding message.

The Kaikōura coastguard was on the channel now and Tom could hear the siren that summoned their volunteers to man the rescue boat. They wanted to gather more information in the time for them to get the boat down the slipway and on its way but nobody could tell them how many people were in the water, whether there were any injuries or how rapidly the boat might be sinking.

Pete caught Tom's gaze and reached for his microphone and identified himself as he joined the conversation. 'On our way,' he said then. 'I've got a doctor on board. And diving gear. ETA five minutes.'

* * *

Two other boats reached the scene at about the same time that Tom and Pete arrived.

They could see the twin hulls of *Time and Tide* just breaking the surface of what was, very fortunately, an unusually calm sea.

'Must be some air pockets inside,' Pete noted, slowing his boat as they approached. 'That's good news for being able to salvage her.'

Tom wasn't thinking about the boat. There were people in the water and he was very relieved to see they were all wearing life jackets. A child was being lifted into one of the other boats and a woman clung to a lifebuoy that had been thrown from the whale watch vessel. The helicopter was hovering overhead, possibly relaying information to the coastguard, but Tom's attention was caught by a man who wasn't far from the unturned boat and was waving frantically at them. They could hear him shouting.

'Help… This guy needs help!'

Pete took them closer. The man who was shouting was holding onto another man, keeping his head out of the water as he was floating on his back. His face was pale and his eyes were closed. Was he unconscious? Or—

'It's Carl.' Pete swore under his breath. He climbed down the ladder at the back of the boat and hooked one arm around Carl. Tom leaned over the side and managed to get a grip on an arm. The man in the water did his best to help and, with a huge effort, they managed to drag the limp body on board and place him flat on his back.

'Carl…' Tom shook his shoulder. 'Can you hear me? Can you open your eyes?'

The man who'd helped with Carl was clinging to the boat's ladder.

'Was he unconscious when you found him?' Tom queried. 'Face down in the water?'

'No. He was swimming. And coughing like crazy. He didn't want me to hold him—it was like he wanted to get back under the water.'

Tom nodded. He could understand that. *Time and Tide* was Carl's livelihood—almost a family member.

Another boat came alongside them, reaching to take the man on board. He turned before taking their hands.

'And then he passed out. Just a couple of minutes ago.'

'Coastguard's on its way,' the crew told them. 'And the ambulance will be waiting on shore. One of the docs from the hospital will be with them.'

Tom gave a terse nod. He'd heard that message on the radio. He looked up at Pete. 'He's got a faint pulse,' he said. 'But he's not breathing.'

He tilted Carl's head back, pinched his nose, took in a breath and then sealed his lips over Carl's to deliver a slow, steady rescue breath, one hand on his chest to feel for its rise.

One breath. And then another.

He needed to start chest compressions because, with no breathing, it was only a matter of time before Carl went into cardiac arrest. But just as he positioned his hand in the centre of the chest, Carl moved, rolling onto his side and retching before spitting out water.

'It's okay, mate.' Pete's voice sounded wobbly. 'You're going to be okay.'

Carl groaned again, trying to speak, but his words were too hoarse to understand.

'Just take a breath,' Tom told him. 'As deep as you can. And another one...' He was checking Carl's pulse, which was gaining strength. His breathing sounded remarkably clear, too. Maybe it had been laryngospasm that had stopped him breathing and he hadn't ended up with any water in his lungs. He still needed to get to hospital as soon as possible, though. To get dry and warm and to be given oxygen and monitored carefully for potential complications, especially to the lungs, like pneumonia or the development of acute respiratory distress syndrome.

The coastguard boat was beside them now and they were the best crew to get Carl to the waiting ambulance. They needed some information first, however.

'How many passengers were on the boat, Carl? Was it eight?'

'Yeah...' Carl still sounded croaky.

'We've got four men, three women and a kid.'

'Anyone injured?' Tom asked.

'Doesn't seem to be. They're cold and scared.' The coastguard skipper turned back to Carl. 'So it was just you and eight passengers on board? That's all?'

Carl shook his head. '...one extra... Claire...'

Tom could feel himself freeze. *Claire* was on board?

'She was...in the toilet...' Carl was trying to sit up as well as speak. 'Tried to...open the door... Had to... come up for air...'

One of the coastguard crew was getting onto Pete's boat with the scoop stretcher they would use to transfer Carl.

Tom should go with him but he was breathing well now and he'd be with the ambulance crew and another doctor—probably Ian—within just a few minutes.

And…and how could he leave if Claire was trapped beneath that capsized boat?

Oh, dear Lord…

The realisation that he might never see Claire Campbell alive again hit Tom so hard the breath rushed out of his body. For a moment, he wondered if he would ever be able to take another one.

He *had* to see Claire, he realised.

He had to be the one to find her.

And even if she would never be able to hear his words, he had to tell her what he'd realised, beyond any shadow of doubt, in that terrible moment.

That he loved her.

That he needed her in his life. Without Claire, his life was never going to be what it could have been.

What he desperately *wanted* it to be.

CHAPTER TWELVE

IT WAS A friendship that was so longstanding and so close that Pete and Tom could work together with the bare minimum of verbal communication. That meant that they could work fast but, right now, it still felt too slow for Tom.

It had already taken too long to persuade others that he should be the one to put scuba diving gear on and get into the boat below the surface. The coastguard crew had a responsibility to identify and manage the risks involved, like the possibility of losing whatever air pocket could be providing the buoyancy to keep the boat afloat and that *Time and Tide* could start sinking, perhaps suddenly, into what was very deep water out here.

Nobody was saying it out loud, but if this was simply a body retrieval it was unwise to be rushing into anything and risking another life.

'But what if there's an air pocket that's keeping Claire alive?' Tom had to make an effort to keep his voice calm. 'I'm not prepared to lose the limited window of time we might have available. I *am* prepared to take that risk.'

He was more than prepared. He wouldn't be able to live with himself if he didn't.

And Pete was totally on board. Literally.

He had all the diving gear they needed on his boat. He was checking that the air tank was full, attaching the regulators and strapping it into a dive vest as Tom was finally given the green light and got himself into a wetsuit, thick enough to protect him from both the very cold water and any potentially sharp hazards he might encounter in a confined space.

Wetsuits were never quick garments to get into but Tom knew that getting it wet by dunking it into seawater over the side of the boat would make it easier and, more importantly, faster. He stripped down to his boxers and then shoved one leg and then the other in and tugged the suit higher bit by bit, up to his knees and then his waist. Then he put his arms into the sleeves and turned, holding his shoulders back, so that Pete could pull up the zip on the back. He put flippers on. His arms went through the shoulder straps of the vest and Pete helped lift the tank and secure it. Tom didn't want to take the time to find and put on a hood or gloves. He pulled a mask over his eyes and picked up the mouthpiece to settle the flanges in place. He double-checked the tank pressure, took a breath of the air to make sure everything was working as it should and then sat on the edge of the boat, his back to sea.

Pete's hand signal asked if he was okay. Tom nodded. Then Pete held up a hand with his fingers crossed to wish him luck, but his expression made it more like he was offering his mate the strength to get through what might be the worst possibility. Tom didn't acknowledge that he might have to bring Claire's body to the surface. He wasn't going to let anything destroy the hope he was desperately hanging onto. He held his mask and regulator in place with one hand, his other hand on the back of his head as he rolled backwards into the water.

He sank, twisted to turn his body and then headed towards the capsized boat that was easily visible in this clear water. It felt like it took too long to get close enough to touch the rails at the back of the boat. Then he had to pull himself towards the cabin. The cockpit door wasn't completely closed, which made it easier for Tom to pull it open far enough to get inside. Larger pieces of debris had to be cleared so that he could move through the cabin—a fishing tackle box, a first aid kit and a large plastic container that looked as though it was full of supplies for an afternoon tea. He had to avoid hazards, like floating ropes and fishing rods that he didn't want to get tangled in, as he moved towards the skipper's seat, which should have been attached to the floor but was now overhead. The step down to the toilet was now above his head and Tom used the sloping rail near the step to steady himself. His heart was thumping so hard he could hear it as he tried to open the door.

And failed.

He thumped on the door. He couldn't even speak with his mouthpiece in, let alone shout Claire's name aloud, but the thought was loud enough to echo inside his head.

Claire...

The initial panic had stopped spiralling completely out of control when Claire had discovered the air pocket. She was between the base of the toilet and the hand basin and there was a pipe she could hang onto to keep her head in the space that was, miraculously, full of air rather than seawater. She had no idea how she was going to get out but she was alive. Maybe all she needed to do was to hang on and rescue would come.

Except it hadn't come and Claire had lost track of time and it was so dark it felt like the middle of the night and she was getting so cold it was hard to keep her grip on the pipe. She tried shouting for help but knew how unlikely it was that anyone would be able to hear her. She couldn't hear anything from the outside. How far underwater was she? She didn't think the boat had sunk to the ocean floor because it was moving—rocking gently, both up and down and sideways.

As minute after minute ticked past and Claire could feel her toes and then her feet and legs going numb, she knew it was only a matter of time before she wouldn't be able to hang on any longer. Or that she would use up all the oxygen available in this trapped bubble of air and that would be the end. Panic threatened to overwhelm her again but she made a deliberate effort to slow her breathing.

She didn't want to have her last moments alive filled with fear so she did her best to try and focus on the things in her life that had brought her the greatest happiness. While there were things in her past that she would always treasure—like the countless times she'd held her beloved daughter in her arms—what sprang to mind right now, with remarkable clarity as she closed her eyes and turned her thoughts inwards, were far more recent memories.

And they all included Tom Atkinson.

That first hug on the beach when the connection was so powerful it felt unbreakable. They both knew how it felt to try and ride a wave of unbearable grief. They both knew how short life could be and how moments of joy and this kind of connection needed to be treasured.

Seeing the 'smoke' of the Milky Way above the ancient brick chimney. It was a gift that Tom had bestowed on her that would be high on any list of the best moments of Claire's life.

That first kiss would have absolutely made it onto that list, as well.

And the night in the cabin up on the mountain. Right from the start, when they knew they were going to be there alone together all night and Tom was breaking up the kindling to get that potbelly stove going to keep them warm and heat up their dinner. Claire could almost feel that warmth now, cutting through the bone-deep chill of having been in cold water for too long. She could almost hear the snap of those pieces of wood.

No…it was more like a thumping sound. So loud she could feel the reverberations.

Claire's eyes snapped open. She wasn't imagining the sound—or the vibrations. Someone was banging on the toilet door. Why couldn't they open it? Did she have to turn the handle from the inside? Oh, no…she'd locked it, hadn't she? She'd pushed a bolt sideways to secure the door.

She'd have to put her head underwater to reach the lock. Claire felt her heart begin to race. She took a deep breath of the air around her head. And then another, her mind racing along with her heart. Where was the door? Opposite the toilet. If she kept one hand on that and reached straight ahead, she could find the door and then feel for the handle and the button that would shift the bolt out of its hole.

The third breath she took was the biggest and then Claire let herself sink into the water and reached blindly forward to find the door. It took two tries to shift the bolt and then, with her lungs starting to burn from a lack of oxygen, she braced herself by holding the toilet seat and put her feet against the door beside the handle to push. Maybe whoever was on the other side was pulling at the same time because it seemed to open easily. Claire propelled herself upwards then, hoping desperately that the air pocket was still there.

It was. She was gasping to fill her lungs again and again as she felt the movement of another body coming into this small space. With the tank of air on the diver's back, the front of his sleek wetsuit pressed against Claire's body. He spat out the mouthpiece that was distorting his facial features but he was still wearing a mask over half his face and it was so dark in here that Claire had to wonder if she was imagining that she could recognise this person.

No... Somehow, Claire had known who this was from the moment she'd heard the banging on the door.

Or had she just hoped beyond hope that it *would* be Tom?

It wasn't just the lack of space pushing them so close together now. Tom was holding her. Tightly.

'I'm going to get you out,' he said. 'Don't be scared. I've got you, okay?'

'Okay...'

He had one hand underwater and Claire could feel him twisting as he located something. She felt his fingers touch her lips.

'This is a mouthpiece. It's attached to my tank. I need

you to seal your lips around it and hold it with your teeth. You can practise breathing with it before we go underwater but we need to be quick. I don't know how much time we've got.'

'But what about you?' How could Claire use his air supply if it put Tom's life at risk?

'This is an Octo—an alternative air source for emergencies. I've got a mouthpiece too. The hose isn't very long, though, so we've got to stay really close, okay? We just need to get out of here and through the cabin and then we'll be safe.' His face was so close to her own. 'I know how scary it is for you to breathe underwater but you're going to be fine. I'll be right beside you.'

That he remembered a snatch of the conversation she'd had with Hanna about how terrifying she'd found breathing underwater was enough to let Claire know how deeply he cared about her. That he would be right beside her while she did something so scary made her feel far braver than she would have believed possible.

Maybe Tom could see that courage she'd discovered she had because his face softened. As if he was proud of her?

'We need to be careful because there's a bit of debris floating around but I'll keep you safe, I promise.'

Claire nodded. She knew he would keep her safe. She'd never trusted anyone as much as she trusted this man.

She'd never loved anyone as much as she loved this man.

'Just don't let go of me,' Tom warned.

'I won't.'

'Are you ready for the mouthpiece?'

Not quite. Because Claire knew she wouldn't be able to talk once it was in her mouth. She could feel Tom's hand gripping hers. She squeezed it back tightly.

'Don't you let go of me either, will you?'

'Never.' There was a note in Tom's voice that was another promise. 'I'm never going to let you go, my love.'

It was a promise that Tom seemed to be taking quite seriously. He kept a firm hold on Claire as he pulled her out of the space she'd been trapped in and guided her through the cockpit of the boat and then into open water and straight to the surface, where there was blindingly bright sunlight and people and boats everywhere she looked. There was a helicopter hovering overhead. He held her close as he swam towards an official-looking rescue boat and as the coastguard crew lifted her on board she could feel Tom's hand trailing down her leg and holding her foot that had lost its shoe for a heartbeat, as if he really didn't want to lose that contact.

He couldn't hold her physically as he stripped off his flippers and the tank of air but he was still holding her—with his gaze—as she was wrapped in blankets and they were both taken back to shore by the coastguard crew. Other medical staff were there now and everybody involved in the incident was being looked after. An ambulance was waiting to take Claire to the hospital and they both changed into clean scrubs after they'd had a hot shower.

They both went to check on Carl, who had been admitted to the ward for monitoring. He still looked pale and shaken but was doing remarkably well after coming so uncomfortably close to drowning.

'I want you to stay in overnight so we can keep an eye on you,' Tom told him. 'We're going to watch that your oxygen levels are stable and you don't start running a temperature or showing any other signs of infection.'

'But…my boat. I can't just leave it floating upside down out there.'

'It's being taken care of. Someone will come and let you know what's happening soon. Your missus is on her way in as well.'

'And the other passengers?'

'They're all fine, thanks to you making sure they were all wearing life jackets. They were cold and wet but nobody got injured and they'll be telling people about their close encounter with a whale for the rest of their lives. I expect they'll be telling the world about it on the news tonight.'

'What about *you*, Claire?' Carl asked. 'Are you all right?'

'I'm fine.' Claire had to blink back tears. This man had almost drowned because he'd been trying to save her. 'Better than fine. I'm feeling like the luckiest woman in the world right now.'

She caught Tom's gaze. Feeling this lucky wasn't entirely due to simply still being alive. It had more to do with the way he was looking at her and the words he'd said when they'd last been alone together. When he'd said he was never going to let her go.

When he'd called her his *love*…

It seemed as if Tom was remembering those words as well but he broke their eye contact to look back at Carl.

'I'm taking care of her,' he said. 'Don't you worry about that.'

* * *

'Breathe in,' Tom instructed as he held the disc of a stethoscope against Claire's chest. 'And again...'

He looped the stethoscope around his neck. 'Lung fields sound clear,' he pronounced. 'I think you're right and you didn't inhale any water.'

'I'm sure I didn't. I remember holding my breath so long it felt like I was going to burst.'

'And you didn't hit your head?'

He was threading his fingers gently through her almost dry hair, feeling for any lumps or bumps on her scalp. When he saw the way Claire closed her eyes and leaned into the touch of his hands he knew that this examination had just crossed a boundary between professional and personal. And this was very personal. His heart was so full of the love he was feeling for Claire that he had to take a breath. She opened her eyes, his hands still cradling her skull, to meet his intense gaze.

'I thought I'd lost you,' he said, his voice cracking. 'And I knew it was the worst thing that could have happened to me.'

He could hear the way Claire caught her breath. And held it.

'I don't want to lose you, Claire.' Tom's voice was a whisper now. 'I love you...'

He heard the whoosh of that breath being released. It sounded like a mix of relief and...happiness. Joy, even.

'I love you, too, Tom. I just couldn't tell you.'

'Why not?' He was still holding her head, his gaze locked on hers.

'Because... I didn't think you felt the same way.'

'How could you think that, after those nights we had together?'

'It was just a trial run, remember? No strings.'

'The first time, maybe. Not that night in the vineyard. Oh, Claire…' Tom leaned down and placed a slow, soft kiss on her lips. 'That was no trial run. That was…' He kissed her again. 'That was as perfect as it gets.'

'It was.' He loved the way Claire caught her bottom lip between her teeth, as if she felt shy saying that.

'I wanted to tell you that, but… I couldn't.'

'Why not?'

'I thought you wouldn't want to hear it. I knew you didn't want to complicate your life by including anyone else.'

'Oh… I can't believe I really said that.'

'I didn't want you to think you had to give up all the adventures you want to have either. And all the new places and people you're going to find along the way.'

'But I've found the place I want to be.'

Tom could feel the movement beneath his hands as Claire swallowed hard and pulled in a new breath.

'And I've found the person I needed to find. The only adventures I need, Tom, are the ones I can share with you. But…'

'But…?'

Tom's heart sank like a stone. Was he still in danger of losing Claire in his life?

He couldn't understand what he could see in her face because it looked like…fear?

'I'm older than you,' she whispered.

And suddenly Tom understood. Her husband had cheated on her with someone half her age. Had she somehow believed that she was partly to blame? That she wasn't young enough. Or beautiful enough. Or just… *enough*.

How could he find the words to tell her that she was so much *more* than enough?

'You're *you*,' he said softly. 'And you're perfect. Age is…' He gave his head a tiny shake. 'Irrelevant.'

'But you could choose someone young and gorgeous. Like the women Hanna and Kerry were picking out for you on the dating site. Like the woman you met at the café today.'

Tom blinked. 'How on earth did you know that I met someone in the café today?'

'It was a blind date. Hanna got me to help set you up, but I felt bad about it so I was trying to catch up with you before you got there and…and I saw you. And her. And… you looked…happy. When you love someone, you want them to be happy, don't you? I couldn't mess with that.'

'I probably looked happy because I thought you were about to arrive and have coffee with me. If you'd waited long enough you would have seen me escaping with takeaway coffees to go and find Pete.'

'I couldn't stay there and spy on you. And, anyway, that was when Carl saw me and said he had room for one more on the boat and…well…you know the rest.'

'I should have guessed that this was Hanna's doing.' Tom shook his head more firmly this time. 'I'm going to have words with my daughter. She has to stop meddling with my love life, once and for all.'

'She won't need to,' Claire said softly. 'If we make it official.'

'That we're dating for real?' Tom felt his heart skip a beat. 'No... I don't think so.'

He saw Claire's eyes widen in shock.

'This is way more than dating,' Tom said. 'I want you in my life for ever, Claire. I want to marry you. I want everyone—and especially Hanna—to know exactly how much I love you.'

He could see the shadows of doubt in her eyes evaporate. And then he could see what looked like a reflection of exactly how *he* was feeling.

'I can't imagine my life without you, Tom,' Claire whispered. 'Or maybe I don't want to imagine it. I love you. I love you so much.'

This kiss was crossing the boundary for needing a lot more privacy. They needed to get out of here and go home. Tom's gaze caught the tympanic thermometer that was still lying on the bed beside Claire. He picked it up.

'I'd better check your temperature again,' he said, keeping his tone serious.

The thermometer beeped seconds later and Tom frowned at the digital screen.

'Thirty-six point four,' he murmured. 'I wouldn't say you're hypothermic but it's still on the low side. I think you could do with a bit more warming up.' It was hard to stop a smile escaping. 'And you know what they say the best way to do that is.'

He could see that Claire knew exactly what he was talking about. A transfer of body heat. Close contact. Skin to skin. Her smile looked as if it was coming straight from her heart.

'Take me home, Tom,' she said softly. 'Please?'

EPILOGUE

Two years later...

THERE ALWAYS SEEMED to be something to celebrate.

Like Hanna getting into medical school. And how she was loving her studies and doing so well. She wasn't sure that she wanted to end up following in her father's footsteps and being one of the GPs in her hometown, but she was sure that it had been her interference that had brought Tom and Claire together.

'If I hadn't set you up on that blind date, Claire wouldn't have been where she was that day and Carl wouldn't have found her and she would never have been on that boat.'

'Which would have been a good thing, Hanna,' Tom said sternly. 'Claire nearly drowned.'

'And that gave you enough of a fright to see how you really felt about her.' Hanna wasn't about to give up the credit. Her smile could be described as smug, in fact. 'I think I can safely say that my work is done.'

There was a community celebration when *Time and Tide* was relaunched after it had been salvaged and restored. Carl used the relaunch of his beloved boat as an excuse for a party where he and his missus renewed their wedding vows and he got to put his repaired wedding ring back on the finger with its missing tip.

A more private but very special celebration was held of a life well lived, when Mabel Jamieson died at the grand old age of a hundred and one. Claire had seen her only the day before and she'd had tears trickling through the channels her wrinkles had created on her face.

'They say that Livvy's in remission,' she said. 'I can die a happy woman.'

And she did.

But the best celebration so far was even more private than Mabel's farewell. It was the wedding of Tom Atkinson and Claire Campbell and they'd chosen to elope.

'So that Hanna doesn't take over,' Tom growled. 'She might create a website just for the wedding.'

'I'm sure she wouldn't. Won't she be upset to be left out?'

'She can arrange the party for when we get back. We can do it at Beachcombers.' He was smiling. 'Maybe that whale will come back and give us a wave with its tail.'

They exchanged rings in a registry office in Blenheim. They used traditional vows, but when they were alone with a bottle of champagne, back in the little cottage in the vineyard for the night, where they'd truly made love for the first time, they added some of their own.

'I promise I'm never, ever going to take this ring off,' Tom said, holding up his left hand so that the white gold band gleamed in the last of the sunshine.

'And I promise I'm never, ever going to throw my ring into a river,' Claire said. She put her hand over his, so that their rings, as well as their fingers, were touching.

Neither of them was looking at the rings, however.

They were caught by each other's gaze and it felt like their souls were touching as well.

They both knew that this was only the first of hopefully a great many celebrations of their love.

This was for ever.

* * * * *

*If you enjoyed this story,
check out these other great reads from
Alison Roberts*

Midwife's Three-Date Rule
Paramedic's Reunion in Paradise
City Vet, Country Temptation
Falling for Her Forbidden Flatmate

All available now!

SECOND CHANCE WITH HIS CITY NURSE

SUSAN CARLISLE

MILLS & BOON

Finnley

You've been a blessing since day one.

CHAPTER ONE

LILY SMYTHE CLIMBED toward the unknown as she stepped up the wooden treads leading to the rustic medical clinic. She scanned toward the tops of the towering evergreen trees and the granite rock face of the mountains of Yosemite National Park. This back-to-nature thing wasn't in her wheelhouse. It had nothing to do with her not liking it but more to do with knowing nothing about it.

Confident she would learn while spending the next three weeks in the park, she still wasn't sure she would fit in any more than she did currently. She'd gotten herself here by making a snap decision so she wouldn't have to think about the rift between her and her secret-keeping parents, who were actually her half brother and sister-in-law. She had been adopted by them when her birth parents had died. Lily just wished her adoptive parents had told her instead of her finding out by accident.

Her woes had been compounded by overhearing a coworker's remarks regarding her entitlement at the hospital because of her name.

"Are you going to apply for the department nurse position?" the younger of the two had asked.

"I had thought about it but decided why bother, if Lily is applying? She'll get it."

The younger one had given the other woman a look. "She might not."

"Are you kidding? There is a wing of the hospital with her last name plastered in huge letters on it. They would be crazy not to hire her if they wanted to keep the money flowing in."

"Yeah, but you have to have a SEMA certificate." The younger nurse had returned to looking at the board.

The older woman said, "I do have one."

"She doesn't, I don't think."

With a sneer in her voice the older nurse responded, "I can't see Miss Country Club doing that type of training."

"Isn't it more about leadership and thinking outside the box?"

With her spirits damaged Lily had hung her head and walked off before they could see her. Was that what they really thought about her abilities? That her family's name had paved her way? The nurses had accused her of using her family name despite all the hard work and effort she had put into being a good nurse and leader.

In an effort to remove any doubt on anyone's part that she was worthy of a new position in the emergency department, and had achieved it on her own merit not her last name, Lily had signed up for this medical program. She needed to stand out. That was the point of extending her education. That the program was built around working in the wilderness had been an accident.

All she had to do was get through the weeks ahead. Then she would have her Special Emergency Medical Assistance certificate. For this class she had signed up using her mother's maiden name—Carter—and flown halfway across the country. No one would know her here.

There would be no doubt she had completed this program on her own ability.

Up until recently she just accepted who she was and not given it much thought. Maybe she should have paid more attention. Had things in her life really come that easily for her? Maybe she had floated along on her name. She knew of at least one aspect of her life that hadn't gone well that had nothing to do with her last name. Her love life. A man breaking off your engagement just weeks before the wedding was demoralizing no matter who you were.

She wasn't as much of a princess as they might think. Lily intended to prove it to herself and them as well. That evening she signed up online for a SEMA class. What she hadn't expected was that the only class with an opening at this late date was being held in California in a remote national park. Some were being held in large inner cities and rural towns but, no, she had to attend one in a place she had no idea about.

Lily opened the door of the Yosemite Medical Clinic and entered. A blond-haired thirty-something man sitting behind a long wooden desk looked at her. The woman beside him did as well.

"Can I help you?" the man asked.

"Yes, I'm here for the SEMA class." She searched the area with its wood plank walls and floor with three plastic uncomfortable-looking chairs positioned against a wall where no pictures hung. No one else was there. Worry filled her. Was she late?

"They're meeting out on the back porch. Just go straight through here." He pointed behind him and down a short hallway. "To the screen door at the end."

"Thank you." She stepped around the desk and walked

toward the back of the building. Her wedge-heeled shoes thumped on the floor as she went. From what she could tell every building around here had been made of wood or stone. It was lovely how the buildings blended into the landscape as if the world outside hadn't invaded. The waterfalls she had seen on her drive in, not to mention the huge one that was the centerpiece of the park, had taken her breath away. She had never before experienced this type of countryside. Her idea and her family's idea of roughing it was a five-star hotel.

She continued down the hall walking slowly enough to notice the pictures along the walls were in black-and-white of the park in bygone years. Hopefully during her time here, she would have a chance to study them closer. Right now, if she didn't keep moving, she would be late.

The sound of people talking reached her ears before she saw them. One made her pause. It sounded too familiar. She pushed opened the door and stepped out on the porch. All five of the people there focused on her but only one made her body stiffen and her heart thump harder.

Cade.

Cade who had been her boyfriend for years. Who had joined her at college. Who she had waited on to finish medical school. The man who had broken their engagement. The wedding that the paper said would be the event of the year. Instead, it was her humiliation of the century.

Irritation flared. Why was he there? He stood with his hands shoved into the front pockets of his jeans, resting his shoulder against the rough-hewn support post of the porch. He gradually straightened. She stepped farther out. His eyes widened. The bottom of the vein along the length of his neck throbbed. She used to kiss him there.

Nope, that wasn't a thought she would allow herself to dwell on. The man had crushed her.

"And you must be Ms. Carter," said an older balding man who stood off to one side on the small porch.

Cade's chin moved to a questioning angle. His look pierced her.

Heaven help her, he still made her heart flutter. He'd been a good-looking man years ago, but age had given him an edge that made him even more appealing and made him favor his father even more. With his piercing, intelligent blue eyes, straight hair cut tight to his head and his slim build, she would bet more than one woman had wanted Cade's attention. A flare of jealousy she didn't have the right to feel heated her.

Wearing a collared shirt under a navy fleece vest with Yosemite National Park on the breast, he appeared the epitome of a man who had found his place in life—all confidence. That she could envy. She seemed to have lost her security with the knowledge her parents had been lying to her for years.

She forced herself to turn away from Cade to the other man. "Uh… Lily, please. I'm sorry if I'm late—"

"No, no, you're fine. We've been expecting you. Since we're all here then we'll get started. Please have a seat."

To take the only seat left she would have to pass close to Cade. Squaring her shoulders, she avoided looking at him as she made her way to the rocker.

The man said, "I'm Lamar Parsons. I'm the co-co-ordinator of SEMA. I'll be leading your program along with Dr. Cade Evans." He pointed to the man she knew all too well, who was now watching her with brooding eyes. "He's the head of the medical clinic here."

Thanks goodness Cade's stare left her to move around

the porch. She had started to sweat in the cool air under his appraisal. Was he as surprised to see her as she was to see him?

That didn't matter. She was here to complete a class. She couldn't let the fact that her ex-fiancé was one of her instructors matter. She would prove she could handle the training and would qualify for the new job despite Cade and their history. She had to consider this the first test in thinking on her feet—how she handled meeting her ex five years later. The corner of her mouth lifted. She bet no one else here had that on their syllabus.

Lily wiped her palms down her thighs. *I can do this.* She would focus on what needed doing and not worry about Cade.

Lamar continued to talk. She turned her attention to the older man.

"This SEMA program is designed to take you out of your comfort zone. We want you to get comfortable with thinking and acting on your feet. Here you're going to be doing it a little differently. You'll be working in the clinic and out in the wilderness as well. With your training here you should gain knowledge you can use anywhere. Now I'd like for us to get to know each other." He nodded toward a man who looked as if he were in his late twenties. "We'll start with you. Tell us who you are and where you are from and what you hope to get out of this program."

Lily tried to concentrate on what was being said but the heat of Cade's look scattered her attention.

Hell. Cade shifted his stance. His skin acted as if ants ran up and down it. Of all the places in all the world, in pops Lily. Even her hothouse name sounded out of place in this isolated area. Never in his wildest dreams would he have ever thought he'd see her here.

Still beautiful with her blond hair pulled behind her head and wide eyes that seemed to always hold humor, Lily made him want to pull her into a hug while pushing her away at the same time. He didn't know what to do. She didn't look any different than the day he'd last seen her. Tall, with a frame that carried enough weight to create curves that made a man want to hold on to her, Lily looked fit and athletic. Was she still playing as much tennis as she used to?

It had been what seemed like forever since he'd told her he was breaking off their engagement. The hurt on her face still squeezed at his heart. He had to let that go. She was part of the past. He couldn't return there. He glanced at Lily for the hundredth time.

A flash of concern went through her eyes before her look skipped away.

"Ms. Carter, it's your turn to tell us about yourself," Lamar said.

Cade couldn't stop the twitch at the corner of his mouth when Lily jumped as if she had been poked in the ribs.

"I'm Lily…uh… Carter."

Cade's brows drew together. Lily's surname was Smythe. Had she married? That shouldn't prick him like it did. She had every right to move on after him.

"I'm from Chicago. And I'm a physician's assistant."

Cade closed his eyes for a few moments. He listened to the sound of Lily's voice. He still liked the tinkling sound. He had always loved it. The softness reminded him of a warm breeze on a summer day. Gentle. Reassuring. Refined.

That had been part of the problem between them. She

had been from one world, and he had wanted another. Or at least that was what he had told himself at the time—he had tried to explain to her, but she hadn't understood or didn't want to. Or he hadn't made it clear enough. Most of all he had wanted to make his own way, get out from underneath his family's expectations. Perhaps that was what he'd failed to explain. That was what had brought him to this post.

His eyelids rose. His look met Lily's. Her last word trailed off.

"Cade," Lamar said, drawing his attention. "Why don't you give everyone a quick tour while I take care of making assignments."

Cade nodded and stepped to the screen door. "This way." When the group moved inside, he said, "I understand you all have solid medical experience so most of this should be very familiar. Along this hall are our three examination rooms." He stood in the door of one room.

Everyone circled around him. Lily hung to the back.

"The clinic is responsible for visitors, rangers, general park staff. All our patients are walk-ins. Along with the three exam rooms there is one overnight room. They're all well supplied. You'll be expected to take your turns helping here as well as undergoing additional training outside of the clinic."

Lily had positioned herself behind the others so there would be no contact between them. That suited him just fine. He needed time to get his head wrapped around the fact she was here, and how he would deal with having to see her daily for the next three weeks. "How are emergencies handled?" Lily asked from behind one of the men.

"Those are taken care of by the EMTs housed with the fire department. They handle 911 calls. Eighty per cent of those patients go by ambulance to the Merced hospital. The more difficult cases will be helicoptered to a trauma hospital in Fresno."

He led the group to the front office, where he introduced them all to Jeff and Meghan, who worked in that area. "We have on staff a doctor, physician assistant, nurse and clerk. There are also seasonal nurses that rotate in for the main season, which is June, July, August and September."

One of the other members of the group asked, "What type of problems do you see?"

"The main issues we see are climbing falls and shoulder dislocations. These include sprains, strains and soft tissue injuries and lacerations of all types.

"Recently we got a young visitor being injured when she approached a buck being fed by other visitors. The buck spooked and its antlers connected with the girl's arm, causing a deep laceration and chest abrasions. We dressed the wounds then sent her on to town for further care at the hospital."

"Is that typical stuff?" Lily asked.

He shrugged. "I hate to admit it, but we do get a lot of issues from visitors just not thinking. The animals here are wild. This is not a petting zoo. People get hurt."

Lily's lips thinned and she nodded. "Stay away from the animals. Check."

"Our day schedule is an equipment check, narcotic count, morning meeting, scheduled shots and the handling of patients. The clinic is open from nine to five, but we also have someone on call overnight for emergencies."

Cade then stepped down the hall to another, smaller one which led to the lab and the X-ray room. He told them his office with a storage area was up front near reception along with the medical records and office space they could use. He finished the tour with "If you'll return to the porch, Lamar should have your assignments ready to hand out."

Everyone filed down the hall. Lily was the last to pass him. As she went by, he reached out but stopped himself. "Lily."

She stiffened. The tautness in her body told him she wasn't pleased with the turn of events either. She faced him.

"I'm surprised to see you," he began.

She glared. "I hadn't planned on you being here."

His voice softened. "How have you been?"

"Fine until now." Her voice sounded hard as the nearest granite wall.

He winced. She wasn't going to make this easy for him. "You look as if you're doing well."

"I am."

"Carter?" He quirked his eyebrow. "Did you…? Are you…uh married? I hadn't heard."

"I'm not surprised. I haven't seen you in five years and as far as I know no one else in Chicago has either. From what I can tell you aren't too interested."

He deserved that jab. "Lily, I've always been interested."

"You have an unusual way of showing it."

He cringed at her bitter tone. This conversation wasn't going in the direction he wanted. "I was just trying to be friendly. After all we were close at one time."

She looked him straight in the eyes. "We were but now you're my instructor and I'm the student. Nothing more."

"That's true." That stung. Cade hated what he had done to her, but he hadn't seen any other way. Saving himself had consumed him. He would have never survived in his father and brother's practice. It just wouldn't have worked. Being under their fingers with no decision-making powers would have slowly destroyed him. After seeing what his father had been doing, he had no doubts he had to get away.

"Let's hope it works out more in my favor than it did the last time we tried doing something together."

There was another jab. One equally well deserved.

She visibly relaxed as if by sheer will she had forced herself to do so. "Now that I think about it, I possibly should be a little nicer to you since you're my instructor."

"I am that."

She looked away from him. "I'll try to keep the past in the past if you will."

"That sounds like a good plan. For both of us."

Cade watched Lily walk away, her firm butt encased in jeans. Yep, she still had a way of getting under his skin, making his blood hum. Both aspects of her personality had kept him on his toes for years and years. In some ways it was nice to see she hadn't changed. It had been good between them in and out of bed. Sadly, he had shattered that relationship.

The change in her last name still disturbed him. He hadn't gotten an answer about a husband. That wasn't his business. He'd missed his chance on that being the case five years ago. He had tried to tell her how he felt back then. That he needed to get out of Chicago. Out from under the thumb of his family. He wanted to help people but do it his way. Not by following in the footsteps of his father and older brother and certainly not under their domination.

No matter how he had attempted to explain it he

couldn't seem to get Lily to understand. She kept saying, "But what about the wedding?" That had been another thing that seemed to take on a life of its own. Bigger, grander and more demanding. Everything had been spinning out of his control.

The more he had worked to explain himself, the more emotional the situation became. Lily had cried. He had raised his voice, making a mess of it. In desperation and frustration, he had told Lily the wedding was off. He left the next morning.

Leaving Lily behind was part of the fallout. Possibly the ugliest part. She had to stay behind and be the talk of the society section, the county club set and friends. Apparently, Lily had recovered nicely and married. He couldn't think of another reason for the name change since she loved being a Smythe.

That brought him back to what was she doing here and in this type of program? She didn't do wilderness or outdoors. She would have days of both over the next three weeks.

Lily climbed into her small car parked in a similarly little parking lot in front of the clinic. She braced her hands on the steering wheel then rested her forehead between them. For once she had truly stepped out on her own and bam, she'd run into her past in the form of Cade. Then he started quizzing her about her name change. That was the last thing she wanted to discuss.

To make matters worse, he would have input on whether or not she earned that certificate. She had to stop antagonizing him and focus on why she was here. Passing this course wasn't only for the job she wanted, but was also to prove there was more to her than others believed. She could only handle so much emotionally. Cade could tip her over the edge, but she wouldn't let that happen. Was the universe plotting against her?

She made a right and drove down the paved road, being careful not to exceed the speed limit. Enormous pines lined the road. Beyond were open fields of grass with hiking paths. She passed more than one set of hikers.

Farther ahead just above the tops of the trees she could just make out the granite face of El Capitan, the mountain famous for free climbing. Lily shuddered. That type of stuff wasn't for her. Who wanted to climb in the first place? With or without a rope? Certainly not her.

The rushing of water falling from the top of El Capitan was beautiful and soothing and could be heard around the valley. She looked forward to walking to Yosemite Falls. The syllabus had listed she would have to camp somewhere above it.

She couldn't deny the area was beautiful. It wasn't just the waterfalls. Even the rushing Merced River intrigued her. The beauty of the area was astounding and indeed worth seeing. Why hadn't her family ever visited anywhere like this? Because they spent their holidays in Europe or on a beach in the southern isles. Those were lovely vacations just not ones that involved a place like this with its rustic beauty.

She needed rest after leaving early that morning from Chicago and flying to Fresno, then driving to Yosemite. Shaking off the tension, surprise and frustration of the morning, she followed the directions she had been given to the room she had been assigned in the park staff village.

Lily stayed to the right on the paved road toward an area called Housekeeping Camp. She had never camped a day in her life, but she looked forward to proving to herself she could do it. Along with the syllabus there had been a list of equipment. She had no idea what 90 percent of the items listed were.

She'd not had time to pick up many things before leaving. Lugging what was on the list across the country sounded daunting, so she had planned to buy what she needed after she arrived in Yosemite. Having no idea now remotely located the park was, she was now ill-prepared for the camping trip. She even thought of ordering online what she needed, but deliveries were not made as frequently here as they were at home. Now she was down to asking to borrow equipment from one of the other students. She wasn't used to being this unprepared.

What she hadn't planned on was having Cade watching her use those items. How she would survive the next three weeks physically she wasn't sure, and she certainly wasn't clear about handling it mentally. It would take all she had to make this work.

Lily had accepted Cade had left her almost at the altar. It had taken her time but seeing him again brought all those disappointed, disbelieving and angry feelings to the surface once more. She couldn't let the past intrude on her future.

She turned into a road leading into a thicker wooded area. On her drive there she passed a grocery, fire department, post office, chapel, park museum and the Ansel Adams Gallery. Amazed, she had no idea the park was a small town. Maybe there was more hope for camping equipment than she thought.

Among the ponderosa pines sat a rustic wood-sided building housing two living areas that shared a wall. Lily double-checked the signs for her number. She located it at the end of the road. Turning into the short drive, she parked in front of her door. Gathering her suitcase, she towed it to the porch. She stopped long enough to look at the wooden rocker. Had she ever sat on a porch and just rocked? Not that she could remember. She wasn't sure she'd ever had the opportunity to do so.

She opened the door to find an efficiency apartment which consisted of one room with a bed, a seating area with a chair, a small sofa and a small TV. In one corner was the door to the bath and in the opposite corner a tiny kitchen including a head-high refrigerator. The entire space was a third of the size of the bedroom she grew up in.

She unpacked her luggage, stored her case and sat on the bed. What now?

Standing, she went to the kitchen and leaned over the sink to look out the window. She could just make out El Capitan and Yosemite Waterfall. Surprisingly she liked her spot. It was cozy.

Going to the table for two, she picked up her schedule for the next three weeks and stepped out on the porch. There she sat in the rocker. She used her toe to start it moving. Her first assignment was working in the clinic. She had to be there at eight in the morning. Emergencies she could handle. At least in that world, she was confident.

Cade climbed the steps to his cabin behind the clinic. One of his staff would take the overnight hours. He would be close by if needed. Going through his evening routine, he settled into bed. He didn't anticipate getting much sleep. Having Lily in the vicinity was more than his emotional wagon could handle without adjustment.

He wanted them to find a way to friendship but if that wasn't possible they could at least be civil to each other. He'd hurt her. It would take time for her to adapt to having him in her life again. He certainly needed time to settle into her being in his.

The change in her last name nagged at him. What did it mean? He couldn't help but be curious about what she had been doing since he left Chicago. He'd wanted to ask his mom about her when they talked but always thought better of it. Despite being the one to break it off, he did care about Lily. He had never returned to Chicago and had no interest in doing so. That part of his life was behind him. He spoke regularly to his mother and saw his family at holidays when he could, but those times had always been at a resort somewhere. He'd been tempted to call Lily but, in the end, felt it was better to let her move on without him.

His mother would have shared information about Lily if he had asked, but he didn't want to get her hopes up he might return to what had been. His and Lily's families had been great friends before his desertion. Both sides had been pleased when he and Lily had finally announced they were going to marry. It was not a surprise to either family. The idea had been hoped for for years. Lily hadn't seemed to mind, but it had got under his skin that they were a forgone conclusion.

His life had been so planned for him that marrying was just one more thing he had no control over. It felt like his family had a handle on everything in his life. At the very least he should've been able to pick his own wife. The shame was Lily would've been his choice, but they wanted two different lifestyles. They had been going in different directions. He knew if he stayed in Chicago their love would die and he would too.

He had been confident somebody would come along and ask Lily to marry him. She would make a wonderful wife. It had never been she wasn't good enough for him. Instead, he hadn't been in the right place to have a wife. But someone had seen her attributes and married her. *Carter.* Who did he know with the last name Carter?

The next morning the question still plagued him. So much so he jerked to attention in his desk chair. Lily had arrived. He just knew she was there without even seeing her. His body had always zoomed to hers when she was around. That hadn't changed even from the time they were middle schoolers and friends just running around with their families. It had become stronger as they grew older. Even after all the time that had passed, Lily still had a way about her.

Cade shook off his reaction. Lily had made it clear she had no desire for them to rekindle even a friendship. Her voice carried from the outer room as she said good morning.

Lamar and he had divided the group of four into pairs for the first week. They would swap the pairs for the second week then the group would work as a team the third week. They would quickly learn how to work with one other and as a whole, along with being out of their comfort zone.

Cade couldn't help but smile. Lily would certainly be out of hers. No spa, and when in the wilderness no shower, and no easy trip to the mall. But the entire program was designed to have the attendees learn from each other and about themselves.

He stepped into the reception area. Lily, dressed in

dark green scrubs and with her long, silky hair pulled back, stood beside a middle-aged man whose name Cade couldn't remember. Cade had been too caught up in the fact Lily had reappeared in his life the day before to make note of it.

Jeff and Meghan were with them as they all held cups of coffee and chatted.

"Good morning." Cade gained everyone's attention. He looked at the man and Lily. "This morning I'd like for you to start by reviewing where things are in the exam rooms. You should have plenty of time to do that. We're pretty quiet in the morning. You can do that together or you can each take an individual room and swap around, however you decide. You'll be working together all this week. While you're working here at the clinic, Lamar has additional activities planned for what happens outside of the clinic, but this week you'll be here."

The middle-aged man walked past Cade. "Good morning, Dr. Evans."

Lily behind him did the same.

"Please call me Cade when there isn't a patient present," Cade said more to her than to the other man.

Lily looked directly in his eyes and said softly, "I prefer Dr. Evans."

"But I don't." For some reason it irritated him for Lily to treat him so formally.

She gave him a long look. "I'm ready to start. Ben is waiting."

Ben? Oh, the other person. Before Cade could say more, she turned and left. He checked his watch. Lily was on time, even a few minutes early, which hadn't always been the case when they were younger. He remembered that and so many of her other personality quirks.

He watched her head down the hall toward the exam rooms. She'd always had confidence. After all she was from one of the most important and well-to-do families in Chicago.

CHAPTER TWO

THE SOUND OF a commotion in the front of the building drew Lily's attention. She headed in that direction.

"I need some help up here," came a voice that Lily now recognized as Meghan's.

Lily picked up her pace. As she passed Cade's office door he appeared and fell in behind her. She entered the reception area to see a hysterical mother with a crying boy of about seven who held his arm, wrapped in a shirt, tight against his chest.

"Don't touch it!" the boy yelled so loud that Lily's ears rang.

Dropping to her knees in front of him, Lily captured his attention. "That looks like it hurts. My name is Lily. What's yours?"

The boy stopped screaming and looked at her then made a loud sniffle. "Rob...by."

Lily resisted trying to touch the arm. "Can you tell me what happened, Robby?"

"I fell." Tears filled the boy's eyes.

"He was climbing on the rocks after I told him not to," the woman with the boy said.

Lily glanced behind her. The first person she made eye contact with was Cade. She nodded her head toward the woman. Thank goodness Cade took her suggestion.

"Lily, why don't you take Robby on back to exam one while I get some information from his mom."

Lily placed her hand on the boy's back. "Come with me and we'll get you cleaned up. When Dr. Evans finishes with your mom he'll come visit you." Lily led the boy down the hall.

Cade moved forward to stop the mother and direct her toward the desk. "You can join Robby in just a minute. I just need to talk to his mom for a moment."

The noise level in the building lowered as Lily helped Robby up on a gurney, allowing his feet to swing over the side. Ben entered the room moments later.

"Ben, would you please bring me a bottle of saline and a pan while Robby and I remove his shirt."

The man went into action.

Lily turned her attention to unwrapping the shirt from the boy's arm. "Robby, I'm going to do this slowly. You tell me when you want me to stop. We don't want this to hurt any more than it has to."

The boy looked at her with watery eyes.

"Okay. Here we go." She lifted the boy's arm away from his body and slowly removed the material.

Lily winced. Bloody scratches and scrapes covered the boy's skin.

"You took a pretty good lick there," a deep voice she knew well said from behind her.

Lily jumped. "Dr. Evans, Ben and I were just getting it cleaned up for you to have a look."

Ben came around to the other side of her and began getting the boy's vitals.

His mother had arrived with Cade in a much calmer mood. Apparently, her and Cade's divide-and-settle approach had worked. The mother calmly took the extra chair in the corner near the gurney.

Cade picked the pan up off the counter and held it below the boy's arm.

"Robby, this may hurt a little. Why don't you hold your mom's hand?" Lily suggested.

The boy accepted his mother's offered hand.

Lily slowly poured saline over Robby's injury, letting it run down the arm. "You okay, Robby? Do I need to stop?"

The boy watched her carefully with glassy eyes, but he didn't ask her to stop. With the washing finished, she took the towel Ben had ready. With all of the blood removed, Robby's arm didn't look as awful as she had feared it might. She felt Cade's bulk and warmth behind her as he looked over her shoulder. She was far too aware of him being near.

"We're going to let Dr. Evans have a look at it now."

Shifting out of the way while making sure she didn't touch Cade, Lily moved to stand at the other end of the exam table.

Cade sat on the stool she had vacated. "Can you squeeze your fingers into a fist?"

The boy did as he was asked. "Good. Now can you wiggle your fingers?"

Robby did that as well.

"Robby, tell me what happened." Cade continued to study the arm, moving it gently one way then the other.

The boy gave his mother an uneasy look.

Lily stepped to the side between the boy and his mother, cutting off any communication between them. Cade needed to know the truth. "Robby, we need to know so we can help you."

Robby glanced toward his mother then looked at Lily. "I got my hand crushed by some rocks falling."

"I told him not to be climbing on everything," the mother's voice rose in defense.

"Boys like to climb. My brothers still like to and they are a grown men."

But Russell and Dave weren't in fact her brothers. She was really their aunt, though they were raised as brothers and sister. She had been little more than a baby when her biological parents had been killed in a car accident. Her brother, half brother actually, Grant, couldn't let her go into the state system. He'd hired Sara to act as Lily's nanny then fallen in love with Sara. They married and started a family; Russell and Dave were their biological sons. Lily had been raised thinking Grant and Sara were her parents, and she was treated as their oldest child.

Lily blinked. She shouldn't be thinking about all that. Instead, she should be concentrating on what she was doing here.

"It looks like it's nothing but bruises and scrapes but let's do an X-ray to be on the safe side." Cade pushed the rolling stool back. "You just might have a break here. Robby, I'd like to put your arm under a machine that will take a picture of your bones. It won't hurt. I promise."

"Can Lily come with me?" Robby gave Cade an imploring look.

Cade smiled. "Sure, she can."

Lily stepped forward. "Come this way, Robby."

Cade spoke to the mother. "If you'll wait here, we'll be right back."

Lily directed Robby into the small room with the X-ray machine. Cade entered right behind them, making the room shrink. She was far too aware of him for her own good. Once again, she reminded herself that she should be focused on the boy.

"Robby, I need to put this heavy vest on you." She held the lead drape as Cade helped Robby put his arms through the armholes.

Cade pointed to a flat tray. "I need you to rest your arm right inside this blue square." Cade positioned the boy's arm where he needed it in order to get a good view of the bones. "You need to stand very still. Lily and I'll step outside in the hall for a moment. Then we'll be right back."

In the hallway Cade punched a button on the wall and there was a buzz. Then they returned to Robby. Lily removed the vest and hung it on a hanger on the wall.

Lily touched the boy's shoulder. "Robby, we're going back to your mom while Dr. Evans looks at your pictures to see if you have any broken bones."

A few minutes later Cade returned to the exam room. He took the stool again. "You're a lucky boy. I don't see any broken bones, but you do have some major scrapes. We're going to cover those. You'll have to keep your arm clean and dry for a few days. We'll have you on your way in a few minutes." He gave the boy a stern look. "But no more climbing on the rocks."

Robby's mother looked relieved at Cade's words.

Cade said, "Ben, why don't you take care of wrapping Robby's arm. I'll leave a prescription for him up front."

"Yes sir," Ben said, turning to the boy. "I know for a fact there's a sucker waiting as well."

That put a smile on Robby's face.

Lily couldn't help but grin.

"Lily, would you mind coming with me?" Cade asked.

His tone wiped the smile off her face. Her eyes narrowed. What had she done? She needed Cade on her side if she was going to pass this program, and she intended to do just that.

When they were both in the hall he said, "Come on back down to the X-ray room. I want to show you how to do them so you can handle it on your own from now on."

"Didn't I do okay this time?" She followed him to the small room.

"Yes, I just need to confirm that you are prepared to take X-rays using this machine. I want to give you a few pointers on positioning."

Cade had seen firsthand Lily knew her emergency medicine. He had been impressed. Somehow, he had to get her to talk to him so he would know a little more about her. Learn what she been doing over the last five years. He couldn't help but be curious.

The Lily he'd watched today had a new aspect to her personality. She'd always been more of a follower than someone who stepped forward. With Robby she had been the leader. Maybe that part of her personality hadn't surfaced because it hadn't had to with her family around. What had happened in her life that made her feel the need to spread her wings here? Something must have set it in motion.

In the X-ray room they went through the procedures once more. Cade spent time explaining how to position the patient for different injuries.

Cade adjusted the machine. "I realize this isn't the normal duty of a PA but here we do a little bit of everything."

"The more knowledge I have, the better I'll be. Do you mind if I practice with Ben when we have time? He'll need to know this as well."

She was still sweet and thoughtful toward others.

Both attributes he'd appreciated before and was glad hadn't changed.

"Not at all. That's a good idea."

"I have one every now and then." She smiled.

It was the first genuine smile he had seen since she had arrived in Yosemite. "You were great with Robby. This side of you I never got to see." He had left Chicago before she had finished her nursing degree.

Lily looked away from him. "That's because you didn't stay around long enough."

That hit him like a punch to the middle. Those statements heaped guilt on him.

"I'm sorry," she said, and sounded like she was. "That was uncalled-for. Antagonizing you won't change anything. Truthfully if that's as hard as the emergencies will be around here then I'll be fine. Nothing like a Saturday night in a Chicago ER."

"I suppose that's true." He grinned. "That's part of this place's appeal."

"You really are happy here, aren't you?" She watched him as if she saw something he wished to hide.

He smiled. "Yes, I love my job."

She moved around the room while making sure she didn't come too close to him. "It's certainly nothing like the one you'd have had working with your father and brother."

"Again, which is much of its appeal." Here he wasn't always doing it someone else's way. Here his suggestions on improvements were listened to and appreciated. Here he wasn't always in his older brother's shadow.

"You weren't going to be able to be yourself in their practice, were you?"

"No." He tensed. Finally, she had seen it clearly when she hadn't before. "I thought I could fake it, that it would get better, but the closer I came to finishing med school the more Dad's and Mike's dictates ate at me. I knew I couldn't stay."

"So that's why you ran away."

Her words were more thoughtful than hurtful, yet he didn't care for them. He stiffened and stood taller. "I didn't run away. I walked away."

"Doesn't seem like that to me. All those years and I never knew how unhappy you were. You used to grumble a bit, but I didn't think you were serious. I've always wondered were you faking us too?" She studied him as if watching for any sign he might avoid her question.

He looked her straight in the eyes. "You and I weren't fake. Leaving you is the one thing I regret."

She didn't blink.

"I was wrong to keep my feelings from you, but I thought I could handle it. Then the walls began to squeeze in on me. Dad and Mike started talking about how it would be with the three of us working together, the type of patients we would see, and I just knew I couldn't face that every day. I tried to talk to them about some inventions and ideas I had. They weren't interested in listening. I knew then they never would be. If I was going to go, do something different, then I needed to do it before I got so far in I couldn't ever leave."

She glared at him. "Why didn't you tell me you were having these feelings instead of springing things on me?"

Cade shook his head, looking down. "I did try, but you were so happily caught up in wedding plans and I just couldn't tell you all of it. I didn't want to disappoint you. I was so crazy about you. I thought it would go away, but it got worse." He couldn't tell her why. "I didn't want to leave you—"

"But you did." Her words were flat and sad.

His chest tightened. He'd been so caught in his own pain he hadn't really let hers affect him.

"I knew you liked camping and being outdoors and all of that, but I never saw you living in a place like—" she waved her hand around "—this."

"Only because I knew that the way I felt would eventually start eating at me and then it would eat at our marriage. You didn't seem to be listening when I tried to talk to you about it, so I thought it best not to share. Hoped it would go away."

"How did that work out for you? You didn't even give me any warning before you blew up everything."

"Because I didn't know where I would end up and I knew how you felt about your family. How much you enjoyed your lifestyle. I couldn't see you in a place like this. I just didn't have the guts to make you choose." He should have confided in her.

"It turns out it wouldn't have been such a big deal."

That was an interesting statement coming from her. "Why's that—"

Ben came down the hall.

"Hey Ben," Lily said. "Come let me show you how to handle the X-ray machine."

Obviously, their conversation of the past was closed. Cade slipped away to his office. What had she meant by it not being a big deal?

That same afternoon, when Lily had cleaned the examination room after the last patient left and she'd finished the paperwork, she exited the clinic with a goodbye and a wave at Jeff. She headed to her cabin, changed into a T-shirt and jeans and put on her new boots, which still needed breaking in. Then she started out along the path leading toward Yosemite Falls.

The light spring breeze rustled the trees and blew a lock of hair into her face. Lily pushed it out of the way. She had planned to make an early evening of it but the pull of the sound of the waterfall made her want to explore.

The activity at the clinic that day had not compared to a metropolitan hospital emergency department, but she'd been plenty busy then there had been the effects of jet lag and seeing Cade again. Despite the difference in the two worlds, she rather enjoyed the slower pace of the clinic. Which surprised her. But now she was glad to be out in the fresh air for a while and clear her head.

She slowed more than once to look up at the wall of granite between the gap in the tall trees to catch a glimpse of the waterfall. It was impressive. She heard the roar of it long before she could see the bottom. A mist drifted around her.

Following the path up to the falls, her mouth dropped open at the full sight. It was gorgeous. The rush of water made it difficult to hear anyone talking. The falls fell a number of feet, creating a rocky pool beneath. From that, a shorter fall rushed under a small viewing bridge into the river beyond.

She spent a few minutes enjoying the sight.

"Such power," she exclaimed in awe.

"Starting to talk to yourself already?"

That was the voice she'd heard in her sleep for weeks after Cade had left. The scent of him cut through her. Cade being so close brought back memories of what had once been between them. Her body heated and tangled to the thought of his touch.

Lily wheeled to face him. She wouldn't let emotions of old take hold of her again. Dressed in running clothes and with his hair damp, he had obviously been running. "Funny. I was just admiring the falls. It's breathtaking."

"It is." Using the tail of his T-shirt to wipe the sweat from his face, he gave her a glimpse of his toned middle.

Her blood tripped along faster at the brief glimpse of his ab muscles. He'd matured and his muscles had become more defined. Lily blinked. She refused to let him get to her ever again. This man had hurt her and didn't deserve her admiration. She didn't need this in her life.

"And to think it goes down to nothing more than a trickle in the summer."

"What?"

He watched her a moment then nodded toward the falls.

"Oh." She gathered herself and went on offense. "Are you following me?"

Cade's eyes narrowed. He waved a hand around. "Have you looked at the size of this place? It's one valley between two sheer granite walls that reach up hundreds of feet with a main road in and out. This isn't New York City or Chicago, where you blend in. It's not hard for people to see each other often. Plus, you're on the main thoroughfare."

Lily pursed her lips and started walking. She didn't want to admit he was right, but he was. "I'm sorry. You didn't deserve that."

A steady stream of cars and trucks pulling campers went by them.

Lily looked for something to say that wouldn't start an argument. "The traffic has picked up."

"Wait until the end of the week. People start pouring in on the weekends from now until the fall. The summer months are the busiest. The nicer the weather, the more people. When the snow starts and roads are closed it is peaceful once more."

"I had no idea Yosemite was that popular. Then again, I can't remember my family ever visiting a national park." Her family favored resorts. She started walking back toward her cabin. Cade fell into step beside her. "Just how long have you been here?"

"This will be my second summer coming up." Pride filled his voice.

"This has become your home, hasn't it?"

He nodded. "It has."

Lily stopped and studied him a moment. "I don't remember you being this relaxed ever."

She continued along the walk. He remained beside her.

"Will you tell me about what has been going on in your life since I left Chicago? Are your parents doing well?"

"Yes." Lily didn't care to share how she felt about them at this point in time. She hadn't figured out how she intended to handle that problem. Hurrying the pace, she moved forward. Cade didn't ask for more.

They walked in silence for a few minutes.

Cade cleared his voice. "I'm sorry I hurt you."

"We've already been over that." Her job, her parents and now this. The hits just kept on coming.

"I want you to believe it." His voice held a pleading note.

She gave him an unwavering look.

"Okay, how about a change of subject. You obviously

don't want to talk about your parents so tell me how you've been."

"Are you really interested?"

He watched her.

Slowly the tension left her body. She shook her head. "I'm sorry. That was uncalled-for and childish."

"Understood. I didn't give you much opportunity to say what you wanted to say to me. I left you all the fallout that you didn't deserve. Along with all the returning of gifts and worse, facing people. I can't blame you and I deserve anything you say. I am really sorry, Lily, but I just had to get out of there. The pressure from my dad, my older brother and everything expected of me was too much."

"I guess that included me too." Lily glared at him. "Why did you wait to tell me you were unhappy until you were ready to leave?"

Cade's chest rose. He slowly released the breath as if trying to form the right words. "I kept trying and then stopped because it felt like you weren't hearing me. Then I guess it was because I didn't want to admit that I was. I want you to know I never was unhappy with you. I was unhappy with what everybody expected me to be. I didn't want big-city hospital stuff. I wanted to be where I felt comfortable. I love medicine but my place to practice it was elsewhere. I felt it in my bones. That's not what my family wanted to hear. Or had planned for me to do."

She looked around them. "Well, you got what you wanted."

"I may have gone a little overboard, but I like it here a lot better than I would've ever liked it in my family's practice. I'm my own person. Not what my father would have deemed right or in his mold. I can't say I have missed the country club or going to a fundraising gala."

"Still you should've talked to me."

"I know. But I did try. I just waited too late. I was selfish. I had to save myself. That you got hurt is my biggest regret. You deserved better."

She tried to keep the hurt from showing but she feared her eyes failed her. "Why didn't you ask me to go with you?"

"Because I couldn't. I didn't know where I was going, but I knew it was different from what you wanted. That would have been more selfish." Could she ever accept the truth of that?

Cade continued quietly, "I hope you're happy. Who is the lucky fellow?"

She gave him a quizzical look.

"Your husband. Your last name is Carter. What did he say about you coming all the way out here? He must miss you."

Lily swallowed. It had been tempting to tell Cade she was married. He deserved to think she'd found someone to care about after he'd left her. The last thing she wanted was to have him think she was still single and pining after him. Only because she had learned the hard way from both Cade and her parents that keeping secrets hurt people. She was a prime example. Which was why she was prepared to tell him the truth.

"It's my mother's maiden name." The mother she had just learned about. It wasn't the name of the woman Lily had believed her entire life had birthed Lily, but the woman who actually gave life to her. Lily sighed. It was all so confusing, disappointing and maddening.

The worst was having everything she thought she knew about herself turned upside down. Who was she really?

His eyes narrowed in confusion. "So why're you using it instead of Smythe?"

Cade had always had a way of getting what he wanted to know out of her. But not this time. She had no desire to share her hurts with him. He'd lost the right to know her personal issues long ago. "Too bad that wasn't a two-way street or maybe I would've known how you felt about living in Chicago. Or you wanting to get out of a big city. Cade, we aren't the confessing kind of friends anymore, but then I guess we never were."

He physically jerked, as if she had punched him.

"Let's just keep the next few weeks on a professional level. I need this class, and you're one of the instructors. I'm not interested in anything beyond that."

Cade didn't say anything for a few more paces then spoke in a soft voice as if easing a scared animal he feared might strike him. "Would you at least tell me why you are here?"

"You know what I'm doing. I'm going through this course."

He didn't look satisfied with her answer. "Then why're you taking this particular course?"

"Because I need it to increase my chances of getting the head nurse position in the ER department. These types of classes are the thing now. It'll look good on my vita." She all but spit the words.

"With your daddy's clout I'm surprised you would have a problem."

That's the last thing she wanted to hear. Lily jerked to a stop and placed her fists on her hips. She leaned toward him, grinding out the words, "I want to earn this on my own merit."

"But here…" He looked around in disbelief.

"I have my masters. I've been working as a physician's assistant in the ER. This job came open and I applied. It's my chance to move into an administrative position. It'll be my chance to improve some areas that need attention but that the hospital and administration are slow to change."

Lily impressed Cade with the determined note in her voice. He'd rarely heard it. More times than not she'd gone along with whatever her parents or friends suggested. Not that she wasn't concerned about people. She certainly had the big heart and the caring personality of a good nurse, but there had never been any real ambition that he had seen. Yet when she spoke of the job she wanted there were notes of fortitude and drive. She had a plan. He liked her before, but he liked this version of Lily even better.

"You've changed."

She glanced at him but continued on. "People change. It's been years since you've even spoken to me."

"I'm sorry about that. Maybe I should have called."

She believed him but that hadn't made those humiliating days afterward any easier.

Cade came up beside her once more. "At the time I thought it best to just cut it off quickly so that it wouldn't hurt you as much as it would if it lingered on."

"Hadn't it already been lingering? You had been keeping how you felt from me. I was in love with you. No matter what you did, I was going to get hurt." She huffed. "I've had enough of this. Stay out of my way, Cade, and

I'll stay out of yours." Lily hurried away without a backward look.

Cade had never gone in for boxing but the way Lily had made him feel bruised and battered must be what it was like to fight bare-knuckled. She had pulled no punches. He'd known she would be hurt but he had no idea how deeply and completely his desertion had wounded her.

After a tension-filled three days of dodging and skirting each other, Cade entered the reception area on Thursday evening. All four students stood talking about going to dinner together. The pair who had come back from a daylong hike talked excitedly about their day. Lily and Ben still had theirs to go on. Then they would go out under Lamar's guidance for their camping trip. Cade couldn't help but wait until then to have some space between him and Lily.

But tonight that wouldn't be the case. As part of the course the students were being judged on how quickly they adapted to last-minute changes.

Cade said, "Lily, I'll need you to man the clinic overnight."

She faced him, her eyes wide. The look of surprise on her face quickly changed to serious. "Okay."

The others headed out the door as if they might be called on as well.

Cade looked at Lily. "You know where everything is. All you have to do is answer the door if anyone comes. I live in the cabin just behind the clinic. If I'm needed text me." He gave her his number. "Or come get me. I'm a pretty light sleeper so you shouldn't have any trouble waking me."

That brought to mind the time she had tried to sneak up

on him and he had grabbed her making her squeal with laugher before he had kissed her with such passion they were soon making love. It still made his manhood twitch to think of those times. What made it worse was he had not had that connection with anyone since. Lily was so close… Moments like those were not to happen again. She made it clear she despised him. He didn't deserve her.

Later that evening, when he exited his cabin, Lily sat on the back porch rocking. He couldn't remember her ever doing something as mundane as peacefully enjoying the surroundings. She had always been busy and in the middle of events. Had he misjudged her all those years ago?

He walked down the steps to join her. "Hey."

She looked up but said nothing.

"Sorry about you missing a night out with the others. Your name just came up that way."

Lily shrugged her shoulders. "No big deal. It happens all the time in my ER."

Had she always been so understanding? Had he been so caught up in himself he had missed that about her? "They make a pretty good burger at the grill in the Village Store. I'm going after one. Would you like me to bring you one?"

"Uh…that would be nice." She moved to stand. "Let me get you some money."

He waved her down. "My treat."

"I don't want you to do that."

"Stop, Lily," he said sharper than he intended. "It's a burger. Let me get it."

She blinked. "Okay. But I buy next time."

"If you insist." He had to figure out a way for them to get beyond this animosity.

"I do." She settled in the rocker again.

"I'll be back in about half an hour." He took the steps that led around the side of the clinic.

Returning, he found Lily still on the porch with a magazine in her hands. He recognized it from one that had been in the waiting area. "I'm back. I hope you're hungry."

"I am." She stood. "Thanks for bringing me something."

Cade stepped on the porch and handed her one of the two brown paper sacks. "No problem." He started toward his cabin.

"Uh… Cade, would you like to join me?"

He turned slowly. Had he heard her correctly? By the look on her face, she had not planned to ask. They had been keeping their distance from each other all week and now she'd asked him to eat with her.

"I can do that." He returned to the porch. "Let's eat out here. With the screen open we can hear anyone who comes in."

He led the way to a small table with two wooden chairs beside it. Seated, he pulled a wrapped burger out of his sack. She did the same out of hers. He dug in again and fished around for the napkins and chip bag.

"I'll get us some drinks." Lily entered the clinic and returned with two canned drinks. "I'm assuming you're drinking the same type of soda."

"You remember correctly." Cade liked she hadn't pushed all knowledge of him away. He wouldn't have blamed her if she had. Unwrapping his hamburger, he watched her. Lily didn't look at him. Anywhere but. He studied her a moment. He would've never dreamed it would be this uncomfortable between them.

"Look, I know this is an awkward situation for us," Lily said. "I'm sorry I've invaded your space. I truly had no idea you were here. My parents might have known, but I asked them not to talk about you to me and they've honored my wishes."

Wow. That stung. "Why's this particular certificate so important?"

"I told you about the job I want. I heard that having a course like this one on my résumé would make me stand out. That the hospital likes that sort of thing."

"Yes, but I'm asking why here, a wilderness situation? You don't even work in this field."

A sheepish look came over her face and she lowered her head. "Because it was the only one that had any openings left when I went to sign up. This one was better than nothing."

He set his drink can on the table. She did too. He leaned toward her until he had her attention and said clearly, "You do realize that this particular program requires camping. Living off the land. Taking care of a patient using only what you have with you. A small first aid kit."

"Well, I didn't exactly when I signed up, but I realized that when I was sent a camping supply list. I just wish I'd had a chance to get everything on the list."

His brows rose as he glared at her. "You don't have all the supplies?"

"I thought I could get them here. I didn't realize there wouldn't be a store just around the corner."

"You aren't in Chicago anymore. Pardon the pun but this isn't going to be a walk in the park."

She sat forward. "I know that."

He relaxed in his chair. "You've done great at the

clinic. I can see you're a great PA, but this course gets harder as you go along. You have to learn to work outside your element. I bet you don't even own the correct clothes for something like this."

She threw her shoulders back. "What do you mean clothes I need? I have T-shirts and jeans. I did buy some hiking boots."

He chuckled. "What about a knife? A sunscreen hat? Sleeping bag? Pans to cook over a fire? A snakebite kit?"

Lily face twisted into something near comical fear. "I told you I still needed to come up with some of my supplies." She paused a moment then looked at him. "Why would I need a snakebite kit? That wasn't on the list."

"In case you or someone else gets bitten." His words sounded as if he were talking to a child.

She looked around like there was a snake just waiting to crawl across her foot.

Cade chuckled and shook his head. "They don't usually hang out around here. It's much too busy. But when you get out in the woods…"

Lily gave him a determined look despite feelings of apprehension. "I have to do this." She hung her head and shook it. "I hate to ask but do you have any supplies I could borrow?"

He hesitated. This wasn't a good example of him trying to keep distance between them.

"Cade, I really need this. Based on what you've been telling me, I'm going to need all the help I can get."

She must be desperate if she was begging him for help. Lily confused him. First the name change, then her dodging act around him and now this need for him to help her. What was really going on with her?

"What equipment do you have?"

She told him the five items she managed to bring with her.

"Right. You are going to need some help." Cade shook his head. What had Lily been thinking when she decided to come to Yosemite?

She lowered her head in a contrite dip. "This isn't the norm for me. I'm usually well prepared. My mind was elsewhere before I came."

Cade waited on her to say more but she didn't.

Lily's face turned anxious. She offered him a begging smile. "Do you have anything I could borrow?"

When she looked at him like that, she could have anything.

Awareness Lily recognized from the past shone in Cade's eyes, causing warmth to fill her body. She wasn't going to let that take a hold on her.

"You can supplement with my stuff. What I don't have we should be able to find at the store."

This wasn't one of her best ideas. Instead of keeping him at arm's length she had pulled him closer. Yet this program was too important to her not to do all she could to pass it. With just a little help and perseverance she could survive. She just had to stay focused on what she wanted. "Thank you for helping me."

Cade studied her. "It's the least I can do."

"Don't sound so excited about it."

"You're here for the medical end. It couldn't hurt for me to share some knowledge of camping. You aren't being graded on those skills. Your ability to cope is what's important. We've got some time this week to get you organized. By the way, you have been great in the clinic."

"Thank you." She wore a proud smile. One of those he'd not seen enough of since she had arrived.

CHAPTER THREE

LATER, SITTING UP in the reception area of the clinic late that night, Lily couldn't help but review the last few days. She hadn't been sure what to expect, but what she got certainly hadn't been it. The last few days had been busy, emotional and tiring. The work had been enjoyable. Staying out of Cade's way had been stressful.

Being around Cade had created a flutter of nerves but by the time the end of the week rolled around, they had settled into him firmly in his area and her in hers. Until this evening. The only time they had mixed was when there was a patient. Then they moved as a well-oiled machine doing what was necessary for quality care. She'd come to trust him.

She had seen twisted ankles, bug bites, sunburn, dysentery and the list of small issues went on. It was refreshing after working in a metropolitan ER with drug overdoses, car wreck victims and gunshot injuries. With each problem Cade had been a compassionate and caring doctor. She hadn't seen him with patients before. After spending a week working side by side, she had been impressed with his skills.

Lily learned to appreciate Ben's skills as well. She depended on him to do his part. She wouldn't have said he was the sharpest tech in the package, but he was eager and gentle and thoughtful. She spent her lunch breaks hanging out with Ben. More than once, she'd caught Cade watching them.

Lamar had stopped in a few times. He would ask everyone how things were going. Then he and Cade would move to the porch for half an hour. She assumed they were discussing how their students had progressed. She had no idea what marks Cade would give her for that week.

He had never given any serious praise or called out her or Ben for something special they had done. The most they got was a brisk nod. Yet by Lily's standards they were more than competent.

Her nerves had turned to worrying about the week ahead. She had to camp for three nights in a tent. She had no experience in that area.

The other students had planned to eat dinner that evening to discuss the week's activities. She had hoped to get some idea of what to expect from those who had returned from the wilderness. She'd missed out on that by having to cover the clinic. Desperate, she'd made a deal with Cade. One she could ill afford.

Finally, she placed her head on her arms and drifted off into sleep.

Startled awake by the knocking on the front door, Lily stumbled hurrying to the front door as she called, "I'm on my way. I'm coming."

She opened it to find a middle-aged couple standing under the yellow light with bugs swarming around it. The woman supported the man with an arm around his waist. He had his arm over her shoulder.

"Come in. Bring him back to an exam room." Lily led the way. "Tell me what's going on and when it started."

The man clutched his chest and leaned on his wife.

The woman spoke, "He started feeling bad about bedtime."

"What time was that?" Lily headed down the hall.

"Around eleven. We just thought he had a stomach bug. Then he woke thirty minutes ago complaining of his chest hurting."

In the examination room Lily helped the man to sit on the gurney stationed against the wall. "Have you taken any aspirin?"

"No."

Lily went to the cabinet, pulled out a bottle and shook out a few pills. Picking up a bottle of water, she handed both to the man. "Take these but don't drink any more water than necessary. You may need tests that require your stomach not to be full."

"It hurts to lay down. I feel like I want to throw up." The man placed his hand on his middle.

Lily grabbed a plastic pan. "Stay right there while I get the EKG machine." Lily hurried out of the room to storage. On the way she pulled out her phone and texted Cade. Possible heart attack.

She sure hoped Cade was right when he said he was still a light sleeper. That he would hear the ding of his phone. Her adrenaline ran high despite the number of times she had helped take care of these types of cases.

Lily rolled the portable EKG machine back to the examination room. She told the man, "I'm sorry but for this test you're going to need to lay down." She helped position the man on the gurney.

She attached the leads to his chest and his side. Returning to the machine, she pushed the button to run the test. Soon the paper tape printed. She gave it a look. Thank goodness the test looked normal.

"What do we have going on here?" Cade's voice, rusty with sleep, came from behind her.

Relief washed over her to have him there to back her up with a man in possible cardiac arrest. She glanced at him. His hair was tussled. A dark shadow covered his jaw. He wore a Chicago Cubs T-shirt that had seen better days, and jeans that looked like they might be his favorite. The man had never looked sexier.

"This gentleman is complaining of chest pain." She handed him the EKG strip and returned her attention to taking the man's blood pressure.

Cade's attention turned to the man. "I'm Dr. Evans. Can we get you to sit up? I'd like to give you a good listening to."

The man nodded and Cade helped him to a seated position. Cade pulled his stethoscope from his back pocket. He placed the ear tips in his ears and the bell on the man's chest. Finished, he looked at the man. "Mr....?"

"Bishop. Henry Bishop."

"Mr. Bishop, your heart sounds fine." He glanced at Lily. "His BP?"

"Within normal limits."

Cade looked at the man. "And your blood pressure is normal. Your EKG looks good." Cade wrapped his stethoscope around his neck. "So could you tell me what you had for dinner last night?"

Mr. Bishop looked perplexed.

The woman with him said, "Some type of Italian dish."

"Yep, that's it," Mr. Bishop confirmed.

Cade met Lily's look. With a nod he returned to Mr. Bishop. "There's nothing to worry about. You have a good case of indigestion."

Lily turned to the cabinet behind her, removed a bottle of antiacids and poured a couple of large tablets into her palm. She handed them to the man. "All you need to do is chew these and stay away from spicy foods."

Mr. Bishop looked at Cade in disbelief while he rubbed his chest. "You mean that's all this is?"

Cade wrapped his stethoscope around his neck. "Hey, this is a good thing. Much better than being in cardiac arrest. Especially this far from a hospital."

The woman took his hand. "Come on, honey. I believe we've had enough excitement for tonight. I know I have. Let's let these nice people get back to bed."

Lily followed the couple to the front door. As they exited she said, "Come back if you need us."

She returned to the exam room. Cade was already in the process of making it ready for the next patient. "Sorry I woke you for that."

Cade faced her. "You were told to."

"That didn't make my powers of discernment look very sharp."

"Hey, a heart attack isn't anything to play with. You did the right thing. This program is about improving emergency thinking, not about putting patients at risk."

Irritation welled in her. She pushed it down. "I know that."

"Look, you're doing fine. Don't worry about it all the time. Now I'm going to see about getting another couple of hours of sleep. See you later." Cade headed toward the back door.

Lily locked up then settled into the squeaky chair once more. Cade might think she shouldn't be worried but that didn't mean she could turn it off. She needed next week to go well.

The next morning, she greeted Jeff when he entered the clinic. "Good morning."

Cade called her name as he entered. She followed him to his office. He sat at his desk behind the computer. "You can take the day off."

"Thanks. Sitting up in a chair all night leaves a lot to be desired."

His eyes twinkled. "You just wait until you're sleeping on the ground."

"Uh...about that. I've been thinking I need to start getting my supplies together today." She hated to ask but what choice did she have. "Will you help me? I promise to be a model student." She looked directly at him. "After all, you owe me."

The shot hit its mark. "Turning to blackmail now."

She grinned. "Isn't this program about using what you've got? Thinking on your feet?"

Cade lowered his head, shaking it. She always had a way of twisting him so she got her way.

She moved close enough he could smell the apple scent of her shampoo. "Come on. Help me get supplies together."

"If I do this you promise to forgive me and not bring up—"

"Leaving me at the altar?"

"Yeah. That. Ever again."

"Agreed."

The eagerness in her eyes convinced him. This Lily

was a new, improved one. Cade liked the change. He sighed. His vow to keep her at a distance had become more difficult than he had expected. He gave another audible sigh. "Come to my place at seven tonight. We'll go through my supplies and see what you need to buy."

Cade held the screen door open to his cabin. He should have never agreed to spend this much time with Lily. Yet he had and he would follow through.

"Thanks for doing this. I'm really nervous about this camping business."

Lily talked quickly. That hadn't changed about her. When she got nervous she rattled on. The first time they made love she would have talked all the way through it if he hadn't kissed her as much as he did. Would she still chatter like that now? Wow, that was an idea he didn't need to spend more time on.

"Why are you so nervous?" Cade asked.

"You're really asking that?"

He shrugged. "Yeah, maybe that was a silly question. I'll pull my equipment out here. I'll get you a chair."

"Don't worry about that. I'll sit on the floor." With the grace of a ballerina, she crossed her legs and sank to the rug and crossed her legs at his feet. When he stood watching her, she looked up. "You going to get your stuff?"

"Uh…yeah." He walked to his room, returning with a large duffel bag and placing it on the floor beside her. "Unzip it and start pulling things out."

He brought over a chair from the dining table and set it across from her.

Lily already had items in a semicircle around her. "I have no idea what most of this is."

Cade chuckled. "I'm not surprised."

"When did you get into all this stuff?" She waved a hand over the camping equipment before her.

"You remember those summer camps Mom and Dad always sent me off to? I learned there." He had loved those weeks in the north Alabama mountains.

Her eyes were wide with interest. "But you never said anything about camping when you got home."

"I asked if our family could go a number of times, but Dad always put an end to that idea. He wasn't interested and said Mother would never survive it. I just never made a deal of it after that. After all, where was I going to go camping in metropolitan Chicago?"

She grinned. "Maybe the eighth hole of the country club."

His heart did a double thump. He still enjoyed Lily's humor. He smiled. "Yeah, that wouldn't have gone over."

Her attention returned to the supplies spread around her. "This is a lot of stuff. What of this do I need?"

"You'll need that bag over there." He pointed to the largest bag. "It's a tent." He pointed to another item. "Cooking pots."

The list went on until Lily said, "I don't know if I can carry all this." She gave him a sideways look as if unsure about what she planned to say. "I don't want to be completely inept out there. I can't afford to fail this course. I just can't."

"You'll do fine. Being creative and taking initiative in all surroundings is the point of my program."

"Your program?"

"Yes, I developed the program. I hope the parks service will decide to implement it in a number of the parks. The people who go through the program will staff the clinics."

"Impressive."

Cade's chest expanded. He liked the idea that he had moved up in her estimation. Being the mud on the bottom of her shoe didn't appeal to him.

Over the next thirty minutes he showed her how to pack. A number of times their hands brushed. Heat shot through him. A couple of times he saw Lily's hand shake as if she felt the electricity as well.

She set back on her heels. "What else do I need?"

"Food, a drinks bottle."

She stood then stretched. The sexy motions made his mouth go dry. "Then we shop at the Village Store for those."

"Okay." The word came out with a frog-sounding note.

"Then we have a plan."

She sounded more enthusiastic about the idea than he was.

"Dr. Evans, Dr. Evans!" Lily shouted, anxiousness in her voice.

Lily's tone and the commotion in the waiting area the next day had Cade flipping off his computer and shoving his chair back to hurry out of his office. He found Lily supporting a woman doubled over in pain. Meghan followed close behind.

"Get her into an exam room."

Lily continued to support the woman as she half led, half pulled her into the nearest exam room.

Cade walked in right behind them. The woman looked as if she was in her thirties and in good health. "Lily, what's the problem?"

She helped the obviously weak woman onto the table.

The woman immediately curled into herself and groaned. At her gagging sound Meghan thrust a bowl in her direction.

Lily rubbed the woman's shoulder.

"What happened?" Cade pulled his stethoscope from his neck.

"I found her in the meadow doubled over vomiting. I hardly made it here with her."

Cade turned to the woman. "Are you allergic to anything?"

The woman shook her head.

"We're going to help you but I'm going to need to listen to your heart and lungs."

The woman groaned and clenched her middle but nodded.

Cade adjusted the earpieces to his stethoscope and placed the bell on the woman's back then moved around to her chest.

Lily took her blood pressure.

He placed his stethoscope around his neck. "She sounds fine."

"BP is high but no more than it should be with her this ill." Lily looked at him as if waiting for an answer.

"Ma'am, can you lie back? I'm going to need to examine your middle."

Meghan helped the woman to stretch out.

Cade watched as the woman tightened her jaw and her hands drew into fists. "I'll be as quick as I can." He carefully palpated her middle. It was tender and distended but all organs were as they should be. The woman's problem remained localized to her stomach.

"Have you eaten anything unusual? Something you've never had?"

The woman drew back into a ball. She grunted. "No."

He looked at Lily. "We need to get some blood drawn to start ruling things out."

Lily turned to the cabinet and started pulling out supplies. She then went about applying the tourniquet and briskly put in an IV line.

As she worked, he checked the woman's glands in her neck, looked at her throat and eyes. Still, he was no closer to an idea of what was wrong.

Lily took tubes of blood for testing then organized for their patient to receive fluid. Minutes later Lily headed out the door to the lab.

Cade's lips drew into a line. He needed to figure out what was wrong. The woman was still in pain.

Meghan placed a wet cloth on the patient's head.

He needed more information. Something. The key to the problem. The woman was in so much pain he could hardly understand the few words she uttered. He stepped out into the hall. Maybe Lily could make it clearer, give him more details. Anything that might help.

She stopped beside him with a questioning look in her eyes.

"Will you tell me a little more about finding this woman? I'm at a loss as to what brought on such abdominal pain without something more presenting itself."

Lily looked off as if visualizing the time in her mind. "She was standing in the middle of the path doubled over."

"There was no one with her?"

Lily pursed her lips and shook her head. "Not that I saw, and she didn't mention anyone, but we didn't talk much on the way here. I was more focused on getting her help."

"Think. Was there anything unusual on her, around her, about her?"

Lily glared. "I am thinking. I saw her from a distance. Saw her double over. I ran to her. She was holding her middle. Groaning and crying. Others stopped. When they saw I was helping they moved on."

Cade sighed, shook his head.

Lily was quiet for a moment. "Come to think of it she dropped something."

"Did you or someone else pick it up?"

Lily shook her head. "Uh...no. It scattered. As if it fell apart."

"Did you see anything when you got to the woman?"

"I was really watching her more than the ground. But I remember for a moment I thought of a wedding. Where the bride is showered by flower petals."

His stomach tightened. Like the ones that hadn't been for her. What might be going on with the woman was becoming clearer. "Can you remember what they looked like?"

"I saw a few on the ground here. Maybe white. No, they were a pale yellow. I've noticed them growing around here when I walk from my cabin over here. Pretty flowers."

"Bingo." He grabbed her, kissed her forehead and released her before hurrying into the exam room.

To the woman he said, "Ma'am, did you pick any of the yellow flowers with thin, waxy leaves that grow wild?"

She nodded.

"Oleander is toxic. Apparently more so for you for them to make you so violently ill so quickly." He didn't even have to look back to know that Lily had entered behind him. "Lily, we'll need to start cardiac protocol. We need to give her activated charcoal and clear her stomach ASAP. Meghan, get oxygen in here in case we need it. After that, call for an ambulance. We need to get a chest X-ray and EKG as well."

Lily and Meghan were already moving before he finished.

When Meghan returned, he left to get the digoxin out of the medicine cabinet. Drawing it up, he returned to the patient and administered it. "We need to remove her clothes then wash her hands thoroughly. Wear rubber gloves. Take no chances on anything the flowers might have touched contacting your skin. May I see your hands, ma'am?"

The lady put out a palm. A rash had already developed.

"We plan on you feeling better soon. But I have to be honest, the plant you held is highly toxic. It can cause death. Some things are meant to be looked at, but not touched."

Lily returned. "Lily, you touched the patient and her clothes and you're going to need to shower and change your clothes right away. Throw what you are wearing away."

Her eyes narrowed. "Isn't that a little bit dramatic?"

"Even the smoke from oleander can be toxic. I can't take a chance you get sick too. Go take a shower at my place. I'll be up in a few minutes to find you something to wear."

"Let me at least help her remove her clothes since I have already touched her. Then Meghan can make sure she is clean."

"I'll agree to that, but it needs to be done now. While

you're doing that, I'll get the charcoal together and call in some help."

Lily headed to their patient. "I need you to sit up. I'm going to help you remove your clothes. We have to get rid of them."

Cade stepped out into the hall. His concern for Lily had rocketed when he'd realized Lily might have come in contact with the plant. The idea she might experience what the woman had made him sick.

Minutes later Lily exited the room. "She says her husband is at the Great Lodge. Meghan will try to contact him when she is finished."

"I wish visitors would take the signs to heart. They just don't understand how dangerous things they don't know about can be. Let's hope her breathing remains stable and she doesn't need a ventilator before the ambulance gets here."

"She's doing fine now. Let's don't borrow trouble."

"I'm trying not to. We're going to need to watch her and you closely. Now you need to get that shower. Ben is on his way in. You can find a plastic bag under the sink in the kitchen. Put your clothes in that. As soon as Ben gets here I'll be up to find you something to wear. Make sure to soap up and rinse twice."

Her mouth turned into a smirk. "Yes, Doctor."

Fifteen minutes later, just moments after Ben arrived, Cade took the steps two at a time up to his cabin. Entering, he could hear humming coming from the direction of the bath.

"Lily?" He received no answer. "Lily?" Still no answer. He hurried toward the bath with all types of harmful ideas in his head about why she wasn't answering.

Cade came to a jerking stop. The bath door was open.

Lily stood in front of the mirror with a towel wrapped under her arms covering her middle. A long length of shapely thighs and legs showed as steam swirled around her. A pink tint touched her cheeks. She had one arm up as she combed her hair back. Had he ever seen anything more beautiful?

"Lily, are you feeling okay?"

Her hand halted midstroke. Eyes wide, she looked at him. "I'm fine." She watched him a moment longer then hooked her foot around the edge of the door and closed it, removing herself from his view. "I need clothes."

Clothes. She needed clothes. Yes, she needed clothes. He would get those.

Going to his room, he dug around until he found sweatpants that could be taken up enough for her to wear safely. He then located a T-shirt and sweatshirt. Lightly knocking on the door, he said, "The clothes are on the floor outside the door. I'm headed back to the clinic."

Lily pulled on Cade's ill-fitting clothes, her shoes and headed back to the clinic. She had to admit his insistence that she shower and throw away her clothes had unnerved her, but she hadn't wanted to end up like their patient. That scared her more.

Almost as unnerving had been the look in Cade's eyes when she'd been combing her hair. She'd opened the door to let the steam out thinking she would hear him coming. That hadn't happened. How long had he been standing there staring at her? Surely not long.

Still that intense, all-consuming flicker of hunger held her spellbound. A zing of awareness shot through her. She had liked his attention. But she shouldn't have. She couldn't allow him the opening to hurt her again.

She entered the clinic. The woman had been moved to the overnight room across the hall. A man sat beside her. Cade stood outside the door typing on a tablet.

"How's she doing?"

"Fine so far. The ambulance is still a couple of hours out. I'll be here until they're gone."

He studied her a moment. "You aren't feeling any effects, are you?"

"No. Stop worrying."

"I'm just doing my job."

Lily lowered her chin and gave him a sidelong look. She wasn't sure there might not be more to it than that.

"You're going to need to be watched for the next twenty-four hours."

Cade's look told her there was no point in her arguing the point.

"You can stay here, or I can go home with you, or you can come to my cabin. You take your pick."

"I don't—"

"One of the three, Lily. You decide."

It was after midnight when Cade held the door open to his cabin for Lily to enter. So much for keeping her at a distance. Now she would be nestled in his home. To his surprise she had picked coming to his place as her resting place for what was left of the night. "Come in."

A determined look had formed on her face as she walked past him. Inside she turned to face him. "I want you to know I picked here to stay only because it would be the most comfortable for both of us. I'll be sleeping on the couch."

When he opened his mouth she raised a hand. "If you argue about it, I'm gone."

Cade clapped his jaw closed. He had no doubt she meant it.

"All I need is a pillow and a blanket. If you'll tell me where I can find those then I'll stay out of your way."

"I'll get them."

She nodded.

He went straight to his bedroom to pull a pillow off his bed and an extra blanket from the closet. Returning to the living area, he found Lily still standing in the middle of the floor. He handed Lily the blanket and pillow.

"Thank you. Good night, Cade."

"Good night." He was afraid to say more.

He decided he would be better off getting his shower and going to bed than arguing with her. He retrieved his pajama pants from his bedroom. Minutes later he paused on his way back to his room. The lights were off in the living area. He could just make out the form of Lily on the couch. She had his pillow clutched to her chest and her head turned to the side.

He had watched her like a hawk all evening, worried she might develop symptoms of poisoning. If she had become sick, he hadn't been sure he could hold it together. He had plans to get up regularly during the night to check on her.

Turning toward his room, he stopped when he heard his name. "Yes?"

"You were brilliant today. You saved that woman's life. Your father and brother would have been impressed. I was."

His chest tightened. Was she right? He liked to think his father would feel that way.

"Thanks, Lily. I couldn't have done it without you."

"Hey, Cade."

"Yeah?"

"Don't wake me up when you check on me."

He chuckled. "I'll try not to."

Lily had woken each time Cade had checked on her, which had been often. She wasn't sure he had even slept. At the first ray of sunlight through the kitchen window she had been up. She folded the blanket, put it on the sofa and placed the pillow on top of it. The pillow smelled of Cade, which was just what she hadn't needed.

She quietly let herself out of the cabin and walked to her place. There she would find real sleep. Cade hadn't shown up on her doorstep during the day. To her surprise and disappointment. The last she had tried not to feel. It had been too easy to have him in her life again. She needed some time away from him. Apparently, he felt the same. She would spent Sunday alone.

But at noon she received a text from Lamar saying that there would be a mandatory meeting that afternoon at the clinic.

That's where she was currently. Sitting in a rocker on the back porch of the clinic along with all the others in the program. Only Cade wasn't there. The fact it bothered her made her angry. She missed him.

"I want to give out this week's assignments."

Lily half listened until her name was mentioned.

"You and Ben will be going out on your short hike with Cade tomorrow afternoon. I have a meeting that has come up that I can't miss. Cade has agreed to use his day off to give you an introduction to the outdoors. He'll contact you and let you know where to meet him."

That evening she received a text telling her to meet him at the Village Store at opening time. She was there waiting on him when he arrived. He showed her what to buy and not buy before she purchased the supplies she needed. All the while Cade imparted advice. After getting what she needed they had headed for his cabin.

There Cade had made her pack and repack her backpack, insisting she tuck every space with some type of supply. Cade had even instructed her in the type of clothing required. She needed to dress in layers with a T-shirt beneath a long-sleeve lightweight shirt, cargo pants or jeans, thick socks and boots. He said she needed a hat. When she told him she didn't have one he provided her with a baseball cap.

They were on their way to meet Ben at the clinic when she said, "I'm still not too sure about this."

"Stop worrying. Our hike shouldn't be a big deal. We'll be back before dark."

CHAPTER FOUR

Hours later, Lily called, "Cade, how much farther?"

"Another couple of miles. I have a view I want to show you."

"I think the view is good here." She wanted to stop. The hiking was fine. Carrying equipment became old quickly.

It was Monday afternoon, and Lily had seen more of Cade's bottom than she had the entire time they were growing up. Not that it wasn't a fine butt encased in tan cargo pants, but she had been following him for hours as they weaved and climbed up and around a mountain.

Her feet were aching and her shoulders as well. She lifted the pack with her hands, adjusting it on her back. What would it be like for her when she had to carry everything? Cade had her sleeping bag and tent. He had insisted that she needed to get a feel for carrying a pack even if they weren't spending the night out.

She did appreciate the hat. She had pulled her hair through the opening in the back. Her hair being up had helped with the heat.

"How are you doing back there?" He glanced at her.

"Well, if you subtract the throbbing of my feet, the burning in my heels, the building of blisters, aching thighs and shoulders hurting from carrying stuff, I'd say I'm about one hundred percent."

Cade chuckled. "That good, huh?"

"I hate to sound like a child in the back seat of a car but how much farther?"

"Try not to think about it and enjoy the sky. Listen for the waterfall. See if you can find an animal."

She drew up her features into an ugly face. "I wish Ben was here. At least we could double-team you."

Ben hadn't been waiting on them when they arrived at the clinic. There had been an emergency in his family, and he had already left Yosemite. Lily hated he hadn't gotten to finish the program. Now it was her and Cade again. Just her luck. The more she tried to stay away from him, the more she was left alone with him.

Her head swiveled with a sudden thought. "We aren't going to see bears, are we?"

"We're in the woods. This is where they live. But we'll be fine. We'll just stay out of their way."

"You can bet I will." A note of hysteria edged her voice.

"Lily, I'm not going to let anything happen to you."

Lily believed him. Despite their past she never doubted he would see to her safety.

They climbed over granite rock, crossed fields and hiked under stands of trees. When she had difficulty Cade reached back and took her hand, helping her up. She followed him between narrow spaces involving rocks and trees. A few small animals scurried off the path into a hole in the ground beneath the pine needles. Still, they trudged on.

She looked behind her. Her breath caught. They had

climbed high enough she could see the entire valley floor. "Amazing."

"It is." Cade came to stand beside her.

"So beautiful." Her words were but a whisper.

"Sure is."

A note in his voice had her turning to look. Her gaze met his. A tingle of warmth went through her. He hadn't been looking at the scenery. Her heart fluttered at his admiration.

Her attention returned to the valley. "I can't believe how far we have come."

"I wish we could stay here longer but we're going to run out of daylight if we don't get moving."

She followed. "Is this what it'll be like on the camping trip?"

"Yes."

Lily's lips went into a thin line. She had wanted to stretch herself and she was certainly doing so now.

"The program is supposed to teach self-sufficiency. How to handle emergencies without modern equipment, using only what you have."

"Where does Lamar fit into the program other than the obvious?"

"He works for the parks department. I don't. I get more support by going through him."

"You should take ownership. I remember you suggested to your father something that would made the clinic more efficient. Then he gave your brother, Mike, the credit. I spoke up for you when it was mentioned after you had gone. You didn't deserve not to get the credit."

Cade jerked to a stop. He studied her. A warmth filled his eyes. "Thank you, Lily. That might be the nicest thing anyone has done for me. I had forgotten how supportive you could be."

She smiled and nodded. "You are welcome."

Cade watched her for a few moments longer then said, "Come on. We're almost ready to head down."

As they went the sky darkened. Lily noticed Cade looking up more than once as if he were studying the gathering clouds. At a roll of thunder he said over his shoulder, "You know those heavy supplies you've been complaining about? I think you are going to be glad we have them."

"It's going to rain on us, isn't it?" Dark clouds were building.

"I'm afraid so. We need to find a place to hole up."

Thirty minutes later Cade announced, "This is our home for the night."

Lily lowered the pack from her shoulders with a relieved sigh. She surveyed the small open area with a circle of rocks in the middle. "Here?"

Cade lowered his backpack. "Yep. This is as good as it gets."

She gave the space another look. "Nothing like the Ritz."

The difference in their lifestyles slammed into Cade once again. Her life he had left behind. "I like that you still have a sense of humor, Lily."

"Sometimes it's not that easy but you might as well make the most of things." Lily wandered around the firepit.

"I have learned that as well." Somehow being around Lily reminded him of the gulf that had grown between his father and him. Every time Cade had gotten the courage up to talk to his father about the future, his dad had interrupted to say how he was looking forward to Cade joining the family practice. That ended anything Cade might have said. The rift between father and son hurt his mother, who desperately wanted the chasm closed. Was something similar going on with Lily or worse?

"What's this circle of rock about?"

Yep. Their lifestyles couldn't be more different. "It's where we'll build the fire. Which we need to get on and putting up the tent. Otherwise, we will be doing them in the pouring rain."

Cade had to give it to Lily; at least she was willing to listen and learn.

"What do we do first?" She walked back to her pack.

"Normally it would be start a fire, but we should get some shelter up. We are going to need it sooner rather than later but before I do that let me call the clinic to let them know where we are and that we won't make it back in until tomorrow."

"What can I do while you do that to get started on setting up camp?" She vibrated with enthusiasm.

Could he make her do the same when he touched her? Those thoughts should be shoved in a drawer, and it closed. He'd had his chance. "Bring the tent over here."

While she went after the bag, he stepped well away from the fire checking the ground for rocks as he walked around the area. "This looks like a good spot."

Lily joined him with bag in hand. "There's only one tent."

"Yes."

He said, matter-of-factly, "Yep. That's all I had. The Village Store doesn't sell them."

She gave the nylon bag an unsure look. "It'll hold both of us?"

It wasn't the ideal situation for him either, but it was the way it was. "I'm not going to jump you or anything. By morning you may be glad to have my body warmth. It can get pretty cool out here this time of year. Especially after a rain."

"We're both going to be in it."

"It gets bigger." He worked to hide a grin.

"I hope so." She didn't sound reassured.

Thunder rolled louder. "I'll show you how to put it up. If we don't hurry, we'll be wet."

While Liz unzipped the bag and removed the items he made his phone call She looked at him from where she had tent parts spread around her. "Now what?"

"Lay the blue tarp on the ground here." He moved his foot in a semicircle. "I've already checked for rocks."

"I can see where sleeping on rocks wouldn't be ideal."

Cade couldn't help but be impressed with Lily's attitude. From the look on her face, this wasn't what she considered a good time, but she made no complaints despite having been pampered her entire life. She'd had anything she ever wanted. Her days had consisted of lying by the pool and shopping. He'd never thought she would become a woman with a will of iron.

He'd been so absorbed in his growing unhappiness he hadn't seen the real Lily. He'd assumed like everybody else she would always take the easy way out. She'd made a mistake in being in this program, but she had dug in and done what was necessary to pass it.

A drop of rain hit his cheek. "We need to move faster. Now we need to put the poles in. They just slide into each other, creating a long, flexible line. We need to feed them through the loops."

Not soon enough to beat the rain they had the poles in position.

"Get the supplies and put them in the tent while I put in the corner pins that will hold the tent down if the wind picks up."

Lily hurried to do as he instructed.

Cade removed the fold-up shovel from his pack.

On her second trip out of the tent she asked, "What are you doing now?"

"I'm making a swallow ditch around the tent to get water to flow away from us. Now get inside. We don't both need to be wet."

It had started pouring by the time Cade pushed the tent flaps back and crawled in the tent.

Lily sat among their supplies looking unsure. She moved into action when she saw him.

"You're soaking." She grabbed her pack and found the small towel he'd told her to pack.

When she handed it to him, he took it. "Thanks."

"What now?"

He looked at her. "We wait."

"Wait?" Her forehead wrinkled.

"Until it quits raining."

She looked around. "In here?"

Cade grinned as he looked through his pack for a dry shirt. "Yep." He unbuttoned his shirt.

"What're you doing?" There was a high note in her voice.

His look met hers. "I'm going to put on a dry shirt."

"Oh."

Cade removed his dripping shirt and threw it in the

corner. He didn't have to look at Lily to know she was watching him. Steam came from the heat generated between them. If she kept that up he would forget his promise to himself and reach for her. "Lily, stop."

"What am I doing?"

"If you keep looking at me like that, I may have to kiss you." He wouldn't. He'd already wronged her, and he refused to lead her on again. Still he enjoyed teasing her.

"Then put your shirt on."

He grinned as he pulled a fresh one on over his head. "That better?"

She nodded.

Neither of them said anything for long, awkward minutes. He needed to do something to defuse the uncomfortableness. "You were great with the tent. Well done."

"Thanks." Her eyes shone with pleasure.

She had removed her cap. Her golden mass of hair flowed over her shoulders. His finger itched to touch what he knew was pure silk. But he wouldn't.

Of course he had experienced other women since Lily, but none had ever affected him as she had. There had always been a special connection between them. It was still there, hovering, stronger and more vibrant than ever before. Conflicting emotions jolted him. They were real and honest, having to do with them instead of their families or what was expected of them. His were adult desire. Yet the specter of what he'd once done to her hung over them. He didn't dare make advances he didn't intend to honor.

"Now you're staring."

He waited until she met his gaze. "I want you to know I never doubted your abilities before, or now, if you put your mind to something."

Moments went by before she said softly, "Then you

should have trusted me enough to tell me how you were feeling."

Her words were a kick in the chest. "It had more to do with my faith in me than my faith in you."

Lily needed out of this too-small tent. Away from the too-compelling Cade. She licked her dry lips. This closeness was more than she had been prepared for. He seemed to surround her. Seep past her defenses. "When do you think the rain will stop?"

He leaned his head to the side as if listening. "I think it's easing up now. Maybe not too much longer. How do you like Yosemite so far?"

If she couldn't get out of here she needed to keep talking so she wouldn't think about other things she could be doing with Cade.

"After my surprise wore off, I find I really like it. I love the canyon, the waterfall, the cozy feeling of it all. I especially like seeing all the stars. You seem to be very comfortable here."

He looked around. "I am certainly more at home here than I ever was in Chicago."

"So how did you end up working in Yosemite?"

"This isn't the first national park I've worked in. After I left Chicago, I went to work for Veterans' Administration in the emergency department. When a position came open in Arizona with the Indian Health Service I moved there. That was an interesting experience. Nothing and I mean nothing there resembled the way we grew up. It was a humbling experience. I saw kids who should have had care a long time before they did and the old going gracefully into their final horizon. I learned a lot about the Native Americans and even more about myself."

"And you left?" The man amazed her. He wasn't what she thought.

"I was sent an email saying this position was open, requesting I apply. I got the job and joined the US Health Services."

Cade held her complete attention. "I don't know if I've ever heard of them. What do they do?"

"They're actually a branch of the armed forces."

"Military? You never said anything about wanting to join the military."

"It's a little-known branch. There are seven branches—Army, Navy, Air Force, Marines, Coast Guard, Space Force and me—the US Health Services."

"Impressive. And now I'm smarter." She fingered the latch on her backpack then continued, "Oddly I can see the appeal for you. You've had a chance to do something different. You couldn't have done anything more different than your father and brother and still remain in medicine. I get it now." She gave him a pensive look. "I wish I had listened. Really listened. I was so caught up in wedding plans and thoughts of our perfect life I didn't want to hear what you were trying to tell me. I hate you were so unhappy. And I hate I couldn't see it for my own selfish reasons."

Cade didn't say anything for a moment, but she could tell by the thoughtful look on his face that he wanted to. "In truth I was so caught up in the misery of my family, so angry with my father I had to escape. We may look alike but we're very different in other ways. I blew up everything. Just to get away."

"That included me."

He touched her arm. "Unfortunately, yes. I'll be forever sorry."

"That's under the bridge now. You've got your life. I've got mine." She gave him a direct look. "But you should've asked me what I wanted back then."

"I know. The problem was that other than I wanted out I didn't know what *I* wanted. I couldn't drag you into that."

Was he trying to justify his mistake or was there more? "We could have figured it out together, but you didn't leave it where I could be involved. You made all the decisions."

"I'm sorry. I know I can't say that enough."

"I may be putting more on you than you deserve. You may be right about me not being able to handle the changes you needed to make. I can't say back then I would have agreed to move to a place like this. I liked my comfortable life."

"That was natural. You felt safe there. I would've been asking for you to turn your life upside down. And on the spur of the moment. With no warning. I'm not surprised by the way you reacted."

"But if I had listened… Really listened. I'm still not sure you could have convinced me that leaving was the thing to do. I have to take some responsibility for what happened. I'm sure I didn't help matters."

Still she hadn't liked being left. She promised herself she wouldn't put herself in a position for that to happen again. Once had been devastating enough. She wouldn't let anyone get close enough for them to have that much power over her feelings. In a twisted way Cade had been controlling her life since he had left her.

She wouldn't let him make it worse by letting their attraction pull her to him. They could remain professional even in this intimate setting. "I'm sorry I brought it up. I promised myself and I told you we would move on. That's what we need to do."

"You were great on the hike today."

"Thanks. I know you didn't have high hopes for me."

She'd had less for herself. With every step she took she'd thought, *I wish those nurses could see me now. What do they know?*

"I didn't say that." Cade met her gaze, his eyes warm with a twinkle.

"Thanks. I wasn't too sure about me either. You know I've found out doing things that you might not think you can is good for you." Like her maybe giving up the bitterness over the past. Her parents, or half brother and sister-in-law, loved her. She never doubted that. What they had done had been from a place of caring. She needed to give that idea more thought.

Cade grinned when Lily's stomach rumbled. "Perfect timing. The rain has stopped and you're hungry. We'll get that fire built and have a hot dinner. Then get some rest."

She pointed to the floor of the tent. "We're staying here tonight?"

"Yep. It's too late to walk out tonight. Too easy to get lost. And evening is when the animals come out to feed. Better chance of running into them." He moved to the tent door.

"I don't want to do that." Her stomach made another rumble.

"Apparently the animals aren't the only ones looking for food."

"Funny man." She stepped out of the tent behind him. "How can I help move things along?"

"By gathering firewood. Which is going to have a degree of difficulty since others have been here ahead of us and it rained We'll need to spread out to find enough."

"Am I supposed to carry it in something?" She looked around as if a carrier might appear.

He chuckled. She needed more detailed instructions. "In your hands and arms."

"Oh." A contrite look came over Lily's face.

"Don't lose sight of the camp. Watch where you step." He pointed. "You go that way, and I'll go this. I won't be out of hearing distance."

He watched a moment while Lily tentatively stepped under the trees looking around her as if something or someone were planning to jump out at her. He headed in the other direction, checking on her often. He found Lily's eagerness endearing. She was giving it her best shot. How could he have underestimated her so all those years ago?

Soon Cade returned with an armload of twigs and limbs. Lily came out of the woods with an armload as well. She unloaded it beside the rocks next to his pile. He squatted next to the circle and placed twigs together.

She laid a twig over his. Their hands brushed. A zip of desire shot through him. He was too conscious of Lily being close. Yet he found it a personal victory when she didn't jerk away.

He went to the tent and pulled his and her backpack out. Unzipping a small pouch, he removed a piece of wood in a plastic bag. "This is lighter wood." He put a lighter to it and soon the twigs were burning. "Lily, add some wood. We need to get it to dry so it will burn. We have dinner to cook."

Lily's brows went almost to her hairline. "We're going to cook our dinner over the fire?"

"Yes. What did you think we were going to do?"

"I guess—" she shrugged, lifting one corner of her mouth "—eat it out of a package."

He grinned. "I like a hot meal when I can get it. Especially after a rain. It will get cold tonight."

Cade stood and offered her a hand. She took it without hesitation. It felt good to touch her again. For her to trust him.

"I'm starting to have fun. What's next?" Her voice held eagerness.

"I'll show you how to use a cook fire."

Her shoulders squared with confidence. "I can do that."

Cade grinned. "I'm sure you can." Going to his pack, he removed their food for the evening along with a stackable pots-and-pans kit.

"That's rather ingenious, isn't it?"

He glanced at her with a quirk of his mouth. "It is."

"It makes it easier to carry and you've got everything you need."

"Not everything." He couldn't have her. Did he need her? He feared he so easily could. "It's just big enough for the two of us." Somehow that sounded more personal than it should have.

"I'm glad. I would have hated for you to be left out."

Cade chuckled. He had missed her wit. Had forgotten how much it lightened his day. "As always you're so funny."

She grinned. "I like to think so. What's for supper? A recipe from the Cordon Bleu?"

Cade pulled four packages out of her pack. "No. Something less dramatic. It's in these packages." He held them up. "The nice thing about these is they don't require more than warming them up. Aren't you glad I insisted you practice carrying your pack? We would be hungry and really wet if we hadn't brought the stuff with us."

"I've just started to wonder if you planned this."

He looked at her. "Lily, I wouldn't do that to you."

"I was just wondering if you were trying to prove a point." She added a piece of wood to the fire.

"And that would be?"

"That you had been right. That I couldn't cut it living in a place like this."

"You have already proven me wrong on that. More than once."

Her shoulders rose. She stood straighter with her chin high. "I have, haven't I?"

"Yes, you have."

Lily wrinkled her nose and twisted her lips looking at the food in his hand. "Will it be any good?"

"Everything is good when you're hungry enough."

She moved around to the other side of the fire. "You have a point there. I've lived off vending machine food for three days before."

"I think you'll be pleasantly surprised at how tasty tonight's meal will be." Cade cut the corner of the package with his multipurpose tool then squeezed the contents into a pot. After spreading out the coals of the fire using a stick, he set the pot on them.

"While I watch the food, how about you seeing to spreading out our bedding? Put one of the silver blankets on the floor and then the sleeping bags on top of it. The other we'll use over the top."

His mouth went dry as he watched her sweet butt swing back and forth as she crawled into the tent. Yeah, that he didn't need to get fixated on. He could remember too clearly his hormones jumping when he watched her walk around the pool in her hot pink bikini bottom years ago. He liked her fuller, more mature body almost as much in her jeans.

From the tent Lily called, "What's so special about the noisy silver blankets?"

"They were invented for use in space. They're light, keep heat in, rain retardant and fold into a small package. They're a must-have while camping in this area. Zip up the door on the way out. We don't want any unwelcome visitors to join us while we're eating. Supper is almost ready."

She returned to the fire.

"Will you get the plates out of my pack?"

"Wow. They are so compact. I love it."

Cade chuckled. He liked her excitement over a new discovery. "The utensils are inside. Don't drop them. Come on. This is ready. Hand me a plate."

"What are we having?"

"Beef stroganoff and peas. Oh, yeah, and there's a biscuit." He pulled a plastic bag from the bottom side pocket of his pants. "These came from the Village Store."

"All the comforts of home." She took one from him.

They stood with their backs to the fire eating.

Her look flashed to him. "This isn't half-bad. I'm glad you like it."

She studied him as if he were an alien. "Who are you? I had no idea you liked this sort of thing so much."

"Some of it I developed after I left Chicago."

Lily shook her head. "I never knew you to cook in a kitchen."

"Never had to. We had a cook."

"That's true. Still, why did you keep that side of you from me? Did you think I would make fun of you?"

"I thought about taking you camping once but you seemed to prefer having your nails done. Or wearing the latest fashion. I just didn't think it would be your thing. So, I just didn't mention it to you."

"You know you can be more than one type of person when you need to be. Now that I think about it you always liked to go to the park, find some natural area and sit."

"But there weren't many of our dates where we could do that. We were always expected to be at the country club for some event. We were told what we were supposed to be doing. In fact, I was always told what my life would look like."

"Was it really that bad? I thought you liked going to the club."

He had her complete attention. "I liked doing anything with you. What I didn't like was being told to do so."

"Like playing golf? You didn't necessarily play—you just liked to walk the course."

"I liked being outside. Even if it had to be on a golf course."

Lily remembered he'd often suggested they take a long walk. She'd always agreed because she enjoyed his company anytime and anywhere. With her meal finished, Lily said, "What do we do about cleaning the pots and plates? And I need to wash up some too before I go to bed."

"We'll go to the river. We must carry out garbage including food scraps. We'll put them in this plastic bag so the bears won't be tempted."

"The bears can be that aggressive?"

"If they smell food they can be. We need to make sure they aren't."

He said it as if it were no big deal. The idea of seeing

a bear terrified her. "I think that's a good plan. What do I need to do to help?"

"Get the garbage together in one bag. I'll get the other food out of my backpack too. We'll close it all up in the bear box."

"Bear box?"

He pointed to the green metal box mounted on a pole near the tree line.

"I wondered what that was. How does this work?"

"The idea is that the box is strong enough to withstand a bear getting into it, but I've seen a bear be pretty aggressive when food is involved." He placed what they had into the box and securely shut it.

"Got it. Now for the dishes and a soak of my feet."

Cade carried their packs to the tent and returned with his towel. He checked the fire before saying, "Come on. I'll show you the prettiest little creek."

Lily ducked under the limb Cade held for her along the path. She had to admit she was having a good time. Being with Cade was fun. She'd missed him more than she had allowed herself to admit.

She feared she would have a difficult time leaving him after finding him again. Did he feel the same way? If he did, would he say so?

Why couldn't people tell her what she needed to hear? What was it about her that made them want to keep things from her? First Cade about his feelings of feeling trapped and now her parents about who she really was. Didn't they believe she was strong enough to handle the truth?

CHAPTER FIVE

CADE WATCHED LILY ahead of him and shook his head. Being around Lily's infectious personality had made it more difficult for him to keep his distance.

That didn't make him feel any better. He had no idea how much he'd missed her until she had returned to his life. Lily had developed into an enhanced person of who she had been. A better, improved and more enticing Lily.

"Who made this nice path?"

Cade took the lead again. "The animals. The forest service does some maintaining but mostly they like to leave things as natural as possible."

They reached a spot where water rushed over and around rocks. It was wide and not deep. A small pool had formed on their side of the creek.

"What a nice place. Lovely." Lily looked around at the unspoiled area. It was one of his favorites in the park.

Cade watched her. The spot wasn't the only thing that filled him with pleasure.

"Hand me those pots. I'll do the cleaning since you did the cooking. It's only fair." She reached out a hand.

Her fingers brushed his as he handed the pots to her. Warmth filled him. He shouldn't have had such a reaction. Nothing had really changed between them. She lived in a big-city world, and he lived thousands of miles away from that.

Lily scooped a pot across the water. "Eek, this is freezing."

Cade laughed. "The water is from the snow runoff. I didn't think to tell you. Now I'm kind of glad I didn't. Can you make that sound again?"

She smirked. "Where's the soap?"

"No soap. You can't use anything like that in the water. Scoop gravel or sand from the riverbed or along the bank and use it to scrub them. Then rinse. Just do the best you can. I'll wash them well when we get home."

"That won't do much good for my manicure." She fanned her fingers out on one hand and studied them. She shrugged. "I never was as into that as my friends were. I mostly went along to be sociable."

Lily continued to wash. "Have you ever thought that some of what you had in Chicago wasn't all bad?"

He swallowed. "You weren't bad."

"Thanks for that." She handed him a pot. "Here you go. All clean. Next one."

He took the pot and handed her the towel.

"What's this for?"

"You said you wanted to clean up some. Use your hand to splash your face and wash your hands then dry off with the towel."

Her head pulled back and looked at him in horror. "Using this freezing-cold water? Is that what you call cleaning up?"

"Lily, I thought you had a sense of adventure." He grinned.

She glared. "Okay, I'll do it your way. Hang on to the towel." She cupped her hand and splashed water on her face. Shivering, she did it again then ran her hands over her face.

He stood watching like a lovesick teen. Something he wasn't any longer.

Lily reached behind her. He placed the towel in her hand. She wiped her face and stood. "Satisfied."

Cade chuckled. This was more fun than he'd had in a long time. He rested his butt on his heels. With his eyes closed he lifted the water in his cupped hands. Before he could splash his face a wave of freezing water hit him in the face and shoulder. He jerked to a standing position.

A gust of laughter filled the air. He looked at Lily to find her doubled over holding her waist. Her eyes glistened with mirth.

"You should have seen your face." Again, she went into peals of laughter.

He glared. "That was cold."

"Yeah, that'll show you not to make fun of me."

"I'm sorry." He didn't even try to sound sincere. Cade grabbed her and brought her hard against him. "That'll show you to be splashing me. Now you'll be wet too."

It didn't take him more than a second to realize he'd messed up. Bringing Lily's soft, pliable, warm body against his wasn't wise. He wanted more of her.

Lily studied him with wonder in her eyes.

"Lily, I've missed you."

"I've missed you too." She didn't move.

Cade lowered his head. His lips lightly brushed hers. They were sweeter than he remembered. He found the right spot and pressed harder. His arms tightened. The beat of his heart that had been missing had joined in once more.

Seconds later she pushed him away shaking her head.

"As nice as that was, I don't think it's a good idea. I can't handle whatever this is—" she pointed at him then her "—right now."

Disappointment flooded him. His arms dropped to his sides. "I'm sorry. I couldn't resist…"

Her eyes avoided his look. "I think it's best we keep things between us professional. I'm here for instruction and you're the instructor."

Cade watched her a moment. He didn't miss the slight tremble of her hand at she pushed at her hair. Had she been as affected by their kiss as he had? He cleared his throat. "We should get back to camp. It'll be dark soon."

They retraced their steps. Neither of them said anything.

Was she playing with him? Why would she? Or had he misread Lily's signals?

Fifteen minutes later they were back in camp.

"We need to secure everything for the night."

Lily turned. "What do we have to do?"

"Bank the fire, double-check the bear box, make sure all supplies are stored in the tent. Get our flashlights and put them where we can easily find them," he said, rattling off the list.

"Do you mind showing me how to bank the fire?" She followed him to where the coals glowed.

He picked up the shovel. "I'm sorry. I should have had you watch me a while ago. I just made an assumption—"

"That I know what's going on."

"Yes, I realize you're out of your element." He pushed the coals up into a neat pile but added no more wood.

"Up until this past week I would've said you were out of yours."

Fifteen minutes later in the tent Lily moved and the thermal blankets crinkled again.

"If you keep rolling around over there, we're never going to get any sleep."

Cade had climbed into his bag. She moved hers as far away from him as the wall of the tent would allow. After that sweet, stomach-fluttering kiss at the creek she didn't think being close to Cade would be a smart idea.

He had said it would get cold that night despite how warm it had been in the day, so at least she wouldn't freeze with her bag around her. He had removed all his clothing but his underwear before he had wiggled into his bag.

When she'd made a comment he said, "When you get out of a warm bed and put on your clothes, you're warmer than getting out of the bed with your clothes already on."

"Thanks, but no thanks for me. I'll just keep my clothes on." She wasn't prepared to strip for Cade even though he had seen her naked. This was different.

"Suit yourself." She'd turned her back and taken special pains to adjust her bag. It hadn't helped. All she could think of was his sexy body just an arm's length away. She was hyperconscious of each of Cade's movements, his breathing. Her entire body vibrated with awareness. It was so thick it could have become a physical thing. She shifted again.

With a resigned huff, Cade turned his back to her.

Using the crook of her arm as a pillow, Lily worked not to move. Her inability to find rest was made more irritating by the fact Cade softly snored. After what seemed like hours she finally fell into an exhausted sleep.

She woke with her teeth chattering and her body curled into a tight ball.

A deep voice said in the darkness, "Get over here. I'm not going to let you develop hypothermia out of stubbornness." Cade's arm roped her waist and brought her against his chest. "You can stay in your sleeping bag if you want, or we can put one below us and the other on top and be really warm."

"I'm never going to be warm again." She huddled against him shaking.

Cade unzipped both bags and spread his beneath them. He pulled her against his deliciously heated chest then pulled her open sleeping bag over them and the thermal blanket as well. He tucked it all in around them.

Lily nestled against Cade, his arms around her, and quaked.

"Shh, it's all right. You'll be warm soon."

His hands ran up and down her back over and over again. Lily clung to him, absorbing his warmth, his scent. His arms tightened. His chin rested on top of her head and he entwined his legs with hers. Lily buried her head in his shoulder. Slowly the chills decreased, and she snuggled into her warm cocoon and drifted off to sleep.

Lily woke to a draft of cold air against her back. She shifted into the warmth on the other side of her. Cade held her tight. His hand resting on the skin of her back between her shirt and the waistband of her jeans moved. The draft was gone.

"Mmm," she murmured against the heat of his bare chest. She was reaping the benefits of him removing his clothes. "You're so nice and warm."

"Thank you," he said softly.

"Is there a turn of weather like this all the time?"

His hand traveled over her shoulder and back, leaving

a hot path behind. "The weather in this part of the world can be unpredictable."

"That's an understatement."

His chuckle rumbled through his chest and rippled throughout her.

Lily liked the effect too much. She ran a foot along his leg. "Thanks for sharing your warmth."

"My pleasure." Rough notes filled his voice.

Lily relaxed against him, saying nothing for a few moments. "Are you asleep?"

"No."

She paused a second. "I didn't tell you the whole truth about me being here."

"That came out of the blue." His words brushed the hair beside her ear.

"I don't like secrets. I want you to know the truth. I've told you about wanting the department supervising position. What I didn't tell you was I overheard two nurses talking. One of them said I only got my positions because of my family name."

"That must have hurt."

How like Cade to understand right off. "In a knee-jerk reaction I signed up at the last minute, not reading the fine print. I wasn't prepared for nights like this. Heck, I wasn't prepared for much of it."

"Ah. I get it now. You have something to prove."

She didn't say anything further for a long time. Neither did Cade. It was as if he knew there was more. "Uh…"

He waited. Finally he said, "You know you can tell me anything."

"At one time I thought I could." She said the words so softly she didn't think he could have heard them.

"I know you don't think you can trust me, but you can." A gruff note clung to his words as if his emotions might be getting the best of him. "I'm not that scared, confused kid I was once. I think you need to talk to someone and I'm here. It won't go past me unless you agree. Please trust me again, Lily."

She did need to say it out loud to someone. Cade was safe. He was all the way across the country from anyone else who really knew her. She cleared her throat. "The man I thought was my daddy turns out to be my half brother and my mom my sister-in-law."

Cade's muscles tightened but he said nothing. Thankfully he couldn't see her. She wouldn't have been able to get it out if he'd been looking at her. "How could they keep that from me? My real mom's last name was Carter. She and my father died when I was a baby."

Cade's arms tightened a second in an encouraging hug.

"My parents died in an automobile accident. My half brother, who I grew up believing was my father, took me to raise. He needed a nanny, and Sara was a nurse taking time off so she took the job. They fell in love and married. They raised me as their child along with who I thought were my brothers. Who are actually my nephews. It's all so mixed up and bizarre."

"Why did they tell you now?"

"I found out. I found my adoption papers when I was looking for something in my dad's office. Cade, did you know?"

His chin moved against the top of her head. "I had no idea either. Why didn't they tell you?"

"They said they were waiting until I was old enough to understand, then it just seemed like there wasn't a right time and after a while it didn't matter. It wouldn't change anything." She shifted so she could look at him despite being unable to see his face. "But it matters to me. I trusted them."

"You've always been crazy about your parents."

She had. They had been the best. "Still, I'm disappointed in them. They should've told me."

"So that's why you're using a different last name."

"Yeah. After what I overheard and along with learning about my heritage, I feel lost. It's like I'm not who I thought I was. I've been using my real mother's maiden name out of rebellion. I don't want this class to have anything to do with the Smythes. I know it sounds crazy but right now it makes sense for me. I was making decisions based on emotions and ended up here. I am in a tent, in Yosemite National Park in freezing weather with my ex-fiancé. If my decision-making is questioned, I could be in trouble."

Lily felt it before she heard Cade's laugh. She smiled.

"You do have a way of complicating your life."

"It must come through genetics. I understand my father and my mother were real messes." Both had horribly mistreated her half brother/father.

"Maybe it was a good thing you didn't grow up with all that hanging on to you."

"Maybe so. I hadn't thought of it like that." She had a sense Cade had something hanging over him. He hadn't talked to her in the past. Would he do so now? Lily twisted so she lay half on and half off Cade's chest. His skin felt wonderful beneath her fingers. Talking to Cade was therapeutic. "So much for having a squeaky-clean family."

"I don't care who your parents are. I think you're special for who you are."

"Aw, that was a nice thing to say. Thank you." She kissed his chest. "I've missed you."

Cade stiffened. His hands stilled. He cautioned, "Lily. Don't start something you don't mean."

She shifted to where her body faced his, lying along him. It was an old memory yet new, exciting. "I want to celebrate us. Now. Who we are. Not who we were. No promises. No regrets. Two people who have become friends again."

Cade took a deep breath and slowly released it. "I should resist you. I don't want to hurt you again. But I can't. I want you too much. Have missed you for too long."

Lily crawled up his body. His hands ran down her sides. She shivered. Her lips found his mouth in a hot, tantalizing kiss. Lily was delicious. Before she'd been timid, unsure. He liked the bolder version. "Are you sure this is what you want?"

She kissed his chest once more. "I'm not asking for promises. I'm talking about two people enjoying each other."

"I can live with that." His hands cupped her cheeks. "I've always been crazy about you, Lily." He kissed the tip of her nose. "When I left you behind it tore my heart out, but I had to go."

She ran her hands over his bare shoulders, appreciating the strength of him. "Enough of that. We said we were going to look forward."

His mouth found hers. At first the kiss was an easy, get-to-know-you-again kiss, finding his way once again. But the memory returned. He wanted more. So much more. He took the kiss deeper. To his satisfaction Lily joined him.

Cade ran the tip of his tongue over the line of her lips. Lily opened and welcomed him with an enthusiasm that had his manhood thickening. Her hands gripped his shoulders then slid around his neck before her fingers fed through his hair. Her soft moan had his tongue curling with hers, a dance of desire.

Lily shifted over him. His hands traveled over her ribs and down to cup her behind. He settled her so his bulging manhood rested between her legs. "You have too many clothes on."

She wiggled. "I was trying to stay warm."

"I'll keep you plenty warm if you take those off."

She sat on his lap, raising her arms. "Maybe you could give me a little help."

Cade needed no more encouragement. His hands found the hem of the T-shirt. With deliberate movements he lifted her shirt. She helped him remove it over her head and dropped it in the corner of the tent. Her palms rested on his chest. His fingers brushed over the skin of her back.

Lily shivered. His thumb and index finger worked in unison to flip the catch of her bra open. Pushing the straps down her arms, he removed the bra, sending it after the shirt. Unable to resist any longer, he cupped her breasts in both of his hands.

"You have always had gorgeous breasts." His hands molded and massaged them, pressing them together in his palms. "May I taste?"

"Please." The word came as a low hum of anticipation.

Cade reached under her arms and pulled her along him until her breasts hung over his mouth like ripe, full melons waiting for him to savor them. He had no intention of disappointing her. Or him. His lips encircled a nipple. "Sweet like fruit off the vine."

Her hot center brushed his manhood. It twitched with longing. Her mouth captured his, bringing her chest against his. Heat and desire shot through him. His hands moved to the button of her jeans, releasing it. She lifted to her knees, allowing him to lower the zipper.

He pushed her pants wide. He slipped his hand under her silky panties to cup her heated, damp center. His mouth went dry. His length jumped.

Lily made a buzzing sound of pleasure. His middle finger entered her. She pressed against his hand while her fingertips bit into his shoulders. Cade didn't have to see her to know she appreciated his attention. He removed his hand and gently guided Lily to his side.

She lifted her hips, and he helped her remove her jeans. Before she had them off her feet his hands had returned to caress her shoulders, moving down her arms with a stop to cup a breast, and then the curve of her hip. His fingertips followed the length of her thigh and returned to her hip.

Lily's hand explored his chest and shoulders, kneading his muscles as she went.

He loved her touch, wanted more of it. Shifting to his side, he said, "Lily, put your leg over mine."

She ran the sole of her foot up his calf, resting her thigh on his.

His dragged his finger along the inside of her thigh from the knee resting on the ground beside him. Lily's skin rippled but she didn't move. Her breath caught the closer he came to her center.

He brushed her curls before moving down the same

leg to the knee and starting the process over again. Lily's nails scraped his chest. As his finger came closer to her core she groaned. His manhood pulsed. His hand hovered.

"Ca-a-a-de..." His name came out as a plea.

"What do you need?" He wanted her to say it, beg for his touch.

"For you to touch me."

"Like this?" His finger found her center. He brushed her nub.

"Mmm."

His finger entered the wet heat waiting for him. Lily flexed into his hand. He pulled way.

Lily grumbled a complaint deep in her throat. He re-entered her. This time she gripped his wrist. His mouth found hers as his hand continued to indulge her. Soon Lily's back bowed. She squirmed, tensed and her ecstasy flowed over his hand.

Cade smiled. She found her pleasure. Satisfaction filled him.

Lily hung on the cloud of bliss for as long as she could. It had either been too long since she'd had sex or too long since Cade. Whichever it was she wanted more. They had been good together before but nothing like what had just happened to her. She lay alongside him, eyes closed, weak as the fluttering tent material.

Cade's arm beneath her shoulders pulled her closer.

Lily kissed his chest. She ran her palm over the soft patch of hair growing in the center. "That was very nice."

"Nice? That doesn't do much for my ego."

"Maybe you should try a little harder," she teased.

"Mercy, you're a hard woman to please, but I'm up to the task." He rolled over her.

She giggled. "You're defiantly up."

"Lily," he said, his lips stopping just above hers. "I've missed you so much."

Her arms circled his neck. His lips found hers in a white-hot kiss that had heat pooling at her center again. She opened her legs.

Cade rolled away from her long enough to remove his underwear.

He was nothing but a blur as he searched for something.

"What're you doing?" She sat up far enough to run a hand over his back before the cold had her digging back into the covers.

"I'm looking for protection." His frustration was clear in his voice.

"Is that part of standard camping equipment?" She both teased and truly wanted to know.

"No, but a man can always hope."

"Have you been planning this between us?" She wasn't sure how she would feel about it if he said yes.

"No, I always try to be prepared. Found it." The last two words were triumphant.

His notes of success made her smile. Then came the tear of the package.

A moment later Cade pulled her down beside him, rested over her and settled between her legs. He returned to kissing her as if he couldn't get enough of her mouth. "Lily, say you want me."

"I want you." She wrapped her legs around his hips and pulled him to her.

Cade pushed at her entrance, slowly sinking until he

filled her. A sigh of contentment brushed across her ear. "Lily."

She shattered at the reverence and desire he gave her name.

Cade's mouth found hers as he drew his hips back. She lifted hers, not wishing to lose the connection. He slid into her. Her fingertips curled into his back muscles. She tightened her legs. His push-pull increased.

Her center flared in her like Cade had sparked a fire. He had started a blaze in her. It grew, brightened, glowed, building until she shimmered, squirmed before exploding into a burst of pleasure that left her dazed. She relaxed. Her hands floated over his shoulders and arms.

He paused. "Lily you are amazing."

She raised her hips.

Cade lifted his chest from hers, supporting himself on his palms. His muscled legs flexed as he lunged once more. His shoulders tensed. Throwing back his head, Cade groaned as he found his release.

Lily welcomed him into her arms when he came down on her. His deep breathing slowed while his body became heavy. She worked to catch her breath.

"I'm sorry. I'm crushing you." Cade rolled to his side and took a moment for himself before he pulled her to him. Reaching down, he grabbed the covers and jerked the sleeping bag over them, cocooning them in the material.

Complete for the first time since Cade had left her, Lily fell into sleep, warm, sated and safe.

CHAPTER SIX

A BUZZING SOUND woke Cade. It came from his phone in the corner. He groaned and stretched as he continued to hold Lily against him. Grabbing his pants, he searched his pocket, pulling the phone out.

He said into the phone, "This is Dr. Evans."

"We've got a missing kid. Nine years old. He's been out all night. We think he's in your area, maybe a mile or two to the northwest of your location. You're at least five hours ahead of us," the lead park ranger said from the other end of the line.

Cade listened. "I understand. How long has he been gone?"

"Since 8:00 p.m., and it's rained. To make the issue worse he's a type-one diabetic."

Could matters get worse? "Great. That complicates things."

"Yeah. He may need you before he needs us."

"That's what I'm afraid of. Let my clinic staff know I am helping search and that Lily Carter is with me. Tell them to be on standby."

"Will do. I'll keep you posted."

Lily pulled at the sleeping bag covering her beautiful breasts. "What was that about?"

"There's a child missing. We have to help look." Cade

already formed a list of what needed doing to get them packed up and moving. He grabbed his pants.

"How old?"

"Nine." He found his shirt.

"He has to be so scared." Lily moved the blankets around, locating her clothing. "And his parents must be terrified."

Cade stood then jerked on his pants. "I'm sure they are. Lily, about last night—"

"We can talk about that later. Don't we need to get started?"

"But—"

Lily pulled her panties on beneath the sleeping bag. "I'll be ready to go in a few minutes."

This wasn't what he wanted their morning-after to look like. He'd wanted them to… He didn't know what, but it wasn't this. He pulled on his shirt. To his satisfaction Lily watched for a moment as he buttoned it before returning to her dressing.

"You know how to do a search?" She pulled her T-shirt on, covering all that glorious bounty he'd explored last night and had hoped to experience again that morning.

"I do. I've done it one other time since I've been here." He quickly put on his socks and boots.

"Lily, stop watching me. If you continue to look at me that way, it'll be a long time before we get moving and there's a little boy out there that needs us."

Her cheeks turned pink. "I wasn't looking at you."

"You were so ogling me."

"I was not." Her shoulders straightened. She glared at him.

* * *

His ego had only recently returned. For some reason that had happened when Lily showed up in his life once more.

"I'll get some water heated." He unzipped the tent and ducked out.

Minutes later Lily backed out of the tent and all he could think about was taking her back in there. Their afternoon hike had taken more than one unexpected turn. Right now, though, his focus must be on a missing child.

"I rolled up the sleeping bags and stored the thermal blankets as well."

He nodded. "You'll become a camper after all."

She took a sip of her drink. "I don't know about that, but I want to do my part. Do they have any idea where the boy is?"

"He was last seen about a mile from here." Cade carefully returned items to his backpack. "This is usually the park rangers' department but since I was in the area they asked me to help until they could get here. They want me…uh…us to hike to where he was last seen and start there."

"What do I need to do to help?"

"We need to break camp. Which is doing everything we've done in reverse. We are going to have to have food bars for breakfast. Maybe lunch."

"Okay."

"While I take care of things here would you be comfortable going to get water by yourself?"

A moment of anxiousness shot through her. Seconds later she straightened her shoulders. "I can do that."

"Just stay on the trail. Animals like to be out in the

early morning." His attention had already turned to packing her backpack.

"I'll be fine."

"Okay. Then fill our containers and one of the pots to douse the fire. I'll have everything ready to go when you return."

She headed toward the river until finally the sound of rushing water reached her ears. A few more paces and she would be able to see it. She stopped short. There, drinking from the creek, was a doe and her fawn. The mother's head rose with ears back. The deer's eyes locked on Lily. She held her breath. Lily had never seen a picture so serene. She had started to understand the appeal of working in this environment. Why Cade liked it so much.

She filled the containers, secured the tops and headed back to camp. She hurried down the path, glad to see Cade standing near the fire. He took the pot. Getting close to the fire, he poured the water over the few remaining coals then, using the shovel, he placed dirt over them. He then stored the shovel in a loop on his pack and hung the pot on a clip.

Lily watched as Cade removed a folded paper in a plastic bag from the side pocket of his cargo pants. They were ready to leave the campsite. He spread it out on the ground. She moved to look over his shoulder. She knew enough about the park to recognize that it was a map of Yosemite. "Where are we?"

He placed his fingertip on a spot. "This is where we're supposed to search." He moved his finger in a circle, indicating an area in the middle of the map.

"Where was the boy last seen?"

Cade pointed to another spot on the map.

"Since he's a type-one diabetic what are the chances he has any extra supplies with him?"

Cade shook his head. "Who knows. Even if he did, he may have had to use them by now and be in need of more."

Fear washed through her. She'd seen patients in the ER in diabetic comas. She didn't want this for this boy. "We need to find him."

Cade folded the paper and stood. "Agreed. We better get started."

His face had turned all business. She missed the slight teasing lift of his lips. She knew this was serious in general, but from the look on his face, it was even beyond that. A child lost in the land she had traveled to get here the day before could not end well.

All semblance of what had happened last night was gone this morning. There had been that brief mention, but no tender touch. Cade was taking her at her word that what had happened was just for last night with no promises of anything beyond that. Or was it just he was worried about this boy, very worried?

She didn't know what had gotten into her the night before. Was it from being around Cade again? Had being close to him caused her to slip back into those old ways? She had had a couple of serious boyfriends, but neither of them had ever measured up to Cade. She could admit that now. A few days ago, she would have denied those feelings. Whatever it had been, the time between them had been special.

This time their packs were more evenly distributed than they had been on their trek up the mountain. She had insisted she carry her weight. Every thirty minutes

Cade stopped to check his compass, which gave her a chance to catch up.

The walk started smooth and easy, but the grade grew higher. Lily pushed at the hair that had fallen out of her hat. Sweat bubbled on her face. Still, she refused to complain. "What's the boy's name?"

"Ricky."

Lily called, "Ricky."

As they walked, she continued to call his name at intervals.

After she'd fallen behind the third time, Cade pulled off his pack. "Let's take a rest. I'm sorry I've been so focused I forgot you aren't used to this."

She gladly sank to a rock. "I know I'm more of a hindrance than a help."

"You're doing just fine. I hope this doesn't put a bad taste in your mouth being dragged all over the forest, but it can't be helped."

"I understand. There's a little boy out there that needs us. How I feel doesn't matter." Had he really thought she felt that way? She wasn't that spoiled. Never had been. "I do understand the bigger picture."

"I know you do. If you're rested, we should go."

Lily's shoulders had hurt from the hike the day before, and her feet as well, but now they screamed. She wasn't used to this type of activity. Swimming and tennis were her usual exercises. Trying to keep up with the longer-legged Cade didn't improve matters. But she couldn't say anything. There was a boy out there who must be scared, and possibly ill or hurt. They had to keep moving. Her issues weren't as important. She understood the seriousness of the search.

She could only imagine the worry the boy's parents must be feeling. Wouldn't hers be just as upset? She had no doubt they would have been. They loved her. What they had done hadn't been intended to hurt her. It had taken stepping out of her comfort zone to realize that. As soon as she made it back to civilization, she would call and tell them where she was.

"You okay?" Cade called back.

"I'm good."

He stopped to ask, "Would you like to lead for a change?"

Her brows came closer, as if she questioned his thinking. "And end up where? We'd be lost too."

"I wouldn't let that happen."

He wouldn't. To the center of her being she was confident Cade would always take care of her. "Yes, I would like to lead for a while."

Another half hour went by before Cade said, "Why don't we stop for a rest."

With relief she trudged to the nearest rock and dropped her pack. "The problem now may be that I'll never get up." She began to unlace her shoes.

"Don't do that. You'll never get them back on. Your feet will be so swollen they'll hurt worse."

Lily squelched her groan. If she could just take her boots off for a moment. Dip them in a cold stream like the one last night. But she resisted the urge.

They took ten minutes to rest then walked for another forty minutes with Cade checking on her often. Lily did her best to keep up but continued to fall behind. She tried to keep the pace, but it became difficult to do so as the terrain became more challenging. They were climbing up at a place where Cade had to reach back and take her hand to help her.

"Surely a nine-year-old boy couldn't make it over this."

Cade huffed. "You'd be surprised. My mother used to complain about me climbing on top of shelves and around the cabinets."

"You've never told me that before." Lily looked at him in wonder. There was so much she didn't know about him.

He grinned. "We had our minds on other things beside stuff like that."

That was the first time since this morning he'd properly alluded to them having sex. It had stepped in and out of her mind all day. "That's a shame. I rather like the idea of you as a monkey and driving your mother crazy."

Cade grinned. "Yeah, I did that."

She turned her attention back to the task at hand. "Ricky," she called. Lily listened for a response and heard none. "What do we do if he's in a diabetic coma? Or can't hear or see us?"

"We can only hope he answers or sees us when you call out."

Worry built in her. "We really need to get to him before he passes out."

"I agree."

"There's so much area here to cover." She stumbled.

Cade reached back to help her. "We'll stop here for a rest at the top of the ridge. Otherwise, I'm afraid that I'll have another patient on my hands."

"I'm made of sterner stuff than you give me credit for." She might not have been years ago but she had learned in just a week she had strength within her she'd never tapped.

He met her gaze. "I have learned that recently."

"Good. Don't forget it."

When the rock became level enough that they could walk across it, they lowered their packs. Cade dug out a power bar from his backpack and handed it to her. As they ate, they took turns calling Ricky's name.

Lily stretched her legs out across the warm rock. The heat seeped into her sore muscles. "I'm sorry if I'm holding you up."

"Don't be. Two sets of eyes are better than one. I hate I'm having to push you so hard."

"I understand that time is of the essence."

He lifted the power bar. "This is all we have time for in the way of lunch."

"I don't mind." She pulled her water bottle out of the pocket of her pack.

Before she could take a swallow Cade said, "Don't overdo it on the water because I'm not sure how far it'll be before we have a chance to fill up again."

"Okay."

He put a finger under her chin and lifted it until she clearly saw his eyes. He studied her for a moment then gave her a gentle kiss. "Lily, you really are being a trouper."

"What did you think I would be? A silly debutante?"

Cade's head dipped to the side. "Well, that's what you were the last time I saw you."

"I've grown up and realized some things since then."

"Like what?" He watched her.

"Like there isn't such a thing as a perfect world. People are imperfect. Like we can't believe people will tell the truth all the time but that doesn't make them bad. And what we expect we want out of life can sometimes not be what we need."

His lips thinned. "I guess we all think that until we learn differently."

"Cade, what are you not telling me about leaving Chicago? I can tell by what you don't say that there was more to it. I know you'll feel better for telling someone. If not me then someone else."

Cade tensed. "You don't want to hear it."

"It can't be any worse than mine."

"Yeah, it can." He paused. "I saw my dad kissing one of his nurses. He denied it but that's what it looked like to me."

"Oh."

"He told me the nurse was upset, and he was trying to comfort her. That she kissed him, not the other way around. I called him a liar."

"Oh, my."

"Yeah. I told him I wanted no part of working at the family clinic and I sure didn't want any part of that environment where my mother would be humiliated. That she deserved better.

"He told me I was in no position to make demands on how he handled his life or business. I knew then that I would never have any say in the direction of the clinic or be looked at as anything but the inconsequential son. My father made it clear what my opinions and feelings on any matter would be—unimportant and disregarded."

Lily understood now. She wished she had listened to him when he'd tried to tell her. "But he did give you a reason to get out and you took it."

"Yes. Whether or not the kiss between him and the nurse meant anything I don't know, but it happening gave me a way out."

"We grew up in this perfect-looking life. Good families, plenty of money, travel and education. Yet behind it were dirty secrets." She sounded like she had grasped a gold key to life.

"When you come down to it, we were like anybody else. Human."

"Do you think we expected them to be more than that?" She watched him closely. Had they expected too much from their parents?

"Could be. My father tried to apologize. Explain. Said he had told my mother, and they had worked it out, but I wouldn't listen."

"I haven't spoken to my parents in weeks. I told them I need to process it then I left town. I didn't even tell them I was leaving or where I was going. I bet they're worried." Guilt washed over her.

"I'm sure they're worried. At the first chance you get you should call them."

She met his gaze with an unwavering one. "And I think you should try to talk to your father again. For your mother's sake if for no other reason."

He lowered his chin and raised it. "You know, I liked the Lily before, but I like this Lily even better. She stands up for what she believes."

She smiled. "You know, I like this Lily better too." She looked out over the valley below them. A feeling of empowerment she'd not known filled her.

Their conversation had been deeper and more emotional than he had expected. As painful as it had been, it had also been therapeutic. He had needed to tell the story, and he wanted Lily to know he trusted her with the knowledge. Somehow their secrets strengthened their relationship, bound them. Something he was starting to want more and more.

In a perfect world, Cade would've enjoyed showing Lily some of his favorite places in Yosemite. The spot where a bird had hatched her chicks. The fox den or his favorite rock by the river. "I'm sorry we're not able to take the time to really enjoy being out here."

She stuffed her wrapper in a plastic bag and closed it then replaced her water bottle. "We can do that again later. Shouldn't we get going?"

"Sit for a few more minutes. The going gets tougher up here. We need to rest and you need more sunscreen. Your nose is pinker than it was."

Lily wiped on the sunscreen and relaxed, putting her hands behind her, palms on the rock as she raised her face to the sun. She really was beautiful. Last night had been moving for him. He realized how much he had missed her. She'd always been the one he compared the others to. The person the women hadn't lived up to. Now Lily had matured, she had really become a force of nature. One he craved.

A few minutes later he said, "We'd better get started."

"Before we do, can you show me on the map where we are and where we have come? And where we're headed now? I have no sense of anything."

"Sure." Cade pulled out his map and spread it on the rock between them.

Her face turned serious. "Do you think he'll be alive when he's found?"

Cade wanted to reassure her the boy would be fine, but he couldn't. Instead, he cupped her cheek and looked into her worried eyes. "The best we can do is keep looking. The sooner we find him the better chance he has."

They hiked across the uneven but wide stone to the other side into a copse of trees, moving across soft pine needles as they gradually descended. A noise grew into the roar of water.

Lily came up behind him and looked around him. "We have to cross that?"

After the rain the night before, the usually tame creek ran wild. Cade let his pack slip from his shoulders to the ground. He studied the water. "During the summer we could hop across this without getting our feet wet but right now with the winter runoff it's powerful. I hadn't counted on this."

"You don't think the boy would try to cross this?" There was a note of fear in her voice. "You never know. But I do know we have to cross it."

She gave the rushing water flowing over jagged rocks a dubious look. "It's running mighty fast."

"Yeah, it is. I'm going to walk around that boulder." He pointed downriver. "To see if there's a better place to cross. You wait here."

Lily found a spot under a tree, removed her pack and sat with her back leaning against the tree. If it hadn't been for the fact they were searching for a lost child, she would have called it heaven. This was the most beautiful place she had ever been. The sun had heated the ground beneath her. The sky was azure with large white cottoncandy clouds. The sound of moving water and the fine mist of spray touching her arms, calmed her. The smell of moss filled her senses, lulling her into a peaceful space. Would she ever have a chance to experience this again?

She watched Cade stride toward her. He truly was a handsome man. His hair blew in the breeze. A hint of color rested on his cheeks from activity and the sun. Everything about him said he belonged here. She couldn't remember ever thinking that when they had been in the pool at the country club. Never would she ever consider encouraging him to be anything less than himself.

"I think our best chance is right here. There's a tree across it we can use to steady ourselves. But I do have an advantage because my legs and arms are longer."

Lily looked at the flow of water, the distance between the rocks and the sharpness of them. Could she even touch the tree when she needed to? She worked to sound confident and failed. "Right here?"

"Yep."

She stood, squared her shoulders. "All right, let's get across this. So, what's the plan?"

"Not to get wet." He grinned.

She liked Cade even more when he showed his sense of humor. "Funny guy."

"I thought you might appreciate some humor before we tried this. Come on, this shouldn't be too bad. There's the tree to hold on to." He offered her his hand.

Lily thought more about holding on to him.

"Hand me your pack and I'll take it across along with mine then come back and help you."

She did so. Cade pulled on his backpack and hooked hers on his chest. He stepped to the edge of the river. Lily held her breath while he maneuvered to the first rock. He rocked back and forward. His hand shot out and grabbed a broken limb of the decaying tree to steady himself. His feet stabilized before he stretched his foot over to the next rock. He made the same maneuvers once again, remaining upright and dry.

Unfortunately, the rocks were not round and flat; instead they were sharp and uneven like cut diamonds, making each step difficult. The dampness of each didn't help matters.

Carefully Cade moved on. In the middle the water washed over his foot, but he didn't linger long enough for her to believe it soaked in. Her anxiousness didn't increase again until he had made it almost to the other side. Lily clenched her hands in front of her. If something happened to Cade what would she do?

There the rocks were almost covered with water and the tree ended. He made quick work with agile balance to the dry ground across from her. He turned and grinned.

"Show-off," she called.

When Cade had worked his way to the center once more, Lily stepped off the bank onto the first rock, holding on to the tree trunk as if it was a lifeline.

Cade's look of surprise to see her meeting him would have been laughable if it hadn't been for the seriousness of the situation.

Lily clung to the tree as she moved to the next rock. She steadied herself, making sure she had a firm stance before she prepared to move again. The next rock was large enough for both of them to stand on. She stretched as far as her legs would allow.

Her booted foot touched the rock but the wet sole slid across it and into the water. Her body lurched backward, pulling her fingers over the roughness of the tree until all she grasped was air.

"Oh…"

Cade grabbed Lily's arm as it flailed by his head. She was going in the water!

His fingers bit into her arm through her shirt. As the

river caught her, her weight increased, jerking her away from him. His shoulder screamed in resistance. His other arm wrapped around the tree limb to keep him from being washed away along with her.

Lily scrambled to right her footing, twisting her body.

The angle only made his shoulder scream louder. He bit through the pain. "Stop moving! Let me pull you up on the rock."

It took Lily a moment to respond then she relaxed. Crossing her ankles, she went straight as a board, pulling her arm in against her side to make herself as streamlined as possible. Smart girl.

It didn't ease the strain on his shoulder but at least he had a chance to save her. If she got away from him she would wash down the river. Could his heart take it if that happened? Who knew if she would survive?

Leaning back as far as he could against the tree, he hauled Lily toward the rock he stood on. The current pulled at her furiously, making the going slow. His muscles twitched and throbbed with the effort to bring her out of the water. At a turtle's pace, Lily came closer to the rock. All the while he feared he might lose her. His shoulder wouldn't last much longer. His fingers already tingled with the need to release her arm.

Lily's bottom reached the rock. She used her other hand to steady herself. "Don't let me go."

That was his plan.

She used her feet to push against another rock, working to get herself farther out of the water. With her free hand, she leveraged her way upward.

Cade continued to hold on to her. The pressure eased in his arm and shoulder, but pain coursed through him. He clenched his teeth not to groan in pain. He had dislocated his shoulder with the lurch that had stopped Lily from washing away. His other arm remained around the tree trunk.

"Climb up my leg," he bit out.

She grabbed his calves. He nodded and tightened his hold on the tree.

"No! A leg. You're going to take us both down." Cade looked down into her terrified eyes. He had been sharper than he had intended.

Lily changed her grip to crawl up his leg. When she made it to her knees, still clinging to him, she rested her face on his thigh while she took gasping breaths.

He rested his aching hand on her head to reassure her. Every movement created a searing pain.

"I thought I was a goner."

The fear and urgency in her voice pulled at the same emotions filling his chest. He couldn't let them be swallowed up in those. They still had to get out of this river. "Climb to your feet. We need to get out of here."

At his words, Lily's look met his. Apparently, she saw the fear, worry and pain in his eyes. She started moving, working herself to standing. While she did, he continued to hold the tree. If she went down again there was no way he could hold her. His arm strength and mobility were gone.

Lily gripped the tree with as much of her arm as the distance would allow.

Cade gave her time to catch her breath. "We need to get to ground."

She looked at him then at the space of water between them and the bank. "Then let's get going before I decide to set up camp here."

There was her spirit again. "I'm going out to the end

of the tree. You use me to steady yourself as you cross the rocks. That last step is a long one, but you can do it."

She squared her shoulders, wrapped herself against his chest and stepped by him to the next rock. He shifted his arm down the tree. She continued to use him to balance. He reached the end of the tree and his hold. With willpower he didn't know he possessed he lifted his arm for her to hang on to.

Cade gritted his teeth when she touched it. He must have made a sound of pain because Lily's head whipped around to look at him. She couldn't stop now, not here. "Move, Lily."

She bent her knees and sprang over the last of the water, landing on the bank on her stomach. She quickly pulled her feet out of the water.

Cade wasted no time in bounding over to land. He fell to the ground, rolling to his back. Lying there, he took deep breaths to try to slow his breathing and work through the pain throbbing in his shoulder.

Lily rotated toward him. "Thanks for saving me."

"Are you okay?" He'd never known fear like he'd felt when he realized he might lose her.

"I'm good, thanks to you. Just wet." She sat up. "How are…?"

She must have seen the angle of his arm.

"You're hurt." Panic filled her voice.

His arm hung worthless beside him. "I dislocated my shoulder."

Lily came to her knees beside him. "Let me see. When did this happen?"

"When I caught you to keep you from going down the

river." He really didn't want to talk about it. He needed time to control his pain.

"Oh, I'm so sorry I hurt you. We need to get that immobilized. Then call for help."

"We can't. My phone got wet. I should have put it in a plastic bag but who knew we would be going swimming. Just patch me up the best you can." He started to rise. "Anyway, I don't want to take any resources away from those looking for the boy. Finding him is the best way for us to get help."

She placed a hand on his shoulder. He winced. "Sorry. Stay seated and let me take care of you. You can't help the boy if we don't see about you first."

The firm tone of her voice had him doing as he was told. "Are you bossing me around?"

"I am. Can you lift your arm?"

Cade tried, only raising it a few inches.

"Man, I hate I did this to you." She worked her hands gently up his arm. "You've not only dislocated it, but I bet you've torn the rotator cuff."

"I think you're probably right. Just put it back into the socket. I'll deal with the other later." He tried to sit up but fell to his back again with a yelp of pain.

She placed a hand on his shoulder and held him in place. "Stay put."

"Lily," he said, and her look met his. "You know you're going to have to put it back into the socket."

She shook her head. "That'll hurt like the devil."

"It hurts like the devil now." The pain pulsed through his body.

"But I've never done this before. Seen it, but not actually done it." He heard the fear in her voice.

"Just do what I say."

* * *

Lily hoped Cade didn't pass out. But there was no choice but to put his shoulder back into place. The treatment would be brief compared to the agony of not doing anything. She'd seen it done a few times in a hospital but never under these types of conditions.

"You'll have to pull hard. You'll need to brace your foot under my arm and pull as hard as you can. It should slip into place."

She looked down on his pain-drawn face. "You should be in the hospital."

"See one anywhere? Just do it, Lily. You've got this."

"Okay. Hold on a minute." She tugged her backpack to her. Opening it, she dug around until she found a T-shirt. Rolling it into a tight log, she handed it to him. "Bite on this."

He took it. To her surprise he didn't question her. She placed her hands just above his elbow and lifted his arm. Cade grimaced but she had no choice in what she did if she was to help him.

A white line of pain formed around Cade's mouth, yet he didn't say anything. "Now put your foot under my arm, but not too high. That's it, against my ribs. While you push with your foot pull my arm and slowly rotate. Hopefully it'll slide into place."

Lily shook her head. "I don't have a good feeling about this."

"I don't have good feeling in my arm right now," he ground out.

She quit stalling and placed her foot against his chest. "Okay, here we go."

Cade braced his feet against the ground.

Lily did as he had instructed. She pulled with all her

might on his arm. When it didn't move she leaned back, using all her body weight. She felt the slide of the humerus bone pop into the socket of the scapula. She laid Cade's arm across her lap and took deep breaths. Cade had taken on a wan pallor as if he might be sick.

"Do not pass out on me." She glared down at him.

She slowly arranged his arm so it rested on his chest at a ninety-degree angle. Cade didn't open his eyes. She hopped to her feet and picked up the T-shirt he had dropped to the ground. Taking it to the water, she wet it and returned to place it across his forehead.

With that done, she unzipped the large pocket on the pack and removed the first aid kit Cade had her place there. She quickly found the small bottle of pain medicine. "Cade, you need to take these."

His eyelids fluttered open. Pain dulled his eyes, making them a creamy color not the clear blue she loved.

"I'll help you sit up. Take these." She placed them in his palm then put her arm behind his back and nudged him forward. "Put those in your mouth and I'll hand you the water."

He did as she asked. Turning the water bottle up, he swallowed the pills.

"These aren't going to do much to help with pain, but they're better than nothing. Now tell me how to contact the emergency guys so we can get you to a hospital."

"We have to go after the boy. Give me five minutes then secure my arm to my side."

Was he crazy? "We need to get you to some real help."

He raised his good hand. "Lily, just give me a minute."

She humphed. "If you aren't going to listen to me then I'll empty the water out of my shoes and put on dry clothes."

Looking through his backpack, she found a shirt and rolled it, placing it beneath his neck. She removed her clothes and shoes and redressed as fast as she could. "Can I put dry socks on your feet?"

"No, I'll be fine. Just get my arm in a sling and let's get going."

The man was tough. She would give him that. He'd had to have been tough to walk away from his family and her. Now she better understood who he was. Why couldn't he have shown her that then? Because he would have scared her if he had.

Going through Cade's backpack once again, she pulled out another shirt. This time a long-sleeved one. She tied the cuffs of the sleeves together, pulling them tight to ensure they didn't come apart.

"I need you to sit up." She helped him then looped the attached sleeves over his head.

"What're you doing?"

"Making you a sling." She took one corner of the tail of the shirt and pushed it under the part crossing his chest. Carefully tying the other corner to the first one, she held Cade's arm in place. Taking the shirt that she had worn earlier, which was now only damp, she folded it into a long line. "Here, hold this."

He took the cuff of one sleeve.

She stood and circled Cade, making sure the shirt rested against his arm so that it would secure it in place. Returning to her original spot, she tied the sleeves together against his chest. She sat back on her heels. "How does that feel?"

"Not bad. You're quite ingenious when you want to be."

Lily smiled. "Thank you. I'm rather pleased with myself as well." She stood. "One more thing."

"You need surgery."

"I figured as much."

She opened her backpack and found a plastic bag. Then went looking for another.

"What're you up to now?"

"You'll see." She filled a bag with water, sealed it and put it into the second bag and closed it. Returning to Cade, she placed it on his shoulder.

"Aw, that feels good. An ice pack."

"I'm glad I could make you happy." She picked up her wet socks and squeezed all the water she could out. Tying them together, she then spread them as wide as she could and positioned the band so it would hold the bag of water in place.

He caught her hand, looked into her eyes with his agony-filled ones. "You have always been able to make me happy."

She kissed the top of his head. "You sure know how to show a girl a good time."

"Thanks. You know you're really incredible in an emergency."

"I appreciate you saying that. I hope you make a note on my progress report. And I'm the one who should be thanking you. I'd have been washed away without you."

"I couldn't, wouldn't have let that happen to you."

His words sounded heartfelt. Warmth washed through her.

Lily picked up his pack and pulled it over her shoulders. Lifting hers, she strapped it on her front like Cade had done hers earlier.

"Let me have one of those. You can't carry them both." Cade reached out.

"I'll figure it out. You need to have a hand free if you

happen to trip." She nodded her head forward. "Let's go find that boy."

Cade pushed himself to his feet, a twist of pain tightening his mouth. "I'm sorry about this."

"Are you going to be okay to travel?"

"I'll make it." He put one foot in front of the other. "There's no choice. My phone is sopping wet. It needs to dry out some before I can use it. We should meet up with rangers soon."

"Then we can get you out of here. You should be at the hospital, and I need a hot shower."

"I'd rather go with you." Her look met his. He managed a lopsided wolfish grin.

That giddy feeling she basked in the night before bubbled up once more.

"We're going to search meanwhile."

"Okay."

Cade took the lead. He weaved a couple of times but stayed upright. The pain in his shoulder must be excruciating.

She called the boy's name. They had to find him soon for all their sakes or the others searching needed to show up soon. All the while she kept an eye on Cade's movements. He couldn't afford to fall. With one arm bound he would be unable to catch himself if he went down. More than that, she feared he was in more pain than he let on. He had refused additional pain medication because he said the pills tended to make him sleepy.

The time passed and when Cade paused, he encouraged her to keep moving, insisting they didn't want to get into the position where they might need to spend another night in the woods.

"Having a one-armed man around is little help. If we don't find the boy and get back to civilization before dark, we might be in real trouble."

They kept marching on in the direction he'd been told the boy was last seen. As they did, Lily called Ricky over and over. When Cade slowed, Lily moved ahead of him as they walked. A number of times she glanced back to get a direction. He would nod forward or redirect her with his head.

After calling the boy's name she would stop and listen for a noise, or to detect the slightest movement. Her ears strained and her heart anticipated. Yet there would be nothing.

Occasionally she took a moment to appreciate the views and the wonder of the country.

"Ricky." She went stock-still. What was that? She could swear she heard something human.

"Why're you stopping?" Cade came to stand beside her.

"Did you hear that?" She cocked her head.

Silence filled the air.

She called once more.

Yes! There it was. "Did you hear that?"

Cade shook his head. "I didn't hear anything."

She hollered, "Ricky."

Moments later a small voice said, "Help. Help. I'm right here."

Lily took a step in the direction of the sound. "Ricky."

"Help," came the small sound.

"Cade, over this way." Lily dropped the packs and started running.

"Be careful. Don't fall!"

"Down here," came a weak voice.

Lily looked back at Cade. "He's over here."

"Keep talking. We're here to help you." Lily went to her hands and knees at the edge of the outcropping.

"Lily, wait."

She belly-crawled to the edge. "Slow down. You don't want to fall."

A call for help came again. His voice was weak. Obviously, the boy was dehydrated.

"I see him. I see him," she said over her shoulder to Cade. Ricky lay about twenty feet below. Lily controlled her voice, keeping it calm. "We're here to help you."

Ricky looked at her with wide, scared eyes.

"We'll have you up here in just a few minutes." She resigned herself to the fact she'd be the one who would have to go down to help him out. She didn't like the idea but there was no choice. The area looked treacherous. Especially since the rock had slid.

The boy sat at an odd angle among the rock. Thankfully, he wasn't far down, but he wasn't in a position where they could bring him up easily. The face of the rock was too smooth.

"Ricky?"

The boy didn't immediately answer. "Yes."

"Stay right there. Don't move," Cade said from beside her. "We've been looking for you. Help is coming."

"The rock fell. I slid down." The boy's voice was turning feeble. "I don't feel so good. I need my medicine."

"Do you have any with you?" With any luck he would.

"No."

There went their luck. "I'm Lily and this is Cade. We've been looking for you."

"My foot is stuck."

"I'll come down and help you up." She scooted away from the edge and came to her feet.

Cade sat back. "You're not going down there."

Lily placed her hands on her hips, glared at him. "Like you're going to be able to with that arm. That leaves me."

CHAPTER SEVEN

CADE COULDN'T DISAGREE with her logic. He studied her a moment. What could he do if she got hurt? "Pull out my phone. See if it'll work."

Lily searched his pack and removed the phone. She pushed a few buttons then put it to her ear. "Cade, we're wasting time. This phone isn't working. You know me climbing down is the only way. We can't wait on help. Ricky could go into a coma by then."

His heart couldn't stand the idea, but he had no choice. "Get the rope. It's attached to my pack."

It didn't take Lily four steps before she snatched up his backpack and began removing the rope.

Cade walked across the rock to a large tree. He stopped, then reached out a hand. Lily handed him the rope. Using his good arm, he wrapped the cord around the tree. He attempted to tie it off. Lily joined him, taking the rope from him.

"You want to do a square knot. You don't need the knot to slip," he coached. "I've stood in on a little surgery along the way. A good surgeon learns to make a solid knot."

She smiled. "I should have known." Under his guidance she manipulated the line into a square knot.

Cade tugged hard on the rope, making sure it was secure. His shoulder roared with pain, but he tried to ignore it. "I wish we had more rope. I'm not confident this will reach."

"We'll figure it out then. I need to get down to that kid. He's scared and sick. Not a good combination."

She hurried to her pack. There she made a pile of what she figured she wouldn't need. "I'll need the first aid kit. Can I get in your backpack?"

"Sure. Take what you think you'll need."

Lily stuffed the kit into her pack before she shrugged it on. "I may need your knife."

Cade handed it to her.

She slipped it into her pants pocket. She stopped long enough to say "Don't worry. I've got this."

His chest tightened as he clenched his jaw. "I don't feel good about this. I should be the one going."

"I'll do what needs to be done so let's stop arguing and get started. Cade, trust that I'm strong enough to do this."

He gave her a long look. "I do. Just be careful. I don't want you hurt."

"I'm not the hothouse flower my name implies. I'm tougher than I might appear."

Cade cringed. How much had he been involved in her learning tough lessons? Cade feared he might have had a major hand it. Right now, he didn't have time to process how he felt about that.

"Tie the rope around your waist." His voice turned gruff.

Lily circled it around her. He held it at her middle while she worked the knot.

Cade dug around in his pack and pulled out gloves. He handed them to her. They were leather, huge, but she put them on her hands. They would be better than nothing when climbing around in the sharp rocks.

The boy called out. His voice had grown weaker.

"Ricky, I'm coming down." The sound of rock falling made her tense. If Lily didn't hurry, they might be involved in a full-on rockslide. That was one thing they didn't need. She called, "Don't move."

"Lily, don't take any chances. Just assess him, and let's get him up here to safety."

Lily lay on her stomach, preparing to go over the side feet first. "Don't worry," she said firmly to Cade. "Just tell me what to do."

He wished he felt as confident. "Slowly shift backward. Get your footing. Make sure one foot is secure before you move the next one. This rock isn't stable."

Rock scattered below her. Lily called, "Ricky, cover your head with your arms."

Cade watched as Lily kept moving, half on her feet and half crawling.

"The rock is hitting me," Ricky whined.

"I'm almost there. Hang in there."

Lily didn't stop moving. If she did, Ricky might be in more trouble. Cade knew she wouldn't let her fear hold her back. What was it she had told him a few days ago? *Just because I work in a city doesn't mean I'm not needed.*

The realization Lily wouldn't be pleased with further argument stopped him from offering more. Still concern for her welfare put a knot in his chest. Lily had been stubborn years ago, but she was even more so now. Especially when she believed she was right. The emotions that assailed him regarding Lily he would have to deal with later. Too many issues stood between them from the past to think of a future.

Cade winced at the amount of rock rolling down the slope. Not only was it hitting Ricky, but the sharp edges must be cutting into Lily's body. Yet she continued.

He should have reasoned more with her to wait on rescue, but it would have done no good. The determined look he'd learned she owned had appeared on her face, her jaw jutted out. There would be no holding her back when a child was in trouble.

With a grunt and a groan, he lowered himself to his side to look over the edge. What he saw did nothing to ease his worries. Lily had found a spot between crawling and climbing as she made her way down. Rock slid as she continued on. Below Ricky covered his head with his arms as debris rained down on him.

Lily made good progress but at the same time the boy continued being pelted. That wasn't good but nothing could be done about it. Eventually she reached the boy. There she had to do some unnatural maneuvering to get into a position where she could sit beside him. One of her legs remained extended to keep her from sliding farther along the mountain.

"I bet I didn't make it here fast enough for you," she said to Ricky.

Cade could hear every word she said, clearly as it echoed in the small canyon.

Lily continued, "Sorry about all the rock falling. I kind of made a mess all over you. You can pay me back on your way up."

Even hanging in a parlous position on the side of a mountain Lily was able to keep an upbeat attitude.

***

Lily settled in as comfortably as she could beside the boy and secured the pack within reach. She removed the gloves, tucking them into the side pocket of her pants. "We're going to have you feeling better and out of here real soon. I understand that you're a diabetic. How're you feeling?"

"What?"

This wasn't good. Confusion had set in. "How're you feeling? Do you hurt anywhere?"

"I'm…uh…not feeling so good. I need my shot. Thirsty. Should eat." Ricky's eyelids dropped then bounced open again.

She needed to get information out of him before he fell asleep. "Can you tell me the last time you had insulin?"

"Before dinner last night," Ricky said just above a whisper.

"Good to hear. Then what happened?"

"I ate and we went star watching. On the way back I got lost. An animal howled and I got scared. I started running." Tears rolled down the boy's cheeks.

Lily gathered him into her arms as much as her vulnerable position would allow. "Ricky, can you tell me the rest?"

"I fell down here. I couldn't climb up. I screamed but no one heard me." He shuddered. "I was so cold and my leg hurts. I missed my morning medicine. My mom will be so mad."

"No, no, your mother isn't mad at you. She just wants you to come home." Lily placed her hand on his shoulder. "That's why I'm here. And Cade up there. We'll get you out of here. You'll see your family soon."

He nodded then his eyelids closed.

Lily leaned close to smell his breath. Relief washed through her at the lack of a sweet smell. At least ketoacidosis hadn't started. If the ketones in his blood had turned toxic, then there might be no return. Giving him more sugar would kill him. Since it hadn't started, if she could get some form of sugar into the boy fast, she could ward off the situation getting worse.

"Cade, I need something sweet."

"Remember you packed a couple of packages of jelly in the small side pocket of your pack."

He had been thinking when she hadn't. What would she do without Cade?

She unzipped the pocket and reached inside. Her fingers touched the packages of jelly. Relief flooded her. Quickly she tore the corner off a package with her teeth. She squirted the sticky grape goo on her fingers. "Open your mouth for me, Ricky."

The boy took a moment to respond. As soon as he did, Lily wiped her fingers against the inside of his cheek. There the sugar would adsorb fast. She watched for a reaction, hoping he would soon open his eyes.

"Lily?" The concern in Cade's voice cut through her worry for the boy.

"Yes?"

Cade's voice carried. "You okay?"

"Yes. I'm waiting on the sugar to work."

The boy blinked. "Where am I?"

He was still disorientated. "You fell. Cade and I are going to get you out of here. Now let's get some of this rock off you. See if we can get you sitting up. But first I need to check you out. I also need to put something around your neck to support it. The EMTs would be mad at me if I didn't." She pulled the backpack toward her and unzipped the largest pouch. Removing a shirt, she rolled it into a log. She placed it around the boy's neck.

Talking to herself as much to Cade, she said, "I need something to secure this around his neck."

Cade said, "Use the small pull on the top zipper of the pack. Push it up over the sleeves until it's tight enough."

"Good idea," she called. Pushing the cord out of the loop, she removed it then widened it enough to secure the material. Soon she had fashioned a makeshift neck brace. Satisfied, she pushed rocks off Ricky's body.

"Lily?" came Cade's voice again. A note of panic filled it.

"I'm pushing rocks off Ricky. We're fine."

"Just be careful. I can't have you sliding into the canyon."

"I'm good. I have myself braced." She pushed her heel deeper into the loose rock until she found a firm hold. She continued to push the larger rocks off Ricky. He woke enough to brush himself off where he could. She soon had his leg where she could see it.

Ricky started to move. She placed her hand on his leg. "Wait just a moment. Let me check it. It might be broken." She ran her hands along the leg from above the knee to the ankle. It wasn't until she reached his ankle he winced. His face drew up. "I'm going to need to splint your foot."

"Cade?"

"I heard. Give me a sec to think. Got it. Hold on a minute."

Minutes later Cade lay on his side and lowered the bundle he had prepared over the edge.

Earlier he'd had to force himself to breathe while watching Lily go out of sight. The sounds of rocks shifting tightened his chest with worry. One slip and she could really be hurt or die. Here he was with a bum arm and no way to help her. She hadn't even flinched at the idea of going to the boy, but he sure had on her behalf.

He'd felt helpless as he'd leaned over the edge watching her. It should have been him going down there. The least he could do was assist as much as he could from here. He picked up the tent bag and dumped the tent out. Collecting the poles, he quickly snipped the elastic cord running through them. That allowed the poles to fall apart. He then cut off the straps of his backpack. Gathering four poles, he bundled them and secured them with the strips.

"I'll need the rope to lower this to you. Find a place where you are safe and don't move."

"I understand." Moments later she called, "You can pull the rope up."

As Cade tied the rope to the bundle, he listened to rock shifting then settling. He leaned over the edge and lowered the bundle. He could see Lily doing another evaluation on the boy, who wasn't moving.

When the bundle had almost reached her, she looked up. Lily gave him a weak smile. He made his expression brighter than he felt. The sooner she and the boy were up with him, the better.

The rope went slack as she removed the bundle. "Got it. You want to talk me through the plan here. I'm not sure what you have in mind."

"Will do. Place two poles on the anterior and posterior sides of the leg. They're so thin I didn't think one will be strong enough. Wrap my straps around at the top and bottom. Then cut yours off and do the same between them. You have the knife."

He watched as she followed his directions to the letter. "Be careful not to cut yourself. That's the last thing we need."

"Cade, don't put ideas in my mind. Think positive."

"I am. But being realistic as well." At least his voice didn't sound as tight.

"Have I said thank you for the wonderful time you've been showing me? I can certainly see why you want to live among nature."

Cade recognized her chatter for what it was. Nervous energy. "I tell you what. The next time I'll take you glamping and have breakfast delivered in. How does that sound?"

"That I can get behind."

Cade hoped there would be a next time between them. He watched as she wrapped her straps around the boy's leg and secured them. This wasn't the flighty Lily he had once known. This was a serious woman with a sense of humor. This woman knew her mind and was determined to do what she thought right. He couldn't help but admire her while at the same time being sick to his stomach she was in such a perilous position. If something went wrong, he didn't even have a way to call the rescue squad.

"Add a hot shower and a massage and I'll be yours forever."

Forever? Could they do forever after all the history they'd shared? Could she really trust him enough for her to open her heart to him again? Would he return to Chicago for her? Those questions he would have to consider later.

"Now you need to wake Ricky. He needs to help himself as much as he can to get up here. Tie the rope under his arms. I'll pull him up."

She looked at him. "How do you plan to do that with one arm?"

"I'll manage." He would somehow. He had to.

"I'll climb up and help you."

"Lily," his tone went firm. "Do as I say. Stay put."

What she had done so far had been close to superhuman, but it was time he did his share. The boy needed to be seen at the hospital pronto. If not, his issues could become more dangerous. The sooner they got him up and to help, the better. The same went for Lily. It was past time he relieved her of all the responsibility. Not that she wasn't rising to the occasion.

And there was his injury. Cade was barely keeping the pain at bay.

Lily yelled, "We're ready down here."

"Direct him away from the rock face as much as you can while he's coming up but do not, do not, put yourself in danger," he called back. "Lily!"

"I promise to behave. I got this down here. Stop worrying. You just get Ricky up."

Cade didn't have a choice but to believe she would do as he asked. Stepping to the rope, he lifted it then made a complete turn, wrapping it around his waist once. Grabbing the rope with his good hand, Cade began to walk away from the cliff, slowly pulling the boy upward. He hoped the rope could withstand the pressure along with the friction created by the edge.

The rope bit into his hand and middle while his shoulder throbbed from the exertion, but he kept moving. Sweat poured along his temples and down his back from the effort. He couldn't stop now.

Cade recognized the moment Lily had stopped helping lift the boy. Ricky's weight tugged on Cade, making the going more difficult. The boy felt heavier. Cade grunted but didn't slow his process. He made half steps backward while watching for a sign the boy had reached the top.

"Only two more feet," Lily called. "You're doing great."

Not soon enough to suit him, Cade saw the boy's head rise over the edge. He was hardly making any effort to help but when he reached the edge Ricky grasped for any hold he could find. With one more large step Cade had him lying on his stomach on the ground.

Releasing himself from the rope, Cade hurried to the boy, rolling him over and pulling him to safety.

"Got him, Lily. Stay put while I get him settled then I'll have you up in a flash."

"Okay."

Cade pulled the sleeping bag to him. Undoing the ties, he opened it. Using his chin to hold it steady, he unzippered it and spread it wide. All of this took more time than he had planned. Lily waited. What if she became impatient and tried to climb up on her own?

"Can you help me get you on the sleeping bag?"

Ricky nodded, rolling until he lay on the cloth.

"That's good." Cade covered Ricky then placed what was left of his backpack under the boy's feet, treating him for shock.

"Thirsty," the boy said through dry, crusted lips.

Cade handed him a plastic water bottle and lifted his head. "Little sips at first."

Ricky took a small amount and swallowed.

"Better?" Cade asked despite his eagerness to pull Lily up.

"Sleepy." The boy's eyelids closed.

"That's understandable." Cade helped the boy to lie back. "I need to do a quick exam of you."

Ricky said nothing. Cade made quick work of taking vitals. They were stable, but just barely within range. The boy was dehydrated and needed his blood sugar to level off, and his ankle needed medical attention Cade couldn't give him. Cade had done all he could do for Ricky. Now it was time to get Lily and reassure himself she was safe.

"Lily, I'm sending the rope down. Tie it around your waist and I'll pull you up." He dropped the rope over the edge.

"I can make it up on my own. You've done enough. You'll ruin the other shoulder if you aren't careful."

How like her to worry about him. Cade needed her back on firm ground. He worried far less about him being further injured than he did about her safety. His nerves couldn't stand any more. "Lily, please just do as I ask."

There was a moment of silence then, "I'm ready."

Once again, he wrapped the rope around his waist and walked backward while pulling on the rope with one hand. The scraping of rock reached his ears. The tug on the rope made him grunt. Every so often there was slack in the rope. Not soon enough for him he saw the top of Lily's head covered in cream-colored dust.

Cade dropped to his hand and knee from relief and exhaustion. Still heaving deep breaths, he gathered himself and stood above her. "Are you okay?"

"I'm fine. I just need to catch my breath."

She rolled over and looked at him. "How about you? How's the shoulder?"

"Let's not talk about it so I don't think about it."

That statement had her coming to her feet. "Do I need to have a look?"

"No. Right now I want to leave well enough alone."

He helped her to her feet, bringing her in for a hug, holding her close. Her arms circled his waist. He kissed her temple. "That I don't want to do again."

"What? Pulling me up?" The words were muffled against his chest.

He eased his hold, meeting her look. "No, letting you go down. I was terrified the entire time."

"I'm safe and sound." Lily removed the rope then leaned over and removed his hat from her head. Using it she slapped the dust from her pants. Straightening again, she repositioned the cap, then brushed at her shoulders and sleeves. Despite her efforts dust clung to her.

"This has not been a normal hike, I promise."

Lily lifted and lowered a shoulder. "But isn't this what your SEMA program is all about? The kind of thing you're trying to prepare medical personnel for? I have certainly been thinking and acting outside my comfort zone."

Cade shook his head. Lily had always managed to see the positive. He had never given her much credit for being resilient. Maybe if he had years ago things would have been different. He should have trusted she would stand beside him when he told her how he felt about his life.

Lily continued to slap at the dirt. That finished, she unbuttoned her shirt. Cade's eyes widened. She removed another shirt from the almost empty and cannibalized backpack. With quick, limited movements, she pulled the clean one on.

"Once again you turn out to be resourceful." Cade handed her the water bottle.

She took a long refreshing draw then handed it back to Cade. He followed suit.

Relief filled her now she was back with Cade and not below on a shifting rock slide with an injured patient. She had watched the slow movement of Ricky up the side of the rock face with trepidation. Being left alone had unsettled her.

More than that she had worried about Cade doing the heavy lifting with only one good arm. She hadn't wanted him making matters worse by hurting himself further. His grunts and groans had reached her as he worked to get Ricky to safety. She had wished she could be of more assistance, but too soon the boy had been out of her reach. Finally, the rocks stopped raining down on her as Ricky went over the edge.

Lily had been so engrossed in helping Ricky she hadn't given much thought to her own safety. Lily had glanced to the valley floor far below. With the boy gone and no rope, panic had seeped in. Her heart had pounded like someone beating on a door.

What if she slid farther? Could Cade get to her? Could she find a way out?

She'd had to work to control her breathing and not let terror intrude. Instead she had looked around at the trees, rocks, the sky then thought about the two injured people she was responsible for helping. This wasn't a place she belonged. She knew nothing about surviving in the wilderness. Yet she had been doing it.

As the minutes crawled by she searched above her. Why didn't Cade come and get her? At least throw her the rope? Should she try climbing? No, Cade had said to stay put. He would get her out of here. Of that, she had been sure.

Instead of negative thoughts she focused on memories of Cade kissing her so tenderly the night before. The way his hands had caressed her skin with such reverence. Or the sound of his pleasure as he entered her.

She refocused on the present when the rope appeared, and she secured it around her waist as Cade instructed.

"I'm ready," she called.

For a second she had thought of the pain Cade must be in while pulling with all his might with only one arm. The frustration he must feel at not being able to do more. Little had he known how much she appreciated his efforts. She had kept moving even when the going became tougher knowing he would be there waiting for her at the top.

Seeing the edge, she had reached over and grabbed what handhold she could find and pulled herself over the lip of the rock to lie on her stomach. Wiggling, she had hauled in gulping breaths after the amount of energy she had expended. Cade had been there to reassure her she had made it by pulling her into a hug as tight as the rope that had been around her waist. She welcomed his attention.

With that ordeal behind them they had another to consider. "How do we get out of here?"

"I have no way to call for rescue so we have to move from under these trees to an open area where the searchers can see us from the sky."

"How's Ricky? Can he be moved?" They both looked at the boy where he lay on the sleeping bag.

Cade stepped toward Ricky. "I'm sure his sugar is still low. He's sleeping a lot. But that could be from exposure after being out all night and scared to death. At least he didn't go into DKA. But we need to get him to a hospital so that doesn't happen."

"How do we plan to do that?" Lily continued to take deep breaths.

She looked at the trees above them. "You aren't carrying him out. You're hurt. We're going to have to figure something else out."

He thought for a minute. "What we need we're going to have to build."

"You tell me what to do and I'll do the building."

"Do you have the skill set for that?" He gave her a probing look, his lips pressed together.

Her hands went to her hips. "Do we have a choice? Do you see anyone else who can?"

"I cou—"

"Not going to happen." She started gathering the rope. "So get started telling me what to do."

"Were you always this bossy?"

She picked up a backpack and placed it beside the rope. "I don't know but it does feel good."

Cade chuckled. "Power going to your head?"

"No, I'm just ready for a hot bath." The dust made her feel grimy all over.

"That'll have to wait a little longer. Right now, we better get to work. We need to be out of here before it gets dark. And I'm going to help you search for supplies." He looked around them as if searching for something in particular.

"Supplies?" she echoed.

"We're going to build a litter. We need two long sticks and two smaller ones to use as crossbars."

She wasn't going to give him time to head off into the

woods. "You stay with Ricky. I'll get what we need. Then you tell me what to do from there."

"They have to be sturdy if they're going to work," Cade called as she entered the forest.

She had to work at it but half an hour later she returned with limbs under her arm and dropped them.

"You did good," Cade said with enthusiasm as he came to meet her.

"These were just lying there waiting on me."

"My guess is the storm last night broke it off. I think we can get everything we need out of this pile."

Cade offered her the water bottle. "Have some and we'll get started on putting this together." He picked up the rope. "This needs to be cut into four three-foot lengths. We'll need what's left to crisscross to hold the boy."

Lily pulled the knife out of her pocket and went to work. While she did that Cade broke the smaller limbs off the larger one. He placed them in a diagonal on the ground.

"Now I need you to make a cross with the rope and back around the two ends to hold them together."

Lily wrapped the rope.

"No. Like this." Cade took the length from her and showed her how he wanted it secured.

She tried again.

"Good. Now all of them need to be tied the same way." He stepped over to check Ricky.

Lily made quick work of doing the rest. She sat back on her heels. "Now what?"

He returned to her. "Take the rest of the rope and lace it across the middle. We'll use what we have left of clothes for support of his head and feet. We don't have enough rope to do the entire area."

"Where should I start?" She looked at the apparatus and then to Cade.

"Right here." Cade pointed a third of the way up one of the longest sticks. "Tie it off here and then go to the other stick and wrap it around then come back to this side. Like making a web."

"I got what you're doing now." Lily went to work and had soon used up all the rope.

While she had been doing that Cade went through the backpacks, pulling everything out. He held up their clothing. "These are going to have to work."

"What're you trying to do?"

"To make supports for the top and bottom area. I thought we could string our clothes in the spaces but I don't have anything but pants left and yours aren't large enough."

"What about cutting the tent into strips?"

He grinned then leaned down to give her a quick kiss. "You are brilliant."

Warm heat washed through her. She liked he thought so. Before yesterday she would have said she would be a hindrance in a situation like this, but it had turned out she had done her share. There was something satisfying in that idea she had not felt before. "I'm glad you think so."

Cade snatched up the tent and brought it to her.

"How should I cut it?"

"In the two largest squares you can. We can then split the corners to create ties."

Under his watchful eye she spread out the tent and began to cut. With the pieces in hand, she made the cuts for the ties.

"Now tie one corner to the other and lay it in the center of the rope webbing. Then tie the other corner to the poles as close to the crossbars as possible."

Lily did as he said.

"That's it. Great, you're doing great." When she finished, he announced, "I believe that will do it." He sounded pleased with their efforts.

"Now we need to get Ricky on it. If you can pick up the top corners of the sleeping bag I can get the bottom and we'll get him on it. But first we need to place the litter close beside him."

They did that.

Cade lifted Ricky's feet by picking up the sleeping bag. "Okay. On three, lift. One, two, three."

With a swift movement they swung Ricky, sleeping bag and all, onto the litter.

Lily looked down at Ricky, whose eyes had wide opened. "You okay?"

He nodded. "I want my mom."

She smiled. "You'll see her soon and get to tell her all about your adventure."

Cade stood over them. "Before we go, I want to give you a quick look over. Lily, will you unzip him?"

She did as Cade asked then went to stuff what was left of their camping equipment into their backpacks. Those she placed on either side of the boy.

A few minutes later Cade pronounced, "He's stable for now but it may not last. We should get moving. Lily, you take one end, and I'll take the other. We need to go as straight as possible for about half a mile. There's an open patch there."

The sound of Cade's voice told her he had drained his energy. She had no doubt he was in pain. She didn't need him passing out. If they didn't get help soon, she would have two problems on her hands. Not counting being out in the wilderness when she knew so little and they had used up so many of their supplies.

She took one end of the litter. "You lead. I can pull Ricky."

"No—"

"We're wasting time, Cade."

It didn't take long for sweat to bead on her forehead and run down the center of her back as she pulled the boy over the rough ground. Still she kept moving forward. Even with the use of gloves she would have blisters upon her blisters before she was done.

Cade stumbled a couple of times but righted himself.

"Time for a stop," she called.

"We need to—" Cade started.

"We need a stop. You need to sit a moment. We'll never make it if you pass out on me or worse, fall and get hurt." She pulled the water out of the pack and offered it to Cade. She then checked Ricky. His eyes were open. "How're you doing?"

He just looked at her.

"It won't be too long now." The poor kid had been through so much. She turned back to Cade. "Let's go."

"I can—"

"I have this. You show me the way." If she hadn't taken a stance, Cade would insist on doing the work even with his shoulder hurting.

With his mouth in a thin line, Cade started walking but not with the strength and confidence she'd known him to have. She went to stand between the poles, took the ends and pulled the litter behind her. Her shoulders strained with the effort. It didn't take but minutes before she started sweating once more. She continued putting one foot in front of the other as she watched Cade's sagging shoulders ahead of her.

Her concern for him grew with each step. They needed to reach their destination soon. He had begun to weave with the effort to stay upright. His skin looked pasty when they had stopped. To her great relief they finally left the trees and entered a large field.

Cade kept moving until they reached the middle. Lily followed. Cade sank to the ground then lay on his back. She lowered the boy to the grass then she threw the gloves to the ground before grabbing a backpack and running to Cade. Putting her hand under his head, she helped him to drink then put the pack under his head. "You stay put. Tell me what I need to do."

"Make a large cross in the grass by stomping on it. Something that can be seen from the sky."

Lily went to work immediately. Finished, she checked the vitals of her two patients. Then she lowered herself to the ground beside them to wait.

Cade took her hand. When she winced, he turned it so he could see her palm. "Your poor soft hands." He brought it to his lips and kissed it tenderly.

Tears came to her eyes. Cade must be in excruciating pain, and he was worried about her hands.

His agony-glazed eyes held hers. "We need to talk. About last night."

She shook her head. "Later. When we both aren't exhausted and can think straight. We said it was one night."

"I know, and…"

The whoop, whoop, whoop of a helicopter could be heard over the top of the trees.

Lily jumped up and started waving. The helicopter

flew over them and her heart sank before the helicopter made a sharp banking turn. Relief welled in her. "Cade, they're coming back. They see us."

Unable to sit up, Cade cupped her calf and squeezed.

She watched the helicopter slowly land. Before the machine had settled, two people wearing navy jumpsuits and carrying large packs over their shoulders popped off. They ran toward them. Seconds later she was busy giving them a report on first Ricky and then Cade.

With that done she stood to the side. Her job was finished. The EMTs had told her she'd done an excellent job. Their praise gave her a sense of purpose she'd not felt before. Would she have it again after she returned home?

CHAPTER EIGHT

CADE SEARCHED FOR Lily around the EMT who was down on one knee next to him. She'd moved out of sight. Was she overseeing Ricky's care? She should be checked out as well. Most of the physical labor had been done by her. Lily would never admit she needed help as long as he and Ricky were here. Her patients would always come first.

When asked briefly about how she was doing, she had assured the EMTs she was fine and encouraged them to focus on Cade and Ricky, as they had serious issues. Lily may be acting as if she weren't hurting, but he knew better. She must be dehydrated, aching and as exhausted as he was. Yet she stood nearby watching like a hovering mother in case she was needed.

Lily had been a real champ during the entire ordeal. Not once had she complained. She'd done what needed doing even though she was completely out of her element. Now the hero stood on the sideline.

Cade looked at the EMT who had just finished doing his vitals. "See to her now."

The EMT, who was resting on one knee beside Cade, glanced back at Lily. "Sir, I need to look at your shoulder."

Cade hated he couldn't go to Lily. He was attached to an IV line providing him hydration. Cade pulled away from the EMT. "Not until you check her out thoroughly."

"Sir—"

"Not until you see about her." Cade glared at the man. "She's the one who did the majority of the physical work. Please see to her."

The EMT stopped in midmotion. "Ma'am," he called, getting Lily's attention. When she looked their way he said, "He's not going to allow us to do anything until I have checked you out."

Lily, with her sweet lips tight in irritation, joined them. "Cade, let them see about your shoulder. What I did was makeshift at best."

"Stop fussing, Lily. Let him check you out first."

"I'm fine." There was a bite to her tone.

"So you say." He could be just as determined.

"Lily, you're going to listen to me this time. I want him to make sure you're okay then he can see about my arm." Cade's voice had turned pleading. For his sake she needed to listen.

Her face eased and she shook her head. "You're not going to have it any other way, are you?"

"I'm not."

She nodded to the EMT. "Okay." She lowered to the ground beside Cade. Her being close made him feel better immediately.

The EMT pursed his lips and went to work. Soon he had checked her heart rate, respiration and blood pressure. He also looked at her nails and hands. He pulled out a bottle of water and handed it to her. "You need to drink this. You're dehydrated as well." He felt around in his bag once more, removing a protein snack bar and giving it to her. "I believe you'll be fine."

Lily lifted her chin and gave Cade a look of triumph. "I told you so."

Cade managed to raise a corner of his mouth. "I don't care. I still think you needed to be seen first."

"Now, you let them take care of your shoulder." She touched his good arm.

"Will you stay here beside me?" He counted on her hearing the imploring in his voice. "And make sure they do it right."

She gave the EMT a reassuring smile when his brows grew together. "He's just kidding."

The man went back to work on Cade.

He took Lily's hand and played with her fingers as the EMT unwrapped the makeshift sling. Everything about each movement hurt. As he held Cade's arm gently, the EMT moved it, studying the range of motion and marking when and where it hurt. "Somebody did a fine job getting this back into the socket."

Lily winced. "That wasn't the most enjoyable thing I've ever done."

"I'm not surprised." The EMT looked at her with admiration. Pride filled Cade's chest as the EMT secured Cade's arm once more. "You have a date with an operation."

"I was afraid of that," Cade bit out between clinched teeth.

"You'll be flying out of here with the boy in just a few minutes. Let me check with the pilot. We're still waiting on the rangers. They'll be here to get you." He looked at Lily. "We don't have room for more than two patients and the crew."

Cade tugged Lily's fingers to get her attention. "You will be okay?"

"I'll be fine. The EMT even said so. Stop worrying.

I'm just relieved we got here, and it looks like Ricky's going to be fine and you are too."

"The rangers will take care of you. You know they're going to take me to the hospital." Cade's eyes slowly lowered. The pain medicine the EMT had given him had taken effect.

"Yeah. They need to. That's where you need to be."

Cade's fingers tightened around hers. She winced. He eased his grip. "I'm sorry."

"For what? You couldn't control what happened."

"For not being who you thought I was so long ago. For not recognizing how wonderful you are."

She huffed. "I think you might be exaggerating some. It's all in the past."

"I know, but I'm not exaggerating. In fact I…" When he could think straight again he would see to it she believed him. Cade wanted more. Did she? What if she didn't? Maybe this could wait till later. He shifted toward her then groaned.

Lily's eyes narrowed. "Did the EMT give you something for pain?"

"He did but—" His eyes were starting to glaze over.

She brushed his cheek. "Cade, I know the camping trip wasn't what either one of us had planned but I wouldn't have wanted to go through the last few hours with anyone but you." Her shoulders straightened. "I can't wait to tell my friends and family that I've been camping. They'll be so impressed."

"You be sure to tell them what a hero you have been. You certainly are mine." And more.

"I just did what had to be done. Just like you."

The EMT walked up to stand above them. "Time to load up. I'll help you to the helicopter."

Lily's fingers slipped from Cade's as she stood.

When the EMT moved to support him Cade stopped him. He wrapped his arm around Lily and brought her against him for a squeeze. "Hold your head high. No one is stronger or more determined than you. You have nothing to be ashamed of—ever."

She tightened her hold on him. "Thanks for saying that. You need to remember people make mistakes. We all deserve forgiveness. Even when it means forgiving ourselves. Have a good life, Cade."

That sounded far more final than he liked. But he didn't have the energy to refute it now. Was that really the way she wanted it? What did he want?

The sound of the helicopter engine covered any chance for further words being heard.

Cade kissed her tenderly on the lips, looked into her eyes for a long moment. Lily gave him what he recognized as a forced smile. He returned it and started toward the helicopter. The EMT helped him into the chopper. Ricky was already there.

In the distance Cade glimpsed the rangers approaching on ATVs. But what really held his attention was the lonely figure standing in the field looking up. His chest ached. He feared he'd just left part of him behind. Was it his heart?

Lily stood watching the helicopter rise with every fiber of her being vibrating. The need to run to Cade and latch on and never let go built. Yet she didn't let her feet move.

There was no future there. If there had been, surely he'd have said something. What had happened between them had been under the cover of darkness and by being forced together. The entire camping experience had been a disaster, a mistake. He'd let her down once and there was no reason to think he wouldn't again. Nothing had changed between them. The only thing that had happened was two friends reminiscing. She had her issues, and he did too.

She still needed to deal with her family. She needed to understand her background to understand her future, her place in the world. Even if Cade wanted her, she must be a whole, complete person before she could move on.

His disconnect with his father, mother and brothers was too large to ignore. If she and Cade were together and he still couldn't reconcile with his father, it would always lay heavy on his heart. What would happen if they had children? Too much heavy baggage.

All of those issues were worries she shouldn't bother with. What made her think that Cade would ever come after her? He hadn't before. Why would she think he would this time?

What if she ran to him and he rejected her? He had pushed her away before and not looked back. She couldn't live through that again. The only thing she knew to do was what Cade had done years earlier—make a clean cut.

Maybe if she told herself that often enough she would start to believe it.

The roar of the ATVs approaching demanded her attention.

Both rangers pulled up beside her. They shut the machines off and climbed down. "Ms. Carter?"

Who else would she be standing alone in the field? Still she hesitated a moment at the unfamiliar name. "Uh… yes."

"Dr. Evans said for us to take good care of you, or we would hear from him."

Lily looked at the tree line where the helicopter had just disappeared then back at them questioningly.

"He took the radio from the EMT and demanded to speak to us. I understand he was adamant about doing so." The female ranger smiled. "I wish a man felt that way about me." With a nod of her head, she indicated the ATVs. "Can you get on yourself or do you need help?"

"I can get on myself. Do you mind if we get going? I'd like a shower."

The woman smiled. "I'm sure you would." She swung her leg over the ATV seat. "Climb on behind me."

Lily picked up what was left of the backpacks. The ranger on the other ATV took them from her and stored them under his seat.

Over the next hour they traveled through paths in the forest, across rock and even forded a stream until they reached a paved road. From there they traveled into the village. The entire trip back Lily reviewed all she and Cade had shared. The last two intense days overshadowed all they had ever experienced before together. Even their lovemaking had been deeper and more meaningful.

"Where're you staying?" the woman asked.

"In the cabins," Lily yelled.

The ranger turned the ATV in that direction and soon Lily stood in front of her cabin door. Alone. With a quick goodbye she was left standing there wondering, as if the last two days had been a dream or a nightmare. Had she ever felt more alone?

Suddenly desperate to know how Cade was doing, she went inside and grabbed her phone. She called the clinic. Meghan answered.

Lily hardly let her speak before she asked, "Have you heard how Cade is?"

"He just arrived at the Fresno hospital. That's all I know now."

"Will you let me know if you hear more?" Lily thought about driving to the hospital.

"I'll call you."

Lily heard the desperation in her own voice. "Even if it is the middle of the night."

"I'll call. Are you okay? I heard it was pretty difficult out there."

Lily sighed. "I'm fine. I just need a bath. Call me."

"Will do."

Who did she call to tell how worried she was? No one in Chicago would believe her or be interested. She just wanted Cade's arms around her. Or to sit next to him and hold his hand.

It wasn't until she was in the shower that she let her tears of worry and loss over Cade flow. What if she never saw him again?

After a night of little sleep and tossing and turning from pure exhaustion, Lily rose and quickly dressed. She was going to the clinic to find out how Cade and Ricky were doing. Someone had to know something. Surely Lamar knew some information.

Lily entered the clinic and all the students and staff turned to face her. All of a sudden everyone circled her and started talking at once.

"How are you doing?"

"What's going on?"

"We heard what happened with you and Cade."

She patiently answered each question when all she wanted to do was ask her own. Finally, she had her chance. "Do you know how Cade's doing?"

Lamar answered from the doorway of Cade's office.

"He'll be having surgery today on his shoulder. Then will need weeks of physical therapy. He should be fine in time."

Her anxiousness lessened. "Good to hear."

Lamar moved to the side, leaving the doorway open. "Lily, may I see you a minute?"

She glanced at the others, who wore concerned looks then nodded to Lamar.

He said to the rest, "You have your assignments. I'll be ready to go as soon as I speak to Lily. I'll meet you in the parking lot." Lamar turned to face her. "You had quite the ordeal. You've done more during your overnight trip than you would have done with the three days you were supposed to be out in the wilderness with me. It has garnered us positive press, which is a good thing. It'll work to the program's favor."

"I'm glad there was something positive to come out of it."

"As I've already stated you have certainly done more in the last two days than you would have under my instruction. I'm not sure any further participation would be to your benefit. You have earned some rest. You're free to go home. I'll be sending along your certificate."

Lily gasped. She needed to be close to Cade. Here's where she felt that. "I can help out here."

"That won't be necessary. The doctor who will be filling in will arrive tomorrow. Personally, I'm very impressed with how you handled yourself out there. You're the epitome of what this program is all about."

"Thank you, sir. Do you happen to know what hospital Cade is in or the number for it? I'd like to personally check on him."

"I understand they're transferring him from Fresno to

a San Francisco hospital. There is a world-renowned orthopedist there who specializes in shoulder injuries who will do the surgery. Cade will be moved this morning. Seems his father wanted him in the best place possible. I'll just have to wait on Cade or a family member to call to know more."

Cade no doubt had something to say about his father making decisions. "And Ricky?"

"He's well. He stayed in Fresno. He's going to spend a couple of nights in the hospital but should be back with his family in no time. Thanks to you and Cade." He placed a hand on her shoulder. "Now, I think you have earned some time off to recover."

"Thank you, sir. I appreciate it and I understand. I hope Cade has no lasting effects."

"Ms. Carter, I hope that's the case as well." Lamar gave her an encouraging smile.

"It's really Smythe."

Lamar tilted his head. His look turned questioning. "What?"

"My last name is really Smythe."

He shook his head. "I'll be in touch, Ms. Smythe."

Lamar opened the door. She walked through it. Out of Cade's office, his world. Why did the idea of leaving his office align with the emotions of believing that what they had shared would be gone forever? The idea hurt. But wasn't that what she had insisted on? She plowed into his life, made requests and been the reason he'd been injured. If he never wanted to speak to her again she wouldn't blame him.

Controlling the tears teetering on the edge of falling, she told the remaining staff goodbye. Outside she spoke to those in the parking lot waiting with their camping equipment around them. They all gave her a hug, then she slowly walked to her car.

At her cabin she arranged for her flight out. If she left right away she could catch a plane later that afternoon out of Fresno. She went through all the scenarios she could come up with to go see Cade, but none seemed practical. Cade wouldn't be out of surgery today for hours. He wouldn't even know or remember she had come by for a few days when the anesthesia drugs were out of his system. He had been moved to San Francisco, which would take her hours to reach. It was best for her to go home and call to check on him. Just having her hanging around wouldn't be helpful to his recovery if he even wanted her around.

Hours later Lily stepped on the plane leaving Fresno without any enthusiasm. This was worse than leaving Cade's office. More final. She had expected, when she came to Yosemite, she would find joy in heading home but instead reluctance filled her. She found her seat with shoulders slumped and feet slow. Despite the shock of seeing Cade again and all that had happened between them she was glad she had visited Yosemite National Park.

Because of the days she spent in the park and with Cade she was a stronger person than she had been. She could handle what people said about her and better understood her parents and their decisions. Hadn't Cade said that was the point of the SEMA program: to develop confidence in a person's leadership, and strength to make decisions and stand by them? In those aspects he had been successful with her.

Now it was time to go home and honor what she had learned. She would tackle going after the new job and hearing her parents out about what they had done. No matter what she would stand on her own two feet when facing the world.

"I'm going to be fine, Mom. Stop fussing," Cade groused as his mother adjusted his hospital bed covers once again.

When he'd arrived at the San Francisco hospital a staff member had told him he would have to have somebody to help him if he wanted to be released from the hospital. There would also be weeks of physical therapy. His first thought was of Lily but that would be pushing their unsure relationship and future too far. Reluctantly he gave them his mother's number. To his great relief she arrived without his father. He needed to feel his best to deal with that parent.

In the last two days he hadn't heard from Lily. But had hoped to. Without a phone he couldn't call her or her him. A couple of times he had missed his room phone ringing. Had those been Lily? Or had she just returned to Chicago and moved on with her life?

He would deserve that. Wasn't that what he had done to her? Worried about his life over hers.

But he didn't think being without Lily would be the answer this time. He was older and wiser. More aware of what he needed in his life. That was Lily, based on the ache in his chest along with the constant thoughts of her.

Cade's mother said, "I think you should consider returning with me to Chicago. You're going to need help for a while."

"Mom, if that's what you think is best," he said.

His mother's look of astonishment was almost laughable. "You're going to agree?"

"I am." Somewhere in his drug-induced state he'd realized he'd messed up again with Lily. He should have shared all he felt for her, that he wanted them to try again. He shouldn't have let her close him down before he had a chance to tell her that. He hadn't said everything he needed to say. He planned to go to her on bended knee and beg for another chance.

His mother immediately picked up the phone and made arrangements for their flights. She even took care of talking to the surgeon about which orthopedist Cade should see in Chicago.

If it wasn't for the fact Lily was in Chicago he would have never agreed. If it took going there and staying in his family home to see her again, then he would do it. He had to talk to her. Let her know how he felt. That he wanted to try again.

The next day his mother packed his few belongings. From across the room she asked, "Are you ready to go, hon?"

"Yes. I've always heard that doctors make lousy patients. I can't disagree with the sentiment." Cade had already passed the point of no return on staying in the hospital. He'd had to stay a couple of extra days just for observation to make sure he had recovered from being dehydrated.

"I've had your father arrange physical therapy. You'll need help dressing and driving for a few weeks."

He would rather Lily be doing it. "Thanks, Mom."

"What's a mother for? It'll be so nice to have you home. It has been too long. We've missed you. Too bad you had to get hurt for you to come for a visit." She picked up his bag when a transporter came with a wheelchair.

They were settled into first class on the airplane when

he asked, "Mom, why have you never said anything to me about Lily?"

She looked at him a moment. "Because I thought you needed to ask first. That it must be too painful."

"But you have kept up with her," he stated.

"Yes. I have."

"How was it after I left?"

Her voice turned sad. "From everything I heard or saw, very difficult. She lost weight, dropped out of school for a while. It took a long time for her to recover."

"Did you know she has been in Yosemite taking a class from me for the past week?"

"I didn't until I saw the news report on TV about the two of you saving a lost child in the park. I was surprised and impressed. I had no idea you and she had been in contact."

"We haven't been. I was as surprised to see her as she was me. Lily was great with the kid. I had no idea of the fortitude she has."

There was so much distance between them. In miles and thought, yet he didn't want a friendship. He wanted her with him all the time. As his mate. He had been an idiot back then. Hadn't recognized what he had. How much he loved her.

Lily captured his heart with how she'd stood up to him. The way she jumped in and tried even when she had no experience. She had a kindness about her that went beyond the normal to angelic. She added her special dose of humor to his life that he had been missing and needed.

"Mom, I really hurt her. Do you think she could forgive me enough to love me again?"

His mother met his look with an intent one. "That's the thing about loving someone—you have to learn to forgive. If Lily loves you, she'll forgive you. You just have to be brave enough to ask."

The pain medicine he took before getting on the flight made him drift off to sleep. Had his father asked his mom for forgiveness?

Cade had been in Chicago three days when Lamar called.

"How're you doing?" his friend asked. "I've been checking on you, but this is the first time I've actually had a chance to talk to you."

"Going to physical therapy and sleeping for the most part. I'm sorry about not having a phone. I'll do something about that as soon as I can." Cade would ask his mother to get one right away.

"No problem."

Cade asked, "How's Ricky doing?"

"Great. All is well. The parents were asking about how they could thank you and Lily," Lamar responded.

"I hope you told them that wasn't necessary."

Lamar said, "I did. But they were pretty vocal about their appreciation. You two made the news. I know we talk about getting the word out about the SEMA program but…"

"Yeah. This isn't the way I wanted to do it, but it is good for us."

Lamar continued, "I'll say you proved the value of the course by what you and Lily did. Especially with how well Lily performed since you were hurt. That's a real positive for the program."

Cade could only hope the parks service saw it that way and gave him a contract.

Lily had returned to Chicago and taken a couple of days off since she wasn't expected back at the hospital for another week. She spent her time recovering from the physical ordeal she been through.

A number of times she called to check on Cade. None of the calls did any good since she didn't actually speak to him. When she managed to get a human, she received the standard information, which was the equivalent of almost nothing. After he was moved to a room, she called a couple of times, but no one ever picked up.

She finally gave up and called Lamar to find out information. Doubts filled her. She should have gone to see about Cade. Did he have someone to help him?

"He's fine. Stable. They did what needed to be done on his shoulder. His mother is with him." Lamar relayed the information with little emotion.

"Thanks. That's good to hear. I'm glad he has someone to be with him." She just wished he'd asked for her.

"He should be getting out of the hospital in a few days."

Relief flooded her at his words. Cade had saved her life. Why was she kidding herself? He was her life. Had been forever. That's why she'd never found someone else. She been hoping Cade would come back for her. Yet she'd been the one to keep a distance between them. Because she'd been afraid she might be hurt again. But didn't she hurt now?

"Has the parks service made any decision about the program?"

"They're still considering it for other parks. You managed to get the program much-needed attention, which is a good thing." Lamar sounded pleased.

"When will you know something?" She wanted Cade to have his dream.

"I don't know. We'll just have to wait and see how things go."

* * *

She was anxious.

Lily had been back at work at Chicago Hospital for three days when she stopped in front of the same bulletin board she had been standing before when the nurse had made all those negative comments.

Satisfaction filled Lily. She had received her certificate. Lamar had sent a copy by email with a printed one due in the mail. Lily was grateful for that. She had already forwarded the email to her superior to attach to her application.

Looking around her at the large, modern emergency department with its gleaming equipment and glowing floors, she missed the slower pace of the Yosemite clinic and the creak of its ancient wood floor. What she wouldn't give for a good rocker.

She had been so sure weeks ago that having the supervisor job was what she wanted. So much so she'd even taken a class at the last minute to prove it. But was staying here really the right move for her? Was it what she wanted now? Would her skills be better used elsewhere? With a taste of time spent in a remote area, she found she no longer belonged in a metropolitan lifestyle.

Lily wanted something more—no, something different.

She missed the trees, the fresh smell of the air, the roar of the waterfall, the coziness of a cabin and the relaxation of a rocker. Mostly she missed Cade. Maybe it was time for her to strike out on her own, to stand alone. To take her own path, one that didn't have anything to do with her family. She'd learned so much about herself, was much stronger than she thought she was. It was time she took that strength and stepped out of her perfect safe world.

She knocked on the supervisor's door. Inside it only took her five minutes to give her two weeks' notice. She would be leaving the emergency department. If she could work it out, she would leave Chicago as well. If Cade would have her, she would go to him. If not, she would find her place elsewhere.

She wasn't sure who was more shocked—her or her supervisor—with her action, but Lily had never felt better about a decision. She had done the right thing.

Before she left again, she needed to talk to her parents…uh…half brother and sister-in-law. It was all so confusing. Was Cade right? Had they only done what they thought best? Regardless of their reasons she still owed it to them to let them know she had quit her job and would be moving. They deserved that. The idea of facing them didn't excite her. She would just have to draw on her newly gained strength and do what must be done.

The next afternoon Lily drove up the brick drive that curved in front of her family home. Nothing had changed. How she saw it had. Half of the mansion belonged to her. Granted, her father had told her that. She didn't want it.

She pulled around to park in her usual spot in front of the extended garage. The spot that had been hers since she had started driving. At the back door, she hesitated with her hand on the doorknob after taking in a deep breath and releasing it. She turned it, letting herself in.

Her mother…uh… Sara. Lily couldn't get used to the fact the woman who had been her mother all her life now was also her sister-in-law. It was all too weird.

Sara stood in the kitchen chopping vegetables just as Lily had expected she would be. They had never had a full-time cook. Her mother had always liked to prepare the meals. She said creating family meals was the glue that held them together. She also made sure her dad was there. If he was running late, they waited until he came home.

More than once, her mother had said this was her favorite room.

Her mother had always been the center of the family, the sun. The rest of them circled around her like planets, held in her sphere. Her father was the moon who worshipped her. They had the type of relationship Lily had longed for. The kind she wanted with Cade.

Her mother glanced Lily's way. She dropped the knife and with a huge smile hurried to pull Lily into a tight hug.

Lily returned it.

Her mother squeezed her one more time before releasing her. "I'm so glad you're home."

"I'm glad to be here too." Lily meant it. A lot had changed since the last time she'd been here.

Her mother had tears in her eyes when she turned back to what she was doing. "How're you doing?"

"I'm fine." Lily went to stand across the bar from her.

"We didn't know where you were until we saw the news about the rescue." Her mom sounded hurt. Lily hated she had put that note in her voice.

"I'm surprised it made it all the way here. I'm sorry I didn't tell you I was leaving or where I was going." Lily hoped she believed her.

"You were upset. I had no idea you and Cade had stayed in touch."

Her mother sounded hurt Lily might not have confided in her. Another mark against Lily. "We haven't. That was purely accidental."

Her mother looked up in disbelief. "That must've been a real surprise."

"That's an understatement." Lily grinned.

"I had no idea that rescue in parks used medical personnel." Her mother turned and dumped the vegetables into a pot on the stove.

"That was purely accidental as well. I've been having a lot of that happening lately. When will…uh… Dad be home?"

Her mother glanced back. "I'm expecting him soon."

Over the next few minutes, they had a pleasant conversation about what her brothers were doing while ignoring the proverbial elephant in the room. "I have a few things to tell you, Mama."

Her father…half brother—there it was again—entered the room through the back door.

He came straight to Lily and wrapped her against his chest. "We've been worried about you."

When he released her, she said, "I'm sorry. I didn't mean for you to do that."

"I can understand why you needed to disappear." He kissed her mother, who had come to stand beside him. He took her hand in his, smiling down at her.

Lily had seen this hundreds of times, maybe thousands, but this was the first time she had registered she was watching two people in love. She wanted that connection in her life.

Her mother nudged her father toward the table that sat in front of a large bay window overlooking the pool and the small house beyond. "Let's sit down. I have some water hot for tea."

Lily and her father took the places they had occupied for years.

"I saw you've been busy," her father said with censure and a note of pride. "We had no idea you were in Yosemite."

"I didn't tell anybody I was going. It was a last-minute decision." Lily felt a need to defend herself.

Her mom set cups of tea in front of them then went after hers.

When her mother settled, Lily looked at both of them. "Mom. Dad. Sara. Grant. I don't know what to call you anymore."

Her parents' eyes turned dark with sadness.

Lily let her hurt out. "I don't understand why you didn't tell me."

Her mother spoke. "When you were young, we just didn't think you'd understand. That it would be too confusing. As you got older, we got caught up in life and it wouldn't have made any difference. You were ours. There just didn't seem like a good time."

Lily's father leaned forward, his earnest look focused on her. "When our dad and your mom were killed and you needed a place to live or go into foster care I couldn't let my baby sister grow up in someone else's house or being passed around. I took you for mine then and you have remained mine. I love you as a sister, but I love you even more as my child." Her father's eyes glistened.

"We fell in love with you and each other. Because of you we have each other." Her mother looked at her father then back at Lily. "We love you, honey. We always have. It doesn't matter if you want us to continue to be your parents or to be your brother and sister-in-law. We were—are—a happy family."

Her father took her mother's hand. "We wanted you to feel secure. We hope you'll keep us in your life. We want you to be happy. We're just sorry you found out the way you did."

Her father said with his eyes sad, "I should have told you. There wasn't going to be a good time."

"I get it. You made a mistake. We all make them. I can forgive you for that. Have you told the boys?"

"Yes." Her mother grinned.

"I bet they weren't glad to learn I'm their aunt."

"Actually, they found it all rather interesting." Her father smiled. "They're expecting special gifts at Christmas."

"That's not happening." That statement brought a smile to all their faces. "I have something else to talk to you about."

Concern re-entered her parents' eyes. They took their chairs again.

She hurried along. "I've resigned from my job at the hospital. I've already put in my two-week notice. I'm going to be looking for another job more rural. I'm going to move away."

"Lily." Her mother placed a hand on her arm. "We didn't mean to drive you away."

"You didn't. This has nothing to do with what you and Dad did. This is about me. This experience both here and in Yosemite has shown me I have lived a very sheltered life. That I need to get out and expand my world. See it from other points of view. To use all my skills. In the best way possible."

"But where're you going?" her father demanded, his protective nature showing.

She shrugged. "I don't know yet. I'm going to spend the next few days looking online for what kind of positions are out there. I'm good at medicine, Daddy." She grinned at him. "It's in my blood. But I need to step out from underneath the Smythe name and make my own path."

Her father's body relaxed. "I can identify with that. I felt the same way when I started out."

"Yeah, I think it must be in the blood too, honey. We'll be here for you no matter what." Her mother hugged her again.

Lily never doubted that a moment.

"Just promise you'll stay in touch," her dad said. "These past weeks knowing you were mad at us and us not knowing where you were were terrifying."

"I'll never do that again. Promise. But I need you not to ever keep a secret like that from me again. I'm so sick of secrets. They aren't good for anyone. They just hang there waiting to ruin people's lives."

Her mother glanced at her father. He nodded. "We'll never keep secrets from you again."

"I love you, Mom and Dad." Lily reached for them.

They hugged her. "We love you too."

"Now tell us about seeing Cade again. How did you handle that?"

Lily gave them the highlights, leaving out their time together in the tent.

"So you've had a change of heart?" her mother asked.

"More of an expanding of my heart. I've always loved Cade. I think that's why I never gave anyone else a chance."

"Even after the way he treated you?" Her father sounded as if he wanted to fight for her. "I didn't know there were that many tears in one person's body until he left."

"Sweetheart," her mother said as she placed her hand on her father's knee. "I know I cried tears over you."

"You did?" Her father's brows rose.

She smiled indulgently. "Sure. I knew how I felt about you long before you realized how you felt about me. The day we met I loved you but it took you a little while longer to catch on." They gave each other a secret smile that made Lily almost jealous. They turned back to Lily. "Are you planning to get in touch with Cade?"

"I am. I'm just not sure how or when. I'm not even sure he wants to see me."

Her father put his arm around her shoulders and gathered her into his chest. "He'll want to see you."

CHAPTER NINE

CADE WATCHED HIS father kiss his mother on the cheek. He noted the way she brightened. Had his father really come clean with his actions and changed his ways? Cade hoped so. He wanted to clear the air with his father. Whatever was or wasn't between his parents, they would have to live with. He would be returning to Yosemite. But before he did, he needed to talk to his dad.

A few minutes later, Cade followed his father to his office. He knocked on the door. The man everyone said Cade looked so much like glanced up from where he sat behind his desk.

"May I come in?"

His father said, "Sure," then waved Cade in.

How many times had he been called in here for a dressing-down or even for good news? Memories swamped him. He had always marched to a different drum than the rest of the family. He should have probably picked a more comfortable place for this discussion, but he was here now.

"Dad, I appreciate you letting me come here to recuperate."

His father gave him a sad look. "I'm sorry you feel you have to say that. This is your home. Your mother and I would not have it any other way."

Cade studied his father. He looked as if he had aged far past what he had looked like when Cade had left town.

"You'll always be welcome here. Do you think I've enjoyed having you gone? This is home where you belong."

Cade flinched. This wasn't where he belonged any longer.

"You'll always be welcome here. In fact, we have an opening at the clinic—"

"Dad. Nothing has changed about me joining your practice. But I do owe you an apology for leaving like I did. I should have been more of a man about it. I should've told you a long time before I left that I wasn't interested in working in a large city environment. Yours isn't the type of medicine I want to practice." When his father opened his mouth to say something, Cade hurried along. "It doesn't make yours wrong or mine right—it just makes us want different things." It had taken Cade years to realize that.

"I thought you understood you were to join my practice. I had planned to pass it down to you and Mike. Give you a start I didn't have."

"Dad, you know Mike would never see me as a full partner with any real influence. He's older and has always wanted to tell me what to do. I would have made him miserable, and he would have done the same to me."

"That I hadn't thought about. Mike has always wanted to boss you around and you have always resisted. I also know he took credit for an idea you had for the practice. It was pointed out rather loudly and pointedly."

"By Lily."

"Yes. You may have left her, but she would have defended you to the death to anyone who said a bad word about you." His admiration was clear in his voice.

That made Cade's guilt heavier. If she would have him again, he would make it up to her and more. "I should have done better by her. I hope she gives me a chance to make it up to her."

"I didn't make that time better for you." He paused. "I want you to know that I don't have to explain my personal life or decisions to you but I'm making an exception for your mother. This will not happen again. I didn't initiate that kiss between the nurse and me. We did flirt and I let things get out of hand. That's too easy to do in the working world, anywhere for that matter. I didn't have an affair with her. I have come clean with your mother. It'll not be mentioned again between she and I or the two of us. Your mom and I are stronger than we ever have been."

His father's forceful words made Cade sit straighter. "That's good to hear. Very good to hear."

"I understand you've been very successful in your chosen path. I've kept up with you the best I could." Obviously, the earlier subject had been closed.

"You have?"

"Of course. Just because you aren't in my practice doesn't mean I don't want to know how you're doing. This SEMA program sounds exciting. You have always been good at seeing a problem or something missing and finding an answer."

Cade couldn't help but appreciate the unexpected praise from his father.

His father's look turned direct. "I should have listened more."

"That's water under the bridge now, Dad."

His father crossed his arms on his desk. "You and Lily had quite an adventure, I understand. I bet it was a surprise to see her."

"That would be an understatement." Cade thought of the shock in her eyes that day on the porch.

"So, what are your plans now?"

How like his father to think of the next step. "As soon as I get this arm well enough I'm going to return to Yosemite. And I hope to convince Lily to go with me."

"Is there anything I can do to help?"

Cade couldn't think of another time in his life his father had asked him that question. "Not right now but I'll let you know if there is."

From a distance Cade heard his mother call, "Mike and his family are here."

Cade and his father stood. His father came around the desk and placed a hand on Cade's good shoulder. "I'm proud of you, son."

Cade met his father's look and saw the sincerity in his words. That was all Cade needed to move on. Now he had to see if he could salvage something with Lily.

The buzz of the apartment doorbell made Lily look up from where she sat at her kitchen table. It was the middle of the afternoon. She wasn't expecting anyone. She had spoken to her parents two days before. When she had left her childhood home, it had felt good to have mended the bridge between her and her parents.

At the door she looked through the eyehole. Her heart skipped. She whispered, "Cade."

Even with the distorted view he looked wonderful. Much better than he had when she'd last seen him. She never expected to see him at her door. He had said he had no plans to return to Chicago.

Why had he?

She pushed at the locks of hair that had fallen from the

band holding it away from her face. She gave the hem of her T-shirt a tug. The cutoff jeans would just have to do. She might not look her best, but she wouldn't turn Cade away.

The doorbell buzzed again as Lily fumbled with the lock. She must get control of herself. Still her heart raced with anticipation.

Cade stood there looking better than an ice cream on a hot day. The blue shirt he wore brought out the color of his eyes, which were bright compared to the pain-filled ones she had last seen. His arm remained in a navy medical sling she had given more than one person in the emergency department.

"Cade. This is a surprise. But then you seem to do that to me a lot."

The wrinkle in his forehead eased and a smile brightened his face. "Hi, Lily."

For a moment had he been worried she wouldn't welcome him? "What brings you to Chicago? To my humble home?"

"I came to get something. May I come in?"

"Uh…yeah." She stepped back, allowing him to enter. He smelled wonderful. Like fresh air and a hint of lemon. She wanted to step close and inhale.

Her spacious living area became smaller with his bulk in it. More than that he looked out of place. After seeing him in nature this man didn't belong in her slick, silver chrome modern high-rise apartment. She closed the door.

Cade strolled to the large bank of windows that looked out over Chicago and beyond to Lake Michigan. "Great view."

"Being twenty floors up will give you that." She moved to stand beside him. This apartment had been a gift from her parents after Cade had left her. They were trying anything to cheer her up. "Different from those views in Yosemite."

"Yeah, but both have their value."

"I think I like the ones in Yosemite better." Mostly because he had been with her.

Cade turned. "Do you really mean that?"

"I don't say things I don't mean." Why did she feel they were talking around what was really on his mind? "How's your shoulder? I called but never got to talk to you."

"That's okay. Me not having a phone was a problem." He pulled a phone out of his pocket. "But I've solved that." He let the instrument slide out of sight again. "I wanted to call but I didn't have your number."

She didn't question the fact he could have asked his mother to get the number from her mother.

He looked away. "I probably should have called before I came here. But I was afraid you might not want to see me, and I wanted to see you."

"You're welcome anytime." Was he crazy? She was positively vibrating with excitement over him being here. "How's your shoulder?"

"It's getting better every day. The physical therapy is grueling but I'm getting there. And of course, my mother is taking too good of care of me. I had to sneak away to come here."

So that's why he was in town. Because he was staying with his family. It had nothing to do with her. Sadness washed through her. She stepped over to a living room chair and sank into it. "I'm surprised you agreed to come to Chicago. You said you never planned to do so again."

He continued looking out the window. "I needed to make it easier on Mom, so I agreed when she asked, but

I was coming anyway. I needed to pick up something that belongs to me."

"So you've been staying with your parents." How long had he been so close and she'd had no idea?

He turned to face her. "The doctors wouldn't release me from the hospital until I had someone to help me. Mom didn't give me a choice of who that would be. She was on the way as soon as the hospital called."

"You're only two weeks out. It must have hurt to travel." Why hadn't he contacted her before now? She'd wanted to hear from him so badly it hurt. But he was here now.

He grinned. "Pain pills come in handy."

Her stomach did a flip when his smile focused on her. She hadn't thought about how much he must have been out of it until recently. "I guess they do."

"It must be interesting being in the house with your father. How's that going?"

"Better actually. We discussed what I saw briefly. He told me Mother knew of the incident and the subject was closed between us. Based on how I see my parents acting when they're together, I believe him."

"That's wonderful. I've always liked your parents. I hate to think all isn't well with them." And she hated to see how his father's actions affected Cade.

"Dad told me he was proud of me. Especially in light of our adventure."

The look of wonder on his face was almost boyish. "I'm so happy for you."

He studied her from head to toe. Heat washed over her at his intense look. She raised her hand to touch him but stopped herself. What if he didn't want her? Wasn't she the one who had said they were going to keep things friendly between them?

He'd pushed her away before. Did she dare let him know how much she cared for him?

Could she survive if he rejected her?

"You look like you have recovered from being in Yosemite. May I see your hands?"

She put them out for his view. He took one and turned it over, looking at her palms. Her heart soared at his touch. His fingers caressed hers as he released her fingers. "I've worried about your poor, beautiful hands."

"They have recovered." She had recovered in every aspect except for where he had captured her heart. "I've been worried about you."

"Nothing to worry about here. You know you were pretty amazing through all of that."

A thrill rippled through her. "I just did what had to be done."

"I hated leaving you behind. It was like taking a date to a dance and leaving with someone else. Just not right."

She smiled. "Interesting comparison but I don't remember you really having a choice." Much like years ago. He'd done what he had to do.

"I've done that too many times to you. I should've insisted you go in the helicopter or wait until another one could come." He sank to the couch facing her.

For some reason she wanted to reassure him she was fine. "The rangers got me home with no problem. See, I'm all in one piece."

"Still, I should have been the one to take care of you." Cade looked beyond her to the table where her laptop and papers were spread around. "I'm sorry. It looks like you were busy. I didn't mean to interrupt you."

Didn't he know she quaked with joy just having him there with her? She would take his interruption any day. "No big deal. I'm just looking for a new job."

His brows rose and eyes widened. "Really. I thought you had already applied for a new job."

"I did, but I decided I didn't want it." Lily hadn't planned to blurt that out. She had enough savings to last her for six months. Her father had offered to help her, but she had told him no. This she needed to do on her own.

"Why?" He watched her closely.

"After my time in Yosemite I thought I should spread my wings some. I can always come back here if I wish but now is the time for me to do something different. Your SEMA program showed me that. We can all get in a rut."

His eyes glowed. "I'm impressed. Speaking of SEMA, I owe you a huge thank-you."

"Why's that?" She sat straighter.

"I got a phone call from Lamar just a little while ago. He said we were all set with the program. It seems the parks service liked the positive press and believes the SEMA program will be good public relations."

"That's wonderful. I'm so proud of you."

Cade settled more comfortably on the sofa as if he planned to stay awhile. "So, you and your parents patched things up."

"I realized after talking to you that I should hear them out. I was in a better place to listen when I came home. They agreed to no more lies and I told them I would never leave without telling them where I was going. I also told them I was moving out of town."

She and Cade were talking like old friends. At least she would have that.

"How did that go?" He sounded particularly interested.

"They hated not to have me close but promised to support me no matter what I wanted to do."

"I'm glad." Cade watched her for a moment. "Do you have some place in mind where you would like to work?"

She wanted to shout *With you. I want to be with you.* But she couldn't bring herself to say it. She needed to have a hint of how he felt. Something that would give her some encouragement. "All I know is that I don't want it to be in a large city."

Cade shifted. "Ouch."

Lily moved to the edge of the chair cushion. "Are you okay?"

"Yeah. Physical therapy doesn't mean no pain."

"Can I get you something? Pain reliever? Ice pack?" She stood.

"An ice pack sounds nice." He leaned his head back against the top of the couch and closed his eyes.

Cade smiled as he heard Lily hurrying out of the room. Getting her into nurse mode would get her focus on him instead of everything else and also get her to come sit near him.

Soon she returned. "This is going to be cold." The sofa cushion sank before she placed an ice pack on his shoulder.

Cade flinched but knew from experience he would be glad to have it on him.

"I'm so sorry you got hurt because of me," Lily whispered close to his ear. Her lips brushed his cheek. His heart thumped against his side. Maybe there was hope for him.

He opened his eyes and met her look. Would she let him kiss her? "Hey, I would've hated to lose you. I was so afraid I might. More than once. One time wasn't even my fault."

"We've already talked about that and settled it. Let's not drag that up again."

His gaze met hers. It was time to get down to why he was here. "If you don't want to talk about the past then how about we finish the conversation we were having before I had to leave on the helicopter."

She blinked. "I thought we did."

"I wasn't through talking about us." He took one of her hands in his and played with her fingers.

"I didn't know there was an us. Then by all means continue."

He ran a fingertip over her pulse. It was speeding along. Lily wasn't unaffected by him. "I sure felt like there was that night in the tent."

"But we agreed it was just a one-time thing. For memory's sake. Old times."

"If I agreed, then I messed up. I don't want you in my life for memory's sake. I've just been existing over the last few years without you. Not really moving forward or backward. I want you in my life because I love you. Would it be possible for you to trust me enough to try it again?"

Lily looked into his eyes. Dread built in him. She said nothing. "Lily?"

She shifted to her knees on the couch then moved so she sat on his lap facing him. Her actions brought him some encouragement. "I should punch you in your hurt shoulder. You've been here all this time and you're just now telling me this. You should have told me that the minute you walked in the door!" She cupped his face and leaned in to kiss him. "I love you too. I always have."

Cade's heart started beating again. His good hand rested at her waist. He brought her closer. The ice pack dropped to the couch, but he paid it no attention. "If you'll take a chance on me, I promise I'll never let you down again. We'll always talk things out."

Lily's look held his. "You'll always tell me how you feel?"

He nodded. "Always. Will you promise to always be supportive of me? I like having you in my corner."

She grinned. "I promise. That's easy to do because you are brilliant."

His chest swelled. "Thank you for that. Will you consider working in Yosemite? If not, I'll see about getting a job where you are. What I want most is for us to be together."

"That's what I want too." She ran her hand down his cheek.

He tightened his hold at her waist. "Hey Lily, do you think you could kiss me now?"

"I don't know of anything I would rather do. I love you."

Just before her lips touched his, Cade said, "You're my world, Lily. I love you too."

EPILOGUE

LILY WENT WILLINGLY when Cade took her hand and gently guided her out a side door of the Ahwahnee Lodge's Great Lounge into the sunlight hitting the side patio.

"Hey, where're we going? Do you have another present for me?"

The night before he had given her a large thin present. With her blessing, Cade had planned a camping trip for their honeymoon. This time he promised to return with her. She had anticipated some type of lingerie. When she had made a comment to that effect Cade told her she would have no need for any clothing in his tent. She unwrapped the gift to find a portable camping shower.

She laughed. "I love it!"

His look had turned wicked. "On our last camping trip, you talked of a hot shower. Even said I could share so I'm going to hold you to it."

"I'm going to hold you to it," she had told him.

He continued on across the yard to where one of the large trees stood out of view of the others. "I need a few minutes with just you."

She would be glad to have some time with just him too. In the flurry of getting ready for the wedding in the last few days they hadn't seen much of each other.

Inside, their family and friends were enjoying the wedding reception in the huge room with its double fireplace and vaulted ceiling with exposed beams. They sat and mingled around the masculine furniture grouped throughout the room to encourage conversation. Two tables that would require six men to move stood loaded with food and drinks. Everyone seemed be enjoying themselves and wouldn't miss her and Cade. At least not for a while.

Cade leaned against the tree and pulled her to him before nuzzling her neck. "You're absolutely beautiful today. You have to be the most beautiful bride ever."

Lily grinned. "I doubt that but it's nice that my husband thinks so."

They had been married in the Yosemite Valley Chapel. It was a small, simple building in the middle of a field of grass with a steeple dwarfed by the surrounding mountains. It had been a perfect venue.

Cade pulled back and gazed at her. "I always will. When you entered the chapel and stood in the sunlight coming through the windows, you took my breath."

"Every bride should be lucky enough to hear those words from her groom." Lily kissed him deeply.

Her knees had nearly buckled when she had stood at the top of the aisle looking at Cade waiting at the other end. He looked so handsome, strong and self-assured dressed in a black suit. She had no doubt of his love. He showed it to her daily in big and little ways.

When she hadn't moved down the aisle, he had held her gaze then reached out his hand and wiggled his fingertips in a come-here motion. The crowd chuckled. She gathered herself, smiled and started toward her future.

Where their first wedding plans had included hundreds

of people, mostly their families' country club friends and business associates, their wedding today only consisted of a few family members and friends. Their parents had been there supporting them all the way. The ceremony had been perfect.

From the chapel she and Cade had driven to the Ahwahnee Lodge, or Great Lodge, for the reception. The historical lodge with its gray stone walls gave a fairytale feel to the day.

She ran her hands along his lapels. "You look pretty good yourself."

"Thank you. I love you, Ms. Evans."

"And I love you too, Dr. Evans."

Cade leaned his forehead against hers. "It took us a while to get here but we finally made it."

Lily looked around. "This is so much better than what we had planned before. This—" she looked around "—was worth waiting on. This was the right time."

He kissed her again. "Lily, I'm so glad you gave me a second chance. You make me very happy."

"We're not going to talk about the past anymore. That's behind us and we're going to move forward."

"Speaking of going forward I got a call from the parks service yesterday."

She circled his neck with her arms. "What did they say?"

"They've accepted my proposal for the SEMA program and would like to set up two new ones in the next year. One in the east and one in the northwest."

"That is wonderful." She hugged him.

"They would like me to supervise the programs until others can be trained or hired. So how do you feel about a bit of travel?"

Lily leaned back in his arms. "As long as it's with

you, I've got no problem with it. Will you be able to keep working at the clinic here?"

"I should be able to keep my hand in if I have an assistant to help me with the SEMA program. Do you happen to know anybody who might be looking for a job? Maybe someone who has had experience with the program."

"Come to think of it I do know someone who might fit those qualifications."

His look turned serious, but his eyes held a twinkle. "Do you think she would consider it? It would mean having to work closely with me every day."

"I think she would like that." Lily gazed into his eyes.

"You'll need to contact her and have her submit an application."

"That'll have to wait because I happen to know she's going to be on her honeymoon for the next week. She's going to be camping with her new husband." Lily grinned. "And doing other things."

The need to have her shot through him. "I'm looking forward to those other things. Today, tomorrow and forever."

* * * * *

*If you enjoyed this story,
check out these other great reads
from Susan Carlisle*

A Kiss Under the Northern Lights
An Irish Vet in Kentucky
Falling for the Trauma Doc
Second Chance for the Heart Doctor

All available now!

MILLS & BOON®

Coming next month

FORBIDDEN FLING WITH THE PRINCESS
Amy Andrews

Dios! A man should not look that good in what were essentially blue pajamas.

'*Xio,*' he greeted as his gaze roved over her face and hair and neck and, god help her, lower.

She'd dressed this morning in her favourite form-fitting, v-necked, pink t-shirt with a glittery tiara stamped across the front, teaming it with a flowy, layered skirt of soft tulle that hid a multitude of sins and flirted with her ankles. For comfort, she'd told herself. Nothing stiff or formal for a long day sitting in the hospital keeping Phoebe company.

But in truth, she'd worn it for him, this man who seemed to have such a preoccupation with her clothes. Because she'd wanted him to look at her as he was now, his gaze brushing her neck and the swell of her breasts. She'd wanted to see his amber eyes darkening.

She'd wanted him to look at her like she wasn't some pretty, unattainable, untouchable princess on a pedestal but like she was a woman who knew her own power. A woman who craved his touch.

And in those long beats she totally forgot herself and their surroundings. And that two of the palace security detail were witnessing this mutual display of ogling that violated all kinds of royal protocols. Commoners should never look upon a royal princess with such unbridled lust. And the princess should definitely not be wondering how easy it was to get a man out of a pair of scrubs.

Continue reading

FORBIDDEN FLING WITH THE PRINCESS
Amy Andrews

Available next month
millsandboon.co.uk

Copyright © 2025 Amy Andrews

COMING SOON!

We really hope you enjoyed reading this book. If you're looking for more romance be sure to head to the shops when new books are available on

Thursday 28th August

To see which titles are coming soon, please visit
millsandboon.co.uk/nextmonth

MILLS & BOON

FOUR BRAND NEW BOOKS FROM
MILLS & BOON MODERN

The same great stories you love, a stylish new look!

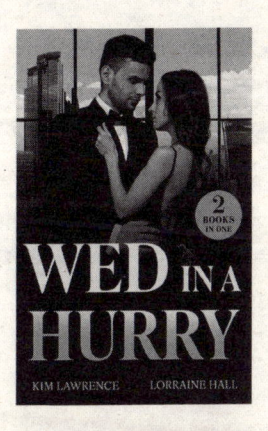

WED IN A HURRY — KIM LAWRENCE / LORRAINE HALL

Bound & Crowned — LOUISE FULLER / CLARE CONNELLY

Love to HATE HIM — JULIA JAMES / MILLIE ADAMS

RECLAIM ME — CATHY WILLIAMS / DANI COLLINS

OUT NOW

Eight Modern stories published every month, find them all at:

millsandboon.co.uk

afterglow BOOKS

Afterglow Books is a trend-led, trope-filled list of books with diverse, authentic and relatable characters, a wide array of voices and representations, plus real world trials and tribulations. Featuring all the tropes you could possibly want (think small-town settings, fake relationships, grumpy vs sunshine, enemies to lovers) and all with a generous dose of spice in every story.

♪ @millsandboonuk
◎ @millsandboonuk
afterglowbooks.co.uk
#AfterglowBooks

For all the latest book news, exclusive content and giveaways scan the QR code below to sign up to the Afterglow newsletter:

SCAN ME

afterglow BOOKS

THE CODE FOR LOVE

Her perfect plan has a gorgeous glitch...

NEW YORK TIMES BESTSELLING AUTHOR
ANNE MARSH

- ✈ International
- ⛅ Grumpy/sunshine
- Fake dating

OUT NOW

To discover more visit:
Afterglowbooks.co.uk

LET'S TALK
Romance

For exclusive extracts, competitions and special offers, find us online:

- **f** MillsandBoon
- **X** @MillsandBoon
- **◉** @MillsandBoonUK
- **♪** @MillsandBoonUK

Get in touch on 01413 063 232

For all the latest titles coming soon, visit
millsandboon.co.uk/nextmonth

OUT NOW!

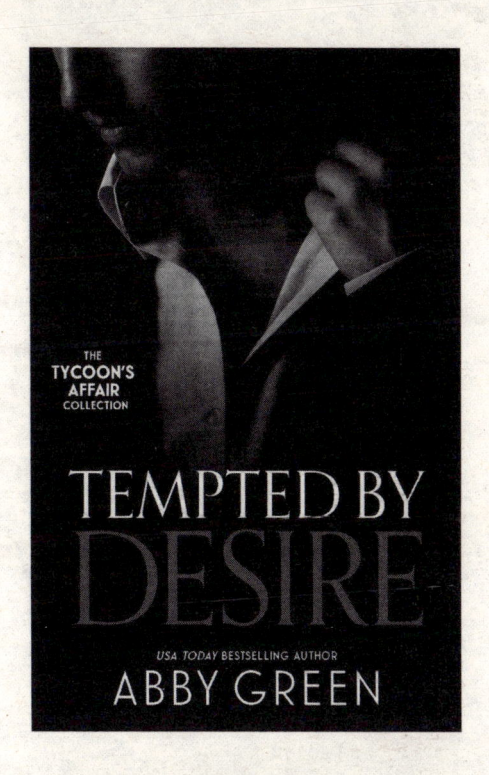

THE TYCOON'S AFFAIR COLLECTION

TEMPTED BY DESIRE

USA TODAY BESTSELLING AUTHOR
ABBY GREEN

Available at
millsandboon.co.uk

MILLS & BOON

OUT NOW!

A DARK ROMANCE SERIES

Thorns of Revenge

TARYN LEIGH TAYLOR · ABBY GREEN · JACKIE ASHENDEN

Available at
millsandboon.co.uk

MILLS & BOON